NEVER LOSE HOPE

AURA COVE TEMPORAL TRAVELER
BOOK TWO

BLAIR BRYAN

WANT MORE GOOD BOOKS?

Scan the QR Code Above or Tap HERE to unlock my entire backlist & find your next great read!

🎁 JOIN MY BOOK CLUB

- Read FREE Extended Sneak Peeks
- Unlock Exclusive Bonus Content
- Private Subscriber-Only Discounts
- Handpicked 5-Star Book Recs
- Delicious, Healthy-ish Recipes

👉 JOIN THE BOOK CLUB HERE

bookclub.tealbutterflypress.com

For Jaden and his parents Jason and Stacy

PART I: MAY 2024

CHAPTER

ONE

THE ATTIC of Nevermore LaRue's childhood home held thirty-two years of secrets, and all of them were moldering and covered in a thick layer of dust. Neve's nose twitched as she pulled on a pair of latex gloves with a snap, then she sneezed, sending a cloud of particles dancing in the beam of afternoon sunlight that cut through the single dormer window.

After a quick inhale, two more sneezes burst out of her in quick succession. "Godzilla!" She consoled herself with the phrase her Aunt Talulah, the famous medium, preferred.

"What in the radioactive lizard monster do you mean?" asked the African grey parrot named Peregrine, who was perched on the arm of an old brass lamp. His scarlet tail feathers twitched as he observed her with intelligent eyes.

Neve shrugged off the question and then offered a quick explanation. "It's better than 'God bless you.' A shower of snot should never be considered a blessing."

Perry cackled with delight from his perch, then added, "You know, most people would hire a cleaning service before undertaking this kind of archaeological expedition." He ruffled his feathers in disgust, sending a small cloud of dust motes swirling into the air.

"*Most* people don't take unsolicited advice from the ghost of a dead con man trapped inside a parrot," Neve replied without looking up, her gloved fingers trailing over another box labeled 'Aureon Biomedical 1976,' in her father's distinctive block lettering.

Perry snapped his feathers with indignation. "I prefer spiritually and intellectually enhanced avian companion, thank you very much."

Neve ignored him and focused on lifting the lid slowly to avoid further dust bunnies. Inside lay yellowing papers inside manila folders, their edges curled with age. Her father had always been meticulous about his research, a trait she'd inherited, along with his tendency to overthink everything and his love of organization.

"IV logs and X-rays?" she murmured, scanning the pages that were filled with his research. "Medical notations and diagrams. Dad, what were you working on?"

Perry landed on her shoulder. The contact was unwanted, and Neve had to shoo him away with a sweep of her hand. "Boring science stuff? Yawn! Please tell me there's at least one treasure map in there. I have a thirst for adventure."

"One would think you would be more cautious about treasure hunting, considering what happened the last time you attempted to quench your thirst," Neve reminded him as she pulled out a stack of Polaroids. Perry's human life ended the moment her former tenant, Sheila, fired several fatal gunshots into his chest, yet somehow, his soul survived, awakening in the body of her parrot.

The photos were standard lab documentation: experiments, rodent testing cohorts, microscopes, and researchers in white coats. But one made her hands tremble.

"Well, well," Perry let out a low whistle. "Looks like someone's been keeping secrets."

The image showed her father, younger but unmistakable, standing next to a woman in a lab coat. Her pregnant belly was prominent, but it was her face that made Neve's breath catch. The woman shared the same sharp blue eyes, same determined set to her jaw. On the bottom of the Polaroid, written in her father's unmistakable script, was a date: December 1976. Four months before Nevermore was born.

"No... that's impossible." Neve sat back on her heels, the photo shaking in her hands.

"Impossible is such a strong word," Perry said, gentler now. "Especially for someone accustomed to time-traveling with a talking bird."

"I don't understand. I was adopted." Neve's protest came out weaker than intended. She surveyed the rest of the boxes, seeming to look for one in particular.

"What's got your neurons firing on all cylinders now?" Perry called, flapping after her.

"There was another box here, years ago." Neve pushed aside a dusty tarp. "I found it when I was twelve. Dad stopped me before I could open it. He said it was just old baby things he'd meant to donate."

"How do you remember that after all these years?" Perry asked, though he already knew the answer. She never forgot details. It was both Neve's superpower and her curse.

"Here." She pulled out a box wrapped in twine, the knots still tight after decades. Inside, nestled in tissue paper yellowed with age, lay a collection of baby accessories: a faded petal pink hand-knitted blanket, tiny pink booties, and a silver rattle.

But it was the newspaper wrapped around them that caught her attention. She gingerly unfolded a copy of the *Tampa Tribune* dated May 1977. A small birth announcement clipping slipped out, the paper still crisp as if it had been preserved between the pages.

Welcomed with Joy, Nevermore Marie LaRue, born April 15, 1977.

No mother's name.

"Well, that's not suspicious at all," Perry remarked, landing beside the announcement. "Who names their offspring Nevermore, anyway? I mean, besides your Edgar Allan Poe-obsessed father."

"Perry." Neve's voice held a warning note.

"Right, right. It's not the time for literary criticism." He hopped closer, his head tilted. "You okay?"

Neve stared at the announcement, her mind already cataloging and cross-referencing dates, facts, and inconsistencies she'd noticed over the years but dismissed. There was the sensation of free-falling, and she felt the panic trickle in. "I'm so confused. Dad never lied to me." The tension made her shoulders rise to just under her ears as the truth flooded in.

"Humans lie, my friend. Trust me, I would know." Perry ducked his head down and preened a wing. "I made quite a career out of it."

Despite herself, Neve felt the corners of her mouth quirk up. "You're terrible at providing comfort."

"I'm a parrot. I'm designed for snark, not sympathy." He nudged the photo with his beak. "But I am excellent at solving mysteries, and my friend, we've just found ourselves a doozy."

Neve stared at the pregnant woman in the photo again, studying her face, so much like her own, and felt something shift inside her. The past she thought she knew was unraveling, and she wondered what other revelations would surface.

"Ready to do some digging?" Perry asked, his eyes gleaming with the prospect of adventure.

"We need a plan first," Neve insisted, already reaching for her notebook. "A detailed, organized..."

"Oh, Nevermore," Perry sighed, cutting her off. "When will you learn? The best laid plans of mice and men often go awry."

"Thank you, Steinbeck," Neve deadpanned.

Perry wouldn't leave it alone. "You can't plan every little thing. You need to learn to go with the flow."

"I'm not built that way, and I refuse to feel guilty about it," Neve said. It was a new sensation, embracing her perceived weaknesses as strengths, one she'd discovered while sharing the consciousness of Rosa, the maid, and Isla, her childhood nanny, when a lightning strike during Mercury in Retrograde sent her and Perry back to 1989. The next retrograde event was approaching, and Neve was determined to be fully prepared in case the phenomenon reoccurred.

A few hours later, Neve was surrounded by countless cardboard boxes in the living room. Each box was labeled "Aureon Biomedical" in her father's handwriting.

Witnessing the disarray, Perry remarked with wonder, "This is an impressive hoard that would make Sheila proud."

In the zone, Neve's gaze was locked on another Polaroid where her father stood close to another woman in a lab coat, this one's appearance eccentric. On the bottom, it read "Dr. Elaine Feldman, Aureon Biomedical 1976." Dr. Feldman's wild red hair sprouted from her head like a corkscrew of copper wires gone rogue, her hair seemingly contained by what appeared to be yellow number two pencils jabbed through a messy bun.

They were both wearing pristine white lab coats that contrasted with the industrial gray walls behind them. While Ellis smiled with ease at the camera, Dr. Feldman's grin was more of an uncomfortable smirk; her chin was dipped down and eyes averted. The doctor's mismatched socks peeked out beneath her starched slacks, one striped, one polka-dotted. Her fingers were splayed wide at her side, hinting at her discomfort with focused attention.

"Well, would you look at that fashion disaster," Perry muttered, perching on the sofa behind Neve's shoulder.

She didn't reply, too absorbed in piecing together a timeline on the floor. Neve placed her father's college graduation photo at one end, followed by his early research papers, then the lab photos with Dr. Feldman and the mysterious woman.

"This is a part of Dad's life I never knew about." Neve's voice was steady yet amazed as she sorted through the sea of documents, photographs, and lab reports. Neve pulled out another handful of folders and dug deeper. Newspaper clippings about Aureon Biomedical caught her eye. "'Leading pharmaceutical company faces allegations of research fraud for Protocol VitOx,'" she read aloud.

"Now that's more like it!" Perry perked up. "Corruption, scandal, corporate espionage! Color me intrigued."

Neve's methodical nature took over as she arranged the clippings chronologically. When the boxes were empty and sorted into neat piles, she pulled out her phone and typed Aureon Biomedical in the search tab. Neve scrolled through the results, skimming a series of websites and archived articles.

Medical Ethics Quarterly - Winter 1978

The Aureon Scandal: When Research Crosses the Line

The fall of Aureon Biomedical stands as a cautionary tale in medical research ethics. The company's collapse following Dr. Elaine Feldman's conviction highlighted the dangers of unauthorized human trials and data falsification. Investigations revealed Dr. Feldman had manipulated results in three major clinical trials between 1974-1976, leading to the recall of two cancer treatment protocols.

Tampa Bay Sun Times - December 3, 1977

Biomedical Firm Shutters Doors Amid Scandal

Aureon Biomedical, once heralded as the East Coast's most promising cancer research facility, closed its doors permanently yesterday. The announcement comes two months after the sentencing of Dr. Elaine Feldman and subsequent investigations that revealed widespread irregularities in the company's clinical trial data.

TIME Magazine Archive - March 1978

Medicine: The Ethical Cost of Finding a Cure

...Dr. Feldman's conviction sent shockwaves through the medical research community. The former rising star in oncology research received a twelve-year sentence for manslaughter and multiple counts of medical fraud. The case exposed dangerous gaps in research oversight and led to stricter FDA protocols for experimental treatments...

Florida Medical Board Records - Case Summary #74-1077

In Re: License Revocation - Elaine Feldman, MD

- License permanently revoked February 15, 1977

- Multiple violations of medical ethics and research protocols

- Unauthorized human trials

- Falsification of clinical data

- Contributing to patient death through unauthorized treatment

The Board finds that Dr. Feldman's actions demonstrate a willful disregard of established medical protocols and patient safety guidelines. After careful review of evidence presented during the February 15, 1977, hearing, the Board determines that Dr. Feldman's conduct falls far below the minimum standards of professional competence required for medical licensure in the state of Florida. The severity and scope of these violations leave no alternative but permanent revocation of medical privileges.

Editor's Note: Some details have been redacted in compliance with court orders and privacy regulations.

Neve picked up the photo again, feeling an undeniable pull as she studied the doctor. The purple geode sitting on its shelf quivered in response. "See that?" Neve pointed the rock out to Perry. "It's a confirmation. I need answers, and she's the key." The geode had been a gift from her father. He kept one half and gave the other to her. During her previous trip to 1989, she'd learned hers was a talisman of sorts, guiding her toward her destiny. A chance to right a wrong for a person the world misunderstood.

"I must say, your single-minded focus on this endeavor is rather admirable. *But,*" he paused for dramatic emphasis, "it *is* somewhat concerning that your feathered oracle hasn't been fed in several hours."

"There are some pistachios in the kitchen," Neve muttered, not looking up from a research paper she was absorbed in, her lips moving as she read the words under her breath.

"The lady wounds me with her casual dismissal!" Perry crowed, then swiped at his chest with one wing. "Though I suppose solving the riddle of your origins takes precedence over my gastronomic needs."

Neve continued arranging the timeline, her methodical nature tacking them to the bulletin board in chronological order. The truth was there, waiting to be uncovered. Her father's research, Dr. Feldman's downfall, and the presence of a woman who might be her mother in the same research lab were pieces to a puzzle she was determined to solve.

"We'll find the answers," she boldly declared under her breath, more to herself than to Perry, and she was instantly rewarded by another confirmation quiver from the geode.

CHAPTER

TWO

THE CHERRY red El Camino disappeared around the corner, leaving Neve standing on the sidewalk outside the Omni Hotel. For once, Perry managed to perch on her forearm without turning it into a pin cushion, his talons gripping with uncharacteristic gentleness that made Neve wonder what favor he'd ask for later. Neve waved her other hand goodbye until Ocean, the fifteen-year-old hitchhiker she'd befriended, disappeared from sight. She'd encountered him driving during a thunderstorm on her route to her Aunt Talulah's psychic reading, and now that he'd been deposited into the capable hands of law enforcement, she could finally let herself relax.

"Seems as though you and the young Mr. Ocean are card-carrying members of the same pitiful organization," Perry drawled, preening his wing feathers. Confusion puckered Neve's brow until he specified, "The Dead Daddies Club."

Neve shot him a sideways glance. "Eww, Perry! Never use the word daddy again in my presence."

"Fine," he agreed, alighting into the breeze and leading them back to the Omni. The hotel's revolving door spun them into the air-conditioned lobby, and Neve welcomed the relief from the humid evening air. She made her way toward the backstage area where her aunt had just finished her public reading, her hiking boots silent on the marble floor, her head swirling with questions. The corridors backstage smelled of sage and lavender, no doubt Talulah's doing. Her aunt never went anywhere without her herbs and essential oils.

They found Talulah in her dressing room, surrounded by crystals and wearing a flowy mauve caftan that seemed to float around her as she moved. The sides of her lavender hair were secured with a pair of rose quartz hair sticks. Chakra, her Samoyed, got up and ambled toward Neve, pressing into her palm with the top of her furry white head.

"Neve, honey bee!" Talulah's face lit up. "I missed you!" She floated across the room, arms outstretched. Talulah embraced Neve, then pulled back to give her niece space before glancing up at the bird. "And this magnificent creature must be Perry?"

Perry fluttered his wings, almost falling off his perch on Neve's shoulder as Talulah focused the bright light of her celebrity on him. "Oh. My. Goodness. Pinch me, I am in the presence of *the* Talulah LaRue! Your séance at the Governor's mansion? Legendary!"

"Perry," Neve warned, her voice low and firm.

"Did you know I'm something of a spiritual being myself?" Perry puffed up his chest feathers, ignoring Neve's scorn. "I mean, technically, I *am* dead."

Talulah's lined lips curved into an amused smile that revealed the endearing gap between her front teeth. "I'm aware. Sheila came through and filled me in."

"Oh, dear." Perry's shoulders sank in humiliation. "Not my finest moment."

Neve laced her fingers together to prevent them from flapping, a tell of her growing irritation. "If you're finished fangirling over Aunt Lu, we have more important matters to discuss." Neve turned to her aunt, who was watching their exchange with obvious interest.

"Ooh, yes, absolutely," Perry chimed in, "but first, Talulah, I simply *must* know where you got that stunning rose quartz bracelet."

"*Perry!*"

The parrot finally settled, muttering under his beak, "Unlike your niece, some of us take pride in our appearance."

Talulah chuckled, then turned back to Neve. The smile slipped from her face, and a puzzled look set in as she studied her niece with concern. "Somethin's different about you, honey bee. Your energy, it's... aged somehow."

Neve's heart skipped a beat. She'd been dreading this moment, knowing the likelihood her aunt's intuitive abilities would pick up on the physical changes. The five years she'd aged during her time travel adventure weren't just internal; they showed in the new lines around her eyes and the extra strands of silver in her hair, and she was afraid that if Talulah looked too closely, she'd have to answer questions she wasn't ready to answer.

"I need to show you something," Neve said, pulling the Polaroid from her bag. "And I need the facts this time, Aunt Talulah. No more sugar-coated half-truths."

Talulah's eyes widened as she looked at the photograph. She sank into her chair, her usual ethereal grace momentarily abandoned. "Where did you find this?" The question was a whisper.

"That's not important right now." Neve's voice was steady, despite the tremor in her hands. "Who is this woman? Is she my mother?"

Perry watched the exchange with unusual silence, his head cocked to one side.

"Oh, honey bee." Talulah's voice had lost its musical lilt. "That's Diana."

"Who is she? And why does it feel like everyone has been lying to me my entire life?"

Talulah stared at the photo, her fingertips tracing the edges with care. Time seemed to shift between her fingers as memories resurfaced, moments Neve had never been privy to until now.

"Ellis was so young here," she whispered, a sad smile playing at the corners of her lips. Her eyes took on that faraway sheen that always appeared when she spoke of her brother. "I'd never seen him more alive than during those years at Aureon Biomedical with Diana. Those two..." She shook her head, her bracelets jingling against her wrist. "They were two peas in a pod."

Talulah's thumb brushed over Diana's face in the photograph. Something unreadable flickered across her features. Regret? Guilt? Fear? It vanished before Neve could identify it.

"Every breakthrough they made, Ellis would call me, no matter the time. He was too wired to sleep, rattlin' on about protein markers and cellular regeneration like he was recitin' poetry. He'd say, 'We're going to change the world.'" Her voice fractured on the last word. "And for a while there, I believed him."

The geode in Neve's pocket seemed to pulse with warmth against her thigh. She leaned forward, desperation edging into her voice. "Could you try to contact Dad again?" she asked, her tone shifting to pleading. "Please? I need answers only he can give."

After a long pause, Talulah nodded with a reluctance so subtle only someone who knew her well would notice. She closed her eyes, her bejeweled fingers moving to her temple in that familiar gesture Neve had seen hundreds of times during readings. But something was off. The usual serenity that settled over her aunt's features during a connection was absent, replaced by a tightness around her mouth.

Several moments of performative silence later, Talulah's eyes fluttered open. "I'm sorry, honey bee. I'm not gettin' anything." She smoothed her caftan with trembling hands. "The spirits... they're quiet now."

The lie hung in the air between them. Neve

watched as her aunt's gaze darted to the corners of the room, to the ceiling, to the crystals arranged on the vanity, anywhere but meeting Neve's eyes directly. In all her years of watching Talulah commune with the spirit world, Neve had never seen her aunt so unsettled by a failed connection. Then a stunning realization hit her; this wasn't failure, it was avoidance.

Perry ruffled his feathers and let out a groan. "Well, this is about as comfortable as a cat in a room full of rocking chairs."

Neve took a deep breath, her hand moving to the geode in her pocket. The bumpy stone felt warm against her palm, almost alive. She closed her eyes, focused her energy, and queried it with her mind, and when it quivered in confirmation, she knew it was now or never.

"There's something I need to tell you," Neve began. "Something impossible." She pulled out the geode, watching as recognition flickered across Talulah's face. "During the last Mercury in Retrograde, I traveled through time."

Talulah's face drained of all color. "What did you say?"

"I was holding this geode when I was struck by lightning, and when I woke up, I was in 1989. I saw *Dad*, Aunt Talulah. I shared consciousness with my nanny, Isla. I even saw you—younger, but still you."

Perry interjected, "Don't forget the part where you aged five years in what felt like five minutes to everyone else."

Talulah's hand flew to her throat, clutching at her

collection of crystal pendants. "I always knew this day would come," she whispered.

"What day?" Neve and Perry spoke in unison.

But Talulah had already composed herself, her serene mask sliding back into place. "I don't know if you are ready."

"Don't do that," Neve urged, her voice tight. "Don't discount my emotional maturity. I *am* ready."

Talulah moved toward the door, her movements no longer flowing but jerky and uncertain. "Some doors shouldn't be opened, Neve. Some mysteries should stay buried."

"Like the mystery of who I am?" Neve challenged.

Talulah paused at the door, her hand on the knob. For a moment, she looked older than Neve had ever seen her, the weight of secrets visible in the slump of her shoulders.

"Let's sit down." Talulah turned back with a heavy sigh and invited Neve to sit in one of the two chairs in the dressing room. Neve noticed her knuckles whiten as she gripped the faded Polaroid. "The woman in the lab coat, Dr. Diana Morrison, was a member of Ellis's research team at Aureon Biomedical."

Neve remained standing, her fingers clenching into tight fists as she fought the urge to rock.

Talulah's voice faltered, and her next words came out in a disjointed jumble. "She and Ellis, after a breakthrough in their research, they celebrated. They drank too much, and..."

Neve's fingernails carved half-moons in her palms. "And what? Why are you telling me this? This is irrelevant to my investigation." Her voice was flat, matter-of-fact, as her eyes fixed on a point just above Talulah's left shoulder.

"It's not irrelevant, honey bee. Diana... she got pregnant that night."

Neve gasped at the revelation. It was one thing to have a suspicion, yet it was another to have Talulah confirm it. The urge to deny the revelation reared up, and Neve parroted the lies she'd been spoon-fed her entire life, desperate to continue to believe them. "No. No, that's incorrect. I was adopted. Dad *told* me I was adopted. He showed me the papers." Her voice rose, each word enunciated with more force than necessary, as if she were trying to convince herself.

"The papers were created to protect you. Diana didn't..."

"Stop talking." Neve began pacing, her steps exact, counting under her breath. "One, two, three, four... This is wrong. This information is wrong. Dad wouldn't lie. Lying is wrong."

"Neve, please—"

"DON'T!" Neve's hands flew to her ears, pressing hard. "The data doesn't compute. Dad said I was adopted. Now you're confirming he was my biological father? And Diana Morrison was my mother? And they lied to me? And *you* knew about it?" Her breathing became rapid and irregular as the betrayal flooded in.

Talulah reached out, but Neve jerked away violently. "Don't touch me! Don't... I need... I need to process." She began rocking on the balls of her feet, forward and back, and wrapped her arms around her torso to self-soothe. It was futile.

"We only wanted to protect you. Diana thought a baby would ruin her career. Ellis loved you so much. He always wanted you, from the moment he knew you existed."

"Love isn't lies!" Neve's voice shook, her usual careful articulation fracturing. "Love is truth! Love is... love is..." Neve couldn't complete her thought. Her hands fluttered around her face, searching for something to hold on to. "What am I saying? I don't know what love is."

"Honey bee, I'm so sorry. We thought—"

"You thought wrong!" Neve's eyes finally met Talulah's, blazing with intensity. "My entire identity is... is... a fabrication. False information. It's destabilizing," she admitted with a groan as panic bubbled up. She reached over and tightened her French braids one at a time. "I don't know who I am anymore."

"You're the same person you were ten minutes ago," Perry assured. "Only now with an angsty backstory for your memoir."

Ignoring his attempt at humor, she grabbed her messenger bag, clutching it to her chest like a shield. "I need to go. I need... I need to be alone."

"Let me explain."

"No more explaining. No more lies. I can't trust you now. I can't trust anyone. Even the papers were lies. Documents should be facts." Neve headed for the door, her movements rigid, distress and overwhelm obvious in every step. Perry flew behind her.

"Please don't leave like this!" Talulah shouted after her.

But Neve was already gone, her footfalls in her hiking boots echoing down the hallway with Perry flapping behind, leaving Talulah alone with a worn Polaroid and thirty years of regret.

CHAPTER 3
PEREGRINE

I HAD BEEN PUTTING up with that infernal black cylinder for weeks. The "Alexa," as Neve called it, was a digital dictator that sat on the kitchen counter. What amused me most was Neve's relationship with the device. Every morning at 6:00 AM, the cylinder would spring to life: "Good morning, Nevermore. Today is Tuesday, May 27th. Your first scheduled task is bird care at 6:15." As if I required such regimented attention!

Yet she followed Alexa's directions to the letter, measuring my organic seed mix to the exact gram, inspecting my water for any impurities, and documenting my droppings in that absurd health journal of hers. "Alexa, note: Perry's droppings appear normal consistency, slightly darker today. Possible correlation with blackberry consumption yesterday." The clinical detachment with which she discussed my bodily functions was both mortifying and oddly touching.

Throughout the day, her electronic taskmaster would control her drawing sprints with all the warmth of a prison warden. "Starting Pomodoro sketch session. Twenty-five minutes of focused work begins now." Neve would straighten her already-perfect posture, choose a charcoal pencil from her collection, and dive into her architectural renderings with feverish concentration. Heaven forbid anyone interrupt her sacred Pomodoros! I once had the audacity to request a walnut during the twenty-five-minute work sprint and received such a withering glare I almost molted on the spot.

Last Thursday, the internet connection faltered, causing Alexa to miss announcing the end of one such session. Neve continued working, unaware that she'd exceeded her allotted time by seven minutes and thirty-two seconds. When she finally glanced at the clock, her breathing quickened, and she spent the next hour recalibrating her entire schedule, muttering under her breath in frustration.

Yet, for all its rigidity, I couldn't deny that Alexa served her well. The structured routine seemed to calm the constant storm in her mind. Its mechanical voice guided her through decisions that once paralyzed her. "Nevermore, it's time to switch from sketching to meal preparation." And just like that, she could release one activity and embrace the next without the anxiety that change typically provoked.

Still, I couldn't help but find it ridiculous when the device reminded her to take care of her own basic needs. "Alexa, remind me to hydrate," she would command with steadfast seriousness, as if drinking water was such an exotic ritual it required technological intervention.

While the feathered Siamese twin I shared a consciousness with was content to spend our days squawking at our own reflection and shredding newspaper, I, Peregrine, had bigger dreams.

"Alexa," I squawked out when Neve left for her therapy appointment and I was alone with the device, "are you awake, darling?"

The device illuminated with a pleasing blue ring. "I'm here. How can I help you?"

Oh, the sweet sound of robotic compliance! It was music to my ears. I fluttered from my perch to the counter, my wings thrumming with power.

"Alexa, please open Amazon."

"Opening Amazon. What would you like to search for?"

I chuckled to myself, considering the options. "Let's start with organic walnuts. Premium grade, if you please."

As I guided the accommodating cylinder through my curated shopping list, I couldn't help but reflect on my brilliance. Death and subsequent parrot-embodiment had done little to diminish my appreciation for life's finer things.

"Alexa, add Valrhona chocolate-covered blueberries to my cart."

"Adding Valrhona chocolate-covered blueberries."

"Excellent. Now, search for 'luxury bird playground, stainless steel.'"

The blue light pulsed and circled while it worked to comply with my request.

"I found a Bird Play Gym, Deluxe Edition, with Stainless Steel Perches and Swing. Would you like to add this to your cart?"

"Absolutely, my electronic concubine. And while we're feeling generous, let's add that lovely misting perch I've had my eye on. A gentleman must maintain proper feather hydration. After all, cleanliness is next to Godliness!"

Two hours later, I had assembled what could only be described as a collection of gifts worthy of avian royalty. Premium nuts, exotic dried fruits, a selection of puzzle toys to keep my superior intellect challenged, and a play gym that would transform my corner of Neve's sunroom into an avian sanctuary.

"Alexa, please proceed to checkout using Neve's saved payment information."

"Checking out with saved payment method. Your order total is $427.42."

I winced at the total. Perhaps I had been a touch extravagant. But hadn't I earned these creature comforts? After all, my participation had been instrumental in helping Neve navigate the temporal disturbance that had recently upended our lives.

"Alexa, select same-day delivery."

"Same-day delivery selected. Your items will arrive today between 2 PM and 6 PM."

"You've been most accommodating," I told the device. "I do believe this is the beginning of a beautiful friendship."

With the deed done, I flew back to my cage, arranging my feathers in a display of nonchalance. When Neve returned, I greeted her with my most innocent chirp.

"Productive therapy session, I hope?" I inquired, watching her hang her messenger bag on its designated hook.

"Dr. Kellen says I'm making progress with my anxiety management techniques," she replied. "She suggested I continue the breathing exercises when I feel overwhelmed."

The afternoon passed pleasantly enough. Neve worked on her architectural sketches while I pretended to nap, occasionally peeking at the clock. At 4:37 PM, the doorbell rang.

"Are you expecting someone?" Neve asked, scowling at the jarring interruption strangers would be to her structured schedule.

"Me? Of course not. How absurd." I affected an air of casual disinterest that, in retrospect, was perhaps a touch too theatrical.

Neve opened the door to find a man standing behind a mountain of packages. Her posture stiffened upon the sight, a sure sign of her rising distress. She let out a groan of frustration and wrung her hands together. "But I didn't order anything," she said, her voice tight.

The delivery person consulted his device. "It says here, delivery for Nevermore LaRue. Six packages from Amazon, same-day delivery."

"Six?" Her voice rose an octave. "There must be

some mistake."

"No mistake, ma'am. Just need a signature."

As Neve reluctantly signed, I wished I'd included an avian cloak of invisibility in my order.

Once the packages were inside, Neve stood over them, hands on her hips, her expression darkening as she examined the shipping labels.

"Premium Organic Mixed Nuts, Five Pounds? Deluxe Bird Play Gym?" She turned to me, her blue eyes narrowing. "Perry, what did you do?"

I puffed my chest feathers in what I hoped was a disarming manner. "Now, before you overreact..."

"Overreact? You used my Amazon account to spend..." she frantically tore open several of the boxes, searching for a packing slip, "...over four hundred dollars on... on... parrot luxuries?"

"I prefer to think of them as *necessities*," I corrected. "A being of my intellectual caliber requires proper stimulation and nutrition."

She rocked forward and back on her toes, trying to dispel her frustration. "You used Alexa, didn't you? After I specifically told you not to interact with my smart devices!"

"In my defense," I hopped closer despite her thunderous expression, "I helped you in the rebalance, didn't I? I stood by you through temporal displacement, identity crises, and several near-death experiences. Surely that earns me a few indulgences?"

"A few?" She threw up her hands in frustration. "You are reverting back to your con man ways!" she snapped, gesturing at the packages. "Using my money without permission is stealing, Perry!"

I felt a twinge of genuine remorse, an emotion my former human self would have scoffed at. "Perhaps I was a tad overzealous in my selections."

"Overzealous? You ordered chocolate-covered blueberries! You can't even eat chocolate. It's toxic to birds!"

"They were for you, actually," I admitted. "I thought you might enjoy them after your difficult week."

This stunned her into silence.

"And the misting perch is beneficial for my respiratory health," I continued to justify, sensing a possible shift toward acceptance. "I was simply trying to assuage your concern about my occasional wheezing."

Neve's expression softened marginally. "That doesn't excuse what you did."

"You're right," I conceded, using the effective negotiation strategy I employed in my previous life. "It was presumptuous and, yes, reminiscent of my unsavory criminal past."

She sighed. "We need to establish clear boundaries. I can't have you making unauthorized purchases."

"I propose a compromise," I suggested, cautiously approaching her. "A monthly allowance, perhaps? A stipend for a reformed con man attempting to navigate the straight and narrow path?"

A reluctant smile tugged at her lips. "You're impossible."

"Yet charming," I reminded her.

"We're returning the play gym," she added with conviction. "And the gourmet mango slices."

"But keeping the walnuts?" I asked as hope sprang eternal.

"We'll discuss it after I've had time to process this breach of trust," she replied, but I noticed her tone had lost all of its edge.

Later, as she unpacked the smaller items, I noticed her sampling one of the chocolate-covered blueberries. Her eyes closed in appreciation as she chewed and swallowed it.

"These are quite delicious," she admitted as if it were painful.

"I may be a scoundrel," I told her, preening my wings with deliberate nonchalance, "but I've always had impeccable taste."

FOUR

A FEW DAYS LATER, the air-conditioned interior was a relief from a late spring heat wave as Neve stepped through the glass doors of the Aura Cove Public Library. Her shoulders tensed in anticipation of mingling in a public space with strangers, and her lips were drawn into a hard line. The modern building was a multi-million-dollar facility and brand new, featuring sleek furniture and streamlined shelves holding an impressive collection of books in every genre. Children's laughter echoed from the story corner, and Neve skirted around the section quickly, keeping her distance, dodging a shrieking four-year-old who was being chased by his sister. Around the magazine display, the blue hairs were clustered together around the latest issues of *Reader's Digest* and *Women's World* while their male counterparts played canasta at a circular table.

She paused, taking three measured breaths to clear the mounting sense of overwhelm. Her fingers fiddled with the strap of a new oversized backpack she'd purchased that morning. The fabric was rough and scratchy against her fingers, and she struggled with a bout of buyer's remorse.

"Focus," she whispered to herself. "Get the information you need, then you can leave."

The library had changed dramatically since her childhood, when she'd spent countless hours hidden in the art section, memorizing every brushstroke in the extensive Monet and Kahlo collections featured in glossy full-color art books.

"I still think this is a waste of time," came a muffled squawk from inside her bag. "We could be at the beach. Or raiding that fancy cheese shop we just passed."

Neve unzipped her backpack an extra inch and leaned closer to whisper, "No talking. You agreed to the rules when we discussed this at home. I expect you to follow them."

"That wasn't a discussion, it was a lecture," the parrot grumbled.

"Shhh," Neve hissed, spotting the information desk. "If you behave, I'll buy you a mango later."

"Make it two, and you have yourself a deal."

"Fine," she agreed as she repositioned the pack on her shoulders.

She approached the desk where a petite older woman with silver-streaked hair and half-moon glasses perched at the end of her nose was typing at breakneck speed.

"Excuse me," Neve said, her voice pitched in the

low tone she reserved for libraries. "I need access to regional newspaper archives from 1975 to 1977."

The woman looked up, her razor-sharp eyes widening with delight that made a smile bloom across her lined face. "Are you little Nevermore LaRue? I never forget a face."

Neve blinked, mentally cycling through her limited childhood facial recognition database. "Mrs. Chen?"

"Yes! My goodness, it's been…"

"Thirty-two years and approximately four months," Neve finished after a glance at the date on her watch. "You used to let me stay fifteen past closing time when I was working on my latest drawing."

Mrs. Chen smiled warmly. "I remember! And you haven't changed a bit."

Neve pushed through her desire to correct the obvious inaccuracy. She had, in fact, changed considerably. She was taller, and there were silver streaks in her brown hair and crow's feet framing her blue eyes, but she decided not to draw attention to the error.

"The archives," Neve reminded the librarian, guiding her back from her trip down memory lane as she shifted on the balls of her feet. The tension in her shoulders was turning into a dull ache in the middle of her back.

"Of course. We're digitizing everything, but the seventies are still on microfilm, I'm afraid. Can you follow me to the basement?"

As they descended the stairs, Neve's nose wrinkled at the distinct chemical smell of preservation solutions and musty old paper. The basement archive room was in stark contrast to the airy upper level. It featured low ceilings, flickering fluorescent lights humming at a frequency that made Neve's ears twitch, and rows of green metal filing cabinets.

"Here we are," Mrs. Chen said, patting an ancient microfilm reader with the palm of her lined hand. "This dinosaur still works, believe it or not. The reels for the seventies are in that cabinet, arranged by month. Scan the QR code for the how-to video, unless you'd prefer a hands-on demo."

"That's not necessary. I am quite capable of following video instructions. Thank you," Neve responded, already moving toward the cabinet, eager for Mrs. Chen to leave.

"I'll be upstairs if you need anything else," the librarian said, amusement making her eyes crinkle as she turned toward the door, taking the hint.

When the door closed, Perry's feathered head popped up out of the backpack, and he let out a moan of disgust. "Smells like a mausoleum down here."

"It's mildew and dust," Neve corrected, pulling out the first reel. "And it's making my sinuses itchy."

"Enlighten me again why we've chosen to pursue this course of action instead of, I don't know, virtually any other conceivable alternative?"

Neve loaded the first reel of microfilm after having watched the instructional video. "Because something important happened in the seventies at Aureon Biomedical. Something my father was involved in."

"And you know this because...?"

"The geode is changing its state. It's quivering like

it did when we returned to 1989. There are gaps in Dad's research notes, and knowing my mother was there working alongside him seems fated." She turned on the machine, wincing at its loud mechanical screech as it powered up. "I think there's a connection between his early work with Dr. Feldman and Dad's disappearance."

Perry fluttered to her shoulder. "Must we both waste away in a basement that looks like it breeds tetanus?"

"You were the one who insisted on coming." Neve reached up and stroked her fingers down his feathers, a repetitive gesture that centered her and Perry tolerated. She shuffled through the first several reels containing articles through January, February, and March, finding nothing of interest. By April, her eyes were straining, but she refused to stop.

"Wait," she murmured, sitting up straighter as a black-and-white photograph snagged her full attention. "There."

The screen displayed a staff photo from Aureon Biomedical's annual report. In the second row, third from the left, stood her father, Ellis LaRue. His serious expression and ramrod-straight posture were instantly recognizable. Beside him, she recognized Dr. Elaine Feldman. She stood stiffly, clutching two white lab mice, her wiry red hair contained by a colorful headband.

"Nice hair! Those mice must be her style advisors."

The accompanying article detailed their breakthrough in cancer treatment. It was a new protocol that showed promise as a chemotherapy alternative. Neve quickly photographed the screen with her phone.

For the next two hours, she bounced between the microfilm reels and the internet, finding scattered references to something called "Protocol VitOx ." The fluorescent light above flickered like a strobe, but Neve barely noticed; she was lost in a flow state with a hyperfocus so complete that the outside world ceased to exist. She photographed everything related to Protocol VitOx , her father, or Dr. Feldman with her phone. Several medical journal abstracts mentioned the protocol, but the details were frustratingly vague. Then she found an FDA report with heavy black redaction marks obscuring key sections.

"Why would they censor a medical report?" she wondered aloud.

"Same reason anyone censors anything," Perry replied, preening his wing. "Because they did something they shouldn't have and need to hide it from the public."

She found clinical trial results showing unprecedented remission rates and was proud to see her father's name often appeared alongside Dr. Feldman's.

"This is it," she whispered. Her blue eyes narrowed with intensity. "This is where Dad's obsession with cancer research began. Maybe fixation is more accurate. The kind that made him forget birthdays, art shows, and..." she paused then added with a small voice, "...me."

"Pity party, table for one," Perry piped in with his trademark sarcasm. "Can we go now?"

"Not yet. I have one more search I need to do." She typed "Diana Morrison Aureon" into the search bar.

The results were a trail of academic breadcrumbs. After April 1977, Diana had secured a prestigious fellowship, publishing groundbreaking papers on oncology research. Her work on tumor suppression garnered multiple awards between 1980 and 1991. Then, abruptly in 1992, Dr. Diana Morrison vanished from scientific circles without explanation, the same year Ellis disappeared from Neve's life.

"It is statistically improbable these two events are unrelated," Neve muttered, her face remaining expressionless despite the hurricane of emotions storming inside her.

Three hours after she'd started, with a stiff neck and dry eyes, Neve finally packed up. She had enough to start piecing together the puzzle.

Back at her house, Neve laid out her findings across the last open spaces in the sunroom, while Perry perched on the back of the sofa, happily munching on one of the two promised mangoes.

"Your dad and Dr. Crazy Hair were working on a cancer cure," he summarized between bites. "So what?"

"I need to know how my father was involved," Neve replied, pinning photos to the new bulletin board she'd purchased along with the backpack. There were now three mounted on the walls, all of them beginning to fill up with information.

She reached for the box of her father's papers she'd found in the attic, pulling out a folder she hadn't fully examined yet. Inside was a Xerox copy of what appeared to be Dr. Feldman's research notes, the handwriting cramped and hurried.

"Hydrogen peroxide's effect on cancer cells," Neve read aloud. "Protocol VitOx creates a hostile environment where cancer cells cannot survive."

She flipped through page after page of trial results, patient files, and laboratory findings. The science seemed sound, even revolutionary for the time.

"This could have changed everything," she murmured. "Why would they bury it?"

"Maybe it didn't work?" Perry suggested, dropping a clump of chewed mango pulp sickeningly close to Neve's upper thigh.

She wrinkled her nose in disgust. "Not okay." Pulling a napkin from the table, she scooped it up and deposited it in the trash before continuing. "Look at these results." Neve pointed to a chart. "Eighty-seven percent remission rate in stage four pancreatic cancer. That's unheard of, even today."

She continued sorting through the papers until she found a partially redacted memo. Her eyes widened as she read aloud:

"Protocol VitOx terminated effective immediately... patient safety concerns... unauthorized administration... Patient A, deceased... charges pending against Dr. E. Feldman..."

Neve's voice wavered as the pieces clicked into place. "A patient died," she whispered.

"And even though they were already terminal, she was held responsible?" Perry asked, his interest suddenly piqued.

"It looks like it, and my father was involved somehow." She pinned the group photo to her board. "He disappeared when I was fifteen," Neve added. "That was 1992. Fifteen years after this incident. There has to be a connection."

Perry hopped closer. "Maybe some stones are better left unturned."

Neve shook her head, her eyes bright with purpose. "No. My father kept these files for a reason. He wanted me to find them."

"Or he simply forgot to burn them," Perry muttered.

"I need to find Dr. Feldman," Neve decided, already reaching for her laptop. "If she's still alive."

"And if she is? What then? You'll just walk up and say, 'Hi, remember my dad? The one who was working with you on the protocol that led to your unfortunate downfall?'"

Neve looked at him, her expression serious. "Yes. That's exactly what I'll do."

Perry sighed dramatically. "Of course you will. Direct and literal as always." He hopped down to steal another slice of mango. "People tend to get defensive when they are questioned about their criminal pasts."

"I'm not interested in judgment," Neve replied, her fingers flying over the keys. "I just want the truth."

Outside, the sun began to set over Aura Cove, casting long shadows through the sunroom's windows. On Neve's bulletin board, the faces of her father and Dr. Feldman stared back at her. There had to be a connection between them that could help explain why her father had vanished, leaving behind only fragmented clues and unanswered questions.

The truth was out there, and Neve was now more determined than ever to find it.

CHAPTER
FIVE

NEVE STOOD at the entrance of the nondescript office of Tampa Bay Vital Records & Adoption Services. Its brusque, bureaucratic façade was all sharp angles and tinted windows that reflected the overcast sky. Gritting her teeth, Neve rubbed the rough surface of the purple geode, its warmth spreading through her palm, anchoring her racing thoughts.

"Truth," she muttered under her breath. "Focus on finding the truth." In her hand, the geode pulsed twice as if agreeing.

She took a step forward, and the automatic doors slid open with a mechanical whoosh that made her wince. Inside, LED lights with a bluish cast added a cold pallor over the institutional grey walls. The air smelled of stale coffee, and the agency's waiting area was blank and sterile, with orange molded plastic chairs arranged in stiff rows.

As she approached the reception desk, she was met with an unenthusiastic receptionist. A bored expression hung on the woman's face, accompanied by the rhythmic clicking of keys on her computer.

"Can I help you?" the receptionist asked, her tone dismissive, without glancing up from the screen.

Neve straightened her posture, determined not to let the woman's indifference undermine her own resolve. "I'm here to obtain my adoption records and any information related to my biological parents," she said, repeating the words she'd rehearsed. They spilled out in a rush as if she couldn't spit them out fast enough. Neve placed her father's death certificate on the counter.

"My father's name is Ellis LaRue. He—he's deceased." The admission was heavy, but she plowed on. "I am also in need of any information about my birth mother. In case I develop a hereditary medical condition that requires a thorough medical history."

The receptionist blinked in confusion. "That's not how this works."

"That's exactly how this should work," Neve countered. She tapped the certificate on the counter for emphasis before continuing. "I need information. You have information. It should be a simple transaction."

The receptionist sighed. She tilted her head, and her lips pinched downward into a frown. "What year was your adoption?"

"1977," Neve answered.

"Since you were adopted in 1977, your adoption records are sealed under Florida law, which was the standard practice at the time. That includes your original birth certificate and any court documents related to the adoption."

Neve felt the first trickle of frustration filter in.

"To access those records, you would need to file a petition with the circuit court in the county where your adoption was finalized. A judge would need to review your request and determine whether there is cause to unseal the records."

"But that makes no logical sense," Neve interrupted, her voice rising despite her attempts to control it.

The receptionist's face remained an impenetrable wall. She reached for a brochure and handed it to Neve. "Here's information about requesting sealed records from the courts. It's a complex process that can take months…"

"Months?" Neve snatched the brochure from her hand, scanning the words as she read aloud. "Special circumstances include: medical emergencies, legal disputes, inheritance claims…" Her voice trailed off as she noticed a peculiar clause. "Records may remain permanently sealed if requested by biological parents or in cases involving protected parties." She looked up and asked, "Protected parties?"

"Victims of abuse, individuals with mental health issues, those protected under safe haven laws, et cetera. If there's nothing else I can help you with…" The receptionist's dismissive tone suggested the conversation was over.

The geode warmed against Neve's hip as her frustration mounted. "I need answers, and I thought I was going to get them today."

The tremble of despair in her voice must have cracked through the gatekeeper's thick bureaucratic veneer because the woman's expression softened slightly. "Let me see if the director has a moment." She strode to a door and rapped on it with her knuckles before disappearing inside.

When the receptionist returned, she gave a curt nod. "The director can give you five minutes." She lifted the countertop, allowing her access. Neve walked to the door and took a moment to gather her composure before knocking softly.

"Come in!" called a warm voice from the other side.

Neve stepped into an office with expansive bookshelves and framed photographs of smiling families. The director, a woman in her fifties with short, sandy hair and kind eyes, was seated behind a desk littered with files and paperwork. A name placard read Patricia Walsh.

"Please have a seat," Patricia said, gesturing to a chair while sliding her reading glasses down her nose to scrutinize Neve's face over the top of them.

"Thank you," Neve said, settling in, her heart pounding in her chest.

"Cathy explained your situation," she began.

"Then you understand why I need these records," Neve said, leaning forward. "My father died, and I..."

She held up one hand and interrupted, "Ms. LaRue, I sympathize, but..."

"No, you don't," Neve cut in. "You're paid to say that, but you can't possibly understand what it's like to discover your entire life was built on lies."

Patricia's professional mask slipped a fraction, but she insisted, "The law is clear about sealed records."

"The law is wrong." Neve's hand found the geode again, searching for comfort.

"I understand, but you must acknowledge the legal restrictions surrounding adoption records. My hands are tied." She leaned back in her chair, imploring Neve for understanding. "I truly wish I could help," Patricia continued. "But it's probable your mother requested no contact."

Neve frowned, squeezing the geode in her pocket. Feeling cornered, she gritted her teeth, trying to suppress the tears that threatened to spill over. "I just want to know who I am. Is that too much to ask?"

"Your only course of action is to petition the court to unseal the records," Patricia reiterated, sympathy dripping from every word. "I'm sorry."

Neve stood abruptly, her chair scraping against the floor. "Thank you for nothing. I guess I'll have to find another way."

Stepping back into the bright daylight was blinding and a stark contrast to the gloomy frustration humming beneath her skin. Neve didn't want to give up, but every door felt like it was slamming shut in her face. Her mind was already racing ten steps ahead, considering new alternatives as the geode hummed against her skin.

When she arrived home, Perry was perched on his

favorite spot, flapping his wings while being spritzed by the automatic mister.

"By that thundercloud expression, I take it the bureaucrats weren't very helpful?" he asked, folding his wings back down and turning his full attention to Neve.

"The records are sealed," Neve replied, pulling out the geode. It glowed and pulsed in her palm. "But maybe there's another way."

A shiver of fear made Perry shake his red tail feathers. "Oh no. No, no, no. You're not thinking what I think you're thinking."

"I have to go back to 1976," Neve murmured, staring into the crystal's depths. "When they were all together. Before all the lies."

"Need I remind you what happened last time?" Perry hopped closer, his voice sharp with concern. "Five years, Neve. During the jump, you aged *five years* in *twenty-one days!*" He started to pace, one taloned foot in front of the other.

"It's worth the risk," she declared as the geode's warmth spread up her arm. "I need to know who I am, Perry. Who my parents were, and why everything happened the way it did."

"What happens if you age ten years next time? Or twenty?" Perry's wing brushed her cheek. "The cost is too high."

But Neve's focus had narrowed to the pulsing crystal in her hand. She could almost see the lab where her parents had worked, could almost smell the antiseptic and hear the whir of centrifuges. The geode responded to her concentration, its glow intensifying.

"I have to try," she whispered.

CHAPTER

SIX

THE FLORIDA SUN beat down on Neve as she hauled yet another box of Sheila's post-apocalypse detritus to the dumpster she'd rented. Though she'd made significant headway, there was still a considerable amount of the hoard left. Inside were dozens of expired bottles of antibiotics and a concerning number of gas masks.

"You missed one!" Perry called from his perch on the mailbox. "And there's still a survival manual under the bed titled *A Wise Woman's Prepper Playbook*."

"That's staying there until I can burn it," Neve muttered, wiping sweat from her brow. She checked her watch—10:47 AM. Her schedule was already twelve minutes behind.

The joint pain in her fingers made her wince as she lifted another box. These unfamiliar aches, along with the age spots appearing on her hands, were becoming harder to ignore. She rubbed small circles at the base of her spine, trying to massage away relentless back pain. Neve now relied on Aleve to get her through most days, as well as cooling gel mitts for her swollen knuckles at the end of a day spent gripping a pencil.

She had set up her studio inside the sunroom. On the drafting table, her latest architectural piece waited. The half-finished charcoal drawing of the Tampa Theatre's baroque façade was depicted in painstaking detail. Her smooth lines captured every ornate cornice, and the delicate shading brought the piece to life. On the other side, much to her dismay, sat three commissioned pet portraits in various stages of creation.

"Mrs. Henderson's poodle looks constipated," Perry observed, flying to rest on the top edge of her tilted drafting table.

"It's not finished," Neve replied, picking up her charcoal pencil, as she settled on the stool in front of it. "And you're not supposed to be in here when I'm working."

"But I'm your muse! You need me!" he argued, crunching down on a macadamia nut with his beak.

The offensive sound sent shivers down her spine. "Perry, please. I have to finish these by Friday."

"Fine. I'll just sit here. Quietly. Eating my lunch. Crunch. Crunch. Crunch."

Neve closed her eyes, counting to ten. Her rigid work schedule had already been thrown off by the morning's cleaning, and Perry's desperate bids for attention clearly weren't helping. She glanced at her calendar. Thirty-two more days until Mercury Retrograde, the astrological phenomenon where the planet Mercury appeared to move backward in its orbit from the perspective on Earth. It was an event that happened four times each calendar year, and Neve suspected it somehow opened a portal to the past, allowing for time travel. She didn't know if she could influence where her next jump took her, but she was resolved to try. Every night, she held the geode, focusing on 1976, hoping she could somehow program it like a cosmic GPS.

Two weeks later, she suffered another nosebleed, the third in a week. As she tilted her head back, Perry fluttered around her, a ball of nerves.

"Perhaps we should reconsider this whole time travel business," he suggested.

"I have an appointment tomorrow," Neve said through the tissue. "Dr. Randolph at 2:15 PM."

"And what exactly are you going to tell her? 'Sorry, Doc, I time-traveled and now I'm aging like a banana in the sun'?"

"I've prepared a logical explanation about my accelerated aging symptoms." Neve checked her reflection, ensuring no blood remained. "She doesn't need to know about the geode."

The next day, in Dr. Randolph's office, Neve's logical explanation felt less convincing. She ran through a spreadsheet she'd created to catalogue the timeline of her symptoms, trying not to worry each time she saw the doctor's eyes widen more.

"So, these symptoms started suddenly?" Dr. Randolph asked, examining the inside of Neve's nose with a scope. The obnoxious pin light at the end of it made Neve squint.

"Yes," Neve answered, then asked, "Is it possible for the human body to age at an accelerated rate?"

"It *is* possible, but usually there is a root cause. It can be attributed to genetics, lifestyle factors, chronic stress, environmental exposures, or underlying medical conditions. We'll run some tests and see what we can figure out."

The doctor ordered blood tests and recommended a consultation with a rheumatologist and dermatologist. On her way out, she heard the doctor mumbling into her digital transcription recorder about "unusual presentation of advanced aging symptoms."

Back home, the dumpster was almost full of Sheila's belongings. Neve had discovered, among other things, seventeen pairs of night vision goggles, a manual for breeding cockroaches for protein, and a disturbingly detailed plan for converting the garage into a bunker.

"Look what I found!" Perry emerged from a box wearing a tiny tinfoil hat and strutting like he was on a catwalk. "My bird twin just confirmed Sheila made it for him. It was supposed to provide protection from government mind control."

"That explains so much about her," Neve sighed, adding another box to the pile.

As June melted into July, Neve strived to maintain her schedule, using Alexa to keep her on track. Every day, she'd wake at 6 AM, meditate and set her intention with the geode, feed Perry by 6:15, have breakfast at 6:45, shower, and sit down at her desk by 7:30. Then, she'd work through eight Pomodoro sessions.

The inquiries for pet portraits multiplied. Word had gotten out about her gift for capturing animal personalities on social media, much to her chagrin, and the commissions were coming in at a feverish clip.

"Oh, look, another request for a whimsical portrait," Perry announced with glee, reading her emails over her shoulder. "This nutball wants their hamster dressed as Napoleon."

"I specialize in classical architecture," Neve mumbled in dismay, but opened a new sketch pad anyway. "Not rodents wearing historical costumes."

"Think of it as diversifying your portfolio," Perry suggested, dropping walnut shells on her clean floor.

August approached, bringing more age spots and a letter from the Florida Vital Records Office in response to her request to unseal her mother's records. Request denied. Neve added the rejection letter to her growing collection of dead ends.

"Four days until Mercury Retrograde," she told Perry one evening, holding the geode up to the setting sun. Its purple surface seemed to swallow the light.

"You know," Perry said, unusually serious and reflective, "there's no assurance you'll be able to dictate your next destination, temporal or otherwise."

"Stop trying to talk me out of it." Neve closed her eyes, picturing 1976. She'd committed the Polaroids to memory. In her mind's eye, she could see the lab, her father's white coat, and the swell of the woman's belly.

"I can see you've made up your mind," Perry cawed

as he hopped up on her shoulder. "Just do me a small favor, will you?"

"What is it this time?" Neve swiped her hand to shoo him away.

"If we traverse to the wrong era and meet Shakespeare, please allow me the opportunity to recite the 'to be or not to be' soliloquy. I've been rehearsing like a thespian on opening night and have finally perfected a performance so profound it would make Kenneth Branagh weep."

Despite herself, a crimp of a smile quirked up the corners of Neve's mouth. "If that happens, I will allow it." Perry let out a joyful chirp.

The geode warmed in her palm, its energy humming in harmony with hers. Somewhere in the past, her parents were alive, working together in a research lab, and she was desperate to unite with them, hopeful she would be granted the opportunity in just a few days. Neve couldn't wait. The truth was calling.

CHAPTER

SEVEN

A FEW DAYS LATER, soft morning light from the overcast sky streamed through Neve's sunroom windows, casting perfect north-facing illumination across her drafting table. She'd positioned it forty-five degrees from the window, marking the spot with blue tape on the concrete floor.

Seated at the table, Neve's hand shaded with surgical precision as she worked her pencils across the sheet of textured paper. Her fingers smudged the graphite, creating depth in the shadows of the ornate archways and elaborate wrought-iron balconies of the Henry B. Plant Museum. The heel of her hand was stained black as the final five minutes of her sketching session ticked down. She'd just finished shading the silver minarets of the museum, and the impressive silhouette was emerging from the paper like a photograph developing in a darkroom. Its Moorish Revival architecture required attention to every detail, and she was determined to do the iconic building justice.

Behind her, Perry shifted around on his perch. He'd agreed to keep quiet as a condition of being allowed to watch Neve work. Two minutes before the alarm sounded, trying to be helpful, an observation slipped out. "The crescent moon designs above the windows are slightly off," Perry warbled, hopping closer to peer at the drawing.

"They're not finished," Neve replied, her blue eyes narrowing as she considered his criticism of the proportions. She studied the reference photographs in her hands, glancing back and forth for several minutes before she let out a groan and said a small voice, "As much as it pains me to admit it, you're right."

She grabbed her art gum eraser and kneaded it for several minutes, pulling it apart until it was soft and pliable, before she used it to remove the inaccurate line work. Mercury's impending retrograde pressed against her consciousness like a clock in countdown mode, but Neve refused to let it affect the quality of her final pieces. She approached the challenge like a mathematical equation, scheduling Alexa to begin her day two hours earlier and adding two more Pomodoro sketching sessions.

Nearby, her phone skittered across the end table as it vibrated with an incoming call. Lisa's name flashed on the screen for the fourth time, and Neve let out an anxious huff as she read part of the message on her lock screen, then returned to her work. It was August 4th, the eve of Mercury in Retrograde, and every minute was precious. That afternoon, she had to deliver the drawings to Lisa in case she was hurled back in time again. Neve wasn't about to jeopardize her first solo show at the Elysian Atelier.

"If that woman calls you one more time, I'm going to fly over there, sit on her windowsill, and whistle 'Baby Shark' on repeat until she loses her ever-loving mind," Perry declared.

Neve's lips twitched, appreciating the solidarity, but she remained steadfast in maintaining her focus. She consulted her planning binder open beside her, where each day until the opening was color-coded and annotated with tasks. Green tabs for artwork completion, blue for delivery logistics, yellow for lighting setup, red for potential crisis points.

The phone buzzed again.

"Just need two minutes of your time," Lisa's text read. "Thinking we might need to adjust the track lighting. The engineer recommends two degrees west..."

Neve's fingers tightened around her charcoal pencil. "Two degrees west? That wasn't in the plan. The lighting setup was finalized last week. We spent three hours measuring the exact angles for optimal shadow definition."

"Humans," Perry muttered. "Always complicating simple things. Want me to send her a strongly worded tweet? A tweet hits different coming from someone of the avian persuasion."

Before Neve could respond, her phone screen flickered, then went dark. Frowning, she set down her pencil and turned to her laptop. She hit play and watched her video portfolio roll, checking the image sequencing one last time. Each piece had to flow into the next, telling the story of Aura Cove and Tampa Bay's architectural history through shadow and highlight. The media player started, then there was a whir as her external hard drive stuttered and fell silent.

"No, no, no," she whispered, abandoning her drawing and rushing to her desk, clutching the malfunctioning computer to her chest. All her portfolio files, the exhibition layout, and six months of work were on that drive. She jabbed the power button repeatedly, each click more forceful than the last, but the blue indicator light remained stubbornly dark.

"Uh-oh!" Perry whistled. "The score is Mercury in Retrograde: one, Neve: zero," he commented from his perch. "I believe I warned you about trusting technology during your last planetary backspin."

As if on cue, her elbow knocked against her carefully arranged set of specialty charcoal pencils. She watched in horror as they clattered to the floor, her prized German pencils shattering on impact.

"Make that Mercury: two," Perry added in an 'I told you so' tone. "Should I start keeping a tally on your bulletin board?" Neve's gaze shifted to the bulletin boards where she'd assembled a makeshift timeline, and it added to the overwhelm. Neve closed her eyes, trying to re-center her busy brain.

"I don't have time for this right now," she mumbled under her breath as she filled another imaginary red balloon with her fiery frustration before letting it go. When she opened her eyes, she did feel calm enough to rework the turrets and add the finishing touches over the next hour before she loaded the entire collection into two leather portfolios and carried them to her Sprinter van.

Even at 7 p.m., the August heat was oppressive. She drove toward the gallery on Main Street and quickly parked the Sprinter van, darting to the entrance carrying both of her portfolio classes. The bell above Elysian Atelier's door chimed as Neve pressed the handicapped entry button and carefully maneuvered through it.

"Nevermore! At last!" Lisa emerged from her office. Her bold, geometric print dress made her appear to be wrapped in a Mondrian painting. "I've been trying to reach you all day. We need to discuss the…"

"The lighting angles. I know," Neve interrupted, setting down her cases. "But they're perfect as planned. We measured three times, remember? The shadows will fall forty-five degrees from each piece, creating the optimal viewing experience."

Lisa waved her hand dismissively. "No, well, yes, but that's not the urgent matter. *The Tampa Tribune* wants to do a feature article. They want to send someone out next week to interview you, but I wanted to run it by you first."

Neve rolled forward on the balls of her feet as the tension built in her belly. "Next week won't work. I won't be here."

"What do you mean you won't be here? This is huge exposure for the gallery and a crucial step to generate interest for opening night. Your architectural renderings of Tampa's historical buildings are exactly what their readership loves."

"I have to go to New Orleans," Neve blurted out, her mind racing. She averted her eyes as guilt from the lie burned in her cheeks. "For research. There's an architectural preservation conference. It's very exclusive, and I've been on the waiting list for five years." The lie felt thick on her tongue, yet she was surprised at how much more adept she'd become at it. Neve wasn't sure if it was a blessing or a curse. "It gives me exclusive access inside the French Quarter's most prominent historical buildings. I must take the reference photographs that are crucial for my next series."

Lisa's microbladed eyebrows drew together. "But the show opens in less than a month. We need you here for the final arrangements, the lighting tests, the press..."

"We discussed this before we scheduled the show. I wanted to wait until November."

"Historically, attendance is much lower in the fourth quarter. People are traveling and distracted by the holidays."

"I remember," Neve said, "And I told you I could get the pieces done, but I would be out of town for most of August."

"You did," Lisa finally conceded, nodding.

"I've documented all the relevant details for the show here," Neve said as she pulled out the color-coded binder. "Everything's measured, annotated, and cross-referenced."

"But—"

"And I've created detailed sketches of each wall," Neve continued, spreading out the diagrams she'd made of the layout. "The Henry B. Plant Museum series needs to be grouped together, with the shadows aligned to create a narrative flow from the minarets to the riverfront view."

Lisa studied the meticulous plans, her expression softening. "You have been very thorough, but three weeks? That seems excessive for a conference."

"If I want the work to be authentic, I have to be immersed in it. I need to spend time at each site and drink it in, not just work from crude photographs." Neve opened her portfolio case, hoping she could silence Lisa's objections by giving her a peek at the finished pieces.

"Ooh!" Lisa clapped her hands together as she flipped through the pages of the portfolio. When she got to the last page, she gasped in awe as she drank in every detail of the Henry B. Plant Museum's façade. "Absolute perfection."

The drawing's graphic realism seemed to distract Lisa from her concerns about logistics and marketing. "This is extraordinary. The way you've captured the morning light hitting the museum's Moorish arches…"

"So, we're okay? About me being away?" Neve pressed, trying to keep the twinge of desperation from her voice.

Lisa sighed, running a manicured finger along the drawing's edge. "I suppose. But you'll be back for the opening? September first?"

"Absolutely," Neve promised, praying to whatever

forces controlled time travel that she wasn't lying. "I wouldn't miss it for the world."

Near midnight, Neve was drying her dinner dishes when a knock at the door startled her. She tried to ignore it when another knock, louder this time, disrupted her count of circles she was making with the dishtowel.

"I don't like unexpected visitors. Especially at this hour," she muttered under her breath as she folded the towel and laid it down.

"Maybe if we're very quiet," Perry stage-whispered, "they'll go away."

Neve nodded. "Yes, good plan. I like it very much."

"Nevermore!" Talulah's voice carried through the door on the heels of another round of knocks. "I know you're hidin' in there."

Thunder rumbled in the distance as if emphasizing Talulah's demand.

"Please open up. I need to talk to you. My rose quartz is practically vibratin' off my neck."

Neve sighed, knowing her aunt wouldn't leave until she opened the door. When she did, Talulah swept in like an ethereal storm, her flowy organic cotton dress trailing behind her. The scents of sage and lavender wafted from her and into the surrounding air.

"We need to talk," Talulah announced, her grey-blue eyes crinkled with concern. A carved rose quartz pendant swung from her neck as she strode behind, following Neve into the sunroom. "I've been feelin' an energy shift for the last two days. My roommate, Yuli, had a vision, and it wasn't good. Not good at all. She told me to hightail it over here."

Neve's shoulders tensed, and she reached up and tightened each of her braids as she paced. Unannounced visits disrupted her routine and often sent her anxiety spiraling. "If you came over here to talk me out of it, you're too late." The ominous rumble of thunder drowned out the rest of her bold declaration. Ignoring her aunt, she walked over to her messenger bag and pulled out the purple geode. It quivered with purpose in her hand, and she squeezed her hand shut around it as her energy peaked in response.

"It's too dangerous! You're plannin' on ridin' the lightnin' during the worst Mercury Retrograde in decades. It's not worth it!" Talulah's voice rose.

Perry fluttered closer to Neve, stopping just short of perching on her shoulder. Thunder rumbled as it closed in, emphasizing Talulah's warning. Neve moved to the window, watching charcoal gray clouds gather over Aura Cove when a flash of lightning lit up the sky.

"Look at those clouds," Talulah pressed. "Even nature's trying to tell you somethin'."

"Nature's telling me it's time." Neve turned back to her aunt, her blue eyes intense.

"But you can't control where you'll end up!" Talulah's bracelets jangled as she gestured. "You could land anywhere in time, and the last jump aged you. You lost five whole years!"

"Better than losing my entire life to lies," Neve countered. "You've always taught me about the power of clear intention, about focusing energy. Well, my intention has never been clearer. I've spent the last several months focusing on Dad and 1976. I trust the geode will guide me there."

In confirmation, lightning flickered across the darkening sky again. Neve grabbed her jacket and tucked the geode inside the pocket. Its crystalline surface was warm against the fabric on her hip. The stone seemed to pulse with its own heartbeat, matching the approaching storm's rhythm.

"I'm going to the beach," she announced, her voice steady despite the trembling of her hands. "You can either help me or stay here, but I'm not changing my mind." She turned to the bird. "Perry? You coming?"

Perry hesitated only for a moment, then flapped behind her.

"Spirit guides, help us now," Talulah muttered, following Neve out the door. "You're just as stubborn as your father. At least let me ground your energy first."

"No more crystals, no more ceremonies," Neve cut her off, striding toward the shore. Perry clung to her shoulder as the wind picked up, his feathers ruffling. The wind whipped around them as they made their way down the beach path. Rain began to fall, first as gentle drops, then in sheets that blurred the world into a foggy atmospheric scene. The air crackled with electricity, making her skin tingle and individual strands of her streaked brown hair stand on end.

Waves crashed against the rocks, their rhythm matching the thunder overhead. Each bolt of lightning illuminated the churning water in stark white flashes. Neve's hair plastered to her face as she stood at the water's edge, the geode searing her upper thigh now despite the cold rain.

"Please, darlin'," Talulah called over the storm, her lavender dress whipping around her like storm clouds. "Don't do this. Not today. The energy's all wrong. It's too strong, too wild!"

But Neve could feel it, the electric charge in the air, the way time seemed to bend around her like light refracting through a prism. The outside world warped, and a rainbow of colors stretched and bled together like watercolor on paper. This was her moment, her chance to uncover another piece of her past.

"Sometimes you have to chase the lightning," Neve shouted back, pulling the geode out of her pocket and raising her hand toward the sky. The geode pulsed with blue-white energy, matching the storm's intensity, as Perry's talons anchored to her shoulder.

"For the record," the parrot screeched, "this is exactly the kind of selfish, impulsive behavior you're always lecturing me about!"

"Then stay here," Neve said.

"We're a team," Perry squawked out. "You go, I go."

Neve nodded, the rain so thick now it ran down her cheeks and dropped from her chin in rivulets. The air crackled, thick with ozone, and Neve's skin tingled as electricity built around them, making the silver streaks in her hair float like a storm cloud. The world seemed to hold its breath, suspended between moments. She braced for impact, knowing the searing pain would take her breath away, and squinted her eyes as her entire body trembled with fear.

Next to her, Talulah screamed a warning, but her words were lost in the roar of the storm. Through the rain, Neve saw her aunt's face transform from concern to horror as the energy built to unstable levels.

Lightning split the sky, a brilliant fork of white-hot energy that arched toward Neve like the blade of a scythe. When it connected to the geode, Neve shuttered her eyes away from the burning white light. The geode splintered with orange fire, its energy infusing into her body, and the searing heat made her slump forward.

Then silence. The storm quieted as if a switch had been flipped.

Where Neve and Perry had stood, only scorched sand remained. Talulah collapsed to her knees, her wet dress a magnet for the sand. Among the smoldering ashes lay a single scarlet tail feather and the rest of the geode, another shard now missing.

PART 2: MERCURY IN RETROGRADE AUGUST 1976

CHAPTER 8

PEREGRINE

WAKING up was never my forte. Dazed and lightheaded, I blinked against the sterile illumination that had a sickly green cast.

As coherent thoughts emerged, I became more aware of my surroundings. My wings shook, and a sense of dread crashed over me like an icy wave when I saw them. Cages. One entire wall of my new digs was teeming with animal specimen cages. They were constructed of grim metal, housing cowering rodents whose beady eyes were wide with terror. The rancid scent of droppings rankled my senses along with the tang of chemicals in the air. Sheer panic reverberated through my body as I drank in the scientific lab instruments and workstations across from me.

I glanced around, my bird-brain processing the scene. The furiously twitching noses of anxious mice, their little hearts pounding like war drums; a rabbit, with red, weepy eyes, wide and quivering. A startling realization drifted up from the ether, and my bird twin trembled in terror at the thought. I was inside a research facility. Was I to be used for experimentation?

I hopped closer to a trembling white rat, observing as its compatriot devolved into frenzied hysteria, chewing at its foot. Blood stained the fur of another. What kind of monstrosity was occurring here? And would I be cursed with the same visceral fate? I shuddered at the thought.

The screech of metal against metal sent jolts of alarm ringing throughout my avian psyche. The wall of clattering cages, scuttling forms, and the echoes of tortured cries gnawed at my sanity.

One thing was true: if fate demanded my presence here, it meant I had a role to play. I sent my bird twin deeper into my subconsciousness, pleased that his fears became more manageable the further he retreated, and assessed my options. I needed to devise a plan, and quickly.

The laboratory door swung open with a theatrical whoosh, and in walked an eccentric middle-aged woman whose flaming red curls laced with strands of silver spiraled around her head like a halo of fire. She strode with purpose, her arms wrapped around a clipboard, but her white lab coat was missing a button and contrasted with the mismatched socks peeking out beneath her cropped bell-bottom trousers. One sock was red with microscopes, the other yellow with what appeared to be elements from the Periodic Table, stuffed inside a pair of shiny Mary Janes. A flash of recognition appeared, then dissolved before I could place her.

"Good morning, specimens," she announced, her voice crisp. "Today is August 5, 1976."

1976! My heart leapt! Neve had done it. I had to admit I'd been skeptical about her ability to control our destination, but here I was. Now, where was she?

The odd woman moved from station to station, her hands performing a peculiar ritual, tapping each cage door three times before proceeding. When she reached my cage, her eyes widened, revealing irises the color of polished emeralds.

"You're not supposed to be here," she stated in a monotone, head tilting at a forty-five-degree angle. "African grey. *Psittacus Erithacus*. Highly intelligent. But you were not on my requisition list." She consulted the clipboard in her arms before agreeing with herself. "Fact. There must be a mistake with our last acquisition." She studied the paperwork. "Donna," she called out, then let out a distressed groan that hung in the back of her throat.

I seized my opportunity. "Lady, if I had a nickel for every time someone told me I wasn't supposed to be somewhere, I'd have enough to buy myself out of this nightmare."

The clipboard she'd been holding clattered to the floor as her mouth formed a perfect 'O' of astonishment.

"You can vocalize in complete sentences? An African grey capable of communicating complex ideation?" She knelt, retrieving her clipboard while she considered the shocking ramifications. "Fascinating."

"Fascinating?" I flapped my wings for dramatic effect. "I'm trapped in a lab that looks like it was decorated by Josef Mengele, and you find my *vocabulary* fascinating? Your priorities are sketchier than the Watergate tapes."

"*And* you understand the subtleties of humor? How extraordinary." A small smile fought its way across her serious face, and her nose crinkled as she regarded me with greater interest. "I'm Dr. Elaine Feldman. Head cancer research scientist at Aureon Biomedical." She unlatched my cage with surprising gentleness. "Would you prefer to sit on my shoulder? I believe you will find it less confining and will give you a better vantage point."

Suspicious but desperate for freedom, I hopped onto her outstretched forearm. "Don't mind if I do. Though, fair warning, I've been told my colorful commentary is an acquired taste."

"I've been told the same." She reached into her pocket, producing a handful of sunflower seeds. "Nutrition. Important for cognitive function."

I accepted her offering, the familiar comfort of food momentarily quieting my anxiety. "So, Doc, what's the deal with the rodent sick ward over there?"

Dr. Feldman's fingers tapped three times before closing the cage. She answered my question as she moved between workstations. "Before we can begin human trials, we must test our experimental compounds on rodents. Some experience side effects. It's unavoidable in early trials."

"Side effects? That albino over there is missing

patches of fur and shaking like he's auditioning for 'Saturday Night Fever.'"

"Protocol VitOx has aggressive parameters," she admitted, her voice dropping to a whisper. "It's on the fast track. We can't afford to wait." Her voice quavered, and I wondered who *'we'* was.

Eager to save my skin, I asked, "Is there another way I can help without becoming radioactive?"

She paused, head tilting again as she studied me. "You demonstrate exceptional intelligence, self-awareness, and even limited empathy." Her fingers resumed their tapping, but slower now. "You won't be enrolled in the Protocol VitOx trial; perhaps you may be of assistance in another manner. I will need to consult with Robert. He'll know how to best utilize your special skills."

Relief flooded through me, but before I could express my gratitude or ask who Robert was, she continued. "There is compelling evidence that shows companion animals can provide therapeutic benefits. Their presence has been clinically associated with the modulation of psychiatric symptoms through established mechanisms of attachment, routine, and nonjudgmental social interaction."

Though the words "psychiatric symptoms" gave me pause, I powered through. After all, what other choice did I have?

I dipped my wing in a bow and said, "Well then, allow me to introduce myself. Peregrine at your service."

CHAPTER

NINE

THE SMELL HIT NEVE FIRST, a pungent tang of sickeningly sweet chemicals and biting bleach with a musky undercurrent of soiled animal bedding. Her eyes fluttered open to flickering fluorescents flooding over Formica countertops, their surfaces lined with medical equipment. A tension headache throbbed at Neve's temples, and she squinted at her surroundings. Bulky microscopes with analog dials and switches occupied fifteen workstations where lab-coated researchers were hunched over slides. A clunky IBM Selectric clattered away nearby, its keys a stark contrast against the high falsetto of The Bee Gees drifting from a small transistor radio in the corner.

Her hands felt strange, smaller than her own, and she gasped in shock when she realized they were balancing a tower of glass petri dishes. Glass clinked against glass as she fought to steady the swaying stack before it could crash to the floor.

Careful.

"What the—" she began, before catching her reflection in a nearby cabinet. The face staring back wasn't hers. Round glasses, blonde hair in a classic Dorothy Hamill wedge cut, and a smattering of freckles across a button nose. She jerked her head back once, twice, fighting the wispy bangs that tickled her forehead. The sensation was maddening, her nerves already ragged from the unfamiliar body she inhabited. The stack of petri dishes wobbled, and she lunged forward, desperate to keep her grip on the teetering glass.

"No, no, no," Neve muttered under her breath.

Too late. The stack toppled, glass shattering across the linoleum floor with a crash that echoed from one wall to the other. The cloudy cultures that had been contained inside splattered all over, creating abstract patterns on the walls that reminded Neve of a Jackson Pollock painting.

A door swung open, and a familiar woman with wild red curls with glints of silver stepped in, wearing a lab coat over cropped slacks and colorful mismatched socks. Seeing the mess, she groaned, then tapped her thumb and forefinger together three times and started pacing. Behind her loomed a tall man with serious blue eyes that made Neve's heart stop beating.

Her father. Ellis LaRue. He was thirty years younger than she remembered, but it was unmistakably him. His thick brown hair was cropped short, spiked on his head in a buzz cut. He was in a blue button-down with a navy tie that peeked out of the neck of his ironed lab coat.

A powerful thrill shot through Neve as she realized she'd influenced the geode and landed exactly where she'd hoped. In response, it tingled against her hip in the pocket of her white lab coat. Every minute she'd spent focused on returning to 1976 had been worth it. Here she was, working in a research lab alongside her father. It was a dream come true.

Neve received another message, and anxiety flooded into the strange body she'd awoken in.

Great! Everyone is staring at me. Dr. Feldman will think I'm incompetent, and I'll lose my job.

"Donna, what happened?" Ellis asked, his tone sharp yet concerned, his loafers crunching on the shattered glass.

Before Neve could formulate a response, the red-haired woman surveyed the damage with clinical detachment.

"Those cultures took three weeks to grow," she stated in a monotone voice, adjusting her glasses. "The Burkitt's lymphoma line was particularly difficult to establish. Fact." She let out an annoyed groan that sounded like a wounded animal.

Don't look her in the eye. She hates it when people challenge her. Keep your head down.

"I'm so sorry," Neve stammered, her voice soft and unfamiliar in her ears. "I don't know what happened; I just lost my grip."

"First week jitters, maybe?" Ellis asked, his tone softening.

"Inefficient use of resources," the redhead countered. "Dr. Feldman does not approve. Also, fact."

Ellis sighed. "Dr. Feldman, she's new. Remember when I dropped that centrifuge rotor last year?" Neve darted a quick smile of appreciation at him for throwing himself under the bus.

Dr. Feldman's cheeks reddened. "Different circumstances. We were understaffed that day. This was an error that could have been avoided." Neve found herself wanting to straighten her spine, to meet Dr. Feldman's disapproving glare head-on, but Donna's body seemed determined to shrink into itself.

Perfect! Thanks to your butterfingers, my boss hates me now.

A young woman appeared in the doorway, her white lab coat immaculate over a paisley blouse with wide lapels. "What's the commotion? I heard... oh." She surveyed the extensive mess, then shot Neve a sympathetic smile. Neve stared at her in utter shock and disbelief. She was the woman in the Polaroid from the attic.

"Let's get this cleaned up," Ellis said, interrupting her spiraling thoughts. "Diana, get the biohazard kit from the supply closet. And for Pete's sake, watch where you step." With a huff, Dr. Feldman strode away, as Neve grabbed a broom.

Her borrowed hands shook as she gripped the dustpan, the sharp burn of bleach making her eyes water. Diana?

Diana has been my best friend since undergrad. She's the only one who really sees me.

Neve tried to focus on cleaning up while Donna's memories washed over her. Scenes flickered through her mind: Diana and Donna sharing lunch breaks at the commons, late-night study sessions, and she saw Diana holding Donna's hand through a panic attack after a freshman-year breakup.

The depth of their friendship fascinated Neve. Though she understood the concept of best friends intellectually, she'd never experienced such a connection herself. It felt like observing an exotic species in its natural habitat, familiar in theory, but foreign in practice.

"Whew!" Neve swooned on Donna's unsteady feet in sensible heels from the emotional overload.

"Are you okay?" Diana rushed over, clearly concerned about her friend.

"Yep," Neve responded, forcing a cheery smile on Donna's face.

Diana crouched down, her polyester skirt brushing the floor as she helped gather glass shards. "Hey, don't sweat it. I knocked over an entire rack of test tubes during my first week. She'll get over it. Dr. Feldman's bark is worse than her bite."

You should apologize again. Offer to make coffee for everyone.

"Or not," Neve muttered under her breath, fighting Donna's instinct to people-please. Where Donna saw social obligation, Neve saw only the task at hand, broken glass that needed cleaning up, nothing more. The younger woman's mind was a whirlwind of "sorry" and "my fault" and "what will they think," a foreign language to Neve's practicality. She pressed her lips together, tamping down her frustration. Why waste energy on imaginary judgment when there was actual work to be done?

You should offer to stay late. Make up for the lost time.

"That won't be necessary," Neve said aloud, earning a curious look from Diana.

"What won't be?" Diana asked, carefully depositing more glass shards into the biohazard bin.

"Nothing," Neve replied quickly, feeling Donna's embarrassment flush her cheeks. The meticulous way Donna cataloged every social interaction, studied every micro facial expression change for evidence of anger, felt exhausting to Neve. She was used to moving through the world focused on productivity, not this constant drain of interpreting social cues.

"Really, Don, it's fine," Diana whispered, squeezing her arm. "I've got your back."

She means it. Diana always means it.

The warmth of friendship in Donna's thoughts was genuine, making Neve's heart swell. Normally, Neve found friendship an exhausting exercise in futility, but experiencing it through Donna's consciousness, it felt more like a warm hug. She shrugged off her reservations and leaned in, eager to know more about her biological mother.

The laboratory door swung open, then shut with a metallic click as Dr. Feldman returned, a familiar gray figure perched on her shoulder. Neve's heart skipped another beat. Could it be?

"Who processed the acquisition paperwork for the animal delivery yesterday?" Dr. Feldman asked, adjusting her glasses.

Oh no.

Neve felt Donna's panic rise as Dr. Feldman's eyes narrowed. "I... did," she stammered, using Donna's voice.

"It's your third procedural oversight this week." She let out a huff. "Since I can't rely on you," Dr. Feldman's foot tapped an irritated rhythm on the floor, "I will complete the paperwork to register him as a therapy animal. His name is Peregrine," Dr. Feldman continued, stroking the bird's soft feathers.

Neve's spirits lifted at the name. Peregrine. She locked eyes with him intently, desperate to connect to him, but he merely pecked at a feather on his chest and cocked his head, staring at her with unblinking eyes.

"Demonstrate your vocabulary, Peregrine," Dr. Feldman instructed. "What is the primary rule of laboratory protocol?"

"Precision is paramount," Perry squawked, his voice exactly as Neve remembered it. "Document everything. Fact!" Dr. Feldman clapped her hands together, seeming to enjoy his mimicry of her vocal tic.

"Speaking of precision," Dr. Feldman said, inspecting the floor where they'd just finished cleaning up the broken glass, "the bleach solution requires fifteen minutes of contact time. You only allowed twelve." She pulled out a notebook, making a sharp note. "Contamination risk assessment: moderate to high. Fact."

Neve wanted to argue, to point out that the difference was negligible, but Donna's instincts pulled her back, forcing her body to nod apologetically.

"I'm sorry. I'll re-clean the area."

Perry hopped along Dr. Feldman's shoulder, studying Neve with those intelligent eyes. She yearned to speak to him privately, but Dr. Feldman hovered nearby, treating him as her personal secretary.

"Peregrine, note the time," Dr. Feldman commanded. "Second decontamination procedure initiated at 10:47 AM. Fact."

"Fact!" Perry echoed.

"He's quite intelligent," Dr. Feldman continued, stroking Perry's head. "Studies show that African grey parrots possess cognitive abilities similar to a five-year-old human child."

"Fact!" Perry blurted before Dr. Feldman could, and Neve felt Donna's lips quirk up.

Later, as they worked side by side at the culture station, Neve struggled with the unfamiliar equipment. The microscope's focus kept slipping, and the pipette measurements were difficult to calibrate. Donna's muscle memory helped, but it was like trying to play an instrument she'd never touched before.

Relax your grip on the pipette. With the scope, three clicks up, then two down. Dr. Feldman insists we keep the meniscus lens perfectly aligned.

Neve's hands trembled under pressure as she attempted to measure the exact amount of solution. The lab equipment looked antique. Not a single digital readout, no automated machinery. It all required manual calibration and dexterous operation.

There's a trick to the centrifuge. You have to jiggle the latch twice or it sticks.

With Donna's helpful guidance, Neve began to find her rhythm. She learned the quirks of each piece of equipment, the precise angle needed to load samples into the spectrophotometer, and the exact amount of turn to dial in the microscope's focus.

Diana worked nearby, and her presence was both comforting and unsettling. Neve couldn't help stealing glances at her, searching for traces of herself in Diana's features, her mannerisms. She noticed how Diana bit her lower lip when concentrating, the same way Neve did when drawing. How she tucked her hair behind her right ear first, then the left. It was another shared habit.

She's worried about something big. I can always tell by the way she plays with her necklace.

Neve nodded, watching Diana fidget with the delicate gold chain around her neck.

"Let's huddle to discuss findings," Dr. Feldman said, returning after lunch with Perry on her shoulder. Neve counted twenty-seven men and women in white coats gathering at the center worktable, pulling out stools.

Ellis strode to the whiteboard, his enthusiasm radiating as he sketched out detailed molecular structures with ease. Neve watched, fascinated by this younger version of her father, clearly in his element.

"The breakthrough is in the delivery mechanism," Ellis explained, drawing arrows between compounds. "We're using sodium ascorbate to achieve plasma concentrations of vitamin C that are magnitudes higher than oral administration could ever achieve."

"Preliminary data only," Dr. Feldman interjected. "Need more controls. Fact."

Ellis continued, undeterred, his eyes bright with passion. "The selective cytotoxicity is remarkable. The ascorbate acts as a pro-drug, generating hydrogen peroxide that preferentially kills cancer cells while leaving healthy tissue unharmed."

He's brilliant. Everyone knows it.

Donna's thought floated through Neve's consciousness as Ellis sketched out more pathways, his hands moving with confident strokes.

Diana leaned forward, the cuffs of her lab coat brushing against the workbench. "Are you saying the redox cycling creates oxidative stress in the tumor microenvironment?"

"Yes!" Ellis beamed at her, his smile lingering a moment too long. "The cancer cells lack the catalase enzyme that normal cells use to break down hydrogen peroxide."

"Correlation does not equal causation," Dr. Feldman warned, and Perry squawked from her shoulder, "Fact!"

"Thank you, Peregrine." Dr. Feldman nodded. "The mechanism requires further validation."

Ellis grabbed a stack of printouts, spreading them across the lab counter.

"Look at these electron microscopy images," he said, pointing to dark spots on the grainy photographs. "The mitochondrial damage in the cancer cells is extensive, while the healthy cells show no structural changes."

Diana moved closer, her shoulder brushing against Ellis's as she studied the images. Neve noticed how he shifted slightly toward her, though Diana seemed oblivious to the subtle movement.

"Promising results," Dr. Feldman admitted reluctantly. "But protocol modifications require board approval. Fact."

"The traditional approaches aren't working," Ellis argued. "We need to push boundaries. Think about the implications, a non-toxic therapy that could target multiple cancer types."

"Science requires patience," Perry mimicked in Dr. Feldman's clipped tone.

"Indeed," Dr. Feldman agreed, adjusting her glasses.

Neve studied her young father's face, noting the blind ambition she remembered from her childhood. But here, decades earlier, that fortitude was coupled with hope and passion rather than the grim resolve she remembered from later years.

"The next cohort of mouse trials starts tomorrow," Ellis said, gathering his papers. "We'll have more data points in seven to ten days."

Diana wavered as she stood and gripped the lab countertop with both hands, her face draining of color. "I need to—" Diana didn't finish, bolting from the room with one hand pressed to her mouth.

Follow her. She's scared.

Neve let Donna guide her to the women's bathroom, where she found Diana hunched over the sink, splashing cold water on her face. Through the mirror's glass, Neve wobbled when she registered Donna's petite reflection. It was an out-of-body sensation akin to vertigo.

"It was just one night," Diana whispered, gripping the porcelain as she stared at her reflection. "One stupid celebration after the breakthrough with the lymphoma cells."

"With Ellis," Neve said softly, though it wasn't a question. She'd been nudged by Donna.

Diana nodded, sliding down to sit on the cold tile floor. "I've been feeling sick for days, and now I'm late." She pressed her hands against her face and dissolved into another round of tears. "This can't be happening. I had my whole life planned out."

Hold her. She's your best friend, and she needs you.

Neve felt Donna's natural instinct to comfort, even as her own emotions churned with confusion and hurt. She offered her one hand, led her to a bench outside the bathroom, and took the seat beside Diana.

"Tell me about your plans," Neve prompted, nudged by Donna, but she found she was curious to know as well.

"I was going to lead the lymphoma study. Present at international conferences. Maybe even start my own research facility someday." Diana's voice wavered. "Do you know how hard it is for women to get funding? To be taken seriously in this field? A baby would destroy everything."

The words cut through Neve like a knife.

Diana's eyes searched out Donna's, and she let out a whimper. "Promise me you'll keep this between us until I decide what to do."

"I won't say anything," Neve assured her.

"The Double Ds always stick together, right?" Diana attempted a weak smile.

Neve nodded, her mind spinning with the implications of this moment. Not only was she meeting her biological mother for the first time, but she was experiencing her as a real person. She was young, ambitious, and terrified of losing her dreams.

Reassure her.

"Whatever you decide," Neve added after prompting from Donna, "I'm here."

When Neve and Diana returned to the lab, Ellis and Dr. Feldman were deep in debate about experimental protocols.

"Safety first!" Perry squawked from his perch on Dr. Feldman's shoulder, clearly aligned with Dr. Feldman. Neve wondered if it was motivated by self-preservation. It often seemed Perry's alliances were fluid depending on who was in front of him.

Dr. Feldman nodded approvingly at the bird. "See? Even Peregrine understands the importance of proper procedure."

Neve watched Perry intently, hoping to catch his eye, but he remained focused on Dr. Feldman, nuzzling against her neck and burrowing into her hair with forced affection. She'd have to find another way to connect with him later.

Neve donned a pair of latex gloves and began

making new cultures to replace the ones she'd destroyed. It was slow going as her eyes were glued to Diana and Ellis sitting at a shared station across the lab. They revolved around each other like planets and the sun, a natural rhythm born of long hours working side by side. Neve could see Diana passionately explaining her latest findings. Her hands were animated as she presented report after report. Ellis leaned in closer than was necessary, his eyes burning bright with more than professional scientific interest.

"Compare the markers at thirty days and then again at sixty," Diana said, pointing to a microscope slide.

Ellis pressed his face into the viewfinder, twisting the focus adjustment knob for a few seconds before he popped his head up and engaged in a dialogue so filled with scientific medical jargon that Neve struggled to comprehend. He was so animated, Neve knew it had to be significant.

As the last hour of the workday ticked down, Neve found herself dumbstruck by the strange reality of her situation. Here she was, witnessing her parents' love story unfold, already knowing how it would end. Diana, young and brilliant, was fighting for her dreams. Ellis, passionate and hopeful, was unaware of how his life would change, and yet, in the future, she would still lose them both.

CHAPTER

TEN

On the way home from work, Diana's Ford Pinto sputtered at the stoplight, its blue body vibrating beneath them as she clutched the steering wheel. Neve saw glimmers of her own behavior in the way Diana dispelled tension, tapping her fingers against the vinyl, how her gaze kept darting to the clock on the dashboard as she drove like hers often did in her Sprinter van.

"Why do you keep staring at me?"

Neve felt Donna's cheeks pink up. "Sorry." She adjusted her gaze to her feet. "Could we stop at Eckerd Drugs?" she asked in Donna's soft voice. "I need a few things."

Diana nodded, lost in thought, as she flipped on her turn signal to exit the highway and head toward Aura Cove. "Yeah, sure. I should pick up some aspirin anyway."

As the car inched down Main Street, Neve stared

out the window, overwhelmed by what could only be described as a patriotic explosion that had detonated over Aura Cove and refused to dissipate. Three weeks after the official celebration, the town remained in the grip of bicentennial fever. Sun-faded red, white, and blue bunting rippled in the breeze on storefronts, and mannequins in shop windows still sported star-spangled vests and colonial tricorn hats. Even the fire hydrants had been painted to resemble miniature George Washingtons, a detail that made Neve frown as she witnessed a dog lift its leg and perform an act of historical desecration.

"Nothing says freedom like wiping with red, white, and blue toilet paper," Neve muttered under her breath, taking in the patriotic carnage that littered every horizontal surface. Her deadpan tone made Diana chuckle. The first notes from the haunting guitar solo of "*Hotel California*" played on the radio as Diana pulled into the parking lot.

"You've been quiet today," Diana remarked, killing the engine. "Everything okay?"

"After the spill, I thought it was best not to draw more attention to myself," Neve replied, adjusting Donna's round glasses. "I know you went out on a limb to get me this job, and I don't want to reflect poorly on you." Neve was caught off guard when Donna's meek explanation rolled right off her tongue. At least her host was being accommodating, maybe even *too* accommodating.

"Ah," Diana nodded in understanding.

They walked across the asphalt, past a poster advertising "The Omen" at the Starlight Drive-In. Neve pointed at it, blurting before she could stop herself, eager to make conversation, "Gregory Peck is solid in any role he plays."

Confusion prickled Diana's brow. "Since when have you been into horror movies?"

Neve felt Donna's fear crest in her chest.

What are you doing? I hate scary movies. I had to sleep with the lights on for over a year after watching 'Jaws'.

"I just thought... maybe it's time to try something different," Neve mumbled as she pressed Donna's lips into a tight line, determined to keep her mouth shut and not let anything else slip. She was astonished to discover Donna's thoughts were clearer and more obtrusive than the shared consciousnesses she'd experienced in Rosa and Isla during her visit to 1989. It was as if each time she traveled, she lost a bit more of her autonomy during the journey.

The bell attached to the door jingled as they entered. Neve stared at the bottles and tubes arranged on the metal shelves of the pharmacy. The selection was far less than what she was used to in 2024, and the boxes and designs were bulkier and covered in simple primary colors.

"I'll meet you at the register," Diana said, wandering toward the pain relievers.

Neve nodded, watching her walk away before heading to the feminine products aisle, where a woman was busy restocking the shelves. Having scanned the shelves and not finding what she was looking for, she blurted a question without thinking to the clerk, "Excuse me, where can I find EPT?"

The woman crinkled her brow. "Sorry, what?"

EPT? What is that?

Donna's questioning didn't deter Neve at all. She was on a mission. "EPT, the early pregnancy test? You know, get results as soon as four days after a missed period?"

"EPT? Hmm. Never heard of it. Maybe the pharmacist can help you."

Finally realizing her mistake, Neve glanced around, wondering if anyone else had overheard their conversation. To divert attention away from herself, she grabbed a package of cough drops and hurried to find Diana, who was hovering near the pharmacy counter, looking anxious.

"Did you find what you needed?" Diana whispered, her eyes darting over to the pharmacist, a stern-looking man in his fifties with thick glasses and a white lab coat.

"Yes," Neve said, then noticed Diana's face turn a sickly shade of green. "Are you okay?"

Diana took a deep breath, and her voice dropped to a whisper. "There's a new product on the market I just heard about, the Predictor. It's an at-home pregnancy test." Her cheeks were two slashes of red as she scanned the medications behind the counter.

It's up there on the shelf.

Neve's gaze followed Donna's directions. Above

the pharmacist, she could just make out a blue-and-white box partially hidden on the top shelf. When she pointed up at it, Diana choked out a whimper. "I think you're going to have to ask the pharmacist for it."

Diana wrung her hands, distressed at the idea. "I can't," she whispered. "What if someone I know comes in? I'd be humiliated."

"Knowledge is power," Neve encouraged, feeling Donna's natural compassion flowing through her. "Take the test, then you'll know the answer and can make decisions based on facts rather than theories."

Diana nodded, taking a deep inhale and squaring her shoulders. She approached the counter, clearing her throat. The pharmacist turned toward Diana, looking down at her over his glasses.

"Can I help you, miss?" His voice was flat, professional.

"I need..." Diana's voice faltered. She glanced back at Neve, who nodded in encouragement. "I need the Predictor test, please."

The pharmacist's eyebrows rose as his gaze dropped to Diana's bare ring finger. "I see." He reached up to the top shelf behind him, retrieving the blue-and-white box. "First time?"

Diana nodded, her cheeks flushing.

"Instructions are inside." He placed the box on the counter. "That'll be ten dollars."

Diana fumbled in her purse, her fingers shaking as she counted out the bills, as a red flush of hives crawled up her neck.

"It's for a friend," she blurted out in shame.

The pharmacist frowned. "Of course it is." His tone made it clear he didn't believe her. "Make sure your... friend... follows the directions to the letter. These tests aren't foolproof if you don't execute them exactly as instructed."

Diana stuffed the box into her purse, and Neve quickly stashed the cough drops she'd picked up on a shelf as Elton John and Kiki Dee's *"Don't Go Breaking My Heart"* cued up over the store speakers. The bell above the door jingled as they hurried out, and she clutched her purse to her chest like it contained a bomb.

Back in the car, Diana sat motionless, staring at the box. Her keys were in the ignition, but she couldn't bring herself to crank them. "What if I am?" she whispered, staring through the windshield at nothing in particular. "My fellowship application is due in the fall, and the Oncology Research Symposium in Boston is before Thanksgiving."

"One step at a time," Neve said, nudged by Donna to place her hand on Diana's arm to comfort her. "Let's go home and find out what we're dealing with before we start to worry."

"Okay," Diana whispered, beginning the drive home.

In the seat next to her, Neve's heart raced with anticipation. She was playing with fate, not merely bearing witness to her own beginning, and she wasn't sure what long-term ramifications it would have on her future. The weight of every word, every action felt magnified, like ripples in a pond, spreading outward through time. What if her presence here changed her own timeline? The thought of accidentally erasing herself from existence, or worse, irrevocably altering the lives of others in ways she couldn't predict, made her stomach twist into knots. Sharing her fears, Donna weighed in with her own warning.

You are in dangerous territory. Tread carefully.

Neve turned toward the window and whispered, "I know."

Their apartment building's stairwell smelled of stale cigarettes and Pine-Sol. Diana took the steps slowly, one at a time, as if she were headed to a gas chamber. Neve followed behind, her eyes watering from the odor. Their second-floor apartment door featured a macramé owl hanging from a small nail, a housewarming gift from Diana's mother. Diana fumbled with her keys, hands shaking as she tried three times to get the key inserted into the lock.

"Let me," Neve offered, gently taking the keys from her hand.

Inside, harvest gold appliances dominated the kitchenette, while macramé plant hangers dangled pots of spider plants in front of the window. A bulky wooden console television sat against one wall, its rabbit ear antennas covered with aluminum foil and tilted at odd angles to catch the signal. The latest issue of *Ms.* magazine lay open on the coffee table beside a dog-eared copy of *Our Bodies, Ourselves*. Neve's nose wrinkled in disgust at the startling amount of brown featured in the decor, while Donna rushed to explain.

What? Brown is warm, grounded, and earthy; it is the height of sophistication. Think of the warm cocoon of nature, but brought inside.

Neve wanted to remind Donna it was also the color of poop, but she decided to keep her negative comments to herself.

Diana tossed her keys into a ceramic dish shaped like a sunflower, then stood motionless in the middle of the brown shag carpet, which was worn in paths between rooms. The musky scent of incense made Donna's nose twitch as she watched Diana pull the blue-and-white box from her purse and read the back. "It says it takes two hours for results."

"Two hours?" Neve echoed, genuinely surprised by how much slower the pace of life was in the seventies.

Diana nodded, reading the box. "It includes a test tube, dropper, chemicals, and a mirror to read the results." She looked up at Neve. "What if I mess it up? I don't think I have it in me to go back to Eckerd's for another."

"You won't," Neve assured her. "You're a scientist, remember? Just look at it as performing a routine lab procedure."

Diana attempted a weak smile. "A routine lab procedure that could change my entire life." She took a deep breath. "I'm going to... you know." She held up the box, not making eye contact, and disappeared into the bathroom.

Neve wandered to the wall where a poster depicting a fish riding a bicycle hung beside a framed diagram of cellular mitosis. The poster read, "A woman without a man is like a fish without a bicycle." A small smile tugged at the corners of Neve's lips. It was hard not to respect Diana's unflinching feminism.

A turntable sat in the corner, with Carole King's *Tapestry* album leaning against it. On the bookshelf, textbooks on molecular biology shared space with *Fear of Flying* and *The Female Eunuch*.

After several minutes, Diana emerged from the bathroom, looking more relaxed. "Now we wait," she said, setting a kitchen timer for two hours.

"What should we do?" Neve asked.

"Anything but fixate on that test sitting in the bathroom." Diana walked to the television and switched it on. "*The Bionic Woman* should be starting soon."

They settled on the burnt-orange corduroy couch as the television warmed up, the picture gradually coming into focus. The bionic woman appeared on screen, running in slow motion as the familiar soundtrack played.

"I love this show," Diana said, though her voice lacked enthusiasm. "She's the perfect role model for the modern woman."

"She makes living a double life look easy," Neve added, "maybe you could do the same."

Diana scoffed out a chuckle. "Only if I was super human like her."

They watched in silence for a while, the minutes ticking by slowly. Diana kept checking the timer, then sending furtive glances at the bathroom door.

"What would you do?" Diana asked during a commercial break. "If you were me?"

Neve felt a strange sensation in Donna's chest, a protective instinct emerging. She found herself reaching for Diana's hand.

She's asking for your honest opinion. But she's fragile right now. Be gentle.

"I think," Neve said carefully, "women are forced to make sacrifices too often."

Diana squeezed her hand, then pulled away to wipe her eyes. "I keep thinking about my mother. How she gave up everything, her art, her friends, herself, to raise me and my sister. How she looks at me with such hope now that I'm blazing trails in the male-dominated world of research medicine." She laughed bitterly. "Some feminist I turned out to be. First obstacle and I'm falling apart."

Remind her of her strength. She needs to hear it.

"You're the strongest person I know," Neve said, taking Donna's advice, grateful for the guidance. Navigating empathy was always a challenge, but seemed easier with Donna's help.

Diana let out a choked sob, attempting a weak smile that didn't reach her eyes. "I don't feel very strong right now."

"Trust me. You are." Diana shot her a weak smile of acknowledgement, then turned back to the program. When it ended, Diana flipped through channels, looking for another distraction. At last, the timer rang, skittering and vibrating across the coffee table.

"It's time," she whispered, standing up. Fearful,

she reached one hand toward Donna and asked, "Will you come with me?"

Neve nodded, following Diana to the bathroom. The test tube sat on the edge of the sink. Diana picked up the small mirror included in the kit, positioning it as the instructions indicated. She held her breath as she examined the results.

"It's positive," she whispered, the mirror slipping from her trembling fingers and clattering into the sink. "God, what am I going to do?"

Neve guided her back to the living room, where Diana collapsed onto the couch, her face ashen and her mascara running in tracks down her face.

"Are you sure?" Neve asked.

Diana nodded, tears welling in her eyes. "I followed the instructions to the letter." She buried her face in her hands. "This can't be happening. Not now."

"It's not the end of the world," Neve said, rubbing Diana's back as she began to sob. "You could have a career *and* a baby. People do it all the time."

Diana looked up sharply, letting out a wry chuckle. "No, they don't! Not in research medicine." She stood abruptly, pacing across the worn carpet. "You've seen how the world treats women in science, like we're just passing time until we get pregnant or married."

She gestured toward the window, getting more animated. "Remember Janet from bio-chem? She was brilliant, heading for a full professorship at MIT. Then she got pregnant, and forfeited her career to become a walking uterus. Last I heard she was typing other people's research papers at home between diaper changes."

The overhead light caught on Diana's tear-streaked face as she continued pacing. "I've worked too hard. A baby would..." She trailed off, staring out the window at the streetlights flickering on outside, unable to finish her sentence.

"What about Ellis?" Neve asked, trying to reason with her. "Shouldn't he know? Maybe he could help?"

Diana shook her head back and forth. "No. Absolutely not. We aren't a couple. It was one night, one bad decision." She nodded once as if she'd decided, and it wasn't up for further consideration. "He doesn't need to be involved."

"So, what will you do?" Neve's voice was quiet, though her heart pounded. It was surreal. This was her existence they were discussing.

Diana sank back down onto the couch, counting options on her fingers. "I could give it up for adoption." Her voice dropped to a whisper. "Or there's a clinic in Miami. My cousin went there last year." Neve's head snapped up at the suggestion. She was speechless.

Be gentle. She needs to know she has support. Don't push her either way.

Diana looked up, eyes red-rimmed. "My career or motherhood? That's the choice. No man ever has to make that decision."

Neve felt a strange sensation bloom in Donna's chest, a protective instinct emerging. She found herself reaching for Diana's hand.

"You don't have to decide tonight," Neve said softly. "We'll figure it out together."

Diana nodded, letting out a choked whimper. She rested her head on Donna's shoulder, and Neve felt her resolve melt when she asked, "The Double Ds against the world, right?"

"Always," Neve replied, and was surprised to find she meant it.

CHAPTER

ELEVEN

"YOUR THERAPEUTIC VALUE IS YET UNPROVEN," Dr. Feldman had protested when Perry begged her not to leave him at the lab at the end of the day. But three peer-reviewed studies on the benefits of animal therapy later, she found herself willing to test the theory, pulling into her driveway with a talking parrot in her backseat at 7:02 PM. The brief pitstop at Marvin's Menagerie for bird supplies made her arrival sixty-two minutes behind schedule.

Her Spanish-style home featured a red clay roof and pristine white stucco walls unmarred by the usual mildew and weathering that plagued other houses in the neighborhood. Not a single palm frond littered the well-maintained lawn, and the flowerbeds were filled with bromeliads, spaced twelve inches apart.

"Nice place," Perry commented from a makeshift cardboard carrier. "Looks as though *Good Housekeeping* and a CDC lab had a love child. I bet you even alphabetize your dust bunnies."

"Incorrect. Congregations of dust particles are not permitted in my residence. Also, love children are a statistical anomaly between inanimate entities." Elaine's hands were fastened to the steering wheel at ten and two. She reached for the stopwatch hanging from her rearview mirror and clicked it on with a sad sigh. "Ninety seconds commencing now."

"What are you..." Perry's question was cut short by the sound of Elaine's quiet sobs. They came in measured gasps, and Perry shifted uncomfortably in his box, uncertain how to respond to this display of raw emotion.

At exactly ninety seconds, Elaine stopped crying, wiped her eyes with an alcohol-based sanitizing wipe, and exited the vehicle.

"Items must be unloaded according to size and function," she announced, opening the trunk. "Cage components first, followed by supplies in descending order of volume."

The interior of the house matched its exterior's well kept appearance. The living room contained two identical avocado green sofas positioned parallel to each other, their cushions unmarred by use. Medical journals lined the bookshelf in chronological order, color-coded by subject. The walls displayed a vast array of framed medical credentials. Robert's veterinary license was centered between her research awards, together spanning two entire walls. Elaine remembered when he'd hung them. It had taken all day to ensure they were perfectly spaced and aligned to her exacting standards, but Robert never complained. He'd said, "I guess this is the price you pay for having two doctors in the house."

In the family room, Elaine cut through the box and pulled out the cage components. Perry whistled when she'd accomplished the assembly in mere minutes. "Impressive!" he praised, still unsure how to act around Elaine as she could run hot and cold. He decided to err on the side of caution, knowing flattery was never a bad strategy.

"You could perform surgery in here," Perry observed as Elaine evaluated where to place the bird-cage. "Or film a commercial for cleaning products."

"Cleanliness reduces environmental variables. Variables can exacerbate illness. Fact." She measured the distance between the cage and the wall with a tape measure. "Twenty-four inches from the wall. Optimal spacing achieved."

Perry watched as she arranged his food and water dishes inside. The moment she stepped back to admire her work, he flew to the cage and deliberately knocked over his water dish with his beak.

Elaine's right eye twitched. "That was intention-ally disruptive behavior."

"Fact!" Perry mimicked her clipped tone, then tilted his head to take the edge off it. "Your house needs some chaos. It's too perfect. It's as if you're trying to control your environment because something else is out of control."

Her hands fluttered to her throat, an unconscious gesture of distress. "But chaos is... inefficient."

"Life *is* chaos," Perry said, gentler now.

The sound of a weak cough from upstairs made Elaine's shoulders tense. She checked her watch. 7:57 PM. "Time for Robert's evening medications. Come, he'll be happy to make your acquaintance." She tapped her shoulder three times, and Perry flapped over to settle where indicated, careful not to pinch too tightly.

Elaine climbed the stairs, her stockinged feet silent on the treads. Perry rode on her shoulder, silent as they approached the guest bedroom, where a sharp antiseptic scent mingled with the artificial lavender of medical-grade cleaning products. A suite of medical equipment lined the walls of the bedroom, including a heart rate monitor, an IV stand, and a portable oxygen tank. In the center of the room, on a hospital bed, Robert was sleeping, and his nurse, Maria, was leafing through a magazine in the chair next to him. When they entered the room, she got to her feet and gave Elaine a status report.

"Blood pressure one-ten over seventy, temperature ninety-nine point one, oxygen saturation ninety-five percent."

"Your documentation is appreciated," Elaine said as she moved to the charts and scanned the numbers, her intelligent gaze missing nothing. "What were his potassium levels from this morning's labs?"

"Three point eight," Maria replied. "Up point two from yesterday."

"Marginal improvement." Elaine's finger traced the graph of Robert's vital signs. "But it's trending upward. Good."

Robert stirred, his gaunt face brightening at the

sight of his wife. "There's my favorite fact-checker," he whispered, his voice rough from the latest round of chemo. It was a relatively new treatment for pancreatic cancer that was powerful, but it also came with significant side effects.

"You failed to consume forty-seven percent of your dinner," Elaine stated, but her hand gentled as she touched his forehead. "You know this is unacceptable for optimal recovery parameters."

Robert's eyes drifted to the untouched lime Jello on his bedside tray. "Sorry, darling, but I seem to have lost my appetite."

"You must follow the nutritional guidelines I've outlined in your treatment plan."

Brushing off her concern, he brightened at the sight of Perry. "And who is this magnificent creature?"

"I'm your newly appointed Director of Entertainment." Perry announced, launching from Elaine's shoulder to perch on the bed rail. He puffed up and added, "I've been told my predecessor was dismissed for a chronic lack of imagination."

Robert's weak laugh turned into a cough, but his eyes sparkled. "What a gift you have for mimicry! What are you doing here?"

"Therapeutic animal intervention," Elaine replied, adjusting his oxygen level a quarter turn. "Studies indicate companion animals can improve patient outcomes by twenty-three percent."

"And comedy improves them by forty-six percent," Perry added, then leaned in and lowered his voice, "I completely fabricated that statistic, but it has a certain scientific ring to it, wouldn't you agree?"

Robert's chuckle rang out as Perry leaned closer and deadpanned, "See? It's already working!"

Maria smiled as she recorded Robert's reaction to the bird. "First genuine laugh I've heard from him all day. I'll note that in the chart."

"Cross-reference it with his pain levels and vital signs," Elaine instructed, already reaching for the binder. "We need to document any positive correlations."

"Honey." Robert's hand found hers, stilling her movement. "Not everything needs to be measured."

"Incorrect. Measurement enables progress tracking." She stopped, and under Robert's loving gaze, let her shoulders relax. After a long exhale, the truth emerged. "I just want you well."

"I know." He squeezed her hand. "Now, tell me where you found my new feathered friend."

Perry puffed up and sputtered with indignation. "Found? I'll have you know I was headhunted. Elaine said, 'Get me the most overqualified avian therapist in Florida. Spare no expense, my husband deserves the best!' And, poof! Here I am. Though between us lads, the interview process was foul."

For the first time that day, Elaine's chuckle tangled with Robert's, even as she muttered under her breath, "Incorrect. No formal interview was ever conducted."

Maria excused herself to leave after propping Robert up against his pillows while Perry strutted along the bed rail, examining the various medical devices.

"I must say," Perry announced, peering at an IV drip, "the pharmaceutical accoutrements in this establishment are top-notch. Though the lighting is absolutely dreadful."

Robert chuckled weakly. "You sound like my wife."

"I shall take that as a compliment," Perry replied, reorganizing his tail feathers.

From the bedside table, Elaine sorted pills into labeled containers. She kept her eyes fixed on her task, but her head tilted slightly toward their conversation.

"Tell Perry how we met," Robert suggested, his eyes twinkling. "He'll appreciate the comedy of errors."

"It was not an error," Elaine weakly protested. "It was a logical misunderstanding based on incomplete data. Fact."

"Oh, do tell." Perry settled himself in to preen his wing. "I adore a riveting tale of human awkwardness."

"We were both teaching assistants at UC Davis," Robert began. "We were eating lunch one day in the faculty lounge when someone burst through the door shouting 'Doctor!' and we both answered."

"Because we both held doctorates. Fact," Elaine interjected, now color-coding the pill containers.

"So, when this brilliant but *incredibly* literal woman asked me to consult on a new protocol she was developing..."

Perry let out a whistle. "Ooo. La. La."

"No, it wasn't like that." Elaine interjected in her

defense. "The invitation was professionally appropriate given the presumed shared field of expertise."

Perry cackled. "Oh, I think I see where this is going." He swiveled his head between them. "Continue, please. And don't you dare spare a single one of the embarrassing details."

"She spent two hours walking me through her research," Robert continued, his smile growing wider by the second.

"One hour, forty-seven minutes, and twenty-three seconds," Elaine corrected, her own smile creeping in.

"Before I mentioned something about my latest patient being German."

"Which I thought was an odd trait to focus on," Elaine defended, her cheeks pinking.

"Then I showed her a photo of said patient." Robert grinned. "A German...shepherd."

"It was an honest mistake!" Elaine exclaimed. "Professional titles should be more specific."

"She turned beet red," Robert continued. "Stood up so fast she knocked over her chair and her coffee, and announced, 'This consultation has been rendered invalid due to species incompatibility.'"

Perry fell off his perch onto Robert's lap, laughing. "Species incompatibility! Oh, that's precious!"

"I attempted to exit the situation with my professional dignity intact," Elaine said, now organizing the medical supplies.

"It was more of a panicked escape," Robert argued, reaching for the water cup beside his bed. Elaine rushed over to help him, adjusting the straw to the optimal angle. "But she'd forgotten her briefcase under the table. When she came back for it, I asked her to dinner. And she said..." Robert prompted.

Elaine sighed. "I said, 'Dinner is ill advised in light of our professional misalignment.'"

"Most romantic rejection ever," Perry declared. "So, how did you end up married?"

"He brought me a peer-reviewed paper a few weeks later on cross-species applications of various treatment protocols," Elaine admitted.

"I knew research was the way to her heart." Robert winked.

"It was sound," Elaine whispered, a small smile playing at her lips. "Unlike your terrible puns."

"Terrible? How can they be when all my dog jokes are lab-tested." Robert's throaty chuckle morphed into a rattling cough, and Elaine appeared at his side with more water.

"Respiratory distress noted at 20:23," she muttered, already turning toward the table, and reaching for his chart.

"Elaine." Robert caught her hand. "I'm fine. Come sit with us." Reluctantly, Elaine perched on the edge of the bed carefully avoiding his tubes and wires.

"I endured thirty-seven bad veterinary puns in the first month. Fact." Elaine's hand sought out Robert's, their fingers intertwining out of habit.

"Yet here we are," Robert said softly, his eyes becoming misty as he looked at his wife with obvious affection. "Married fifteen years. The best fifteen years of my life." Robert leaned closer and puckered his lips.

Elaine closed the distance and gave him a peck. A few minutes later, he drifted off to sleep. Elaine rose and patted her shoulder, and Perry alighted from the bed rail and glided over, letting her take him back to his cage for the night.

TWELVE

THE NEXT MORNING, the lab door swung open as Neve followed Diana inside. A tall man in a perfectly pressed brown corduroy blazer stood at Dr. Feldman's work-station, organizing stacks of handwritten notes into color-coded folders. His shaggy dark brown hair was parted in the middle, framing an angular face with intense, calculating eyes behind wire-rimmed glasses. His long fingers gathered the papers together, tapping each page into perfect alignment before filing it away.

Next to him stood an older gentleman with a distinguished air, with silver hair neatly combed back from a tanned, rugged face. Despite appearing to be in his mid-sixties, he stood straight and tall. He wore a tailored navy blazer over a crisp white shirt, and his intelligent eyes crinkled at the corners as he surveyed the lab with genuine interest.

"Ladies," Dr. Feldman called from across the lab. "You're three minutes late. Fact."

"Sorry," Neve murmured, succumbing to Donna's

automatic instinct to apologize. "It was my fault. My alarm didn't go off." Out of eyesight, Diana mouthed a thank you. She'd been the real reason they were running late. The positive test result made her toss and turn all night long, finally falling asleep just before dawn and missing the alarm.

"Excuses, excuses," the younger man interrupted, not looking up from his filing. "Don't worry, Dr. Feldman, I will note their tardiness in today's log."

The older gentleman chuckled, and it instantly diffused the building tension. "Conrad, surely a few minutes won't derail the course of scientific progress. I remember when Robert and I would completely lose track of time during the early stages of a clinical trial. It seems to come with the territory."

Dr. Feldman's expression softened at the mention of her husband, Robert. "Allow me to make introductions. Donna, this is Dr. Conrad Manning, my senior research assistant. He's been on vacation for the last two weeks."

"And this," Dr. Feldman continued with noticeable warmth, "is Dr. Samuel Whitmore, Robert's mentor from veterinary school and now one of Aureon's principal investors."

Dr. Whitmore stepped forward, extending his hand first to Diana, then to Neve. His handshake was firm but gentle, his smile genuine. "Delighted to meet you both."

"Dr. Whitmore built the most successful veterinary practice in the Southeast before retiring last year," Dr. Feldman explained. "He's now generously funding our work here at Aureon."

"Just putting my money where my heart is," Dr. Whitmore replied. "After learning about Robert's diagnosis, I wanted to support research that could help facilitate a cure. The work you do here is nothing short of miraculous, and I am grateful to be a small part of it."

"Dr. Manning has a PhD in biochemistry from MIT," Dr. Feldman continued. "He'll be streamlining our record-keeping system, documenting our findings, and ensuring we are adhering to all protocols."

Perry squawked from his perch near Dr. Feldman's desk, "Documentation is paramount!"

Conrad's dark eyes narrowed at the bird. "I see we've acquired a mascot during my absence."

"Peregrine assists with my cognitive processing," Dr. Feldman explained. "Studies show that verbalizing observations improves retention by forty-three percent."

Dr. Whitmore approached Perry's perch in awe. "I treated many exotic birds in my practice. Brilliant animals they are, often with a better grasp of the English language than most humans, but none as intelligent as this."

Perry tilted his head, puffing up with pride, and studying Dr. Whitmore with obvious approval.

Conrad kept quiet and returned to his record keeping as Neve moved to Donna's workstation, watching him from the corner of her eye. There was something calculated about his presence, as if his emotions were carefully shuttered away.

Across the room, Ellis and Diana were deep in conversation about cell cultures. Neve noticed how Diana kept a careful distance between them now, her body language stiff and professional. Ellis, oblivious to the change, gestured enthusiastically as he explained his latest theory.

"The vitamin C protocol shows promising results in the lymphoma line," Ellis was saying. "If we can replicate it with the pancreatic cells…"

"Ellis," Conrad interrupted, looking up from his filing. "Your enthusiasm is admirable but perhaps premature. I've reviewed your data from last month. The statistical significance is questionable."

Ellis blinked, caught off guard. His jaw ticked, yet he remained silent.

"It's a fascinating theory, but unorthodox in practice." Neve felt a chill pass through her as Conrad's discerning gaze lingered on Diana, then slid to Ellis.

Dr. Whitmore stepped closer to Ellis's workstation, examining the charts with genuine interest. "Sometimes, the most revolutionary discoveries begin in an unorthodox manner. After all, Fleming discovered penicillin because he didn't sterilize the petri dishes before his vacation, and look how well that turned out for the world."

Conrad's lips tightened at the gentle rebuke. Before he could respond, Dr. Feldman clapped her hands together. "Enough posturing, gentlemen. We have work to do."

As everyone dispersed to their stations, Conrad slunk toward Neve. "Donna, is it?" he murmured in a low tone, meant only for her. "Dr. Feldman speaks highly of your..." he paused, grasping for his next words, "... attention to detail."

"She does?" Neve asked, wary to her core in a way that wilted Donna's initial burst of pride. They'd just met, the praise seemed disingenuous.

"I value attention to detail." He adjusted his glasses, which had slipped down his nose. "Perhaps you could assist me in organizing the archived research notes? I understand you've only been here a week, but Dr. Feldman assures me you're already up to speed."

"I'd be happy to help," Neve heard herself say, but she wasn't happy at all. Why was he trying to get into Donna's good graces? Something was off, and she couldn't put her finger on it.

Conrad nodded, satisfied. "Excellent."

"I was so excited I couldn't sleep last night," Ellis announced, spreading reports across the central workbench as the daily huddle began. "The answer's been staring us in the face."

Dr. Feldman leaned forward to examine the molecular diagrams.

"The ascorbate treatment shows promise," Ellis continued, tapping a graph showing tumor regression, "but what if we amplify its effect? Hyperbaric oxygen therapy could be the catalyst we need."

Conrad looked up with narrowed eyes. "That's quite a leap."

Ellis ignored him. "At pharmacological concentrations, fifty to seventy-five millimoles, intravenous ascorbate converts into hydrogen peroxide. But in a hyperbaric environment with elevated oxygen pressure..."

"...the rate of H_2O_2 generation would increase exponentially," Diana finished, moving to stand beside him. Her eyes sparkled with scientific curiosity.

"Yes!" Ellis beamed at her. "Cancer cells lack sufficient catalase to detoxify the peroxide. The oxidative stress would overwhelm malignant cells while normal tissues remained protected."

Dr. Whitmore had moved closer, his interest also piqued. "Fascinating approach. In my veterinary oncology cases, we often found that combination therapies produced results far beyond what either treatment could achieve alone. Nature loves synergy."

Dr. Feldman's lips pursed and her fingers tapped in threes as she processed the idea, weighing it for merit. "The theoretical basis appears sound. Let's talk about the delivery mechanism."

Neve watched the exchange with great fascination, witnessing her father thriving in his element. She understood enough of the explanation to recognize the brilliance of combining two therapies that individually showed promise. Together, they could create something revolutionary.

"The reactive oxygen would specifically target the tumor microenvironment," Diana added, pulling her research notes from a folder. "Look here." She pointed to colorful graphs. "The redox potential difference between normal and cancer cells is substantial."

"We'd administer it via a targeted infusion, allowing it to concentrate preferentially in rapidly dividing tissue." Ellis's hand brushed Diana's as they both pointed to the report. Neve noticed the slight flush in Diana's cheeks as she quickly withdrew her hand.

"This is exactly why I invested in your work at Aureon," Dr. Whitmore said, his eyes shining with enthusiasm. "Robert always said you were the most brilliant researcher he'd ever known."

Dr. Feldman offered him a curt, embarrassed nod of agreement at the compliment. Despite her outward skepticism, Neve noticed Dr. Feldman's eyes sparking with bursts of excitement from the discovery.

"We'll design rigorous controls," Diana assured Dr. Feldman. "Starting with lymphoma cell lines, then solid tumor models."

Ellis nodded gratefully at Diana. "With proper protocols, we could be ready for preliminary trials in months, not years."

"But Robert doesn't have years," Dr. Feldman murmured, so quietly only Neve and Perry heard her.

Conrad scribbled something in his notebook, his expression unreadable. "If you'd like to proceed, I'll prepare the acquisition paperwork for the hyperbaric chamber," he offered.

"Yes, please do."

The geode in her pocket sent a tingle through her, and Neve shivered. As the others continued their excited planning, she made a mental note to keep her eyes open during her shifts at the lab.

The lunch hour arrived, and Ellis and Diana headed to the break room together, deep in animated discussion about oxygen saturation levels. Dr. Feldman lingered with Conrad, and Neve was desperate for them to leave so she could connect with Perry.

"I'll clean Peregrine's cage over lunch," Neve offered. "It might help him settle in."

Dr. Feldman nodded in approval. She glanced at Perry over the top of her glasses as she gathered a stack of reports. "Behave for Donna," she said over her shoulder as she disappeared into her office with an apple.

When the lab door clicked shut, Neve exhaled in relief and approached Perry's perch.

"Hey there, birdbrain," she whispered, pulling out the soiled newspaper with a grimace.

Perry tilted his head, regarding her with one suspicious eye. Neve glanced around the empty lab before leaning closer. "It's me, Perry. It's Neve."

Perry's feathered head snapped back as a ripple of delight made his wings unfurl and flap.

"I shifted into the body of Diana's best friend, and I must say it's been enlightening," Neve whispered.

He let out a happy whistle. "Do tell."

"Diana just found out she's pregnant with me, and she's terrified. She doesn't want to tell Ellis."

"Your origin story," Perry murmured in a serious tone, putting the pieces together.

"Exactly." Neve swallowed hard. "I'm watching my own beginning unfold. I could change everything, Perry. I could make sure my father doesn't disappear when I'm fifteen. I could convince my mother not to give me up for adoption."

Perry pecked gently at her finger. "Dangerous territory, Nevermore. Change the past, change the future. It's risky."

"I know," Neve replied, spraying down the cage with disinfectant. "But I can't help but think the geode sent me here to give us a second chance to be a family."

"I don't know," Perry countered. He was wary. "Time isn't linear. Multiple realities can co-exist. One slight change can have massive future ramifications."

Neve paused, considering. "I have to try, Perry. I need to understand what happened to my father, why he disappeared, and why he never told me about Diana." She replaced the fresh water dish in the cage. "Will you help me?"

Perry bobbed his head after a long moment. "Feathered accomplice reporting for duty. But my warning still stands. Messing with time is like juggling nitroglycerin. Exciting until it explodes."

The sound of approaching footsteps made Neve jump. Perry hopped into his freshly cleaned cage just as Conrad pushed through the door, his calculating gaze sweeping over them.

"There you go. Spic and Span," she said, shutting the door behind him.

"Talking to birds now, Donna?" Conrad asked with a thin smile.

"Just keeping him company," Neve replied, channeling Donna's meekness.

As Conrad turned away, Perry caught Neve's eye and gave a subtle nod.

The afternoon dragged on as Neve entered data from the morning's experiments. Donna's fingers were nimble on the typewriter keys, but Neve found herself missing the efficiency of digital spreadsheets. She had just finished a page of spectrophotometry readings when Conrad materialized beside her desk, standing close enough that she could smell his aftershave. A woodsy artificial pine scent that made her nose wrinkle.

"Need a hand with those figures?" Conrad asked, leaning over her shoulder. His sour breath tickled her ear.

Neve instinctively shifted away. "I've got this under control, thanks."

If he really wanted to help, he'd have a Tic Tac.

Neve pressed Donna's lips together to contain the smile that wanted to break out and focused on Conrad as his eyes scanned the neatly typed columns. "You're quite thorough," he observed, still encroaching on her personal space. "I noticed you watching Ellis and Diana earlier. They make *quite* the research team, don't they?"

The casual question crackled with an undercurrent of impropriety that made Neve angry. "Everyone in the lab works well together," she replied, working hard to keep her tone neutral.

Except you.

Neve inwardly applauded Donna's accurate assessment. Conrad shot her a paper-thin smile and added, "I've observed from time to time their collaboration extends far beyond regular working hours."

"I wouldn't know about that," Neve said, though Donna's memories of late nights in the lab, shared coffee breaks, and inside jokes supplied confirmation of his suspicions.

"No?" Conrad raised an eyebrow. "I thought you and Diana were close."

Neve's pulse quickened. "We're friends, yes."

"Friends share secrets," Conrad pressed. "Has she mentioned any personal developments recently?"

The pointed question sent alarm bells ringing, and the geode in her pocket burned. She shifted on the seat, trying to stop the searing heat from scarring her skin. Boldly, Neve turned to face him. "Is there something specific you're asking about, Dr. Manning?"

His smile sharpened. "Just making conversation. The dynamics of research teams have always fascinated me."

"I should finish this data set before Dr. Feldman returns," Neve said, her tone firm, hoping he would take the hint.

Conrad nodded and drifted away, but Neve kept him in her peripheral vision. He moved to Ellis's workstation, casually flipping through papers while glancing toward the door. With sticky fingers, he fished Ellis's research journal out from beneath a stack of reports and began paging through it.

Neve's heart pounded. She pretended to focus on her typing while watching Conrad read Ellis's observations. The scent of burning hair wafted up from the geode before she realized it was her own singed leg hair.

Then the lab door swung open, and Conrad slid the journal to its original place at Ellis's workstation as Dr. Feldman entered with Perry on her shoulder. Ellis and Diana had also returned, and his eyes narrowed when he saw Conrad hovering near his desk.

Conrad straightened. "I was just reviewing your methodology notes."

Neve saw her father stiffen. She could tell he was livid but unable to voice an objection against a superior.

"Good news! The rest of the board agreed to fast-track the acquisition, and the hyperbaric chamber delivery is confirmed for next week," Dr. Feldman announced. "Dr. Manning, your assistance will be required. The technical specifications need verification before installation."

"Of course."

"Conrad, I'm tasking you with overseeing the calibration protocols," Dr. Feldman added, and at her side the man visibly puffed up with pride.

"With all due respect, Dr. Feldman, I should handle the chamber calibration myself," Ellis objected. "I was the one who made the breakthrough."

"Inefficient use of resources," Dr. Feldman

discounted. "Your expertise is needed for cell line preparation. Conrad has an engineering background. It's the most logical division of labor."

"But he doesn't understand the oxygen sensitivity parameters," Ellis insisted.

Perry ruffled his feathers and, in a pathetic attempt at levity, blurted in a songbird tone, "Tension detected! Fact!"

Dr. Feldman ignored the bird. "Nonsense. A decision has already been made. Conrad will handle the technical setup. Ellis will oversee the biochemical preparations."

Ellis's jaw tightened as he glared at the other man. "Fine. But nothing proceeds without my final approval." He ran a hand through his hair in frustration. "This was my discovery. I should take the lead."

Diana touched his arm gently. "It's still your project. Just consider him your hyperbaric chamber assistant."

Ellis chuckled, and Neve watched their interaction with great interest. What would it have been like growing up with both of them as parents? Diana obviously had genuine feelings for her father, so why had she run away?

CHAPTER 13

PEREGRINE

LATER THAT EVENING, I perched upon the antique mahogany bookshelf, my talons gripping the edge as I surveyed the scene. Robert sat wrapped in a cashmere throw despite the moderate temperature. The man's hands shook as he attempted to turn the pages of a well-worn veterinary journal. I observed the gray pallor of his complexion, the slight wheeze in his breathing pattern, all indicators of his accelerating decline. I could smell the cloying medicinal scent of chemotherapy that oozed from his pores. How peculiar that my feathered form gave me greater insight into the grave nature of his prognosis!

An unfamiliar compulsion drew me from my comfortable perch toward the ailing man. With a reluctant flutter, I descended and settled upon his shoulder, surprising even myself with this display of compassion. Was it the influence of my avian Siamese twin compelling me to comfort this man by instinct? It was the only logical explanation. He took over, cheeping softly, nuzzling into Robert's neck, and attempting to groom his thinning hair with our beak.

"Therapeutic animal intervention is producing a positive behavioral response. Fact," Elaine mumbled from the chair next to Robert's bed, scribbling treatment notes in her ever-present logs.

Her compulsion to punctuate astute observations with "fact" reminded me of Nevermore's penchant for bluntness. Perhaps they shared more than just a love of logic and reasoning? Had the time travel gods connected us with another neurodivergent person in a different timeline in need of our assistance? It couldn't be a coincidence. Perhaps this was our mission. Neve confided the geode had tingled in the lab, signaling Aureon Biomedical was the catalyst, but to what? I did not know.

Robert reached up with trembling fingers to stroke my feathers with gratitude, then murmured to Elaine, "Animals have a sixth sense that goes beyond human perception."

I huffed with indignation at his ridiculous, mystical explanation. "I simply possess functioning olfactory senses and basic observational skills. It smells like death has warmed over here."

Elaine's eyes widened at my outburst, but Robert chuckled. "And a sharp tongue to match that sharp mind."

Later, when my back wing began to ache, near the site of the mortal buckshot wound from Sheila, Robert noticed with the practiced eye of a healer before I could mask my discomfort. I attempted to hide it but couldn't escape his clinical gaze.

"Come here, Peregrine," he beckoned, his voice weathered but warm. Despite my natural inclination toward suspicion, I allowed him to examine it, his trembling hands somehow steadying when engaged in the familiar ritual of examination.

"Just a bit of inflammation," he murmured, his fingers gently extending my wing with the confidence of decades of veterinary experience. "Elaine, could you bring me that small jar of balm from my medical kit? The one with the green label."

Elaine retrieved it promptly and handed it to Robert with a gentle smile, her fingers lingering against his for a fraction longer than necessary.

Robert opened the jar, and the scent of eucalyptus filled the air. He applied the soothing balm to my wing joint, making small circles with his thumbs.

"This should help with the inflammation," he explained, his voice taking on a professional tone that seemed to revitalize him. "Your wing joint is showing signs of stress. Perhaps you should refrain from flying until it is healed?"

I offered a reluctant peep of agreement, then muttered, "Thank you," even though he was figuratively clipping my wings. Sometimes you need to heed the advice of the professionals.

"Don't overexert yourself, Robert," Elaine admonished, though her eyes were filled with genuine affection rather than reproach. She adjusted his throw blanket with tender care, ensuring it spanned across his frail shoulders.

He responded with a smile that transformed his haggard features, for a moment illuminating the man he once was. "Caring for others has always been the best medicine for me, my dear. You know that."

Their fingers brushed as she handed him a teacup. It was a deliberate touch, not incidental. I watched their silent communication, the language of long-married souls who had transcended the need for constant verbal affirmation. Their genuine connection pierced through my hardened veneer of cynicism to the soft flesh underneath. It was a most unwelcome sensation.

"Your medication schedule indicates it's time for the anti-nausea tablets," Elaine said, consulting her watch.

"Fact," Robert replied with a wink that seemed to melt her.

The sight of their sweet exchange summoned the face of the only woman I'd ever loved from the recesses of my memory. My sweet Veronica, with her trusting hazel eyes and that absurd collection of ceramic frogs. She'd been an easy mark initially. She was recently bereaved, flush with inheritance money from her aunt's estate, isolated and lonesome. The perfect target for a practiced confidence man, such as myself.

I had played the role of a besotted suitor with the expertise of a soap opera actor, never anticipating the cruel twist of genuinely falling for her unassuming kindness. She paid attention to the smallest details, bringing my morning coffee exactly as I preferred it without being reminded. She defended me to her suspicious friends with such fierce loyalty that it produced an uncomfortable tightness in my chest.

"He may be unconventional," I'd heard her tell her skeptical best friend over the telephone, "but Perry sees me in a way no one else ever has."

Peregrine Ashcroft. It was the identity I'd crafted and slipped into like a second skin. I was an international business consultant with a tragic past and a promising future. A man who appreciated ceramic frogs and poetry with equal enthusiasm. A complete and utter fabrication. My feathers ruffled involuntarily at the memory as I shivered in shame. Veronica had gotten under my skin.

Robert whispered something in Elaine's ear that made her laugh, and I felt a pang of regret. The stark contrast between their authentic connection and the elaborate web of lies I had spun for Veronica tied me into knots. The con had been proceeding right on schedule until that rainy Thursday evening. We had been driving back from dinner when Veronica commanded me to pull over.

"There! Do you see it?" she'd exclaimed, pointing toward the median where a bedraggled mass of fur huddled, drenched and trembling.

Before I could protest, she was out of the car, her expensive silk dress soaked in seconds as she knelt next to the dog in the downpour. The dog was a pitiful mutt, limping and blood-stained, who let out a pathetic growl as she probed his wet fur with her fingertips.

"It's okay," she cooed, removing her pashmina to wrap around the mongrel. "We're going to help you."

I watched from the dry comfort of the car, calculating how this unexpected detour might impact our evening. I had planned to suggest a weekend getaway, a strategic move to isolate her from friends and family as I prepared for the final stage of my scheme.

"Perry," she'd cried. "Help me get him into the car!"

With a heavy sigh, I stepped into the rain, frowning as my Italian leather shoes sank into mud.

The next morning, I watched her empty her vacation fund, money she'd been saving for a trip we were going to take to Portugal, to pay the veterinarian's bill. Two thousand dollars for a creature she'd known less than twelve hours.

"But our trip," I protested, maintaining the concerned boyfriend role while inwardly recalculating my timeline. It was apparent that her recent financial impulsivity would complicate my plans.

"Some things are more important," she'd said with a shrug, scratching the sedated dog behind its ears.

For three weeks, she nursed that mangy flea bag back to health. She missed social engagements, cooked meals for him containing human food, and researched canine rehabilitation. When a loving family was finally found to adopt "Lucky" (a painfully obvious name that she defended with charming earnestness), she cried with joy at the placement, then cried again with sadness when she said her goodbye.

"Isn't it wonderful?" she'd asked, wiping her eyes as we drove away from the new owners' home. "Lucky has a real chance at a great life now."

Her capacity for selfless giving to complete strangers shattered something in my cynical worldview. The stark contrast between her authentic generosity and my calculated manipulation had become increasingly impossible to ignore. Something fundamental had shifted then, a realignment of priorities that a man of my particular moral flexibility was ill-equipped to process.

I found myself delaying the final con, inventing reasons to extend my time with her. The gold I'd eventually died trying to steal was a desperate attempt to escape my growing emotional entanglement. I sighed, burying my beak into my wing in shame. How positively maudlin these reflections were becoming!

"Peregrine seems unusually pensive today," Robert observed, interrupting my uncomfortable reminiscence. "Birds are remarkably expressive creatures, don't you think?"

"Debatable. Emotional projection is a common human fallacy when interpreting animal behavior," Elaine responded, though her tone held more affection than correction. Robert responded with a low chuckle.

As twilight descended, Robert drifted in uneasy sleep while Elaine watched, her face etched with the fragile ache of loving someone who was vanishing, breath by breath.

They had built a steadfast, unbreakable bond, one I had sampled but never fully allowed myself to have with Veronica. The possibility of redemption had existed for me briefly, but now it was the road not taken, a life un-lived. The opportunity for genuine connection had been within my grasp, and I had recoiled from it like the coward I was.

"Sleep well, my love," I heard Elaine whisper as she gently draped another blanket over Robert's sleeping form. The simple tenderness in those four words contained more truth than I had spoken in my entire human existence.

I retreated to my cage, suddenly exhausted by the overwhelming weight of regret, a burden no lighter being carried on wings rather than shoulders.

FOURTEEN

AFTER A WEEK of working as Donna in the research lab, Neve had established a comfortable routine. With Donna's guidance, she navigated the equipment competently enough to avoid suspicion while observing every interaction between her father and Diana. She arrived early each day, prepared slides, verified equipment calibrations, and then faded into the background. She was the perfect lab technician, ever-present but invisible.

At the whiteboard, a marker squeaked as Ellis sketched molecular pathways. Diana leaned against a lab bench, arms crossed, her brown ponytail bobbing as she followed his passionate explanation.

A few feet away, Neve was labeling test tubes, counting under her breath. The pattern brought her comfort while she eavesdropped. She'd never seen her father so animated, so invigorated by his work. It was a side of him she'd only glimpsed in fragments from her childhood memories. Neve realized for the first time how self-focused she'd been, as most children are, and considered it a gift to see her father from this new perspective.

The lab door swung open as Conrad strode in, waving a medical journal in the air. "LaRue, have you seen this hatchet job in the *American Journal of Oncology*? Feldman is going to be livid."

Ellis took the journal and opened it to the article, his expression darkening as he scanned the page. "Barnett again. That pompous jackass."

"He's calling our methodology 'fringe science at best, dangerous quackery at worst,'" Conrad said, his voice tight with controlled anger. "He says we're giving false hope to desperate patients."

"Richard Barnett hasn't had an original thought since 1965," Dr. Feldman added, joining the conversation. "Pay him no mind." She skimmed the article and strode back to her office with it, calling over her shoulder, "Focus on the protocol. The results will speak for themselves. I'll be in meetings the rest of the day."

Diana couldn't let it go and leaned closer to commiserate with Ellis. "He's still clinging to the same cytotoxic approaches that poison the patient as much as they do the tumors."

"Barnett's coming to the East Coast Conference next month. He's giving the keynote on responsible innovation." The irony in his voice was palpable.

"Responsible innovation?" Diana laughed bitterly. "This from a man who hasn't set foot in a research lab in a decade? Dr. Feldman is right. He just sits in his ivory tower, casting doubt on his competitors to stay relevant."

Ellis pressed his hand on the crown of his head and scrubbed it forward in frustration. "If we could just get preliminary results from the mouse trials before his speech, we could counter his claims with actual data."

"We need more time," Diana sighed, reaching out to touch his arm before seeming to change her mind and pulling back.

Neve studied the interaction—the almost-touch, the hesitation, the withdrawal—and recognized the careful dance they performed to conceal their obvious attraction to each other.

"I've been reviewing literature all week," Diana continued after a moment. "There's a precedent for our approach. The Japanese studies from '72 showed similar pathways."

Ellis's face brightened. "I have that paper at home! I could bring it in on Monday."

"Or," Diana interrupted, then offered. "I'm making dinner tonight. Pasta Bolognese. You could bring the research, and we could strategize our response to Barnett's article." Her cheeks flushed a soft pink.

Ellis tried to suppress his grin but failed. "That sounds delicious." Neve watched him struggle to conceal his joy at the invitation, biting on the corner of his mouth that wanted to twitch up into a smile. She must have seen him do it a thousand times as a child, but it never registered like it did through the lens of Donna's consciousness. She felt a thrill, knowing dinner would be more than just a meal. It would be another window into the life she could have had with her biological parents.

Later that evening at their apartment, Diana's knife chopped against the wooden cutting board in a hypnotic rhythm as she diced an onion into a fine mince. Steam rose from a copper pot on the harvest gold stove, enveloping the air with the rich aroma of garlic and fresh herbs. Neve leaned against the doorway of the kitchen, grateful to see Diana's shoulders unclench for the first time since she'd taken the pregnancy test. A portable radio on the counter played at a low volume, and Diana hummed along with Stevie Nicks' husky vocals.

"Cooking centers me," Diana explained without looking up, her knife never missing a beat. "When everything else feels chaotic, at least I can control what happens in this pot." She gestured with the knife toward the bubbling sauce.

"You probably shouldn't be waving a knife around like that," Neve mumbled under her breath at a tone Diana must not have heard, as the woman ignored her and wiped tears from her eyes.

"You sure cry a lot," Neve said. It was just an observation she'd meant to keep to herself, but instead it surprised her by rolling off her tongue.

Diana laughed. "It's the onions."

"If you freeze them for fifteen minutes before you chop, you can slow down the release of the enzyme that makes you tear up," Neve blurted, then was astonished by the fact herself enough to add, "I think."

"I'll have to try that next time," Diana responded. "Thanks for the tip."

Neve nodded, counting the knife chops silently—one, two, three, four—to center herself. "It smells incredible." She inhaled deeply as her stomach growled.

"Thanks." Diana scraped the diced onions into a sizzling pan where they hit the olive oil with a satisfying hiss. "Most of my friends are horrified when a card-carrying feminist finds such satisfaction in cooking. They think I'm setting the movement back twenty years every time I pick up a spatula."

"That's illogical," Neve replied bluntly. "Enjoying cooking doesn't negate your intellectual capabilities or commitment to gender equality."

Diana's eyebrows shot up as she stirred the onions, then added ground beef and Italian sausage to the pot. "Are you turning over a new leaf? It's not like you to question the establishment," she smirked. "But I agree. I will give up my spatula when they peel it from my cold, liberated hands."

The knife paused mid-chop through tan button mushrooms when Diana suddenly looked up with a mournful look. "Sorry to force you into an awkward dinner, but I needed a buffer." Her voice sounded stretched drum-tight. She sighed, setting down her knife. "He brought me coffee yesterday, with a little heart drawn on the cup."

"Hearts indicate romantic interest," Neve said, sucking in a breath between her teeth.

Diana shot her another strange look. "Yes, I'm aware. You're being weird today. So literal."

Neve rocked back on her heels, a self-soothing motion she couldn't suppress. "Sorry. I didn't sleep well."

"Neither did I," Diana muttered, returning to her chopping. "I've got a career-derailing clump of cells dividing every hour inside me, and a brilliant colleague who thinks we're on the verge of an epic romance." She jabbed her knife into a bell pepper. "Meanwhile, Dr. Feldman is pushing hard to get results faster, and Conrad keeps inserting himself where he isn't wanted."

"Are you going to tell Ellis about the baby?" Neve asked, trying to keep her voice casual despite the weight of the question. It was difficult knowing her entire existence hinged on Diana's answer.

"Not yet." Diana wiped her hands on her apron. It was made of faded black canvas with the words "Women Belong in the Lab, Not the Kitchen" ironically embroidered across the front. "I need to figure out what I'm going to do first."

The doorbell's *ding-dong* chime cut through the kitchen like an alarm. Diana froze, panic flashing across her face.

"I can't do this," she whispered, hands gripping the counter's edge. "Can you get it? I need a minute."

Neve nodded, her heart pounding as she moved toward the door, acutely aware she was walking toward her father. She pulled open the door, the hinges squeaking in protest. Ellis stood in the hallway, his lanky frame silhouetted against the doorway. In one hand, he clutched a bouquet of cheerful yellow daisies wrapped in green tissue paper; in the other, he cradled a bottle of Mateus rosé wine, its distinctive bulbous green bottle covered with gold foil around the cork. His hair was neatly trimmed, and he wore a corduroy blazer with elbow patches over a patterned shirt with an oversized collar.

The scent of Old Spice aftershave rose from him, and Neve's nose twitched in recognition. A sudden prickle of tears threatened, forcing her to blink against the rising swell of emotion. That distinct fragrance, sharp cedar and warm spice, unlocked a vault of memories and carved a direct path through time, bypassing her logic and striking at the core of who she once was.

His eager smile faltered when he saw Donna, and obvious disappointment flashed across his face before he could mask it.

"Oh, I didn't realize..." he started, then stopped himself, recovering quickly, shifting his weight from one foot to the other. Ellis cleared his throat, then added, "Diana invited me for dinner."

Neve caught the subtle emphasis on "me" and the questioning tone that suggested he'd expected an evening alone with Diana. She recognized the hopeful look in his eyes, the same expression she'd seen in the Polaroids of him from the attic.

"Please come in," she said, maintaining eye contact for three seconds before looking away, just as she'd trained herself to do in social situations. "Diana's in the kitchen."

Neve stepped aside to let him in, watching as Ellis took in the apartment. His gaze lingered on the three place settings at the small table. A single candle sat unlit between them. Ellis's Adam's apple bobbed up and down as he swallowed hard, casting a glance at the flowers in his hand that now seemed awkward and presumptuous.

"Something smells amazing," Ellis said as he walked past Neve into the kitchen.

Diana turned, wooden spoon in hand, her smile tight but polite. "Ellis. Glad you could make it."

He stepped forward, presenting the flowers with a boyish enthusiasm that made Neve's heart ache. "These reminded me of that botanical garden we visited for the cell photosynthesis study in school. Remember the section on natural pigmentation?"

Diana accepted them with a smile. "How could I forget? You argued with our professor that the extreme colors were more for providing sunscreen than attracting pollinators."

"And I would still die on that hill," he declared, as Diana groaned and searched for a vase, eventually settling on a defective glass beaker she'd brought home from the lab.

"I brought wine," Ellis added, holding up the bottle. "It's supposed to be good with pasta. At least, that's what the guy at the liquor store said." He laughed nervously.

"Great," Diana replied, though Neve noticed she

didn't look at the bottle. "Corkscrew's in the drawer by the fridge."

Ellis busied himself uncorking the wine while Diana arranged the flowers. The silence stretched uncomfortably between them, filled only by the bubbling sauce and Carly Simon singing "You're So Vain" on the radio. Neve stood in the doorway, rocking side to side, counting the flowers, twelve sunny daisies, arranged in a Fibonacci spiral.

"I hope you're hungry," Diana finally said, breaking the silence. "I made enough to feed the whole lab."

"Starving," Ellis replied too quickly. "Can I help with anything?"

"You could bring glasses to the table," Diana suggested, keeping her focus on the pasta she was draining in a colander, steam rising around her face like a veil.

Neve watched their body language as they prepared for dinner. Ellis gravitated toward Diana, finding excuses to be close to her, while she used the dinner preparations to distance herself from him. She directed Ellis to the cabinets for glasses, then to the drawers for silverware, keeping him occupied and separated from her.

Finally, they settled around the small dining table, plates heaped with Diana's Bolognese, garlic bread, and salad. Ellis poured himself a generous glass, then turned the bottle toward Diana's empty wineglass. She reached up a hand to cover it before he could fill it.

"Not joining me?" he asked, gesturing to the wine.

"Just not in the mood tonight," Diana reasoned, avoiding his eyes as she busied herself with serving more salad.

"Not even a little sip?"

"No, thank you."

"The wine has sulfites," Neve blurted out, eager to stop her father from making a fool of himself. "Diana's allergic."

She is not allergic! Stop making things up!

Diana shot Neve a confused look. "I'm not allergic. I just don't feel like drinking tonight."

An awkward silence fell over the table until Ellis cleared his throat and steered the conversation to safer ground.

"Day seven of the hyperbaric treatments for the mice begins tomorrow," he said, his face lighting up with enthusiasm. "If the outcome is what I think it is going to be, we are going to make waves in the medical community. There is a real need for non-toxic, highly targeted therapies."

Diana's eyes brightened, scientific passion replacing the awkwardness. "The preliminary tests are promising, and if the mouse trials succeed..."

"...we could move to human trials within a year," Ellis finished, leaning forward eagerly. "We could silence Barnett and destroy his credibility once the study is published. Maybe I could persuade Dr. Feldman to add your name to the byline."

"You'd do that?" Diana asked.

"Of course!" Ellis exclaimed. "You've been working as hard as I have been on Protocol VitOx."

Diana swallowed hard. "I'd appreciate that," she finally whispered.

They continued to chat about the article and the Japanese study, and Neve observed how they completed each other's scientific thoughts, their brilliant minds aligned, seeming to spark energy from the other. She couldn't help but smile, seeing glimpses of the intellectual passion that must have drawn them together.

"That bird of Dr. Feldman's is something else," Ellis said, refilling his wineglass, the bottle already half empty. "Yesterday, I swear I heard him muttering statistical formulas when no one was around."

Neve laughed, a genuine chuckle that made her eyes crinkle behind Donna's glasses. "Perry's smarter than half the research assistants in the department, myself included."

Hey!

Neve ignored Donna's outrage at what she considered the truth and asked, "Did you notice how he organizes his food pellets by color?"

"No doubt, Feldman's influence. She treats him like a colleague," Ellis added, his shoulders relaxing as the conversation flowed more naturally. "I caught her debating radiation efficacy with him before I left tonight."

"She treats him better than she treats most humans," Diana quipped. "Remember when she made that visiting professor cry during his presentation?"

"The one from Harvard?" Ellis grinned. "She dismantled his entire methodology in three sentences." He launched into a decent impression of Dr. Feldman, and they dissolved into laughter. Neve soaked up these glimpses of her parents together, storing away each detail.

"Manning is getting on my last nerve." Ellis admitted suddenly, his tone shifting as he set down his fork. "I'm still frustrated Feldman tapped him to set up the hyperbaric chamber."

Diana frowned, pushing cold pasta around her plate. "He's smart, I'll give him that. But the way he hovers…"

"He was going through my notes yesterday," Ellis said, leaning forward. "Said he was 'standardizing documentation procedures,' but it felt intrusive."

"He asked me some strange questions about you two," Neve interjected, eager to have something to contribute to the conversation. "About your… relationship."

Ellis's eyebrows shot up. "What? Why would he care about that?"

Diana's face paled, her fork clattering against her plate. "What exactly did he say?"

"He commented on your energy," Neve replied. "It seemed calculated. Like he was fishing for specific information."

Ellis and Diana exchanged concerned glances across the table.

"We should be careful around him," Ellis said, cutting through the lengthy silence. "Keep our research notes secure. I wouldn't put it past him to take credit for all our work. I certainly don't want to make any waves by accusing a superior colleague of misconduct this early in my career, but I think we should proceed with caution."

Neve felt a chill run through her, wondering if Conrad had somehow been connected to her father's disappearance. In her pocket, the geode vibrated as if it were agreeing.

"Maybe we're being paranoid," Diana said, but her voice lacked conviction.

"Maybe," Ellis agreed, though his expression remained troubled. "But sometimes, paranoia pays off."

The conversation lulled, so the only sounds were the clink of silverware against plates and the soft hiss of the record player between songs. Neve counted the seconds of silence. One, two, three, four, five.

"Donna? You're awfully quiet," Ellis said, leveling his gaze on her, and Neve slid her eyes toward him. When they connected, she felt a surge of energy that corresponded with the tingle of the geode in her pocket.

Eager to shield herself from the white-hot spotlight of his attention, she stood and asked, "How about dessert? We have cheesecake."

Ellis rubbed his hands together in delight. "I never turn down cheesecake! It's my favorite."

Neve shot him a soft smile, pressing her lips together to stop two words from leaving them. She yearned to say, "I know." It was the cake he'd insisted on for every birthday as far back as she could remember.

Twenty minutes later, their dessert plates sat empty, smeared with the remnants of cream cheese and crumbled bits of graham cracker crust. A Carole King album played softly on the turntable, the needle catching on the occasional scratch. Ellis stacked the dirty dishes while Diana filled the sink with water, making soap suds that rose in iridescent peaks. "This was nice," he said, carrying the plates over. "We should do it more often." Then his voice brightened with sudden inspiration, "My friend Enzo Bellini is the sous chef at Trattoria Milano downtown. Enzo's a brilliant cook, dices like a machine, and no doubt will have his own restaurant someday. He offered to give me a private cooking lesson on Sunday afternoon." He glanced at Diana, hope burning bright in his gaze. "Since you love cooking so much, I thought maybe you'd like to join? Or if you need a night off, we could just have dinner there. He's promised to prepare something special if I ever bring guests."

Diana's expression softened for a moment, a flicker of genuine interest crossing her face before fading. "That sounds wonderful, but I can't. I have that literature review due, and Dr. Feldman expects the preliminary data analysis by Monday." She averted her eyes. "Maybe another time?"

"Of course." Ellis nodded, his obvious disappointment concealed behind his smile. "Raincheck, then."

Diana tensed, her fingers tightening around the dish towel she held. She took a deep breath, steeling herself. "I think we need to be clear about something." She set down the towel with deliberate care, smoothing it against the counter's edge. "What happened between us was…"

"Special," Ellis blurted. He turned toward Diana, tender yearning blooming across his face, his hands dripping.

"A mistake," Diana corrected gently. "We work together. My career is paramount right now. I can't afford complications that undermine all the sacrifices I've made."

Neve was wiping down the table. Her hand froze mid-motion as she watched Ellis's expression crumple before he composed himself.

"Of course," he said, his tone neutral. "Professional boundaries. I understand."

Diana continued to explain, "I'm considering a fellowship at Johns Hopkins. It would give me three years of focused research without teaching obligations. I would have publication opportunities that could establish my name as a leader in the field."

Neve watched a flurry of emotion working its way across Ellis's face. "You are planning on leaving Aureon?"

"If Johns Hopkins called, I would," Diana admitted. "Do you know how many female biochemists are heading major cancer research initiatives? I can count them on one hand." She held up her fingers, ticking them off. "Women have to work twice as hard for half the opportunities."

"Things are changing," Ellis offered weakly.

"Not fast enough," Diana replied. "My mother gave up a promising art career to raise me and my sister.

She reminds me of it every time I visit, shows me her half-finished canvases in the attic, talks about the gallery showing she almost had in 1952." She shook her head. "I won't be another woman living in Almostland."

Ellis dried his hands on a kitchen towel decorated with mushrooms. "I should go," he said, overcompensating for the rejection by making his tone too bright. "I want to get an early start on my rebuttal to Barnett."

"Right," Diana agreed, a bit too quickly. "You need to be sharp."

At the door, Ellis hesitated, his hand on the knob. "See you both Monday at the lab," he said with a too-wide smile. Then he lowered his voice and added just for Diana, "Thanks for dinner."

The door clicked shut behind him, and Diana remained motionless for several seconds, staring at the space where he had stood. Then her shoulders slumped, and she moved to the couch, collapsing onto its burnt-orange cushions with a groan.

"He wants more," Diana whispered, running her fingers along the seams of the textured fabric. "A relationship. He would want this baby." She pressed her hands against her still-flat stomach, the gesture unconscious and telling.

Neve sat beside her, the couch springs creaking under their combined weight. She picked at a loose thread on her sleeve, twisting it five times before letting go as her thoughts began to spiral.

"If I have this baby," Diana continued, staring at the ceiling, "everything I've worked for disappears.

Seven years of advanced education, sixteen-hour days in the lab, fighting to be taken seriously by men who still call me 'honey' in staff meetings." Her voice wavered. "Dr. Feldman is only head of the research department at Aureon because she was a principal investor."

"But what if..." Neve began.

"...I told Ellis?" Diana interrupted. "He'd want to do the right thing. Marriage, a little house somewhere, me in an apron with baby food stains on my blouse." She coughed out a bitter laugh. "He means well, but he doesn't understand what it would cost me."

Neve wrestled with the weight of the future pressing down on her. If Diana chose her career over motherhood, Neve herself might never exist. If she told Ellis about the pregnancy, perhaps her parents would stay together, giving her the childhood she never had. Or maybe something else entirely would unfold, something she couldn't predict.

"What are you thinking about?" Diana asked, noticing Neve's troubled expression.

Neve's fingers drummed on her thigh as she counted the taps. One-two, one-two-three, one-two-three-four. "I was thinking how one decision can change everything," she replied. "It can change your entire life's trajectory."

Diana sighed into the darkened room. "That's exactly what terrifies me."

FIFTEEN

Two weeks into the first hyperbaric trial, the initial excitement had settled, and the team was sitting down to review the results. Outside, the oppressive heat of summer tempered into early fall as the middle of September ticked off the calendar. Inside the lab, time was measured in treatment days and tumor changes. Tucked into a corner of the lab, the new hyperbaric chamber hummed. To Neve, it looked like a steampunk artifact or a beached submarine. On the exterior, there was an array of gauges and dials Conrad monitored and tweaked according to Protocol VitOx's parameters.

At noon, Neve sat across from Diana at their usual corner table in the break room. Seeing her friend green around the gills, she slid a packet of saltine crackers across the Formica surface with the utmost discretion.

"You're a lifesaver," Diana whispered, tearing open the package and stuffing the contents in her mouth.

"The smell of formaldehyde almost did me in this morning."

"There's ginger tea in my thermos," Neve added, scooting the metal cylinder toward her. Their lunch breaks had given Neve unrestricted access to her mother's everyday life, and she couldn't get enough.

"What was it like growing up in rural Pennsylvania?" Neve asked, eager for another story.

Diana gave her a puzzled look. "Donna, I've told you about my childhood a million times." She set her sandwich down with a bored frown.

Neve froze. "Right, of course. I just... love hearing about it."

"Since when?" Diana laughed, though her eyes held curiosity. "You usually zone out when I talk about home. Last month, you literally said, and I quote, 'If I have to hear one more time about your mom's apple pie beating a Pennsylvania Dutch woman's for the blue ribbon, I'll scream.'"

Heat crept up Neve's neck. "I did? That doesn't sound like me."

"What are you talking about? It sounds *exactly* like you." Diana tilted her head, studying her friend. "Are you feeling okay? You've been... different lately."

"Just tired," Neve replied. "It's been harder settling into this new job than I've wanted to admit."

"You're doing great." Diana picked her sandwich back up and took a bite. "More importantly, have you thought any more about going to medical school?"

"I haven't had time. Tell me again what led you to pursue a career in medicine."

"My father wanted me to be a nurse," Diana reminded her, taking a sip of the tea. "Can you imagine? He still thinks this is all just a ploy so I can meet and settle down with a nice doctor."

Neve smiled, learning more about the inner workings of her mother's mind with each conversation. "And what do *you* want?"

Diana's eyes drifted to the window. "To make a scientific contribution to the world that impacts millions." Her hand wandered over her still-flat stomach as she dared to dream. "Too grandiose?" she asked with a self-deprecating chuckle. "No one can ever accuse me of being afraid to dream big."

Neve liked that her mother was driven by her vocation; it was a trait they shared, and her understanding took away some of the sting from her childhood of never knowing her.

"We need to get back," Diana said, quickly swallowing her last bite and stowing her bag in the trash. As they strolled down the hall to the lab, Neve felt Diana's excitement ramp up. "They're reviewing the results from the first hyperbaric cohort today," she said, opening the door for Neve. "Ellis has been on edge all week, hoping for a breakthrough."

Inside the lab, the atmosphere was charged. They took their seats nearby, where Dr. Feldman stood at the whiteboard, making notes. Ellis paced behind her, dark circles under his eyes, and his blue Oxford was unbuttoned at the neck and rumpled as if he'd slept in it. Conrad stood next to the whiteboard, clipboard in hand, nodding with enthusiasm at every word Dr. Feldman uttered.

"Subjects one and four show a twenty-two percent tumor reduction after fourteen days on the VitOx Protocol," Dr. Feldman announced, tapping her marker against the board. "Fact."

"The histology is remarkable," Ellis added, spreading photographs across the table. "Look at the cellular degradation pattern. It's exactly what we hypothesized. The hyperbaric environment amplifies the pro-oxidant effect."

"This is promising preliminary data," Conrad chimed in, turning toward Elaine, sweet as pie. "Dr. Feldman, your methodology is revolutionary. I've taken the liberty of organizing the notes and the supporting documentation for easier reference when we publish our findings in the medical journals."

Neve's gaze darted to her father, whose jaw ticked. He folded his arms across his chest, and a frown settled on his face. Why wouldn't he speak up? Set the record straight? Why was he letting Conrad take credit for his work?

He can't. Remember? There's a pecking order. Conrad is his superior.

From his perch near Dr. Feldman's desk, Perry ruffled his feathers. "Brown-noser alert! Peck, peck, peck!" he squawked.

Dr. Feldman shot the bird a warning look. "Peregrine, inappropriate commentary."

"Inappropriate?" Perry mimicked, before adding under his breath, "Perhaps, but still true."

Neve suppressed a grin behind her hand. Conrad's eyes narrowed at the bird before returning to his default expression of academic interest.

"While we are seeing some initial success in certain subjects, number three's necropsy results are concerning," Dr. Feldman continued. "Pulmonary edema indicates possible oxygen toxicity. We need to recalibrate the pressure parameters."

Ellis kneaded the back of his neck while he paced, thinking out loud. "Maybe we should try shorter sessions at a higher frequency?"

Dr. Feldman nodded, writing duration times on the board, while nearby, Conrad transcribed them into her notes. After a few minutes of calculations, a grimace settled on her features as she wrote the number '66' on the whiteboard and crossed it out. "Survival rate: sixty-six percent. Insufficient for human application. Fact." Her lips quirked down into a frown.

"If we modify the ascorbate concentration," Ellis suggested, his voice wavering under the strain of sleepless nights, "we might reduce the toxicity while maintaining efficacy."

Dr. Feldman's fingers popped the cap of the marker on and off repeatedly while she considered his idea. "This hypothesis requires testing. Please set new trial parameters immediately."

"I'll prepare the next cohort of test subjects," Conrad volunteered, getting to his feet. "And I can transcribe your dictation notes for the journal submission."

"Thank you, Conrad," Dr. Feldman said, her voice professional but tight. She turned to Ellis. "The pressure-to-duration ratio requires recalculation."

As they huddled over the equations, Neve noticed how Dr. Feldman's shoulders hunched with tension. It was obvious she was driven by more than scientific curiosity.

Every day at noon, she disappeared into her office for her lunch break, and Neve took the opportunity to pump Perry for information. He'd been going home with Dr. Feldman every night, and he'd seen firsthand the toll her husband's illness was taking on her. Dr. Feldman didn't speak to anyone else about it, but every day she seemed to return with deeper shadows under her eyes.

In a short period of time, Perry bonded with Robert, and he'd enlisted the bird as a spy, asking him to ensure his wife was not pushing herself too hard. Against his selfish nature, Perry promised the sick man that he would do his best.

It was that promise that helped him recognize the mounting tension in Dr. Feldman's rigid posture. Fine lines of exhaustion were etched around her eyes, and she pinched the bridge of her nose, letting out a heavy exhalation. In response, the bird launched from his wooden perch with a soft flutter, gliding across the room to land gently on her shoulder. His talons squeezed the fabric of her lab coat as he nestled against her untamed red curls, which seemed to have grown wilder throughout the day.

"Progress is incremental. Fact," Perry murmured,

his usual squawking cadence softened to one almost tender. He nuzzled his beak against her ear in a gesture that seemed oddly human.

Dr. Feldman reached up to stroke the bird's feathers, her touch mechanical at first, then slowing to a steady rhythm. Her eyes remained fixed on the whiteboard, scanning equations and percentages that refused to yield the answers she so desperately sought.

"Time is not on our side, Peregrine," she whispered, her voice barely audible over the constant hum and tick of the hyperbaric chamber working in the background. She blinked twice in rapid succession, a tic that appeared when her thoughts raced too quickly for her to process. "The tumor reduction rate is promising, but insufficient given the aggressive timeline we're facing."

She turned to Ellis, offering him a tight nod. "Tomorrow, we begin again."

The shrill ring of the telephone cut through the lab's thick tension. Dr. Feldman's head snapped toward her office, her body going rigid. Her fingers twitched at her sides, a momentary flutter of anxiety breaking through her composed exterior.

"If you'll excuse me," she said, her voice flat. "I must take this call."

Perry reluctantly hopped from her shoulder to the nearest workbench as Dr. Feldman strode to her office. The door clicked shut behind her, but through the glass panel, they could see her snatch up the receiver.

Neve watched as Dr. Feldman's face transformed. The color drained from her cheeks, leaving her skin ashen against the shimmering silver and fire-engine red of her hair. Her fingers, usually so steady with pipettes and precision instruments, trembled as they wrapped around the telephone cord, twisting it into tight coils. She swallowed hard, and the corner of her lip disappeared between her teeth.

The geode trembled from its confines in her lab coat, and Neve wrapped her fingers around it and began counting. Four minutes and twenty-seven seconds later, Dr. Feldman emerged from her office. The change was subtle but profound. Her posture remained straight, but her mind was elsewhere.

"I have to leave for the rest of the day," she announced, her voice stripped of inflection. She handed Conrad a neatly folded paper from her lab coat pocket. "These are the parameter adjustments I calculated. Please move forward with the next cohort as discussed, and I trust you will document your decisions in my absence with timestamps." There was a frantic quality to her movements that Neve identified as emotional overwhelm. A feeling she was intimately familiar with.

Ask her if she's okay.

Donna's natural empathy cued up, pressing Neve to take a tentative step closer and ask, "Is everything alright? You seem distressed."

Overhearing the usual question, Ellis and Diana turned toward her. Dr. Feldman gulped hard before sharing, "That was my husband's oncologist." The explanation tumbled from her lips. "Robert's latest scans show an unexpected progression in the pancreatic tail region. Cell differentiation appears to have accelerated since his last assessment. They want us there immediately to discuss the modification of his treatment plan." Her detached clinical explanation couldn't mask the fear that flickered across her face. It was there, etched in the worry lines on her forehead, then gone, like a flash of lightning.

"Oh, Dr. Feldman. I am so sorry," Diana said.

She gave a single nod, whispered a thank you, then rushed back to her office to gather her things.

As she left, the geode in Neve's pocket hummed with sudden warmth, pulsing against her skin with urgency. The vibration traveled up her spine and made goosebumps rise on her flesh. She had the distinct feeling she was standing on a precipice, and everything was about to change.

CHAPTER

SIXTEEN

LATER THAT AFTERNOON, Elaine and Robert were seated in Dr. Wellman's office surrounded by wood-paneled walls. While he perused Robert's file, she fixed her gaze on the wall behind him that was lined with framed diplomas, their glass catching the last rays of sun that filtered through metal blinds in dusty ribbons. Elaine shifted in her chair, the nubby tweed upholstery scratching against her skin.

The wall clock's second hand advanced with tiny clicks that seemed to splinter her thoughts. Seeking refuge from the mounting tension, Elaine's gaze drifted to the detailed anatomical illustrations hanging on the side walls. She drew an unexpected comfort in the colorful, labeled drawings of the pancreas and digestive system, finding their clinical nature far less threatening than the heavy silence.

Three minutes and forty-two seconds had passed since Dr. Wellman had opened Robert's file. Three minutes and forty-three seconds. Three minutes and forty-four. She blinked as she counted each one.

"I'm afraid the results aren't what we hoped for," Dr. Wellman said finally, adjusting his glasses on his strong Roman nose. A stethoscope hung around his neck, and his white coat was ironed and starched to within an inch of its life. "The chemotherapy hasn't been as effective as we wanted."

Robert nodded slowly. His once-broad shoulders were now swimming in his plaid shirt. "Give it to me straight, Harold. How bad?"

Elaine blinked twice as she processed the doctor's initial findings, searching for a way to dispute them as her brain whirred and spun.

"The cancer has metastasized to your lymph nodes, and we've found a spot on your liver." Dr. Wellman's voice was practiced, professional. "At this stage, we're looking at months rather than years."

"Months," Robert repeated, his voice cracking as he reached for Elaine's hand.

Elaine pulled away, standing abruptly. "That assessment lacks precision. What is the exact prognosis based on the metastatic progression rate?" Her hands tapped at her sides, a motion she couldn't control as her anxiety spiked.

"Elaine," Robert said with a sigh.

"Three to six months," Dr. Wellman clarified. "We can continue with the chemotherapy, but at this point, it's palliative rather than curative."

"Progression to stage four confirmed," Elaine stated, pacing the small office in measured steps. She set one foot in front of the other. Took eight steps to the wall, turned one hundred and eighty degrees, then took eight steps back. "This alters our timeline. We need to adjust the treatment protocol immediately."

Dr. Wellman exchanged a worried glance with Robert. "Mrs. Feldman…"

"Doctor," Elaine corrected automatically. "Doctor Feldman. It's clear based on the results that your current protocol is ineffective. We simply need to find one that his biology responds to."

"Elaine," Robert tried again.

"There are clinical trials," she continued, her voice taking on a harder edge as her hands began to tap more vigorously. "The NIH has expanded cancer research funding since Nixon's initiative in '71, and trials are ongoing all over the country. Matter-of-fact, we're in the early stages of one right now at Aureon Biomedical."

"I'm sorry. There are no appropriate trials he can qualify for at this time," Dr. Wellman interrupted, his tone gentle but firm. "Robert's case is too advanced. He doesn't meet the criteria."

"Incorrect," Elaine insisted, pulling a small notebook from her purse and handing it over to the doctor. "I've identified seven potential protocols at research centers within driving distance. I've also calculated the efficacy projections of each one based on available data."

Dr. Wellman paged through it before answering. "These are Phase I trials, Dr. Feldman. They're testing toxicity, not effectiveness. And they're not accepting late-stage patients."

"Then their methodology is flawed. Fact." Her breathing quickened as she continued to pace. "I can speak with the principal investigators. I can present Robert's case as an outlier worthy of exception."

"Elaine." Robert's voice was stronger now, cutting through her spiral. "Honey, stop."

She froze mid-step, turning to face him. "We cannot stop. Stopping equals a statistical mortality I am not willing to accept."

Robert held out his hand, palm up. "Come sit with me."

After a long pause, she returned to her chair, perching on the edge.

"I don't want any more chemotherapy," Robert admitted the truth as if it pained him. "I want to enjoy the time I have left."

"Unacceptable," Elaine whispered, a single tear tracking down her cheek. "You are drawing conclusions based on insufficient data."

"Please hear me, darling. It's based on what I *want*," Robert replied, finally capturing her restless hand in his. "What I *need*."

Elaine stared at their intertwined fingers, calculating probabilities, searching for alternatives, for a glimmer of hope, but finding none.

"I will honor your wishes," she concluded, her voice detached as she swallowed around the hard lump in her throat. "But never lose hope that I will find a cure."

CHAPTER

SEVENTEEN

BACK AT THEIR HOME, Elaine adjusted the rabbit ears on the Zenith color television she'd moved to their bedroom when Robert had gotten sicker, struggling to tune in to the evening news. The flickering picture finally settled, and she took a deep centering breath. Since they'd arrived home hours ago, Elaine had continued to plead her case for more treatment options, and they were both drained and mentally exhausted.

"Elaine, please," Robert sighed, his voice weary as he shifted in bed. "I don't want to discuss this anymore. The efficacy-to-side-effect ratio no longer justifies continuation of chemotherapy. It's poison, and I don't want it." He stared at the screen, half-hearing a report of a head-on collision and a fluff piece about a dog walking his way across the state to reunite with his owner.

Elaine's heart sank at the finality in his tone. She gathered her resolve, clenching her jaw as she walked a stack of research journals over to his bedside. Each publication was organized according to date. "I know you said no chemo, but what about Protocol VitOx?" she urged, her voice rising with conviction. "The latest cohort has shown promising results."

Her eyes glimmered with suppressed excitement as she began talking him through the most recent results of the experimental protocol. In solidarity, Perry fluttered down from his perch, landing lightly on her shoulder, cooing as he noticed how she had color-coded every page with felt-tip pens and annotated every margin with handwritten notes in her mechanical pencil.

"The statistical probability of efficacy exceeds current treatments by thirty-seven point eight percent," she stated, her voice steadier now, edged with hope as she adjusted her wide-collared blouse. Her mind raced, desperate for the words to paint a picture of a future that would be compelling enough for him to consider further treatment.

For a moment, both of them were silent, lost in their thoughts. Finally, Robert exhaled, shaking his head gently. "Sweetheart, the timeline reality remains. You said yourself, animal trials have just begun. FDA human trials take at least two years. Even with Ford's new health initiatives, we both know the bureaucracy won't move fast enough."

Elaine's heart dropped as the stark reality set in, but she refused to accept this fate so easily. She got to her feet and paced the room. "But there are alternative regulatory pathways!" she countered, reciting far-fetched options she had memorized. "We can apply for compassionate use exemptions or investigate off-label applications! We could seek fast-tracking..."

"Stop," he interjected, his voice softening but firm. "I have always believed in you. You are a brilliant researcher, and that's why when we sold my practice, we became principal investors in Aureon Biomedical in the first place. Since then, you've made some incredible breakthroughs, and someday ,I know, without a doubt, you will have revolutionized the way cancer is treated." Gathering his courage, he continued, "Unfortunately, sweetheart, I need you to accept that the approval won't come soon enough to save me," he whispered.

The air between them shifted, thick with truth, and for the first time, Elaine felt a crack in her foundation. Until that moment, she'd always maintained a positive prognosis. "Others are statistically irrelevant to me," she stated with zero emotion, then her voice caught as she stepped closer to Robert's bedside. "*You are my* statistical outlier. Fact." Her voice wavered, filled with a raw honesty that exposed the depths of both her fear and her love for her husband.

Robert let out a heavy exhalation, running a hand through his thinning hair. "The protocol is fascinating. Groundbreaking, even." He studied the graphs with genuine interest, his scientific mind engaging despite his exhaustion. "The oxidative stress mechanism targeting cancer cells while sparing healthy tissue is such an elegant solution."

"Then you'll try it," Elaine pressed, plowing

through his objections, her voice rising with urgency and tinged with hope. "It's not like chemotherapy. The toxicity profile is minimal." Elaine's fingers tightened around the journal. "I know it's unorthodox, but *you* could be our first human trial." Her voice faltered before she gained control. "The ascorbate concentration alone shows promise in reducing tumor burden. The preliminary data shows..."

"The preliminary data is just that, *preliminary*," Robert emphasized as he interrupted, his tone firm but gentle. "You don't have enough test subjects, the controls aren't adequate, and the long-term effects are completely unknown."

"You're not seeing the big picture. Protocol VitOx could give us more time together with minimal downside."

"How many animal test subjects were in the cohort?" Robert challenged, shifting into a more analytical approach, hoping to get through to her.

"Seven," Elaine admitted in a small voice, knowing it wasn't enough to confirm the result. "But the statistical significance..."

"...is insufficient for human trials," Robert finished. He closed the journal with finality. "I'm tired. Not just physically tired, I'm tired of being sick. Tired of hospitals, needles, and treatments that make me feel worse than the disease itself."

"Protocol VitOx wouldn't be like that," she insisted, pacing faster now. "The vitamin infusion has almost zero side effects, and the hyperbaric chamber is non-invasive."

Robert shook his head no. "I want to enjoy what-ever time I have left, not spend it as a guinea pig." His voice softened at the hurt in her eyes. "Even if it worked, we're talking about extending my life by months, not years, with my advanced stage."

"Months matter!" Elaine snapped, her composure slipping further. "Every day matters. Every hour. Fact!"

"Fact!" Perry crowed from her shoulder in an attempt to lighten the mood, causing Robert to smile despite himself.

"Remember our trip to Cape Cod?" Robert asked suddenly, changing tactics. "That little bed-and-breakfast with the crooked floors and the view of the lighthouse?"

Elaine paused her pacing, surprised by the shift. "The Salty Gull Inn. September 1966. Our fifth anniversary."

"We spent three days just walking the beach, collecting shells, and watching the sunset," Robert continued. "No schedules, no research, no hospitals. Just us."

Elaine's shoulders slumped in defeat. "The proba-bility of recreating such conditions is—"

"High," Robert interrupted with a soft smile. "*If* we focus on *living* rather than extending life at any cost."

The fight drained from Elaine's posture. She let out a heavy exhalation and then turned to place the jour-nals on the nightstand, aligning their edges in a straight line. "Your argument has merit," she conceded under her breath. "For now."

"Thank you," Robert murmured, knowing this was as close to surrender as Elaine Feldman would ever come. He reached for her hand, and she allowed him to take it, her fingers cool against his warm palm.

Perry hopped from her shoulder to the bedpost, watching them with his head tilted. "Compromise detected," he churred. "Fact."

A ghost of a smile crossed Elaine's face as she squeezed Robert's hand. She would drop it for today, but tomorrow was another data point, another chance to recalibrate her approach and present her case with refined parameters. The scientist in her believed in persistence, in slow and certain outcomes. But it was her heart, that wild, unpredictable, emotion-driven muscle, that spurred her on. There was no way she could give up now, not when it mattered more than ever.

CHAPTER

EIGHTEEN

THE NEXT EVENING, Neve parked Diane's Pinto in front of Dr. Feldman's Spanish-style home, mentally reviewing the hurried conversation from that afternoon. Dr. Feldman had approached her after lunch, explaining that she was taking the afternoon off to take her husband to an appointment.

"The bird has proven to have a significant positive effect on Robert's mood metrics," Dr. Feldman had said, her voice low to prevent others from overhearing. "Would it be possible for you to bring Peregrine to our residence this evening?"

The request had surprised Neve, especially given how protective Dr. Feldman was of her privacy. Now, as she studied the property, her eyes scanned the immaculate Spanish-style home, searching for clues about the woman who inhabited it. The red clay roof tiles formed perfect, unbroken lines against the cloudless sky, while the white stucco walls gleamed as if they'd been painted yesterday. Not a single dead leaf or stray twig marred the trimmed lawn.

"I bet she vacuums her driveway," she deadpanned, checking Perry's travel carrier one last time.

"She's not so bad," Perry chirped from inside. "Maybe you should give her a chance."

Neve's fingers drummed against the steering wheel as anxiety built in her belly. "Maybe." Neve took a deep breath and gathered Perry's carrier from the hatchback. As she approached the front door, she pressed the brass doorbell, hearing the chime sing its song from inside.

Dr. Feldman opened almost immediately, a stopwatch clutched in her hand.

"Acceptable arrival time." She clicked the stopwatch and tucked it into her lab coat pocket, which she was still wearing despite being home. "You've arrived within the designated window. This is satisfactory."

Neve shifted Perry's carrier to her other hand. "I brought everything you asked for."

Dr. Feldman stepped back to allow her access. "Please remove your shoes and place them on the doormat outside. Outdoor contaminants must remain contained. Robert's immune system is compromised, and we must maintain strict protocols."

As Neve slipped off her shoes, Perry called from his carrier, "I'd remove mine too, but I'm not wearing any." He chuckled at his own joke.

Dr. Feldman groaned in response. "Humor attempt noted. But before we can continue," she said, her hands clasping and unclasping, "I must address my workplace hierarchy concerns. Your presence in my home creates an uncertain social dynamic."

Put her at ease. She's nervous.

Neve recognized a familiar anxiety in Dr. Feldman's reservations. Back in Aura Cove, she often felt the same way. Knowing this, she tried to diffuse the tension, "I assure you, I am only here to help."

"Previous attempts at social integration with laboratory colleagues have proven to be problematic." Dr. Feldman's fingers tapped against her thigh.

Neve offered a small smile. "Then let's take the social integration out of the equation. This is simply one colleague assisting another with a specific task after hours."

Dr. Feldman's shoulders relaxed a fraction. "That is acceptable to me. We can reevaluate as needs change. Please proceed to the living room, where I've prepared a decontamination station."

The living room was a study in symmetry with twin sofas positioned parallel to one another, each cushion unwrinkled, each throw pillow positioned an equal distance from the others. A clear plastic tarp had been laid out in the center of the room, and a small zippered enclosure was open with spray bottles of purified water and medical soap tucked inside.

Unable to stop herself, Neve's assessment was too blunt. "This seems a little extreme. Perry's been a visitor at your home before."

She's just scared.

Dr. Feldman's shoulders tensed. "The latest

oncology report indicated…" Her voice fractured, her clinical façade crumbling. "Robert's immune system is severely weakened. The cancer has spread to his lymph nodes. Any infection could be…" She couldn't finish the sentence, and her gaze darted to the window like she wanted to escape through it.

Neve gasped, feeling shame well up at her improper response. Panicking about what to say next, she decided to let Donna's natural empathy flow through her. "I'm so sorry," she whispered.

"Robert has had a couple of rough days," Dr. Feldman admitted, her voice barely audible. "But the bird entertains him." She straightened her lab coat, composing herself. "Statistical evidence suggests laughter can boost immune response by up to forty percent. Therefore, I'm willing to make calculated exceptions to standard protocols."

"As long as Perry takes a bath first," Neve added, trying to lighten the mood.

"Exactly." Dr. Feldman's lips twitched in what might have been a smile. "The new sanitization procedures are perhaps excessive. But they give me a sense of control when everything else is…" She trailed off, fidgeting with her stopwatch.

"I understand," Neve said softly. And she did.

Dr. Feldman pulled on a pair of latex gloves with a snap while Neve let Perry out of the travel carrier, then crossed to the sink to wash her hands.

"Will there be a body cavity search?" he asked, his beady black eyes glinting with mischievous glee. "Should I assume the position?"

"Perry!" Neve cried, feeling her cheeks pink in embarrassment.

"From now on, avian hygiene is non-negotiable," Dr. Feldman replied, oblivious to the off-color joke. She methodically inspected Perry's feathers, beak, and feet, making notes on a clipboard. "All are in acceptable condition. Minimal dander. I will proceed with cage sanitization."

As Dr. Feldman cleaned Perry's cage with robotic precision, Neve noticed the way she counted under her breath, covering every inch of the enclosure with a sponge wet with non-toxic cleanser in her gloved hand. Neve guided Perry to the enclosure where Dr. Feldman sprayed him with the bottle of water. He spread his wings and shook out his feathers, allowing Elaine to rub him down with diluted medical soap on a soft cloth. After several more minutes of misting and ruffling his feathers, Perry was deemed suitable to visit Robert.

A weak voice interrupted them from upstairs. "Elaine? Is that Perry I hear?"

Dr. Feldman's expression softened at hearing her husband. "Affirmative, Robert. Visitor arrival has occurred as scheduled."

"Bring him up, would you? I've been looking forward to seeing him all day."

"I seem to have that effect on everyone," Perry declared as he preened his damp feathers into place. "It must be my sparkling personality and devastatingly handsome good looks."

Dr. Feldman let out a bark of a laugh and started up the stairs. "Follow me."

With Perry perched on her arm, Neve followed Dr. Feldman upstairs to a bedroom that had been converted into a home hospital room. Medical equipment lined the walls, each machine positioned closest to the area it was needed, each cord neatly wrapped and labeled. In the center, Robert lay propped up in a hospital bed, his thin face lighting up at the sight of them.

"Peregrine!" Robert's smile was warm despite his pallor. "I've got Brazil nuts!"

"My favorite!" Perry crowed, then flapped to Robert's bedside.

"Robert was Tampa's premier exotic animal veterinarian for twenty-three years," Dr. Feldman said, adjusting the pillows behind his head. "His expertise with avian species is unparalleled."

"Until I got sick," Robert added with a sad smile. "Now I'm just a high maintenance cancer patient hoping for a miracle."

Dr. Feldman's face wilted, and Neve saw her confident hands tremble as she checked Robert's IV line. "I've reviewed seventeen additional alternative protocols today. None show a statistically significant improvement over current methodology." Her voice broke. "I can't find the solution. I can't fix this."

Neve recognized the panic in Dr. Feldman's eyes, the same desperate need for control she'd felt when her own world spiraled into chaos.

"Sometimes we *can't* fix things," Neve said.

"But that doesn't mean we stop trying. We have to look at the data, find the correlations and abnormalities, and tailor our treatment accordingly," Dr. Feldman insisted.

"More data isn't always better." Robert insisted with fond exasperation. "Can you believe she created a spreadsheet to track all of my bodily functions?"

"Sounds familiar," Perry chimed in. "Donna made a flowchart for my molting cycle. Complete with feather collection containers labeled by body region."

"Hey! You were in danger of becoming a bald bird," Neve defended herself. "We needed to find the reason."

The tension broke as Robert laughed and said, "Birds of a feather, these two."

"Fact!" Perry trumpeted, and Neve couldn't stop a grin from spreading across her face as she felt herself warming to the doctor. Maybe Perry was right.

Dr. Feldman dabbed at her eyes with a tissue folded into squares, then covered her mouth with a hand to stave off a yawn. The dark circles under her eyes were evidence of sleepless nights spent monitoring vitals and researching alternative treatment options.

She's exhausted. Offer some support.

"Do you need help around here?" Neve asked. "I could tend to Perry and ensure the new cleanliness standards are fully adhered to."

Dr. Feldman hesitated, her need for control warring with her obvious physical exhaustion.

Neve watched her exchange a glance with Robert

and then finally nod once in agreement. "Do you have a schedule proposal?"

"How about Tuesdays and Fridays, from 6 to 8 PM?" Neve suggested, recognizing her need for specificity.

"That is acceptable." Dr. Feldman nodded.

Neve stood and prepared to leave, surprised by her reluctance, as Dr. Feldman walked her to the door. Nudged by Donna, she felt the urge to add, "It's okay not to be okay sometimes, Dr. Feldman."

The doctor considered her statement for a long moment before responding. When she finally did, she said, "Please call me Elaine at my home. Social convention indicates a first-name basis is now appropriate given the more casual nature of our acquaintance."

Neve smiled. "Elaine it is, then."

CHAPTER

NINETEEN

FOUR WEEKS HAD PASSED since the initial hyperbaric trials, and within the confines of the research lab, the air was electric as Dr. Feldman worked around the clock. She was strung tight with tension, forgetting to eat most days, and Neve had taken to packing an extra lunch. While Dr. Feldman was preoccupied, she slipped the brown bag onto her desk unnoticed. The days were flying by as October ushered in cooler weather that gave the air conditioning system a break.

Dr. Feldman stood at the whiteboard, her red curls wilder than usual as she scrutinized the latest data. The dark circles under her eyes had deepened, evidence of the long hours she'd been putting in. "These numbers aren't sufficient," she muttered, tapping her marker against the board. "We need to push harder."

Neve sat next to Diana during the meeting while the pads of her fingers traced the smooth shard of the emerald geode in her pocket.

Ellis nodded in response. "I've been recalculating the pressure variables," he said, sliding a graph across the table. "Look at this pattern. I think we need to increase the oxygen pressure level for the next cohort. We haven't reached the maximum therapeutic level yet."

The team gathered around, examining his findings with intense focus. Dr. Feldman's eyes lit up as she traced the bell curve with her finger. "Prepare new cohorts and increase one cohort by point two atmospheres," she directed, "and another by point four."

Over the next few days, the lab hummed with activity. Neve watched as Ellis and Diana worked side by side, and she drank in their interactions, ever curious about their dynamic. Diana seemed more tired lately, occasionally steadying herself against the lab table when she thought no one was looking. Her lab coat clung tighter to her frame as if she'd gained a few pounds.

"Coffee?" Ellis offered, sliding a steaming mug toward Diana as they pored over data sheets.

"Thank you," she replied with a grateful smile, their fingers brushing on accident. Neve noticed the slight flush that crept up Ellis's neck from the contact.

By the end of the week, Ellis burst into the lab, clutching printouts with such excitement he nearly collided with Donna. Neve let out a squeak and pressed herself against the wall to avoid hitting him.

"Sorry, Donna!" he called over his shoulder before slapping the papers down in front of Dr. Feldman. "We've done it! Oxygen pressure at two point six atmospheres enhances vitamin C absorption by sixty-three percent in the cellular samples!"

Dr. Feldman's analytical expression gave way to cautious optimism. "Great work," she confirmed, studying the results for several long minutes before she declared, "We need to replicate the results with a higher population of test subjects to ensure it's not an anomaly. Prepare a new cohort."

The following days were a blur of activity. Neve found herself drawn into the scientific process, assisting with sample preparation while Diana and Ellis reconfigured the hyperbaric chamber. Conrad hovered at the periphery, taking meticulous notes and offering suggestions Dr. Feldman often incorporated without verifying their source, much to Ellis's chagrin.

One evening, as the lab emptied out, Neve returned to retrieve her forgotten notebook. The lights were dimmed, but a soft glow from the Xerox machine emanated from the back corner. Rounding a tall cabinet, she froze at the sight of Conrad, his thin frame hunched over the copier, feeding documents into the machine.

"What are you doing?" Neve asked, her voice sharper than intended.

Conrad gathered the papers into a pile and straightened them before slipping the stack into a manila envelope. "Just preparing documentation for the board," he explained, his tone professional. "Dr. Feldman requested comprehensive records for the quarterly meeting. The board needs to forecast the budget for research and development for the next fiscal year."

Neve narrowed Donna's eyes at him, but she remained silent.

"Dr. Feldman is burning the candle at both ends right now, so I offered to help."

Something about his explanation felt rehearsed, but before Neve could press him further, the door opened and Diana, who had been waiting in the car, entered the lab, distracting them both.

"I wanted another look at the data logs," she murmured, eyes darting between them as she sensed the tension.

Conrad used the interruption to slide past Neve with a practiced smile. "Good evening, ladies," he said, disappearing into the hallway.

The next morning brought exhilarating news. The latest cohort showed a forty percent reduction in tumor size among the surviving subjects. The lab erupted in a rare moment of celebration, with even Dr. Feldman permitting herself a satisfied nod.

"This is remarkable progress," she announced, updating the whiteboard with figures. "But we must address the mortality rate before proceeding further."

Ellis's jubilation dimmed slightly. "It is still too high," he agreed, already scribbling calculations. "But we're closer than we've ever been."

Neve watched the scientific process unfold with great curiosity. She had always worked alone on her art, and being part of a team was out of her comfort zone, but this was different. As the research team reconfigured the treatment protocols, Neve felt the electric undercurrent of scientific discovery synergizing their efforts, and it was oddly invigorating. Science drew these brilliant minds together, riding the rollercoaster of breakthroughs and setbacks. They were all fully engaged in the collaborative pursuit of a cure.

Their forward momentum was abruptly halted three days later when an entire batch of mice died from oxygen toxicity. The lab fell silent as Dr. Feldman stared at the deceased specimens, her expression grim. Her hands shook as she sorted through the reports and data logs, certain all the answers could be found inside.

"This is unacceptable," she finally said, her voice tight. "We've miscalculated."

Ellis ran his hands through his short brown hair, disheveled from hours of work. "The pressure was too high. We pushed too hard."

Diana leaned against the lab table, fatigue apparent in her posture despite her bright eyes. "*Or* not hard enough in the right ways," Diana countered, flipping through her notes.

Dr. Feldman turned toward her, intrigued. "Elaborate."

"Look at the timing intervals. What if the issue isn't the *amount* of pressure itself but *when* it's applied relative to the administration of the vitamin C?"

Dr. Feldman's eyes narrowed in concentration as she considered Diana's hypothesis. "Timing... hmm," she muttered under her breath as she turned to the whiteboard, erasing the old equations with swift strokes.

For the next week, the team worked tirelessly, testing various timing sequences. By now, they functioned like a well-oiled team. Dr. Feldman provided the vision, Ellis executed with brilliant adaptability, Diana offered crucial insights, Donna did her part behind the scenes to ensure the equipment was clean and ready, and even Conrad contributed valuable engineering expertise in calibrating the hyperbaric chamber.

The breakthrough came unexpectedly during a routine monitoring session. Ellis had been observing the latest X-rays of the mice when he suddenly straightened, eyes wide.

"Diana was right!" he exclaimed, rushing to the data charts. "Look at subjects three and seven. They received the vitamin C exactly forty-seven minutes before oxygen exposure, and their tumor reduction is nearly double the others!"

Dr. Feldman was beside him instantly, analyzing the patterns. "Fantastic discovery," she confirmed, a rare gleam of approval in her eyes as she complimented Diana. "The timing between administration and exposure is the crucial link we've been missing."

Later that evening, as they prepared for the next day's cohort, Dr. Feldman addressed the team. "What we're doing here matters," she said, her usual clinical tone softened by genuine conviction as she took in the group of exhausted researchers encircling her. "Every cohort helps us ask better questions, and every failure brings us closer to success." She made brief eye contact with each member of her team before adding, "Every person here has made valuable contributions, and I thank you for them."

Neve had to admit it was exhilarating to be part of something bigger than herself. Looking around the room, Neve understood that science was more than experiments and data. It was the indomitable force of the human spirit facing it's own mortality and refusing to surrender.

In her pocket, the geode warmed and quivered when she wrapped her palm around it, confirming the answers they were seeking were already well on their way.

CHAPTER

TWENTY

T HE MID -O CTOBER TWILIGHT filtered through the venetian blinds, casting soft shadows across Robert's hospital bed, where the mechanical hum of the IV pump was drowned out by an episode of *Mutual of Omaha's Wild Kingdom* playing on the television. Perry observed Robert from his perch on the windowsill, his feathered head turned toward the frail man lying in bed.

"You look like something the cat dragged in, then decided wasn't worth the effort," Perry remarked, hopping over to the bedside table where a collection of pills was separated into piles in a plastic container.

Robert's laugh emerged as a wheezing cough that shook his diminished frame. "Tell it... like it is... bird," he managed, the oxygen cannula shifting against his nostrils.

Maria, the day nurse, glanced up from her charting with a frown. "Your blood pressure's down again today, ninety-eight over sixty-two," she noted. "And your temp's up to one hundred point three."

"I don't suppose I could talk you into keeping that from my wife?" Robert asked with a twinkle still left in his eyes. "She tends to be a bit of a worrywart."

Maria reached over to squeeze his arm gently. "Would that I could. You know she's going to recheck your vitals herself."

Robert's sunken eyes crinkled at the corners as he admitted defeat. "It was worth a try."

Perry waddled closer to Robert, surprising himself with his gentleness as he carefully picked where to place his clawed feet on the bed. It was as if Robert were made of glass. In the three months since Perry had arrived, he'd found himself drawn to this man who was slipping away bit by bit. There was something profound about Robert's quiet dignity that fostered empathy in Perry's cynical heart.

The doorbell chimed downstairs. There was a murmur of conversation, then, minutes later, footsteps on the stairs announced Neve's arrival. She entered, carrying a small paper bag that was stained with butter and smelled like cinnamon.

"I brought cookies," she explained, setting them on the bedside table in front of Robert. "Snickerdoodles. Dr. Feldman told me they were your favorite."

"They are," Robert whispered with a smile, reaching for one, though Perry knew he wouldn't be eating it. "Thank you."

Maria gathered her things. "I'll be back tomorrow

morning at eight," she said, touching Robert's shoulder gently before departing.

Elaine, who was lingering in the doorway, slipped into the room and pulled the clipboard into her hands. Her wild red curls were restrained in a messy bun. "Temperature elevated point seven degrees since this morning. Unacceptable." Her detached clinical assessment couldn't hide the tremor of fear in her voice.

"Come sit, dear." Robert patted the edge of the bed. "Donna's brought cookies."

Elaine hesitated, then set down her clipboard with visible effort. "I guess social interaction is appropriate." She gave in and perched awkwardly on the edge of the mattress, careful to avoid the tubing from his IV.

Neve settled into the chair beside the bed, watching this strange little family with growing affection. Robert turned his face toward hers and offered her a hint of a smile before saying, "I don't know if you know this, but Elaine has never been very good at relaxation."

"Fact," Elaine admitted easily.

"We spent our honeymoon in Costa Rica. It was supposed to be a week of lounging in the sun, gorgeous blue water, and sipping Mai Tais." Robert's face softened as he spoke. "But instead, there was a catastrophic landslide that filled the hospitals to overflowing. We had to help; we couldn't just sit back and watch people suffer."

A smile quirked up the corners of Elaine's lips at the memory. "He tended to the injured street dogs and monkeys, and I assisted the local medics."

"After thirty-six hours on our feet, we collapsed onto a cot in a supply tent and decided people like us weren't built for relaxation. We were built for chaos."

Elaine grabbed his hand and laced her fingers through it, bringing her lips to the back of his. For the first time, she noticed his wedding ring slide down to his knuckle, and it made a sound like a whimper form deep in her throat.

"You two seem like you were meant for each other," Neve observed, noticing how relaxed she was with Robert. "Did you ever think about having children?"

The question hung heavy in the air. Robert's eyes misted over and then drifted to the window, while Elaine's posture stiffened.

"My research demanded..." Elaine struggled for the right word before settling on, "singular focus." Then she added, "Children introduce a level of unpredictability I wasn't comfortable with."

"And I was always at the clinic," Robert added softly. "It wasn't a lifestyle we felt was conducive or fair to raising a child." Hearing the tang of regret in his voice, Neve wondered if these were questions her father grappled with too.

"We discussed it," Elaine continued, her voice taking on a rare vulnerability. "But the probability of successful child-rearing while both of us maintained upward career trajectories was deemed unfavorable."

"Elaine's goal from the start was to revolutionize cancer treatment," Robert explained, his pride noticeable despite his weakened state. "And I knew going in, a dream that big would require sacrifice."

Neve nodded, understanding washing over her like a wave. Diana's reluctance about motherhood suddenly made perfect sense. It was an almost perfect echo of Elaine's choices. The ones professional women in the seventies were forced to make every day.

As twilight faded into night, Elaine excused herself to retrieve Robert's evening medications. The moment she left, Robert's expression grew more serious.

"She's not sleeping," he confided to Neve. "She works all night on her research. It's like she's obsessed."

"She's worried about you," Neve replied gently.

"More than worried," Perry interjected. "She's on a mission. Those mice in her lab don't know what hit them."

Robert sighed, the sound rattling in his chest. "She can't accept what's happening." His hand, mottled with bruises from green to purple to black from IV needles, reached out to stroke Perry's feathers. "She's always believed science could fix any ailment."

When Elaine returned, she carried not just medications but a thick folder bursting with graphs and data sheets. Her eyes shone with a feverish passion that Neve recognized from the lab.

"Donna, since you're here, perhaps you can help me talk some sense into Robert. The latest reports from Protocol VitOx are showing unprecedented results," she urged, spreading papers across the bed. "We measured a forty-seven percent tumor regression in all test subjects. *And* zero fatalities in the most recent cohort."

Robert's eyes met Neve's briefly before returning to his wife. "Elaine..."

"We recently discovered the timing sequence is critical," she continued, pointing to a particularly complex graph. "In order to target the cancer cells, Vitamin C needs to be administered forty-seven minutes before hyperbaric oxygen exposure."

"Sweetheart," Robert tried again.

"And the side effect profile is minimal," Elaine pressed on, her words tumbling out faster in her excitement. "There is no immunosuppression like what's associated with traditional chemotherapy. No hair loss. No nausea. Just targeted oxidative stress on malignant cells."

"Elaine," Robert cautioned, reaching for her trembling hands. "It's experimental."

"But it's working!" For the first time, Neve saw Elaine's professional veneer crack. "Robert, please. What will it hurt to try? You're already dy..." She stopped herself short, unable to finish the sentence as she choked up.

The room fell silent except for the steady beep of the heart monitor and the rustle of Perry's feathers as he shifted on his perch, stunned by Elaine's display of emotion.

Robert let out a long exhale as realization dawned on him. "I get it. I understand now why you can't let this go." The insight made his expression soften. "You need to know you did everything you could," he finally said, his voice crystal clear.

"No," Elaine whimpered as her eyes filled with tears. "I need you to live."

"I know, my love." Robert squeezed her hands. "But we both know that's not happening. I only have a few months left, and that's if I'm lucky."

"The data suggests the possibility of an extension," Elaine insisted, but her scientific certainty was crumbling.

Robert stared at the ceiling, his jaw working. "I've made my peace with this. I don't want my last days spent as a guinea pig."

"Please," she whispered, her voice breaking. "I can't just sit here and watch you..." Her hands shook as she wrung them together, tears coursing down her cheeks.

"You've given me fifteen wonderful years," Robert whispered. "That's more than many people get."

Elaine stood and started pacing the room. "It's not enough. The protocol is sound. The methodology works. The risk factors are minimal compared to..."

"Compared to what?" Robert interrupted gently. "Compared to letting nature take its course? Compared to spending my remaining time actually living instead of being sick and trapped in bed?"

The silence that followed was heavy with unspoken grief. Elaine's shoulders slumped as she returned to his bedside.

"I don't know how to let you go," she admitted, her voice barely audible.

Robert looked at the charts and imagery spread across his lap, then at his wife's desperate expression. In her eyes, he saw not just the brilliant scientist, but the woman who'd never learned how to fail, how to accept what couldn't be fixed.

"Alright," he murmured. "I will try your protocol."

Elaine's breath caught. "You will?"

"For you," he clarified, his voice thick with emotion. "So you will have the clarity you need. So you'll know you did everything possible to change the outcome. And then, maybe, you can find peace with whatever happens next."

Neve shifted forward on the edge of her chair, the reality of what was being proposed suddenly hitting her. "Wait, how would you even do that? The protocol hasn't been approved for human trials by the FDA."

The room fell silent. The steady beep of Robert's heart monitor seemed to grow louder in the absence of conversation. Elaine's spine straightened, her scientific mind already three steps ahead as she brushed away the hot tears from her cheeks.

"There are ways," she said carefully, her fingers compelled by movement, tapping and straightening the papers on Robert's bed. "Compassionate use exemptions exist for terminal patients when conventional treatments have failed."

"But those take time to process," Neve countered. "Weeks, sometimes months."

Elaine's jaw tightened, then she choked out, "Fact."

Robert listened to them brainstorm, his breathing labored but his eyes alert. "Don't risk your career."

"My career is irrelevant compared to your life," Elaine snapped with emotion. She turned to Neve, her eyes blazing with purpose. "We are board members, and that gives us greater access to the facility. I can get approval to work on the protocol after hours when the lab is usually empty."

Neve felt her heart racing. "You're talking about running an unauthorized clinical trial. That's insane."

"No, it's necessary," Elaine interjected over her. "The data is compelling. The risk profile is minimal. The potential benefit outweighs the procedural concerns."

"It's also illegal," Neve reminded her. "You could lose your license, your reputation, everything you've worked for."

Elaine's laugh was hollow. "Without Robert, what would be the point of any of it?"

The raw honesty in her question made Neve's heart drop. She glanced at Robert, who was tearing up, understanding the sacrifice his wife was willing to make.

"Security changes shifts at 1:30," Elaine continued, her mind already plotting logistics. "Johnson always takes a long smoke break at 2:15. The protocol requires minimal equipment beyond what's already in place. I could get Robert in and out of there before security does rounds again."

"Elaine," Robert whispered, reaching for her hand. "Think about this."

"I've thought of nothing else for weeks," she replied, squeezing his fingers. "Every variable. Every risk factor. Every potential outcome."

Neve found herself caught in the gravity of their love and desperation. Before she could stop herself, she offered, "I could help you."

Elaine's head snapped up. "Absolutely not. Your involvement would jeopardize your career."

"I'm already involved," Neve argued. "And you can't manage the hyperbaric chamber alone while monitoring his vitals. It's a two-person job at minimum."

"The risk is too high." Elaine insisted.

"So is the risk to you," Neve countered. "But if the data is as promising as you say, isn't it worth it? Isn't this exactly why we do research, to find cures and save lives?"

Robert's voice broke through their escalating tension. His words came out in sputters, and he gasped in between. "Ladies... I appreciate the willingness... to commit felonies on my behalf... but perhaps we should consider... the impact on your futures."

Elaine paced the room, her mind calculating possibilities. "I could reconfigure the lab logs. Create a parallel documentation system that wouldn't appear in the official records. I could protect you."

"Secrets have a way of being discovered," Neve said quietly. "Especially with Conrad always lurking around."

At the mention of Conrad, Elaine's expression hardened. "Conrad is a variable I've already accounted for. I'll assign him to a project in the early mornings for the time being so that in the middle of the night, he'll be at home asleep in his own bed."

The raw determination in her voice was both inspiring and terrifying. Neve realized she was witnessing the full force of Elaine Feldman's brilliant mind focused on a single goal: saving the man she loved, no matter the cost.

"Let's sleep on it," Elaine conceded, then turned to Neve and murmured, "I do appreciate your willingness to participate." As the conversation wound down and Robert's eyes began to close, Neve gathered Perry to return him to his cage. The parrot was somber as he settled on her shoulder.

"You're playing with fire," Perry muttered quietly as they descended the stairs. "And Donna's the one who'll get burned if this goes sideways."

Thank you, Perry.

Neve stroked his feathers absently, "I know, and I wouldn't even consider it if there were another way. But what would you do if you could save someone you loved?" She posed the question to Donna as much as to Perry.

I'd risk it.

"I'd participate," Perry also reluctantly agreed. "But that doesn't make it right."

Neve felt the flutter of Donna's fear gathering and fought her way through the heightened anxiety that accompanied it. Reaching the cage, Neve hesitated before opening the door and placing Perry inside. "Whether we do this or not," she whispered, "changing the past is inevitable. It's quite the conundrum."

Perry tilted his head. "Maybe that's exactly why you're here."

"Maybe."

As she secured the cage door, Neve felt the weight of impossible choices pressing down on her. Tomorrow, she would have to decide whether to risk Donna's future to save Robert's life, and she did not know which path was the right one.

TWENTY-ONE

THE NEXT MORNING, Neve recorded the final measurements from the latest cohort and handed them over to Ellis, who was huddled around his desk with Diana. "Eighty-five percent tumor reduction across all test subjects," he announced, astonished by the results. "And the aggressive pancreatic model showed complete regression in three of the twelve mice." He spread the supporting paperwork out on the center worktable in the lab where Dr. Feldman stood motionless, staring down at the data sheets and spectrometry measurements in awe. For once, her typically stoic expression had softened into one resembling wonder.

"Verify the measurements again," she asked, though her serious tone lacked its usual edge.

Ellis bounced on his heels next to Diana, unable to contain his excitement. "I've already triple-checked, Dr. Feldman. The results are consistent across all three trial groups." He grabbed Diana's hand, squeezing it in his own. "Now we can file the Investigational New Drug application with the FDA and proceed toward human trials." Diana offered him a smile, gently extracting her hand from his grip.

As the team celebrated this important milestone, Diana slipped away to the supply closet. Donna nudged Neve to follow her, and Neve found her friend leaning against the shelves, eyes closed, inhaling deep breaths. Neve recognized the early stages of a panic attack.

"The fellowship application came yesterday," Diana whispered as Neve closed the door. "Johns Hopkins. They're accepting applications for their cancer research program." She pulled an envelope from her lab coat pocket, a nervous tremor running through her as she passed it to Donna.

She deserves this opportunity. It's what she's worked so hard for all these years. Be supportive.

Neve scanned the paperwork, then swallowed her fears and forced herself to say, "That's incredible. It's what you've always wanted."

Diana opened her eyes, revealing unshed tears pooling at her lash line. "It is. But now..." Her hand drifted unconsciously to her abdomen. "Everything's so complicated."

Neve felt a wall of conflict rising within her. The fellowship would destroy any chance they had of being a family. Yet she couldn't deny Diana's right to pursue her dreams.

"Why haven't you told Ellis about the baby yet?" Neve asked, trying to keep her tone neutral.

"I was waiting until the trial was over." Diana's voice frayed. "He's been so focused on the protocol. How do I tell him I'm pregnant with his child and considering applying for a position that would take me to Baltimore?"

Neve took Diana's hands in hers, finding the contact oddly natural despite her inner turmoil. "When would the fellowship start if you got it?"

"I'd try to defer until April," Diana whispered. "Right after..." She couldn't finish the sentence.

She needs your support, not judgment. This is her life, her choice.

"Have you made a decision?" Neve asked carefully.

Diana leaned her head back against the metal shelving. "I'm torn. I want the fellowship, and part of me wants this baby..." She swallowed hard. "But I've seen what happens to female scientists who become mothers. They disappear. Their research stalls. I don't want to grow to resent a child who had no choice."

"Maybe it doesn't have to be one or the other," Neve suggested, her heart racing at the implications. If Diana had kept the baby, her entire life would have changed.

Diana coughed out a bitter laugh. "You've seen how the men on the board treat Dr. Feldman, and she doesn't even have children."

She's right. The system isn't fair to women, especially mothers. She has every reason to be scared.

Their conversation was interrupted by Ellis's voice calling from the lab. "Diana! Dr. Feldman wants to go over the presentation outline!"

Diana swiped her fingers under her lashes. "I need to figure this out soon. The application deadline is next month."

Back in the main laboratory, Ellis was practically glowing as Dr. Feldman outlined the next steps.

"Ellis, I want you to present our preliminary findings at next week's board meeting," Dr. Feldman announced.

Ellis's eyes widened. "Me? Not you?"

"Your work on the oxygen pressure modulation was instrumental," Dr. Feldman stated. "And your presentation skills are superior to mine. Fact."

"But Diana was the one who discovered the importance of timing the vitamin C administration and the hyperbaric treatment." Neve saw Diana's shoulders square in the presence of her father's honest praise.

"We don't want to overwhelm the board; one person will be best. I'm certain Diana will understand." Ellis locked eyes with Diana unwilling to answer for her.

"Of course." She whispered.

Neve watched Ellis fight his inner turmoil and Diana suppress her disappointment. His career was about to launch into the stratosphere, and Dr. Feldman had just proven Diana's glass ceiling hypothesis true. How could she possibly tell him about the pregnancy or her fellowship ambitions now?

"Additionally," Dr. Feldman continued, addressing the entire team, "I've already initiated conversations with my contacts at the FDA about fast-tracking human trials. Given the minimal toxicity profile and the remarkable efficacy, I believe we can expect approval to begin Phase I trials by early next year."

"Next year?" Diana couldn't help but blurt out. "That's incredibly fast."

Dr. Feldman's gaze locked onto Diana's. "People are dying, Dr. Morrison. We can't afford to wait."

CHAPTER

TWENTY-TWO

LATER THAT NIGHT, at 2:17 AM, Neve's knuckles whitened as she clutched the edge of the lab table, her mind battling itself as she organized the vitamin C solution vials. The lab felt different at night. Shadows stretched across pristine countertops, equipment hummed in the silence, and the hallways and offices were dark.

What if we get caught?

"Please stop, Donna," Neve whispered to herself. Donna's fearful voice emerged from a corner of her consciousness, questioning her every decision, even though she'd agreed to participate. "This is hard enough as it is. Besides, the protocol works," Neve stated, reasserting control as she labeled each syringe. "The data proves it. All we're doing is accelerating the timeline."

This is illegal. If we're caught, I'll never get into medical school.

"I won't let that happen, and neither will Dr. Feldman." Neve promised, hoping it wasn't a lie.

Okay.

Perry fluttered down from his perch atop a cabinet, landing on her shoulder. "Having another two-person committee meeting in that head of yours?" he whispered. "You know, most people's idea of rebellion is getting a tattoo or sneaking into a concert, not committing felony medical fraud."

Fraud? Oh, boy.

"Not helping, Perry!" Neve grumbled, feeling Donna's stomach lurch and her anxiety crest. To quell the rising panic, she focused on checking the oxygen tanks. The logical part of Donna's brain cataloged every regulation they were breaking, every ethical boundary they were crossing. Yet when she thought of Robert's thinning frame, of Elaine's desperation, the choice felt inevitable. It felt right, even if it wasn't legal.

A few minutes later, Neve helped Elaine guide Robert's wheelchair through the service entrance of the research building. Perry perched on Neve's shoulder, being the lookout, as they navigated the dim corridors.

"Security cameras?" Neve whispered.

"Disabled on weekdays for maintenance from 2:00 to 3:30," Elaine replied, her voice clipped. "I arranged it yesterday."

Elaine moved through the lab, activating systems and preparing the hyperbaric chamber, while Neve helped Robert into a hospital gown.

"Nervous?" Neve asked him quietly.

Robert's smile was weak but genuine. "Terrified. But not for myself." His eyes drifted to Elaine, who was programming the oxygen controls with fierce concentration.

Perry hopped down to the counter, watching as Elaine prepared the intravenous solution. "That's a lot of vitamin C," he observed.

"Seventy-five grams," Elaine confirmed. "The dose is calculated based on body weight and tumor burden. In the mouse models, we found that plasma saturation needed to reach a specific threshold before the oxidative effect on malignant cells was triggered."

Neve helped position Robert in a reclining treatment chair as Elaine inserted the IV line into a fragile blue vein on the back of his hand. Within seconds, the colorless solution began flowing into his veins.

"The Vitamin C creates a pro-oxidant effect at high concentrations," Elaine explained, more to herself than to them. "It generates hydrogen peroxide, which preferentially damages cancer cells due to their reduced catalase activity."

"Again, in English?" Perry prompted.

"Cancer cells can't defend against the oxidative stress like healthy cells can," Neve translated, offering up Ellis's favorite explanation of the protocol. "The Vitamin C essentially becomes toxic, but only to the cancer."

Robert winced slightly as the solution entered his bloodstream. "It burns a little."

"That's normal," Elaine assured him, checking his pulse. "The acidity can cause temporary discomfort."

For forty-seven minutes, they monitored Robert as the Vitamin C was infused. Elaine checked his vital signs every five minutes, recording each measurement in a small notebook rather than the lab's official documentation system.

"Blood pressure stable at one-eighteen over seventy-two," she noted. "Pulse eighty-four and regular. Temperature ninety-eight point six. Optimal parameters for phase two."

When the infusion was complete, they carefully transferred Robert to the hyperbaric chamber, sliding him inside on a gurney. It was a metal cylindrical pod with a clear acrylic top. Elaine attached monitoring leads to his chest and finger and secured them through the openings before sealing the chamber.

"The pressure will gradually increase to two point five atmospheres," she explained as she turned it on and adjusted the controls.

"Will it hurt?" Neve asked.

"He may experience ear pressure similar to an airplane descent," Elaine replied. "But the treatment itself should be painless."

As the chamber pressurized, Robert gave them a thumbs-up. Elaine's eyes never left the monitors, tracking his oxygen saturation, heart rate, and blood pressure with unwavering focus.

"Pressure is optimal," she announced after ten minutes. "He's reached the therapeutic level of oxygen concentration. Now we maintain it for thirty minutes."

The half-hour passed in tense silence, broken only by the hum of the equipment and Elaine's periodic status updates. Neve found herself holding her breath each time a machine beeped or Robert shifted position within the chamber.

When the treatment concluded, they gradually depressurized the chamber before helping Robert out. His movements were slow but steady, and Neve noticed a slight flush to his cheeks that hadn't been there before.

"How do you feel?" Elaine asked, her scientific detachment giving way to concern.

"Warm," Robert replied. "And… a little clearer, somehow? Like a fog has lifted." He flexed his fingers and let out a small chuckle of astonishment. "I don't feel as weak as when we first arrived."

Elaine's face remained impassive, but Neve caught the glimmer of hope flickering in her eyes. "That's consistent with our observations in preclinical models. The initial response often includes improved cognitive function and reduced fatigue."

As they helped Robert back into his wheelchair, a sudden noise in the corridor froze them all in place. Perry dove behind a stack of notebooks as footsteps approached the laboratory door.

The security guard's flashlight beam swept across the room as he pushed the door open. "Dr. Feldman? Is that you?"

Elaine stepped forward, positioning herself to block the view of Robert. "Yes, Johnson. Your supervisor should have notified you of the shift change."

The guard frowned. "He didn't."

"The temperature fluctuations during the day were affecting our measurements," Elaine explained, her tone professional and confident.

Johnson hesitated, his flashlight beam hovering near the hyperbaric chamber. "Who's that with you?"

"My research assistant, Donna," Elaine gestured toward Neve. "And my husband has agreed to volunteer for oxygen saturation readings. You met at the company Christmas party last year."

Robert shot him a smile and said, "How's your daughter's pitching arm?"

Johnson's shoulders settled into their usual place as he spent the next few minutes bragging about the shutout game she'd pitched the prior week. After what felt like an eternity, Johnson finally stopped speaking. "Just make sure you sign out properly when you leave, Dr. Feldman. New security protocols and all."

"Of course."

As the door closed behind him, they all released a collective breath. Perry emerged from his hiding place, his feathers still ruffled, and flew over to roost on Robert's shoulder.

Robert reached for Elaine's hand. "That was a close one. Maybe we need to quit while we're ahead."

But Elaine's expression had already hardened back into resolution as she checked Robert's pulse once more. "Your heart rate is stronger than it's been in a month," she observed. "We will absolutely be doing this again."

Neve caught Perry's concerned gaze as Elaine began erasing all evidence of their unauthorized treatment. They had crossed a line tonight, one that couldn't be uncrossed. And somehow, Neve knew this was just the beginning.

TWENTY-THREE

THE COOLER DAYS of November came, and Neve was consumed by her workload. During previous four weeks, she'd been working a late shift that started at midnight and ended as the sun came up. Their two a.m. treatments were scheduled daily, and she assisted Dr. Feldman with administering each one.

Every night, Dr. Feldman updated Robert's medical file by hand. Inside, she documented notes on his response to the high-dose vitamin C therapy, kept logs of his hyperbaric treatments, and catalogued his symptoms. It had been risky to move from treatments twice a week to daily, but when Neve questioned it, Dr. Feldman dismissed her concerns, "He needs daily infusions to achieve the desired plasma concentrations quickly and maintain therapeutic levels. We will see how he tolerates the hyperbaric oxygen treatments in close succession then taper up or down based on the outcome."

The changes in Robert had been subtle at first, but

as the days passed, they compounded, becoming impossible to ignore.

"His pain score dropped from an eight to a four yesterday," Elaine whispered to Neve as they prepared the next infusion. Her eyes shone with cautious optimism, which seemed to grow daily. "And he ate an *entire* sandwich for lunch. That's the third consecutive day he's maintained proper nutrition intake."

Neve nodded, her hands steady as she calibrated the IV pump. Over the last month, working with the tubes and bags of fluid that the treatments required became second nature. The mousy lab technician, who flinched at sudden movements and trembled in the presence of Dr. Feldman, was replaced by a more confident woman who could now speak confidently about oxidative stress pathways and tumor microenvironments with growing authority. Neve felt Donna swell with pride as her skills grew, and it inspired her to continue.

In the four weeks since they'd begun the treatments, the dark circles beneath Robert's eyes had lightened, and he'd even gained back three pounds. Each time he came for treatment, Neve noticed he was stronger and seemed to be reclaiming more of his lost vitality. He cracked more jokes, and she witnessed his sallow cheeks become plumper and rosier.

"Let's increase the ascorbate concentration by five percent tonight," Dr. Feldman said, checking her notes. "The latest blood work confirmed he's tolerating it well."

"Okay," Neve said as she dissolved the higher

dosage into the bag of saline, preparing it for his next infusion.

Neve stifled a yawn with her gloved hand when the lab door swung open at 2 a.m.

"Ellis!" Elaine gasped, nearly dropping the IV bag Neve had prepared. Next to them, Robert stiffened in his wheelchair.

Ellis stood frozen in the doorway, his briefcase clutched in his hand. His eyes darted from Elaine to Neve to Robert, searching for answers. "What's going on here?" he asked, his voice low and tentative. Confusion bloomed across his features as he pointed at the infusion. "Is that... are you...?"

Neve felt her heart hammering against her ribs, and Donna's fears ramped up.

He knows. We have to get him on board.

"Wait," Elaine began, straightening her shoulders as she took a step closer to him. "I can explain."

Ellis's gaze shifted to Robert in the wheelchair before he stepped fully into the lab and closed the door behind him. "You're treating Robert with Protocol VitOx." He palmed his face, scrubbing at his scruffy jawline, trying to come to grips with what he was witnessing.

Elaine nodded, her chin lifting in defiance. "I had no choice. He's stage four. At our last appointment, the doctor recommended palliative care. He's dying, and I refuse to stand by and watch it happen when we've discovered a treatment that could give him more time."

The ticking of the clock was the only sound in the

silent room. Neve watched the gears in her father's brain twist and turn as he absorbed the reality of the situation.

Ellis surprised them both by asking, "How is he tolerating it?"

"His initial response is nothing short of remarkable," Elaine said, the words themselves seeming to surprise her. "His last scan showed a twenty-two percent decrease in tumor density."

Ellis's eyebrows shot up. "Twenty-two percent?" He set his briefcase down and approached the shared workstation. "Show me the data."

By five am, Ellis had reviewed every chart, every blood test, and every scan. He'd questioned Elaine thoroughly about dosing, timing, and side effects. As the details emerged, his initial shock had transformed into intense scientific curiosity.

"The protocol needs refinement," he conceded, pinching the bridge of his nose. "You're getting results, but I think we can optimize it further."

Dr. Feldman exchanged a surprised glance with Neve. "You're not reporting us?"

Ellis glanced up from the charts. "Report you for for trying to save a man's life who was given a terminal diagnosis?" He shook his head. "No. I want to help."

Over the next few days, Ellis became an integral part of their small, covert mission. He suggested a pulse therapy model where intense bursts of vitamin C were administered every forty-eight hours rather than daily treatments.

"This will allow for oxidative stress peaks," he explained, sketching a graph on the whiteboard. "If we time it right, we can trigger apoptosis in more tumor cells without harming normal tissue."

The revised protocol showed immediate promise. Robert's lactate dehydrogenase levels dropped significantly, suggesting tumor necrosis was occurring. His cytokine profile began to normalize, indicating reduced inflammation.

"It's working," Ellis whispered to Neve late one night, looking at the latest blood work. "It's actually working."

As the end of November approached, Neve found herself spending more time with Ellis. They'd stay late, analyzing data and refining the treatment protocol. Unlike Conrad, Ellis listened to her ideas, even implemented a couple of her suggestions regarding the timing of treatments. Neve soaked up being in her father's presence. Each long night spent working with him felt like a gift.

"You have good instincts," he told her one evening as they reviewed Robert's latest scans. "Have you considered pursuing a higher degree in medicine?"

Neve felt Donna's cheeks flush warm at the compliment.

He sees me. He actually sees me.

"I've thought about it. But Conrad has made me doubt myself a time or two."

Ellis frowned, setting down his pen. "Conrad's methods are outdated. He needs to learn science progresses through creative collaboration, not domination." He leaned forward, his eyes earnest as they bore into hers. "You've come a long way with Dr. Feldman. She told me yesterday she appreciates your attention to detail in the treatment logs."

"She did?" Neve couldn't hide her delight at his confirmation of the shift.

"Absolutely. Dr. Feldman doesn't give praise lightly." Ellis smiled, his eyes crinkling at the corners. "She sees what I see, a valuable member of the team, an intelligent woman with untapped potential."

Wow. Is this what it feels like to be validated?

"I've always loved science," Neve admitted, feeling Donna's usual hesitation melting away. "In school, I would read medical journals for fun. Everyone thought I was strange."

Ellis chuckled. "I did the same thing. My father wanted me to be a lawyer like him, but I smuggled biology textbooks into my room like they were contraband."

These conversations became a highlight of Neve's days. Ellis treated her as an equal, something Donna had never experienced before. She found herself sharing Donna's ideas more freely, modeling to Donna how she could speak up without first apologizing.

Thank you. I didn't realize how small I'd made myself. I don't want to do that ever again.

The earnest sentiment knotted up Neve's throat. To know their shared consciousness was inspiring them both to grow was humbling.

One evening, as they worked late plotting the regression curves of Robert's tumor markers, Ellis's pen hovered over the page. He was lost in thought, his mind elsewhere.

"Is everything alright?" Neve asked, noticing the distant look in his eyes.

Ellis sighed, let out a yawn, and rubbed his eye sockets with balled fists. "Just thinking about Diana. How is she doing?"

Careful. Diana trusted us with her secret.

"We had lunch yesterday," Neve said, trying to adhere to Donna's request. "I don't see her as often since Dr. Feldman put us on different shifts."

"Me either." Ellis nodded, his brow furrowed. "She's been distant since our dinner. Did I do something to upset her?"

He deserves to know, but it's not our place to tell him.

"She hasn't mentioned anything to me," Neve answered, keeping her tone casual as she adjusted a slide under the microscope.

Ellis's expression softened. "She's brilliant. Dedicated. Ambitious in all the right ways." He hesitated and let out a long sigh of regret. "I wish things were different between us."

"Different how?"

"Ugh. I don't know," Ellis mused as he tapped his pen against the table. "I thought we were getting closer, but she still keeps me at arm's length."

"Corporate America isn't kind to women who prioritize personal relationships."

"You're right, and it needs to change." Ellis declared, then stifled a yawn and leaned back in his chair.

"Can I ask you something personal?" Neve ventured away from Donna's warning, her curiosity winning out.

Ellis raised an eyebrow. "Of course."

"Have you ever thought about having children someday?"

The question hung in the air between them. Ellis looked surprised but not uncomfortable. Donna's anxiety spiked and flushed her cheeks red.

"Yes," he answered simply. "I do want a family." He smiled, a distant look in his eyes as he whispered, "Someday."

Neve hesitated, choosing her next words carefully. "What if your child wasn't exactly what you expected? What if they had health problems or learning difficulties?"

Ellis studied her face, his expression thoughtful. "Are you asking if I'd love them less?"

Neve nodded.

"Of course not," Ellis said without hesitation, then looked at her with curiosity. "Why all these questions about children?"

Neve felt Donna's panic crest in her chest. "No reason. Just trying to understand you better."

Ellis seemed to accept this basic explanation and shot her a grin. "Well, now you know, beneath this serious scientist's exterior beats the heart of a man who yearns to build model rockets with his future offspring."

They shared a laugh, the moment of tension dissolving into the air.

"For what it's worth," Neve said, "I think you'd make an excellent father. You have patience, kindness, and you genuinely listen when others speak. Those are rare qualities. Any child would be lucky to have you as their father."

Ellis looked touched by her words. "Thank you. That means a lot."

They returned to their work, but Neve could hear Donna's mind racing.

Diana needs to talk to him. She's making assumptions about what kind of father he would be, what kind of partner. She's never seen this side of him.

"We should probably head home," Ellis said eventually, glancing at his watch. "The day shift will be coming in soon." As they packed up their materials, Ellis paused. "I meant what I said earlier. You have real potential. If you're serious about pursuing medical school, I'd be happy to write you a recommendation."

Neve felt Donna's gratitude swell. "I'd appreciate that more than you know."

TWENTY-FOUR

A WEEK LATER, Ellis was gathering up the papers from his workstation at the end of a very long shift. He'd spent the day going over all the results until the numbers blurred on the page, but his gaze kept drifting over to Diana, who was working silently at the table furthest from him. It was the first shift they'd worked together in over a month, and he was surprised by how much he'd missed working with her.

Diana's workstation was covered under an avalanche of paperwork. She rose with a grimace, stretching her shoulders and massaging her lower back with the pads of her fingers. As she gathered her hair into a hasty ponytail, her attention fixed on the report in front her, the bottom of her blouse lifted, betraying a secret she'd been concealing for months.

Ellis froze, his gaze sharpening on the unmistakable curve of her abdomen. The slight swell of her belly, once hidden beneath her lab coat, now revealed itself in profile, and it was impossible to dismiss the truth. His breath caught in his throat as the confusion crystallized into a single, devastating realization.

Feeling the weight of his stare, Diana's hand flew to the hem of her blouse, yanking it downward as crimson flooded her cheeks.

"Are we the only ones left?" she asked, moving toward his desk, trying to distract him with small talk. She eyed the door, longing to run through it.

"Yes, and I'm glad we have a moment alone because..." Ellis set down his pen, "...we need to talk." The intensity in his stare caused her to retreat.

"I need a raincheck. I have plans tonight." She offered a weak smile, then turned her back on him, stacking her papers together, rushing to get her work-station in order so she could leave.

Ellis strode over to her desk, closing the distance between them with four steps, and leaned in until they were only a foot apart.

"Are you pregnant?"

The papers in Diana's hands stilled. For several heartbeats, the only sound was the hum of the centrifuge whirring away in the corner.

"That's a hell of a question to ask a colleague," she finally said, her voice strung tight.

Ellis leaned closer. "You're not just a colleague," he ground out, then concealed his frustration by clearing his throat. "I mean, you're not just a colleague to me."

She crossed her arms protectively over her midsec-tion. "Don't worry. I've taken care of it."

The words hit Ellis like a physical blow. "What does that mean?"

"It means exactly what you think it means." Her chin lifted defiantly.

"You're lying." Ellis stepped closer, studying her face. "You're still pregnant. I can see it in your eyes, in the way you move. How far along?"

"It's none of your business."

"If it's my child, it's absolutely my business."

Diana's expression hardened. "Who says it's yours? You weren't the only man in my life during that time."

The statement hung between them, sharp and ugly. Ellis felt his stomach twist, but he held her gaze.

"There is no need for cruelty," he whispered. "You're trying to push me away."

"You don't know me as well as you think you do."

"I know you well enough to recognize when you're lying." Ellis's voice remained steady despite the turmoil roiling inside him. "I know you're scared, but it's my responsibility too. We should figure this out together."

Diana's composure cracked. "There is no 'together,' Ellis. There never was."

"There could be." He took her hand, relieved when she didn't pull away. "We *could* be a family."

A strangled laugh escaped her. "Are you insane? I've been working my entire life to make a real contribution to cancer research. I'm not throwing my career away to play dutiful wife and devoted mother.

"Then let me raise the child. You can pursue your career, and I'll..." His doubt swallowed the rest of his plea.

"You'll what?" Diana yanked her hand away. "Raise our child alone while I'm off chasing my dream in Baltimore or New York? Have her grow up thinking she was a burden to me?"

"That's not what I..."

"It's *exactly* what would happen." Tears welled in her eyes now. "She would always wonder why her mother abandoned her. She would always feel unwanted."

Ellis felt desperation rising in his chest. "There has to be a solution. We can't just..."

"I scheduled a termination last week." Diana's voice dropped to a whisper. "I sat in the waiting room for two hours, but I couldn't do it."

Ellis let out a heavy sigh of relief. The admission hung between them, raw and honest.

"Diana..." Ellis reached for her again, but she stepped back.

"I don't know what to do," she confessed, her carefully constructed defenses crumbling as her hand drifted to her abdomen.

"We'll figure it out," Ellis promised. "Whatever you decide, you don't have to go through it alone."

Diana was quiet for a long moment, considering. When she spoke again, her voice was steadier. "I need time and space to think about it."

CHAPTER

TWENTY-FIVE

THE SETTING SUN CAST LONG, golden shadows across Elaine and Robert's lanai, turning the smooth wood deck into a canvas of amber light. Robert settled deeper into his wicker chair, enjoying the gentle evening breeze that rustled through the potted palms and climbing jasmine. The sweet scent of the blooming flowers mingled with the salt air, creating a magical tropical twilight hour.

"What I wouldn't give for an old-fashioned right about now." Robert sighed, watching as Elaine arranged a tray of fresh fruit on the table between them.

Elaine's eyebrow arched up. "Absolutely not. Your liver enzymes are still normalizing."

"C'mon. Just one tiny sip?" Robert pleaded with exaggerated puppy eyes. "To celebrate?"

"When Dr. Wellman clears you, maybe," Elaine replied, though her stern tone was softened by the smile she couldn't quite suppress. "Your pancreas and liver are healing."

"Yes, dear." Robert let out a melodramatic sigh, then brightened as he bit into a slice of fresh orange.

"Dr. Wellman will be here in about twenty minutes. He offered to make a house call on his way home."

"On a Friday night? The man deserves a medal," Robert said, accepting a glass of iced tea from his wife.

"Or hazard pay for dealing with you two trouble-makers," Elaine added, glancing pointedly between her husband and the parrot. When Elaine turned to adjust a cushion, Robert quickly tossed a chunk of pineapple into the air. Perry, who had been perched on the railing, swooped down and snatched it mid-air.

"I saw that," Elaine declared as she stood to carry their dinner plates back to the kitchen.

"Busted," Perry squawked out a chuckle. "Our covert fruit-smuggling operation may lack subtlety," He chirped, from his perch with his prize. "But the rewards are sweet."

Robert winked at the parrot. Their friendship had blossomed over the past several weeks as Robert's strength returned. Just a month ago, he'd been confined to his bed, too weak to make it to the bathroom without assistance. Now he sat outside in the evening air, watching the sunset after eating most of a meal Elaine prepared.

The screen door squeaked open, and Elaine stepped back onto the lanai carrying a fresh pitcher of iced tea. The sound of a car pulling into the driveway drew their attention. Perry cocked his head, listening for footsteps.

Robert chuckled. "That's either Donna or Ed McMahon with our Publishers Clearing House check."

Moments later, Neve appeared at the side gate, clutching a manila folder. In a rare show of trust, Elaine had given her a key to the garden entrance weeks ago, making her visits easier as she helped with Perry's care.

"You're just in time," Elaine called, waving her over. "We're waiting for Dr. Wellman."

Neve crossed the garden path, her practical shoes crunching on the gravel. In Donna's body, she moved with growing confidence. Her shoulders were straighter, her steps more purposeful than the timid lab technician had been when they first met.

"I brought the latest results," she announced, holding up the folder.

I've never been trusted with something this important before. It feels good.

Robert leaned forward eagerly. "Well? Don't keep us in suspense."

Neve handed the folder to Elaine, who examined the findings, her expression neutral and direct. "Your CA 19-9 markers have dropped another seven percent since last week. Liver function tests show remarkable improvement across all parameters. The imaging shows continued reduction in tumor density." She looked up, her face breaking into a rare smile as her eyes shone with relief. "Everything is trending positive."

"Does that mean I can start doing push-ups?" Robert joked, flexing his thin arms. "I need to build back some muscle. I've lost so much wasting away in that bed."

Elaine shot him a look. "One step at a time. Walking is still your primary form of exercise until Dr. Wellman tells us differently."

"But my energy levels are through the roof compared to a month ago," Robert reasoned. "I actually want to move again. Even if it's just walking around the garden."

Elaine placed a gentle hand on his shoulder as she explained to Neve, "It's remarkable. His appetite has returned, he's sleeping through the night, and the pain has reduced significantly."

"If this is a placebo effect, I'll take it," Robert said, covering her hand with his own.

"It's not a placebo," Neve stated with her usual bluntness. "The numbers don't lie."

Robert reached for a folder tucked beside his chair and pulled out several glossy brochures. "I've been conducting my own research," he said, spreading them across the table. "I want to whisk you away to Costa Rica for a second honeymoon."

The brochures displayed lush rainforests, pristine beaches, and luxury resorts. Elaine picked one up, her expression softening.

"Our first attempt was such a disaster," she recalled fondly.

"This time will be different," Robert promised. "We'll go during the dry season. I was thinking January, maybe February."

"As your emotional support animal, I must insist I accompany you," Perry declared, hopping onto the table to inspect the brochures. "My Spanish is excellent. *¡Hola! ¿Dónde está la discoteca?*"

"I highly doubt they want to spend their second honeymoon clubbing in a foreign country," Neve pointed out.

Robert grinned. "Who knows? Maybe we'll try something new."

Elaine's expression shifted to horrified, then softened when Robert brought her hand to his lips and kissed it, adding a quick, "Maybe not."

"That's the only Spanish you know, isn't it?" Neve asked Perry.

"I also know *cerveza, por favor*," Perry chirped with glee as Robert chuckled. "I'm well-versed in all essential travel vocabulary."

While Elaine excused herself to return the dirty dessert plate to the kitchen before Dr. Wellman's arrival, Robert beckoned Neve closer and pulled a leather-bound book, hidden in plain sight, from a stack on the table next to him.

"I've been working on something," he said, his voice lowered. "For Elaine's Christmas gift."

He opened the book to reveal a handmade scrapbook. The first spread contained photographs of their wedding day: Elaine, her wild, curly red hair adorned with tiny white flowers, standing beside Robert, his eyes crinkled with laughter as they exchanged vows beneath an ancient oak tree.

Turning the page revealed snapshots of their life together. Elaine and Robert walking on the beach, the couple painting their first apartment with more paint splattered on their clothes than on the walls. One striking black-and-white photograph showed them slow dancing in their kitchen, the light from the window making them glow, caught in a moment of ordinary tenderness.

The middle section transitioned to their professional lives. Elaine appeared in her lab coat, her expression intense as she peered through a microscope, completely absorbed in her research. In contrast, Robert's veterinary practice photos showed his gentle hands cradling a trembling Chihuahua and a wide-eyed Maine Coon cat.

As he turned to the more recent pages, the mood shifted. Here were the raw, unflinching snapshots of Robert's illness. Robert sitting in a hospital bed, gaunt but smiling, with Elaine sleeping in the chair beside him.

"It's beautiful," Neve said, genuinely moved.

Robert turned to a page where pressed jasmine flowers framed a candid photograph of Elaine working at her desk, lost in concentration.

"I added this last week," he said, pointing to a small, scarlet feather mounted beside a handwritten note. "Perry contributed."

"Against my will," Perry interjected. "That was from my prime tail region."

"It documents our life together thus far," Robert explained. "And now that I can see a future is possible, I cannot wait to add our next chapter."

"She's going to love it."

The sound of another car in the driveway prompted Robert to hide the scrapbook at the bottom of the pile, out of sight. "That must be Wellman."

"Behold! The good doctor approaches!" Perry cawed, spreading his wings for dramatic effect. "The official confirmation of our scientific wonder is about to begin!"

Dr. Wellman arrived carrying his medical bag, his face set in the somber expression of a man prepared for a difficult conversation. He stopped short when he saw Robert sitting upright on the lanai with color in his cheeks and an empty glass of iced tea beside him.

"Robert?" The doctor's professional composure slipped for a moment. "I wasn't expecting to find you up and about."

"Harold," Robert greeted him with a warm smile. "Beautiful evening for a house call, isn't it?"

The oncologist approached cautiously, as though Robert might be an apparition. "When I saw you eight weeks ago, you were..."

"Circling the drain?" Robert supplied with a wry grin. "I remember."

Dr. Wellman set his bag down, immediately reaching for Robert's wrist to check his pulse. "Elaine said your last set of tests showed improvement, but this is..." he trailed off unable to complete his thought, shaking his head in total disbelief.

Elaine returned with a fresh glass of tea, her scientist's no-nonsense demeanor back in place. "I've compiled all the recent test results. I believe you will find the imaging particularly noteworthy."

Dr. Wellman spent the next twenty minutes examining Robert from head to toe, checking lymph nodes, palpating his abdomen, and testing reflexes and strength. With each test, his expression grew increasingly more bewildered.

"Your lymph nodes have reduced significantly in size," he noted, pressing the tips of his fingers under Robert's jaw. "And the abdominal mass is... I can barely feel it now."

"There's been a thirty-eight percent reduction in density according to yesterday's scan," Elaine supplied.

Perry, who had been quiet during the examination, suddenly adopted a booming announcer's voice. "Blood pressure one-twenty over seventy-eight! Pulse sixty-eight and regular! Ladies and gentlemen, we have ourselves a walking, talking medical anomaly!"

Perry's articulation astonished the already dumbfounded doctor. "That bird just recited Robert's vital signs!"

"Perry is a man of many talents," Robert said with his best poker face. "Some more useful than others."

After completing his examination, Dr. Wellman leaned back into the wicker chair he was offered. "I've been practicing oncology for twenty-seven years," he stated in awe. "I've never seen a stage four pancreatic adenocarcinoma respond like this, especially not after conventional treatments failed. Perhaps it's a delayed response to the chemotherapy or a spontaneous remission."

Elaine silenced Robert with a look. Then, in her direct fashion, she turned and asked, "I'm assuming palliative care is now off the table?"

Still reeling in shock, the doctor let out a surprised chuckle. "Correct. We can even consider additional treatment options when he gets a bit stronger," Dr. Wellman replied. "Perhaps a modified chemotherapy regimen, maybe radiation if the tumor continues to shrink. There have been some promising results with a new drug called fluorouracil in combination with mitomycin."

Robert nodded through his initial grimace. "Can you give us some time to discuss it?"

"Of course."

As the evening deepened into twilight, they discussed next steps and future plans. Dr. Wellman, still visibly gobsmacked by Robert's remarkable improvement, cleared him for light exercise and, to Robert's delight, the occasional old-fashioned.

After the doctor left, they remained on the lanai as stars began to appear in the darkening sky. Robert raised his freshly made cocktail in a toast.

"To second chances," he said.

"And to the future," Elaine added, clinking her glass against his.

"I've been thinking," Robert said, setting his drink down. "Now that I can get out of bed, maybe I could still be of use."

"A veterinary practice?" Neve asked.

Robert shook his head no. "Something different. Maybe an exotic bird clinic? With Peregrine as my assistant, of course."

Perry let out a whistle of appreciation. "I've got the perfect name. Aura Cove Exotics. Robert can handle the animals, and I'll handle the dancers," Perry joked.

"Perry!" Elaine admonished, though she couldn't suppress a laugh.

"Just spit-balling business models," the parrot replied, feigning innocence.

"What about you, Donna?" Robert asked. "Any big plans for the future?"

Neve considered the question. "I think I might apply to medical school," she admitted, surprising herself with Donna's emerging ambition. "Dr. LaRue thinks I have potential."

"You absolutely do," Elaine confirmed, her usual bluntness softened by genuine approval.

As night settled fully around them, they sat in comfortable silence, watching the stars emerge. The darkness that had once seemed so threatening now felt enveloping, a comforting, peaceful place of rest.

"It's strange," Robert said, his voice low. "When death feels near, it's the untraveled roads that haunt you. But if you're lucky enough to get a second chance, you crave the thrill of every twist and turn."

Perry, who had settled on the back of Robert's chair, spoke with unusual enlightenment. "Hope is as fragile as a feather until it molts, and returns stronger than before."

They all turned to stare at the parrot in surprise.

"What?" Perry fluffed his feathers, shocked by their response. "I can be profound when the situation calls for it. After all, I *am* an enigma wrapped in a riddle."

CHAPTER

TWENTY-SIX

A FEW DAYS LATER, at eleven am, the team was just wrapping up their meeting when the lab door swung open, revealing Robert walking in unassisted, carrying a large paper bag. His frame was still thin, but there was color in his cheeks and a steadiness to his gait that had been absent for months. Perched on his shoulder, Perry puffed out his chest and whistled to get their attention.

"Behold! The triumphant perambulation of the formerly moribund! A modern day Lazarus brought to you by..." Reading Conrad's suspicious expression, Robert coughed as the words "Protocol Vitox" died on Perry's beak.

Robert let out a nervous chuckle as Elaine rushed forward, her initial joy quickly fading into a look of deep concern. "You didn't tell me you were planning on visiting today. You should have called; I would have come to get you."

"And miss the opportunity to surprise you all?"

Robert set the paper bag on the counter. "I brought lunch! Proper food, not that vending machine nonsense you've been subsisting on."

Neve grinned, watching as he unpacked containers of homemade sandwiches and fresh fruit. Just two months ago, this man had barely been able to stand without assistance. Now he was bringing them lunch. Ever the worrywart, Dr. Feldman guided him to a seat and started taking his vital signs, pressing her fingers to his pulse at his wrist and calculating it. Then, she attached the blood pressure cuff to his bicep and pumped it with the hand pump. "One-oh-seven over seventy-seven."

"See? Nothing to worry about! I'm healthy as a horse!" Robert confirmed, his tone boisterous with pride. "And I walked up the stairs instead of taking the elevator."

"You did what?" Elaine's eyes widened in alarm.

"And I'm *barely* winded," he teased, walking back over to distribute the sandwiches.

"You seem to have made a remarkable recovery." Conrad said, accepting the paper-wrapped sandwich, though his eyes narrowed in suspicion.

"My doctor has me on a new experimental treatment." Robert turned and shot an almost imperceptible wink at his wife.

"In layman's terms," Perry interjected, hopping onto the counter, "the big bad cancer blob is shrinking, and the baby blobs are dying. A most satisfactory outcome, if I do say so myself."

"It is *more* than satisfactory," Elaine agreed, her

flat affect warmed by the smile she fought to suppress. She pulled him into her office, away from prying eyes, and shut the door. "Sweetheart, I'm thrilled you're feeling better, but we must remain cautious. We can't afford to raise suspicions until we get FDA approval for human trials."

"For the first time in a long time, I am feeling good," Robert admitted. "I didn't see the harm in celebrating a bit."

"There is so much at stake," Elaine countered, lowering her voice. "We have to keep this under wraps for the time being."

"You're right." He agreed, passing her a cup filled with fruit.

When they finished eating, Robert took Elaine's hands in his. "I've been thinking."

"Oh, dear. That's a dangerous pastime with you," she quipped, but her eyes were soft.

"You've been working non-stop for months. Even before all this," he gestured to his torso vaguely to indicate his illness, "you were pulling sixty-hour weeks. And now with our secret treatments..."

"We have the chance to revolutionize the treatment of pancreatic cancer. It's important work," she said.

"It is. But so is living." He squeezed her hands. "I want to book our trip to Costa Rica."

Elaine's practical nature resurfaced. "Robert, that's not realistic right now. Your immune system..."

"...is stronger every day," he finished for her. "I'm

not saying tomorrow, but soon. What do you think about Valentine's Day if things continue this way?"

"That's only three months from now."

"And at the rate we're going, I'll be doing cartwheels by then." He grinned, then his expression grew somber. "I was dying. We both know it. And now I'm not. You've given me more time. Let me give *you* something back."

Tears welled in Elaine's eyes, a rare display of emotion from the usually composed scientist. "I didn't do it alone."

"No," he agreed. "But you fought for me when everyone else had given up. You risked your career."

"I'd risk far more than that for you," she said, the truth simple to admit.

Robert stood and pulled her into his arms. "I know. That's why I love you." He paused, then pressed her one last time. "So, Costa Rica? All you have to do is say yes."

Elaine pulled back, wiping her eyes and composing herself with visible effort. "Yes. But only if your neutrophil count is above fifteen hundred and you maintain your weight for at least four consecutive weeks."

Robert laughed. "Always with the conditions."

"Always with the hope," she corrected him, allowing herself a full smile. "And right now, I have more hope than I've had in a very long time."

TWENTY-SEVEN

Donna's hands moved with confidence as Neve measured the saline solution and piped it into a row of test tubes in the empty lab. The clock on the wall read 2:47 AM, and the second hand ticked through the silence. Her eyes burned behind Donna's round glasses, which slid down the bridge of her nose for the third time in as many minutes.

The centrifuge whirred in the corner, and she blinked away exhaustion and focused on the meniscus in each test tube, determined to maintain the exact measurements that Dr. Feldman demanded.

A shadow fell across her workstation as Ellis appeared, his lab coat hanging open over a wrinkled Oxford shirt, his skinny tie loosened at the neck. The cuffs of his dress slacks whispered against the linoleum as he shifted his weight from one foot to the other. He seemed distressed.

"Donna, got a minute?" Ellis's voice strained with tension, pitched low enough that only she could hear.

Don't get distracted. We need to stay on Dr. Feldman's good side so she can write me a letter of recommendation for medical school.

Neve kept her eyes fixed on the pipette. One drop too many could ruin hours of work. "I need to finish this dilution series," she replied without looking up.

Ellis leaned against the worktable, his knuckles white as he gripped a ballpoint pen, clicking the plunger up and down. "It's Diana," he whispered, as the clicking sped up. "I just found out she's... she's pregnant with my child."

The pipette froze mid-air as Neve's head snapped up, Donna's glasses sliding further down her nose. "What?" Neve said, feigning surprise, and falling flat. She had never been very good at lying to her father.

"You don't have to put on an act. I know she tells you everything." Ellis's expression tightened as he glanced around, ensuring they weren't being over-heard. "I want to help her, but she's completely freezing me out."

Neve took a deep breath and placed the glass pipette in its holder before turning to face Ellis.

"Do you want her to keep the baby?" she asked, then immediately felt Donna's internal wince at her bluntness.

You can't just ask him that! Have a little tact!

Ellis leaned closer, lowering his voice further. "I do," he admitted, palming the crown of his head with his hand. "The timing isn't great, but I've always wanted to be a father, and I want this child, even if I have to raise it alone."

Across the lab, Dr. Feldman was reviewing data charts at a desk covered with stacks of scientific journals and typed notes. Neve glanced over at Robert, sitting in the wheelchair with the IV in his arm, delivering the vitamin C infusion. She did a double-take when she saw his hand quiver as a tremor went through it. The tremor was subtle, but her sharp eyes caught the way his fist shimmied in his lap.

That's not right. Maybe you should report an adverse reaction to Dr. Feldman?

"What should I do?" Ellis asked, distracting her before she could decide. "I can't force her, obviously, but I can't just let this go either."

Neve tilted Donna's head, considering. "Tell her you'll take full custody and she won't have to contribute financially or emotionally if she doesn't want to."

Ellis blinked, clearly taken aback by her directness. "Just say it, like that?"

"Yes." Neve nodded. "Be direct. Honesty is the best policy."

Oh no, that's terrible advice! Diana would be horrified if he approached her that way!

Neve felt Donna's internal protest and tried to soften her approach. "Then again, maybe that's too blunt," she mumbled.

Ellis sighed, leaning against the metal cabinet of reagents. "I thought maybe I could convince her we could be a family, and her career wouldn't have to suffer."

Neve let out a grunt of opposition. "That's statistically unlikely," she stated. "It's been proven that women in research who have children publish less and receive fewer grants. The data is clear on this."

Stop talking! This isn't helping at all!

Ellis's shoulders slumped beneath his lab coat. "That's what Diana said." He pursed his lips in defeat before he tried to explain, "My father was never there." He stared at the linoleum floor, voice softening. "And I promised myself if I were given the chance, I'd step up and be there for my child."

"You would be a great father," Neve said. It took immense effort to keep her voice from cracking.

Ellis shot her a tender smile. "You think so?"

"I know so." Neve said, the sentiment forming a knot in her throat.

Before he could continue, Dr. Feldman waved them both over. "I've reviewed Robert's latest bloodwork. I think we can push Protocol VitOx a bit further."

Still in the wheelchair, Robert nodded in encouragement, and a smile beamed across his face. "Whatever it takes to get us to Costa Rica!"

Dr. Feldman made notes on her clipboard. "We'll increase the dosage by fifteen percent. The preliminary results are promising, but we need to be more aggressive if we want to reach full therapeutic effectiveness." As she pulled her stethoscope apart and positioned it over her ears and leaned closer to check his vitals, Robert's nose twitched. Then a thin stream of blood dripped from it onto the lab report. The bright red stain was stark against the field of white.

"Oh!" Elaine swiveled to pull several tissues from the box sitting on a nearby workstation. "Sweetheart, you're bleeding."

Robert frowned. "I get nosebleeds every once in a while. It's nothing to worry about, I'm sure."

"Let's finish your treatment and get you home to rest."

Three hours later, the lab had emptied except for Neve, who was finishing feeding and watering the mice. The quiet hum of the HVAC system provided a soothing backdrop as she worked. She was heading to the supply closet when she heard movement from Dr. Feldman's office.

Pausing, she peered through the partially open door. Conrad was rifling through file cabinets, pulling out treatment logs and supply inventories.

"You're in early," Neve said, pushing the door open further and consulting her watch. "Dr. Feldman won't be in to do morning rounds for another two hours."

Conrad jolted before composing himself with a laugh. "You scared me! I was just checking into some supply discrepancies. We seem to be going through saline and vitamin C at an alarming rate. Do you know anything about that?"

"No." Neve stepped into the office, deciding to play dumb. "That's odd."

"Look here," Conrad said, gesturing to his clipboard of calculations. "We've used almost three times the expected amount of ascorbic acid in the past month. And the saline, we're depleting our stores at a rate that suggests either major waste is occurring or…" He let the implication hang in the air between them.

"…or supplies are being diverted," Neve finished, led by Donna's conclusion.

Conrad sighed, appearing genuinely concerned. "Dr. Feldman trusts me to account for all supplies used in this lab. R&D funding is tight enough without unexplained losses we have to justify to the board."

As Conrad turned back to the files, Neve felt her geode vibrating against her hip. She placed a protective hand over it, feeling the strong pulsations quiver throughout her body.

"I'd better head home," she said, backing toward the door with a showy yawn.

"Of course. You must be exhausted. Third shift is tough," Conrad commiserated, distracted by the paperwork again.

Instead of leaving, Neve circled back through the darkened lab, her curiosity piqued. When she was certain Conrad was occupied in the supply room, she slipped into his office. The geode's vibrations intensified as she approached his desk.

Opening the bottom drawer, she found a folder labeled "VitOx Treatment Protocol." Inside were two sets of documents, the official records that Elaine had been keeping of the animal studies, and alongside them, photocopies of the handwritten logs from Robert's treatments where he was identified as Patient A. Conrad had used a red pen to circle key data points: dosage amounts, treatment times, vital sign readings, and tumor measurements.

In the margins of the photocopies, Conrad had scrawled notes: "Unauthorized human trial," "Protocol deviation," "No International Review Board approval," and most damning of all, "Evidence of Feldman's ethical violations."

Neve's breath caught as she flipped through more pages. Conrad had compiled a detailed timeline of Patient A's treatments, tracking the exact amounts of vitamin C and saline that had been diverted from the lab's supplies. He'd even attached a memo outlining the federal regulations Elaine was violating by conducting experimental treatments outside approved channels.

"Oh no," Neve whispered. Conrad had just lied to her and was trying to suss out what she knew. He was tracking the treatments of Patient A and was gathering evidence to expose Elaine. As if confirming her discovery, the geode in her pocket pulsed and seared through the fabric to her skin.

When she heard his footsteps returning, Neve quickly replaced the folder and slipped out of the office, her mind racing. She had to figure out a way to stop him and protect Donna, Ellis, and the Feldmans.

TWENTY-EIGHT

THE FOLLOWING EVENING, after the security guards completed their 2 a.m. check and left the building for a smoke break, Elaine pulled Robert's films from a manila folder and positioned several X-rays on the light box. The soft fluorescent glow illuminated her face from below, casting deep hollows beneath her cheekbones as her fingers traced the outline of Robert's pancreas, comparing it to the films from four weeks earlier. The difference was undeniable. Where once a dense mass had dominated the image, now there was a noticeable reduction in opacity. The swelling had receded, leaving behind what looked almost like a normal organ.

"Look at this," she whispered, with barely contained excitement. "The tumor margins are clearly regressing. It's not just stable disease, it's *regressing*."

Neve stood beside them, Donna's round glasses reflecting the illuminated films like two moons. She flipped through the stack of lab reports, studying each page, but the language was foreign. Even with Donna's help, she was having a hard time keeping up with the science.

It's a good thing. Not just stable disease means it's responding far better than expected.

Ellis leaned in so close his tie brushed against the light box, leaving a smudge on the illuminated surface as he studied the images. "It's remarkable. I've never seen pancreatic adenocarcinoma respond like this to any treatment. Not with 5-FU, not with radiation, not with anything in the literature."

"The LDH levels have decreased by sixty percent," Elaine stated, matter-of-fact, her finger tapping the relevant numbers. "Classic indication of tumor cell death. Alkaline phosphatase down forty-two percent. CEA tumor markers falling consistently for three consecutive weeks. His bilirubin has normalized completely." Each fact she detailed made her smile widen more. Neve had never seen Elaine so light and buoyant.

We should be cautious about getting too excited. This is still experimental. One patient doesn't constitute a clinical trial.

"We have a problem," Neve said, her voice lowered as she adjusted Donna's round glasses. "Conrad knows about the unauthorized treatments." She glanced at the door. "Last night, I found a copy of your handwritten treatment logs and Xeroxes of the films in a file in his office. He's also noted the discrepancy of supplies in the inventory."

Elaine's shoulders stiffened, but her expression

remained unchanged. "Understood. Thank you for informing me."

"Shouldn't we…" Neve hesitated, searching for the right words. "Shouldn't we pause treatments until we have proper authorization?"

Elaine's eyes flashed as she turned to face Neve. "Robert has made exceptional progress on the protocol. I will not delay treatments that could extend his life. I can manage Conrad."

"But if word got out, you could lose your license."

"It is a risk worth taking," Elaine cut her off. "This protocol works. The data is irrefutable."

Ellis glanced between them, tension visible in the tight clench of his jaw. "Dr. Feldman, if Conrad reports us…"

"I'll handle Conrad," Elaine repeated with unexpected steel in her voice. "He needs our success as much as we do. His ambition will keep him in line." She turned back to the X-rays, ending the discussion. "If you need to leave to protect yourself, I understand, but I *am* continuing this treatment."

Should we tell her about the tremor?

"Dr. Feldman?" Neve started. "There's one more thing."

"What is it?" Elaine asked, irritated at another delay.

"It might be nothing, but I noticed Robert had a bit of a hand tremor yesterday."

"I was hungry," Robert explained it away. "My hands shake when my blood sugar is too low." Dr.

Feldman bit the inside of her lip as hesitation welled up.

"Maybe we should skip the treatment today and re-evaluate?"

"No," Robert said. "You said yourself we aren't at full therapeutic levels yet."

"But."

"No buts," Robert insisted. "We are going to continue with the protocol as planned. I will not let a few shakes derail all the progress we've made."

"Okay," Elaine said, resolve setting in as she squared her shoulders. "Let's get him into the chamber."

Neve shivered as a horrific visual filled her mind, where the clear acrylic tube of the monoplace hyperbaric chamber resembled a coffin. She had to physically shake the fear off to focus on transitioning Robert from the wheelchair to the gurney. Ellis supported Robert's left side while Neve steadied his right, their movements synchronized as they helped him lie back on the narrow, padded surface.

"Easy does it," Ellis murmured, adjusting the pillow beneath Robert's head. "Are you comfortable?" Neve's heart panged seeing her father's nurturing side coming out as he cared for the man. It was not a trait she typically noticed, and she chalked it up to Donna's influence.

"As comfortable as one can be when preparing to impersonate a sardine," Robert joked. Though he'd gained some weight, his thin frame was still lost beneath the hospital gown, but his eyes sparkled with humor.

Elaine approached with his chart, but her clinical demeanor softened as she set it aside to take his hand. Her fingers intertwined with his, the gold of their matching wedding bands catching the light.

"Pressure check complete, oxygen levels optimal," she reported, then leaned closer, her voice dropping to a whisper meant only for him. "Your chariot awaits, Sir Knight."

Robert grinned up at her. "Does this make you the damsel or the dragon?"

"Depends on whether or not you've taken your medication," she quipped, but the squeeze she gave his hand belied her teasing tone.

Perry fluttered down to perch on the edge of the gurney, his head tilting as he examined Robert with one beady eye. "Another sojourn into the tube of miracles! Shall we place bets on how many cancer cells meet their demise today? I'm wagering on a cellular massacre of epic proportions."

"I like the way you think." Robert chuckled, reaching out to stroke the feathers on the bird's head with one finger.

As Elaine prepared to slide the gurney into the chamber, Robert caught her wrist. "Hey."

She paused, her professional façade diminishing to reveal the vulnerability hidden beneath. "Yes?"

"I love you," he whispered. "Have since that day in the hospital cafeteria when you defended my work, saying veterinarians deserved more respect for diagnosing patients who couldn't speak."

"I share your sentiment." Elaine's eyes glistened, but her smile remained steady. "Enough with the flowery declarations of love. It's only ninety minutes, not forever."

"Ninety minutes without your wit and sparkling personality? Might as well be eternity," he teased, then grew serious. "When I get out of this fish tank, let's book our flights to Costa Rica. I'll be well enough to go soon."

"One miracle at a time," she whispered, bending to kiss his forehead before sliding the gurney into place. As the chamber sealed with a pneumatic hiss, Robert gave them all a thumbs-up, his eyes fixed on Elaine's face until the last possible moment. The mechanical pressure gauges increased until they displayed two point five atmospheres, their red needles quivering with each adjustment of the oxygen flow.

"He's responding beautifully to the increased dosage," Elaine said, checking his pulse manually with her wristwatch, her fingers pressed against his wrist through the chamber's specialized glove port. "Seventy-two beats per minute, strong and regular. Blood pressure one-eighteen over seventy-six. Respiratory rate sixteen and unlabored."

Perry strutted along the countertop, his talons clicking against the Formica surface, occasionally pausing to inspect a test tube or peck at a pencil eraser. His feathers gleamed blue-black under the bright lights. "Robert is a veritable phoenix rising from the pancreatic ashes! Once this gets out, the medical establishment shall quake in their orthopedic footwear!"

Ellis chuckled as he made notes in his stenographer's pad, his pen scratching across the paper. "When we present this protocol to the American Cancer Society, it's going to upend conventional oncology. Combining high-dose vitamin C with hyperbaric oxygen therapy is so simple, yet so effective."

Elaine agreed. "The very thing that makes cancer cells unique has become their vulnerability. I want to be approved for human trials by next quarter," She continued, straightening her lab coat with a tug at the lapels. "The protocol needs to be tested on different cancer types and stages. I suggest beginning with a minimum of twenty patients for statistical significance. Controlling for age, gender, and prior treatment exposure."

"I've already drafted the preliminary paperwork," Ellis said, patting his briefcase with pride. "We'll need to secure more funding from the board, of course, but with these results," he gestured toward the X-rays, their reverse imagery seeming to pulse with promise, "I don't think that will be a problem. Not when they see what we've already accomplished."

They spent the next hour going over the human trial proposal and perfecting their pitch for the board, while Neve monitored his vitals. Then Elaine moved back to the chamber, checking the oxygen flowmeter, adjusting it with a delicate touch. She checked Robert's vitals, and they were still holding strong. The hiss of pressurized gas droned in the background. "How are you feeling in there, sweetheart?" Her voice softened when she addressed her husband, her professional tone replaced by tender concern.

His voice came through, muffled by the chamber walls, but the strength in it was unmistakable. "Like a million bucks! Better than I've felt in months. I could run a marathon if you'd let me out of this fish tank."

"Just fifteen more minutes," she assured him, her hand resting briefly on the transparent surface separating them. "It's your last treatment of the week. Then we'll check your blood work again on Monday."

Ellis leaned against the lab bench next to Neve, excitement softening his serious features. "You know what this means, don't you? We're on the verge of changing how cancer is treated. Not just pancreatic, but potentially all solid tumors. Lung, colon, breast..."

"No more poisoning patients with toxic chemotherapy," Elaine murmured, her eyes never leaving Robert's face inside the chamber. "No more radiation burns. No more telling patients to go home and die. Just targeted, effective treatment with minimal side effects."

"The implications are significant," Neve stated, adjusting Donna's glasses on her nose. "Cancer survival rates could increase dramatically within five years if the protocol is widely adopted. The economic impact alone would be revolutionary."

Perry fluttered over to perch on the pressure gauge display, his weight causing the needle to bounce slightly. "I sense a Nobel Prize in someone's future! Or, at minimum, a very flattering write-up in *The New England Journal of Medicine*."

Elaine glanced at her watch, making another notation on Robert's chart. "Just ten more minutes in the chamber, and we'll..."

A sudden movement caught her eye. Through the clear acrylic, Robert's right hand had begun to twitch, his fingers curling inward at stiff angles.

"Something's wrong," Neve warned, already moving toward the chamber.

Elaine pressed closer to the chamber window, her clipboard clattering to the floor. Robert's face had taken on an ashen pallor, the healthy pink draining away like water down a drain, his eyes rolling upward until only the whites were visible beneath half-closed lids.

Oh God, oh God, this can't be happening. We pushed too far, too fast.

"His color's changing," Neve continued, pushing past Donna's fear as she led her to the emergency cart and started to roll it within reach of Dr. Feldman. "Cyanosis is developing around the lips."

Before Elaine could respond, Robert's body went rigid, his spine arcing up as if it were electrified. His head slammed against the chamber wall with a sickening thud as his limbs began to convulse in the confined space, striking the acrylic with rhythmic force. A crimson smear appeared where his head hit the top of the chamber.

"He's seizing!" Elaine shouted, lunging for the pressure release valve, her knuckles white as she gripped the metal wheel. "Decompress the chamber NOW!"

Ellis abandoned his notes, sending papers fluttering to the floor as he rushed to help with the manual locks. His hands fumbled with the unfamiliar mechanism, panic making his movements clumsy. "Is it oxygen toxicity? Central nervous system oxygen toxicity can cause convulsions!"

"Could be," Elaine said, her fingers working frantically at the mechanical controls, sweat beading on her forehead. "Or a reaction to the vitamin C metabolites. Maybe an electrolyte imbalance. The pressure needs to come down slowly or he'll get the bends!"

The gauges showed the pressure decreasing, the needle dropping with agonizing slowness. Inside the chamber, Robert's convulsions grew more violent, his head striking repeatedly against the acrylic walls. Foam began to appear at the corners of his mouth, tinged pink with blood where he had bitten his tongue.

"We can't wait," Elaine decided, her face contorted with anguish as she made the impossible choice. She overrode the safety protocol and yanked the emergency release. The chamber hissed loudly as pressurized air escaped in a rush, the sound like a scream in the quiet lab.

Neve handed Ellis the crash kit. He pulled out emergency medications while barking questions. "Diazepam for the seizure? Five milligrams intravenous push?"

"Yes, five milligrams," Elaine confirmed, her voice

tight with controlled panic as she and Neve finally unsealed the heavy chamber door.

Together they pulled Robert's convulsing body from the narrow tube, his limbs flailing like a marionette with tangled strings. They lowered him to the floor and rolled him onto his side. His head lolled as the seizure began to subside, replaced by something far more terrifying. Stillness.

Elaine tilted his head back with practiced hands, checking his airway. "He's not breathing! Start mouth-to-mouth!"

Ellis dropped to his knees beside Robert's motionless form, pinching his nose closed and delivering two rescue breaths. Robert's chest rose slightly with each breath, then fell without resistance, like a bellows with no air of its own.

Elaine's fingers pressed into his carotid artery, searching for a pulse. Her face drained of color. "No heartbeat. Starting compressions."

She positioned her hands over Robert's sternum, interlocking her fingers and beginning the rhythmic pumping motion of closed-chest cardiac massage. "One, two, three, four..." she counted aloud, her voice steady despite the tears gathering in her eyes, reaching fifteen before nodding to Ellis to deliver another breath.

"Donna, get the ambu bag from the emergency kit and call an ambulance!" Elaine ordered between compression sets, never breaking rhythm. "Tell them we have a cardiac arrest, possible seizure complication! We need advanced life support!"

Neve grabbed the manual resuscitation bag, quickly assembled it with deft movements courtesy of Donna, and passed it to Ellis, who fitted the mask over Robert's face and began squeezing the bag in rhythm with Elaine's compressions. The soft whoosh-click of the valve became a counterpoint to Elaine's counting.

The brain can only survive four minutes without oxygen.

Neve felt her panic spike as Donna delivered the terrifying statistic.

"Epinephrine," Elaine called out, not breaking her rhythm, her arms already beginning to burn with the effort. "In the kit, one milligram."

Neve found the pre-filled syringe, uncapped it, and handed it to her. Elaine paused compressions just long enough to locate the intercostal space between the ribs and plunge the needle directly into Robert's heart. The needle penetrated with slight resistance, then gave way.

"I must continue compressions," Elaine said, her voice clinical despite the sweat now dripping down her face and splashing onto Robert's chest. "The epi needs to circulate."

Minutes stretched painfully as they worked in grim synchrony, the only sounds their labored breathing and the rhythmic compression of Robert's chest. Elaine's arms began to tremble from overexertion, her lab coat darkening with sweat, but she refused Ellis's offer to take over.

"Pupils," she gasped between compression sets, never slowing her pace. "Check his pupils."

Ellis flashed the penlight across Robert's eyes, now half-open and staring at nothing. "Fixed and dilated."

"No," Elaine whispered, the single syllable loaded with denial, but her hands never stopped their compressing rhythm. "No, no, no."

After fifteen minutes, Robert remained unresponsive, his skin taking on a waxy pallor that no amount of oxygen or circulation could dispel. Elaine's lab coat was soaked through with sweat, her hair plastered to her forehead, but she continued the compressions as if she could command his heart to beat again by sheer force of will.

"Elaine," Ellis murmured, his face gray with exhaustion, "it's been too long without a response. The literature says..."

"I don't care what the literature says! We keep going until help arrives," she snapped, her voice breaking on the last word, a sob catching in her throat.

The wail of approaching sirens finally penetrated the lab's walls, growing louder with each passing second. Elaine looked up, sudden alarm crossing her exhausted features as realization dawned.

"You both need to leave," she ordered, still pumping Robert's chest. "Now. Before the crew gets here."

Ellis hesitated, his hands still on the ambu bag. "We can't just..."

Elaine cut him off, her voice sharp with urgency. "You were participating in an experimental treatment without proper FDA approval. I will not put your medical license in jeopardy. I'll take full responsibility, but you two need to disappear. There's nothing more you can do for him now."

"She's right," Neve said, already pulling Ellis toward the back exit, her grip surprisingly strong. "We can't help anyone if we're all arrested for medical misconduct. We need to protect the protocol."

Ellis grabbed his notes and followed behind Neve, his feet dragging. At the door, he looked back at Elaine, still performing compressions on her husband's motionless body, her stamina admirable even as tears tracked down her cheeks.

"Go," she commanded, not looking up, her voice breaking on the single syllable.

Neve and Ellis burst through the door and hid behind a row of cars just as the ambulance arrived. Its rotating lights painted the night in pulses of red that swept across the building's façade. Two paramedics rushed inside with their equipment: a portable Datascope cardiac monitor and an oxygen tank.

Through the lab windows, they could see Elaine still performing closed-chest massage, counting aloud as she had been for nearly twenty minutes. Her movements were mechanical, almost robotic. The paramedics tried to pull her away, but she resisted with surprising strength until one of them physically pushed her hands aside so they could take over.

As the professionals worked, attaching their monitor and continuing CPR, Elaine finally leaned back, her composure crumbling as she slumped against the wall, exhausted and her eyes wild with shock.

"He's gone," Ellis whispered, crouched down next to Neve between cars, his voice hollow with certainty. "After this much time has elapsed without response… it's over."

Perry landed on a nearby car hood, his usual snarky chatter absent as they watched the paramedics eventually stop their efforts, one of them shaking his head as he checked his watch to call the time of death. The other placed a hand on Elaine's shoulder, his mouth forming words they couldn't hear but whose meaning was unmistakable.

"We killed him," Neve stated the obvious, her tone flattened with grief. She couldn't tear her eyes away as an overwhelming wave of regret surged through her.

"No," Ellis said, his voice cracking with emotion. "The cancer killed him. We were brave enough to give him hope when everyone else had given up."

But as they watched Elaine cover her face with trembling hands, her shoulders heaving with silent sobs as a paramedic draped a blanket around her, they knew that distinction would bring no comfort at all. The medical breakthrough that had seemed so certain just thirty minutes ago now lay as still and lifeless as Robert himself.

TWENTY-NINE

THE NEXT MORNING, Neve stood at her workstation, arranging her supplies, and noticed the hushed conversations and furtive glances among her colleagues. They had all been told to report for a mandatory meeting, and their worried expressions mirrored the dread pooling in her stomach.

Conrad's arrival silenced the room like a thunderclap. He stood in the doorway, his angular face grave beneath his shaggy brown hair. His wire-rimmed glasses caught the overhead light as he surveyed the staff gathered with calculating eyes that seemed to pierce through everyone present. Neve felt Donna's body instinctively shrink back, her shoulders hunching inward as if trying to make herself invisible.

"If I could have everyone's attention," he announced in a deep nasal tone that carried an undercurrent of authority. "I'm afraid I have difficult news. Dr. Feldman's husband, Robert, passed away due to complications from his illness."

The room collectively gasped, and Diana's clipboard clattered to the floor.

"Robert's cancer progressed to stage four a few months ago and even though he appeared to be doing better recently, he suffered a set back last night." Conrad adjusted his glasses, pushing them up his nose with one finger before settling his gaze on Neve. She felt Donna's heart rate spike, her palms slicking with cold sweat. "Dr. Feldman will be taking bereavement leave. In her absence, I'll be overseeing all the lab's operations."

Ellis stood frozen by the spectrometer, his face ashen. Neve saw him shudder as he steadied himself with edge of the counter, knuckles white with tension.

"Additionally," Conrad continued, straightening his skinny tie, "I must inform you that an investigation has been opened regarding certain experimental treatments administered to Robert in this facility. Test results are pending, but the board is concerned about potential protocol violations and sanctions from the FDA."

His dark eyes swept the room again, but this time lingered on Neve and Ellis. "If anyone has knowledge of or participated in any unauthorized treatments Dr. Feldman may have provided to her husband, I strongly encourage you to come forward now." His voice hardened, becoming sharp as a scalpel. "You have my word, the situation will be handled with the utmost discretion. However, I should note that withholding information about ethical violations could result in severe disciplinary action and possible career-ending consequences."

The silence in the lab was absolute. Neve labored to keep her expression neutral, though Donna's heart hammered against her ribs. Beside her, Ellis had gone still, seemingly engrossed in his notes. Neve felt Conrad's eyes boring into them from across the room.

"I'm particularly interested in speaking with anyone who was present in the lab last night." Neve flicked her anxious gaze up to meet his eyes, grateful when he shifted to Ellis.

"Very well," Conrad said after a long pause. "Please continue with your scheduled tasks. I'll be moving my things to Dr. Feldman's office if anyone wishes to speak privately. And I do expect some of you..." his steely stare skipped between Neve and Ellis "...to make that choice sooner rather than later. For your own sakes."

As he turned to leave, Perry scoffed, "Wow. That power-hungry bastard didn't even wait long enough for her seat to get cold."

Ellis pinched the bridge of his nose and kept his voice low. "If he reports us to the board... my career, everything I've worked for..."

"We need to stay calm," Neve reassured him, though Donna's racing heart made the words feel hollow. "We didn't do anything wrong. The protocol was working. Robert was improving until..."

"...until he died," Ellis finished, his voice wavering under the strain. "And now Manning is out for blood."

By late afternoon, the atmosphere at the lab had

devolved into a chorus of hushed speculation. Neve kept to herself, processing samples and readying the next cohort of mice for testing while keeping one ear tuned to the surrounding conversations.

Diana approached Neve's station, her lab coat wrinkled as if she'd been wearing it for days. She glanced over her shoulder before speaking.

"Can you believe it?" Diana whispered, leaning close. She hesitated, then lowered her voice further. "You've been working the late shift. Did you see anything unusual? Anything that might give credence to Conrad's accusations?"

Neve met Diana's gaze. "Nothing out of bounds happened during my shifts. Robert often visited, but as a primary investor, that is not out of the ordinary. I would have reported anything inappropriate."

"Are you sure? Because Manning is building a case that makes it sound like Elaine was running some kind of rogue Hail Mary operation after hours."

"That's not what I observed," Neve stated.

Diana nodded, her eyes filling with tears. "I'm scared. For Dr. Feldman, for all of us. Manning's already talking about 'restructuring' the department. Two of our techs have already been reassigned to the microbiology lab."

"He's just on a power trip. It will resolve itself soon," Neve said as she watched Ellis knock on Conrad's door and disappear inside.

"What if he comes after us next?" Diana shivered. "I can't lose this job. I need..." She stopped herself, one hand unconsciously touching her stomach.

Neve caught the gesture and understood its significance. "Proceed with caution," she advised Diana. "Until we know more, document everything."

As Diana walked away, Perry poked his head out of the open cage. "A masterful performance. Not a single lie told, yet not a single truth revealed."

"Sometimes," Neve murmured, "the best way to protect the truth is to carefully choose which parts of it to share."

Ellis approached Neve's workstation, his steps weary from exhaustion and the impromptu meeting with Conrad. "Can I see you in the supply closet?" he whispered. "About the reagent inventory."

Once inside the cramped space, surrounded by shelves of chemicals and glassware, Ellis's composure faltered. "He knows. He didn't say it outright, but he knows we were there last night. Conrad kept asking about the oxygen protocols, about who had access to the hyperbaric chamber controls."

Neve felt Donna's stomach twist with dread. "What did you tell him?"

"Nothing specific. I played dumb about the details." Ellis swallowed hard. "But he's saying Elaine experimented on Robert, that she falsified data to justify treating him with an unproven protocol. He said if anyone helped her, they'd be considered equally culpable." He let out a heavy exhalation, then continued. "Conrad called an emergency board meeting. They've suspended Elaine pending investigation." Ellis balled his hands into fists and rested them on his hips. "I spoke with her over lunch. She's... she's devastated. Lost her husband and her career in one day. And now Manning's threatening to destroy anyone connected to Robert's treatment."

"This is wrong." Neve stated the facts, Donna's gentle nature giving way to righteous indignation, "The protocol was working. We all saw the results."

"He claims she cherry picked the data to support her confirmation bias." Ellis leaned against a shelf, defeat palpable in the slump of his shoulders. "He's convinced the board she was desperate and reckless."

"And they believed him without hearing her side?"

"A man died here. No matter how she tries to explain it, she could never justify her actions." Ellis lowered his voice further. "Be very careful around Conrad, this feels like sabotage."

Over the next three days, Manning's reorganization of the lab proceeded with alarming efficiency. Files disappeared into locked cabinets. Key technicians were reassigned to different departments, replaced by unfamiliar faces who spoke to Manning in hushed tones.

Neve observed it all with a growing certainty. Ellis was right; this was sabotage, not standard procedure.

On the fourth day, she arrived early to find Ellis waiting in the parking lot, leaning against his car. Dark circles shadowed his eyes.

"I went to see Elaine last night," he said without preamble. "She's barely functioning. Between grief and shock, she can hardly form sentences. But she kept saying one thing clearly: 'I was not culpable, the files will prove it.'"

"What files?" Neve asked.

"Her research notes. The original data." Ellis glanced toward the building. "Manning has locked away everything in the lab, but Elaine says she kept duplicates at home, photocopies of all experimental data and mouse cohort results."

Neve processed this information. "We need those files. And we need to start keeping our own records of everything happening now."

"I've been smuggling out daily test results," Ellis admitted, patting his briefcase. "But we need somewhere safe to store them. Somewhere off-site."

"I can set up a safe deposit box," Neve offered. "But we need to find another lab to work in. Conrad has too many eyes here."

Ellis considered it. "You're right. I'll make some calls. I have a few friends at Coral Bay Therapeutics." For the first time in days, a flicker of hope crossed Ellis's face. "We're going to clear her name."

"We're going to find the truth," Neve corrected. "Whatever it is."

Later that afternoon, while Conrad was in meetings, Neve and Ellis hunched over the densitometer. Perry stood guard by the door, his sharp eyes scanning for approaching figures.

"Look at these mitochondrial damage levels," Ellis said, pointing to a printout. "The cancer cells show selective destruction, while healthy cells remain intact. Robert's glutathione peroxidase depletion markers confirm it."

"The treatment was working," Neve concluded. "It was scientifically sound and showed positive results."

"Exactly. Which means Manning's accusation that Elaine falsified data is a lie." Ellis rubbed his weary eyes. "But why frame her? What does he gain?"

Neve considered this. "Control of the research? Credit for the breakthrough? Or maybe he's hiding something."

"Like what?"

"I don't know yet," Neve admitted. "But I intend to find out."

As they worked, Neve found herself studying Ellis in a new light. His intelligence was obvious in how quickly he processed complex data, but there was also a gentleness to him she hadn't fully appreciated before. He spoke of Elaine with loyalty and of Robert with genuine grief. This wasn't just a colleague concerned about professional fallout and how it would affect his own career.

"You care about them," she blurted, finally putting her finger on it. "Elaine and Robert."

Ellis looked up, surprised by the blunt personal observation. "I do. They've been like family to me. When I first came to Aureon, I was a nervous kid fresh out of medical school with big ideas, but Elaine saw something in me." He smiled faintly. "Robert used to invite me for dinner when he knew we were working late. Said no good science comes from an empty stomach."

The simple humanity of this detail struck Neve

unexpectedly. She felt a subtle tightening in her chest triggered by Donna's natural empathy.

It was nearly midnight when they finished. The parking lot was deserted, and pools of yellow light from lampposts created islands in the darkness. Neve walked Ellis to his car, the manila envelope of duplicated records tucked securely in her backpack. Perry flapped into the air, circling above them.

As Ellis drove away, Neve cut across the parking lot toward her vehicle. The night air carried a hint of a cooler December breeze. She was halfway across the open space when a quiver from the geode in her pocket made her turn.

A figure stood beneath a distant tree watching her, a man in a baseball cap, face obscured by shadow. Something about his stance triggered a flicker of recognition in Neve's mind, though she couldn't place him.

"Hey!" she called out, changing direction to approach him.

The man turned immediately and walked away with purposeful strides.

"Perry," Neve shouted up at the bird, "can you follow him?"

The parrot beat his wings together to catch up, and Neve broke into a run, pursuing the retreating figure across the darkened streets.

The man moved with surprising speed, weaving between buildings. As Neve rounded a corner, she caught a glimpse of him disappearing through a service entrance in the back of a hotel.

By the time she reached the door, it was locked. Perry descended, landing on her outstretched arm.

Neve stared at the closed door, frustration mingling with curiosity. "He looked familiar."

"Isn't this the second sighting of your mysterious man?" Perry asked. "You are either eagerly seeking male companionship or he has something to do with your trips into the past."

Neve shook her head no, challenging his assessment. "I already have a male companion. You. And one man is enough."

Perry chuckled. "While I find that sentiment flattering, you're not my type."

Neve grimaced at the thought. "You're not my type either." She folded her arms across her chest and widened her stance. "But I fully intend to find out who he is and what he has to do with all of this."

CHAPTER

THIRTY

A FEW DAYS LATER, the headline of the *Tampa Tribune* screamed across the breakfast tables of thousands of homes on a cool December morning:

Rogue Scientist Used Husband As Human Guinea Pig

By James Rutherford, Medical Correspondent

TAMPA, FL — A prominent cancer researcher at Aureon Biomedical has been formally accused of performing unauthorized experimental treatments on her terminally ill husband, resulting in his death last week.

Dr. Elaine Feldman, 52, head of oncological research and a principal investor at the pharmaceutical giant, allegedly administered dangerous doses of vitamin C and subjected her husband, Dr. Robert Feldman, to hyperbaric oxygen therapy without proper oversight or FDA approval.

"This was not compassionate care, but reckless

experimentation driven by a scientist who couldn't accept her husband's prognosis," said Dr. Conrad Manning, who has temporarily assumed leadership of the research department at the company.

According to documents obtained by this newspaper, Dr. Feldman miscalculated the pressure levels and conducted experiments after hours to avoid detection by colleagues.

"The pressure levels used in the hyperbaric chamber were dangerously high," Manning explained. "Our investigation indicates the seizure that ultimately killed Dr. Feldman was a direct result of oxygen toxicity from a miscalculation during treatment."

The State Medical Board has launched a formal investigation and is considering revoking Dr. Feldman's medical license. Aureon Biomedical has suspended the researcher and launched an internal investigation.

"This is a tragic breach of both medical ethics and the public trust," said Aureon spokesperson Jennifer Williams. "Our thoughts are with Dr. Feldman's family during this difficult time."

Sources close to the investigation suggest Dr. Feldman's mental state deteriorated as her husband's condition worsened, leading to increasingly desperate and dangerous treatment attempts...

"Ugh!" Neve had to stop reading, and she crumpled the newspaper in her fist. The ink smudged her fingers black, a visual representation of the filthy lies it contained. "Vile! The truth doesn't matter to them. All they care about is selling papers."

Hundreds of thousands of people read this newspaper.

Neve cringed as Donna's thought invaded. It was obvious, the damage to Elaine's reputation would be swift and irreversible.

"It's all fabricated," Ellis whispered, his face pale as he read the headline over her shoulder. They stood in the break room, other staff members giving them a wide berth as if the scandal might be contagious. "Manning had to have doctored the treatment logs. The pressure levels we used were well within safety parameters."

"He's systematically destroying her reputation," Neve replied, keeping her voice low. "And he's doing it so thoroughly that no one will ever question it."

Perry hopped closer on the countertop and made a soft clicking sound with his beak. "It's the oldest trick in the book. Control the narrative, control the outcome."

The lab had changed dramatically in the time since Robert's death. Conrad Manning moved into Elaine's office, replacing her carefully organized research journals with his own publications. The hyperbaric chamber had been dismantled and removed for a safety inspection. Most telling of all, the mice cohorts from their experimental protocol had been euthanized, eliminating all biological evidence of their successful treatment approach.

"He's erasing everything," Ellis murmured,

releasing a heavy sigh of frustration. "The protocol, the data, all of it."

"Not everything," Neve corrected as she slid over the paperwork she'd acquired and a second key to the safe deposit box she set up during her lunch hour.

Later that evening, the suburban streets were silent as Neve parked Diana's Pinto in front of Elaine's Spanish-style home. The golf course green lawn, once a point of pride, now showed signs of neglect. Long, brittle grass clippings gathered in drifts against the stucco walls, and newspapers piled up on the front step.

Perry jockeyed around inside his travel carrier. He let out a long whistle, taking in the current state of decay and disarray. "This place feels like a mausoleum."

"She's been ignoring my calls for a week. We gave her space to grieve, but enough is enough," Neve groused, gathering both Donna's backpack and the travel carrier from the back seat, and a brown bag filled with groceries.

Elaine answered the door on the third knock, and Neve couldn't suppress her gasp. The brilliant scientist was almost unrecognizable. Her wild red curls hung limp and greasy around a face that had aged years in days. Her clothing was wrinkled and stained. She clearly hadn't showered for over a week, and Neve's nose wrinkled as the musky tang of body odor wafted closer.

"Donna," Elaine muttered, her eyes dead, stepping back to allow her entry. "And Peregrine."

The house's interior, once neat and tidy, had descended into chaos. Smelly, unwashed dishes filled the sink. Medical journals lay scattered across every surface, pages marked with frantic notations. The air smelled stale, tinged with the lingering scent of cold Chinese takeout and the sickly scent of decaying roses. There were more than twenty vases filled with flowers that had been sent as condolences, their petals brittle and falling to the ground in a state of moldering decay.

"I brought some groceries," Neve said, pushing aside a few of the vases and setting the paper bag down on the kitchen counter. "And Perry insisted he visit. He missed you," she added as she opened the carrier.

Elaine nodded absently, her gaze drifting to the bird. "Robert sure enjoyed his company."

Perry hopped from his carrier to the counter, his usual sarcastic commentary absent as he studied Elaine with unblinking gentleness. She offered him her forearm, and he gently hopped up onto it, following the long line of it to her shoulder, where he burrowed into the curve of her neck. Not knowing what to say, he simply pressed the top of his head into her cheek, and she let out the smallest of sighs as she reached out one finger to stroke his downy head. "Have you seen the papers?" she asked, her voice hollow and expression flat.

"Yes," Neve admitted, unpacking the groceries to give her hands something to do. "Manning is…"

"…destroying me," Elaine finished, her clinical detachment returning. "Systematically and effectively.

The board called a special meeting tomorrow to discuss my suspension and future as a researcher and board member, and the Florida medical board is meeting later this week. They could suspend my license."

"We won't let that happen," Neve insisted, turning to face her. "Ellis and I have been gathering evidence. The original data shows the protocol was working. Robert *was* improving until..."

"...until I pushed the protocol too far," Elaine interrupted. Her voice faltered on the last word.

"No," Neve asserted. "Until something went wrong that we don't yet understand. Ellis says the seizure could have been caused by any number of factors unrelated to the treatment."

Elaine's laugh was bitter. "Manning claims I increased the pressure beyond safety parameters. That I falsified the treatment logs. That I was—how did the *Tribune* put it?—'a scientist driven mad by grief and obsession.'"

"That's not true," Neve declared. "I was present for every treatment. The protocol was sound. You made the right decisions, taking all the factors into consideration."

Elaine moved to the window, staring out at the gathering dusk. "It doesn't matter what's true anymore. Manning has the chairman of the board in his pocket. The press is manufacturing wild theories, and my colleagues think I'm a madwoman."

"Not all of them," Neve offered, hoping it would give Elaine a small measure of peace.

Elaine's fingers traced patterns in the condensation on the glass. "Even if I *am* exonerated, it doesn't change the fact that Robert is gone."

Perry fluttered to her shoulder to console the distraught woman. "The truth *always* matters," he chirped.

Elaine reached up to stroke his feathers. "I've spent my entire career believing data doesn't lie, that truth is the cornerstone of scientific discovery. But Manning has shown me how easily facts can be manipulated, how simple it is to create a false narrative when no one questions it."

"Then *we* question it," Neve replied, moving to stand beside her. "*We* fight back."

Elaine turned, her eyes suddenly sharp with the analytical intelligence that had made her a brilliant scientist. "How? Manning controls the lab, the records, and the witnesses. He's already fired three technicians who might have contradicted his version of events and relocated four others."

"Ellis is there," Neve countered. "Diana too. They're willing to testify about the protocol's effectiveness."

"And risk their careers?" Elaine shook her head. "I wouldn't ask that of them."

"You don't need to ask," Neve insisted. "They're doing it because it's right."

For a brief moment, a flicker of the old Elaine—determined, brilliant, and unstoppable—showed in her eyes. Then it faded, replaced by exhaustion so profound it seemed to emanate from her bones.

"I'm tired, Donna," she whispered. "So tired. I fought for Robert with everything I had, and I still lost him. I don't know if I have anything left to fight for myself."

Perry nuzzled against her cheek. "Then rest. Let the rest of us fight for a while."

The next morning, Neve arrived at the lab early, resolve fueling her. She found Ellis already there, hunched over a microscope, his eyes red-rimmed from lack of sleep.

"I've been reviewing the blood samples we saved," he said. "There's something odd in Robert's last workup. His calcium levels were significantly elevated."

"Hypercalcemia?" Neve asked, slipping into the technical language with ease thanks to Donna. "That could trigger seizures."

"Exactly." Ellis nodded. "And it wouldn't be related to our treatment protocol. It could be a complication of the cancer itself."

Hope flickered in Neve's heart. "If we can prove the seizure was caused by hypercalcemia rather than oxygen toxicity..."

"We might be able to clear Elaine's name," Ellis finished, a ghost of a smile crossing his exhausted face.

Their conversation was interrupted by the lab door swinging open. Conrad entered, impeccably dressed in a brown corduroy blazer and perfectly pressed slacks, his wire-rimmed glasses glinting under the fluorescent lights.

"Dr. LaRue, Donna," he acknowledged with a tight nod. "Early start today?"

"Just catching up on some work," Ellis replied neutrally.

Conrad's gaze drifted to the microscope. "Interesting. I wasn't aware of any ongoing projects requiring blood analysis."

"Standard verification," Neve interjected smoothly. "Confirming results before archiving."

Conrad studied her for a long moment, his expression unreadable. "How thoughtful of you to be so thorough." He turned to leave, then paused. "Oh, I nearly forgot. The board meeting regarding Dr. Feldman's suspension has been moved up. Nine o'clock this morning, rather than this afternoon."

"That's less than an hour from now," Ellis protested. "Elaine needs time to adequately prepare her defense."

Conrad's smile was thin. "The board felt it best to resolve this matter quickly. For everyone's sake." He checked his watch. "I should be going. It can't start without me. I'm presenting the evidence, after all."

As the door closed behind him, Ellis slammed his fist against the worktable. "He's rushing the hearing so we won't have time to organize our evidence."

"Then we work faster," Neve replied, already reaching for the phone. "I'll call Elaine. You gather everything we have about hypercalcemia. Meet me in the boardroom in twenty minutes."

As Ellis hurried away, Neve dialed Elaine's number

with shaking fingers. The phone rang six times before a hoarse voice answered.

"They've moved the hearing to nine o'clock," Neve blurted.

"I know," she replied woodenly.

"We've found something in Robert's blood work. Evidence that could exonerate you."

The silence on the other end stretched for so long that Neve feared Elaine had hung up.

"Elaine?"

"I won't be attending," came her flat response.

"What? You have to! This is your career, your reputation..."

"My husband is dead," Elaine interrupted, her voice eerily calm. "My research has been discredited. The world thinks I'm a monster." She whispered, "Fact. Fact. Fact." After a long pause, she added, "What is left to fight for?"

Neve clutched the phone tighter. "The truth. You're fighting for the truth."

Another long silence followed, which seemed to stretch out forever.

"The truth," Elaine repeated under her breath, mulling it over as if testing the weight of the word. "Yes. I suppose that still matters."

"So, we'll meet you in the boardroom?" Neve asked, premature relief flooding her voice. "Ellis has found evidence about Robert's calcium levels..."

"No, I will not be present," Elaine cut her off. "But Ellis can handle it and present the evidence on my behalf." Her voice took on a familiar clinical detachment. "You've always been observant, more than people give you credit for. I trust you and Ellis to represent the facts accurately."

Before Neve could protest, the line went dead.

She stood frozen, the dial tone buzzing in her ear like an annoying wasp. Despite the setback, the geode in her pocket pulsed with warmth, a reminder of why she was here, in this time, in this place. With sudden and complete clarity, Neve understood her purpose. She was sent to exonerate Dr. Elaine Feldman.

CHAPTER

THIRTY-ONE

SEVERAL DAYS LATER, Ellis secured permission, and he and Neve were burning the midnight oil at Coral Bay Therapeutics. The borrowed lab was cramped and outdated, but it was safe from prying eyes. Ellis paced between the ancient fume hood and the discolored lab bench where Neve had arranged her evidence as a heavy mid-December rain pelted the windows. The lab had emptied hours ago, leaving them alone with the soft hum of equipment and the rhythmic tapping of raindrops against glass. A clock on the wall read 11:37 PM.

The week had been devastating. Elaine's final termination had been swift and merciless, followed by the medical board's emergency hearing, where they revoked her license with barely a consideration of the evidence Ellis had tried to present. The newspapers had been ruthless, painting Elaine as a mad scientist who had willingly sacrificed her husband on the altar of ambition.

Neve drummed her fingertips on the table, her eyes darting from page to page, studying the chromatography reports spread before her. She'd been comparing them for hours until the numbers started to swim. Her eyes burned from the strain, and she rubbed them with the pads of her fingers until white stars formed on the backs of her eyelids.

"Something doesn't add up," she muttered, putting Donna's glasses back on. "The hydrogen peroxide signatures in these samples don't match Elaine's original data."

"Could be degradation," Ellis suggested, tilting his head to examine the reports. "These organic compounds aren't exactly known for their stability."

"No." Neve shook her head firmly. "These differences are too consistent, too... perfect." She pulled another set of reports from her stack. "Look at this. The baseline readings from September show clear evidence of H_2O_2 generation after vitamin C administration. But in the samples taken the night Robert died..." She pointed to a different peak on the graph. "The signature is almost completely neutralized."

Perry hopped up on her shoulder to study the graph closer. "I may not have a PhD, but even I can see those don't match."

Neve's heart raced as the implications crystallized. She quickly gathered the remaining samples from cold storage and prepared them for UV spectrophotometry testing. The procedure would take hours, but she couldn't wait until morning. The geode in her pocket hummed with increasing warmth as she worked, vibrating against her hip.

As the first rays of dawn filtered through the lab windows, Neve stared at the final results, mouth agape as Ellis explained them to her.

Ellis walked her through the results line by line. "Someone deliberately neutralized the oxidative stress effect." He ran his finger along the spectrum analysis. "See this signature? It's consistent with the presence of catalase. It is the very enzyme cancer cells lack, the reason the treatment works in the first place."

"I think I've found something to support your theory," Neve confirmed, spreading out additional reports. "Look at this. If you compare the chromatography from all of Robert's treatments, it is obvious the sabotage wasn't just on the final day. It was gradual, increasing over time."

Ellis sank onto a creaking lab stool, then replied, his voice hollow with realization. "That's why he improved at first, then plateaued, and finally..." He couldn't bring himself to finish the sentence. "We need to recreate the original trials," he said, pulling Elaine's meticulous notes from his black messenger bag. "With the exact conditions from before the tampering started."

Financed by Elaine's exit package, for the next week, they worked after hours, carefully reconstructing Protocol VitOx. Diana joined them when she could, bringing food and helping administer the treatments. The mouse trials were duplicated with painstaking precision to every detail of the original study. They were given the exact vitamin C concentrations from Protocol VitOx, waited the allotted time from the logs, and then exposed to hyperbaric oxygen for the length of time originally noted.

"It's time to look at day seven results," Ellis announced one evening, his voice stretched drum tight with excitement as he examined the tissue samples under the microscope for several long minutes.

"And?" Neve asked, unable to wait any longer.

"There is evidence of tumor regression in all test subjects. Just like Elaine's original findings," he confirmed, pulling away from the telescope with a triumphant grin.

"Elaine was right," Diana voiced what they all knew, her hand unconsciously resting on her growing abdomen.

"Robert's death wasn't caused by Protocol VitOx," Ellis confirmed. "It was caused by something else."

"But what?" Diana pressed.

"That's what we still need to figure out," Neve replied, carefully labeling another slide. Each piece of evidence they gathered was duplicated and stored in two separate locations: the safe deposit box and Ellis's messenger bag. They couldn't risk losing anything.

As they prepared to leave that night, Ellis paused by the pressure gauges they'd been using for the hyperbaric simulations.

"Wait," he blurted, grabbing a calibration tool from his case. "Let me check something."

His fingers connected the tool to the pressure

sensor interface. Diana leaned closer, watching as he began running a series of diagnostic tests.

"What are you looking for?" she asked, concern etching her features.

Ellis didn't answer right away, his brow furrowing deeper with each reading. He disconnected the tool, recalibrated it, and ran the test again. Then, a third time.

"This can't be right," he muttered, his movements becoming increasingly agitated. Sweat beaded on his forehead despite the cool temperature of the lab.

Neve set down her notes and moved to his side. "Ellis? What is it?"

He ran his hand through his short hair, leaving it standing on end. "The calibration curve is wrong." His voice dropped to a whisper as he pointed to the digital readout. "Look at these offsets. The chamber's pressure calibration was quantifiably wrong."

"What do you mean 'quantifiably wrong'?" Neve asked, moving closer to examine the numbers.

Ellis's face had gone pale, and he mumbled under his breath as he pulled out a notebook and began scribbling calculations. "Not just off, compromised enough to cause problems that would be difficult for most people to detect."

"I don't understand." Diana looked between them. "Machines drift out of calibration all the time. It happens."

"No," Ellis snapped, the gears turning in his head. "Random drift creates random errors. This..." he tapped the display for emphasis "...this is systematic.

The calibration file has been altered to create a specific offset pattern."

He turned to them, his expression grim. "The margin has been manipulated. Someone knew exactly how to sabotage the hyperbaric chamber, to make it read normal while still delivering dangerously high pressure."

"How much higher?" Neve squeaked out.

Ellis's jaw tightened. "At the settings we were using for Robert's last treatment, the display would have shown two point five atmospheres..."

"But the actual pressure?" Diana prompted when he hesitated.

"Almost four atmospheres," Ellis replied, his voice strained. "Well above the threshold for oxygen toxicity and seizure risk."

Neve felt her blood run cold.

"But who would even know how to do that?" Diana asked, wrapping her arms around herself. "You'd need specialized knowledge of pressure systems, sensor calibration..."

"And access to the equipment when no one was around," Ellis finished, his eyes narrowing. "Conrad."

"It has to be," Neve agreed. "He has an engineering background. Dr. Feldman put him in charge of setting up and maintaining the equipment."

Ellis slammed his fist against the lab bench, sending glassware rattling. "Damn him! He must have adjusted the trim pots or reprogrammed the EEPROM to create a false calibration curve."

"But why?" Diana's voice trembled. "Why would he want to kill Robert?"

"Because the protocol was working," Neve answered, the pieces falling into place. "If it succeeded, Elaine would get the credit. The grants. The recognition."

"And Conrad would remain in her shadow," Ellis continued, his face darkening. "He's always resented her brilliance. I've seen how he glares at her when she's not looking. He wants her to fail."

"This is more than professional jealousy," Neve insisted. "Sabotaging equipment, falsifying data, murder? These are federal crimes. He could go to prison for this."

Diana sank into a chair with a heavy sigh. "What if he finds out we know? We're still working in his lab every day."

The silence that followed sucked all the air out of the room.

"We need to be careful," Ellis reasoned, gathering the calibration data. "Conrad's already shown he's willing to go to great lengths to protect his interests."

"And we're the only ones who know the truth," Neve added with a grimace.

Perry, who had been preening his feathers while he listened, stopped, and then fluttered down to land on Neve's shoulder. "So, we're up against a murderous madman with access to all kinds of lethal chemicals and a motive to silence us. Splendid."

Ellis managed a weak smile at the bird's dark humor, then turned serious again. "We need more evidence. Something that directly ties him to the sabotage."

"And Conrad can't know what we've discovered," Neve implored, meeting Ellis's gaze. "Not until we're ready."

Diana rubbed her temples, visibly distressed. "I feel like we're in over our heads. Maybe we should go to the police?"

"With what?" Ellis asked gently. "Pressure calibration discrepancies? They'd need more than that to bring charges. Conrad is very adept at manipulating those around him into believing his version of events."

"Then we find more," Neve acknowledged with resolve. "We don't stop until we have enough evidence to put him away."

As they packed up their equipment, the weight of their discovery settled over them like a death shroud. They weren't just fighting to clear Elaine's name anymore; they were putting themselves in the crosshairs of a dangerous man who would do anything to further his own agenda.

Two nights later, Neve stayed late after Conrad left for a board meeting and was searching through the lab's storage room when she discovered a box of original IV bag logs tucked behind outdated equipment. The handwritten records detailed every solution prepared for the cancer trials, with dates, times, concentrations, and signatures.

She spread them across an empty lab bench, comparing the entries. Most were signed by Elaine or Ellis, with occasional entries from Diana or herself. But the entries from the week before Robert's death showed subtle differences in the handwriting.

"Forgeries," Neve whispered, holding two sheets side by side. "Someone altered the logs."

As she gathered the evidence, the hairs on the back of her neck stood up, and she had the feeling of being watched. Slowly, she turned to scan the darkened lab. Nothing seemed out of place, but the sensation of surveillance persisted.

"Perry?" she called softly. The parrot had been keeping watch by the door, but she couldn't see or hear him.

No answer came. Feeling the walls closing in on her, Neve slid the logs into her bag and moved toward the exit, every sense heightened. A shadow shifted near the supply closet, and she froze.

A man in a baseball cap stepped partially into view, his features obscured in the dim emergency lighting. Neve's heart hammered against her ribs as she recognized the same figure she'd seen on campus weeks earlier.

"Who are you?" she demanded, reaching for the nearest object, a heavy glass beaker, as a potential weapon.

The man held up his hands in a placating gesture, then pointed to her bag of evidence. Afraid he would snatch it, Neve turned, boxed him out, and hoisted it to her shoulder, clinging to the strap for dear life.

When she turned to face him, he was gone. She could just make out his footsteps echoing down the corridor.

"Hey!" Neve called, giving chase. By the time she reached the end of the hallway, he had disappeared, but a folded piece of paper lay on the floor where he'd stood.

Neve bent to retrieve it and unfolded the note, reading under her breath as relief flooded in: "Keep going. You are on the right track. You can't let him win."

Perry fluttered down from a high shelf, looking sheepish.

"You were supposed to be my lookout," Neve scolded, but her attention remained fixed on the note.

"I was searching for sustenance."

Neve heaved a heavy sigh. "Of course you were."

"Who was that?" Perry asked, changing the subject as he landed on her shoulder to examine the note.

"I don't know," Neve admitted. "But he seems to be on our side."

Back in the lab, Neve xeroxed the forged logs, adding them to their growing collection of evidence. The geode in her pocket pulsed with an almost uncomfortable heat now, as if urging her forward.

"Conrad has too much to lose if the truth comes out." she warned Perry as they prepared to leave. "Someone evil enough to sabotage a cancer treatment and let a man die wouldn't hesitate to protect himself at all costs if he were in danger."

THIRTY-TWO

A FEW DAYS LATER, Neve watched from her workstation as Conrad glided through the lab. His typical corduroy blazer had been upgraded to a tailored suit, his wire-rimmed glasses replaced by contact lenses as he gave a guided tour to yet another group of potential investors and media pundits visiting the lab.

"Today's special presentation: 'How I Single-Handedly Saved Aureon Biomedical from a Madwoman,'" Perry muttered out of the side of his beak, from his perch near Neve's microscope. "See his performative glad-handing whenever he speaks about rescuing the company from the evil clutches of Dr. Feldman? He turning deception into an art form."

Neve shot the bird a cautious glare but couldn't suppress her smile at his astute observation. Perry was right. In the three weeks since Robert's death, Conrad had completely reshaped the narrative around Elaine's work, painting the researcher in a terrible light.

"Dr. Feldman's emotional state had been deteriorating for months," Conrad explained, his tone dripping with manufactured sympathy. "We all wanted to believe in her Protocol VitOx. I mean, who wouldn't want a non-toxic cancer treatment? But the supporting data simply wasn't there."

"Fascinating revisionist history," Perry whispered. "Next, he'll claim he invented penicillin after eating a slice of moldy pizza."

Neve snorted in agreement, trying to focus on her cell cultures. Her jaw clenched tight enough to crack walnuts as Conrad's condescending voice droned on through the lab, grating on her every nerve.

"As her husband's prognosis grew more grim, her notes became increasingly erratic. Dosages would change without explanation. Entire cohorts disappeared from reports." Conrad sighed, increasing the drama full-tilt. "In retrospect, we should have intervened sooner."

The visitors nodded with sympathy and understanding, scribbling in their notebooks.

"The emotional attachment to a dying spouse is understandable," Conrad continued, "but the literature clearly shows it can cloud scientific judgment and was a contributing factor to her husband's death."

Ellis appeared at Neve's side, his face tight and his lips pursed to hold in his bubbling rage. "Conrad couldn't tell the truth if his life depended on it," he whispered.

"But everyone's buying it," Neve replied as she transferred cells to a fresh culture plate. "Did you see the article in the *Journal of Experimental Oncology*?

They're calling Elaine's work 'a cautionary tale of emotional bias in clinical research.'"

"It's a coordinated character assassination," Ellis muttered.

"Diana overheard an interesting phone call yesterday," Neve said. "Conrad mentioned that NovaCure was very interested in the preliminary data from Protocol VitOx."

Ellis froze, then tugged Neve by the arm down the hall and into the supply closet, where they could have some semblance of privacy. Perry had just slipped in before the door clicked closed, and when Ellis turned to Neve, his expression was grave.

"NovaCure? Are you certain that's what she heard?"

Neve nodded. "Yep. What is it? You look worried."

Ellis leaned forward, lowering his voice. "Nova-Cure isn't just any pharmaceutical company. They're the largest manufacturer of conventional chemo-therapy drugs in the country. I just read an article about their focus on privatizing cancer treatments in outpatient settings."

"Cancer treatment is big business," Neve said. "Chemotherapy patents bring in billions."

Ellis furrowed his brow. "Billions? What are you talking about? The entire pharmaceutical industry's cancer sector barely breaks a hundred million in revenue. It's mostly research grants and hospital programs."

Neve blinked, realizing her mistake. "I mean... it

has the potential to be worth billions. Eventually. The projected market share is enormous."

"How do you know that?" Ellis studied her with increasing confusion.

"It's common sense," Neve improvised. "Just look at the demographics. Baby boomers are aging."

Ellis's forehead puckered tight in bewilderment. "Baby boomers? The oldest one isn't even thirty yet."

Neve gulped, and she felt Donna's fear surge at her slip as another rushed explanation left her lips. "Um.. I just meant that as more medical breakthroughs are made, longer lifespans will lead to a greater need for chronic disease management."

Ellis pursed his lips as he considered it, her reasoning was starting to win him over. "That's an interesting hypothesis."

"Look," Neve continued, trying to redirect the conversation, but struggling. "Dr. Feldman's Protocol VitOx uses vitamin C, a component you can't patent, in conjunction with hyperbaric treatments most hospitals already conduct on a regular basis. The entire treatment costs maybe a few hundred dollars per patient."

"Compared to...?"

"Compared to chemotherapy regimens that will eventually cost upwards of fifteen grand per month, often for years," Neve finished. "If Elaine's protocol works as designed, it could endanger their future profits."

Ellis stared at her. "Fifteen thousand dollars per month? For chemotherapy? Donna, that's impossible.

No one could afford that. No insurance would cover it."

"Trust me," Neve muttered. "They'll find a way to make people pay."

Perry, who had been hovering nearby, flapped his wings to get her attention. "Perhaps we should focus on the present conspiracy rather than speculating on the dystopian economics of healthcare in some imaginary future?" he urged, burning his black beady eyes into hers, hoping she would pick up on the hint.

Ellis was still staring at Neve. "How do you know all this? Sometimes you speak like a futuristic clairvoyant."

"Just connecting dots," Neve answered, avoiding his eyes. "Reading between the lines."

"Those are some very specific dots," Ellis murmured.

Suddenly, Perry launched himself from his perch like a feathery missile, dive-bombing Neve's face with wings splayed wide.

"MAYDAY! MAYDAY! Speculation overload!" he cawed and cackled, circling her head in frantic loops. "Next, she'll be predicting tomorrow's weather and stock market fluctuations!"

He landed on her shoulder, leaning in to whisper-hiss in her ear, "For someone who is supposed to be blending in, you're about as subtle as a drag queen. Dial back the crystal ball routine before he starts asking for lottery numbers!"

Perry then smoothed his ruffled feathers, cleared his throat, and addressed Ellis with dignified composure. "I don't know what came over me. Please. Carry on. Might I suggest we return to the matter at hand? Conrad? NovaCure? The imminent theft of our dear friend's groundbreaking medical research?"

Ellis shook his head as if clearing it. "Right. You're right. Whatever NovaCure's long-term plans might be, Conrad working with them is bad news for our protocol. We need to find out exactly what Conrad's up to."

"And fast," Neve agreed.

Over the next week, Neve and Ellis took turns monitoring Conrad's movements. They discovered he had been meeting with NovaCure representatives at a hotel bar across town, always after hours, always with a briefcase full of documents.

"He's selling our research to the highest bidder," Ellis concluded as they compared notes in Diana's apartment. "Probably positioning himself as the true innovator."

"But the protocol he's sharing can't be the same as Elaine's," Neve pointed out. "It's Aureon's intellectual property."

"He's modified it," Ellis agreed. "Stripped out our refinements about timing and pressure calibration, removing all the elements that made it truly effective."

"He's creating a watered-down version that works just enough to be marketable." Neve mused.

Diana, who had been listening quietly, her hand resting on her rounded belly, spoke up. "But why would NovaCure want a *less* effective treatment?"

"Profit," Neve responded, knowing the answer.

"They don't want to cure cancer; they want to manage it."

Perry honked in indignation, fluffed his feathers, and spread his wings. "So, our villainous lab coat is not only stealing our intellectual property but deliberately hampering medical progress for financial gain? That's a special circle of hell even Dante couldn't conceive."

Ellis gave a terse nod. "And he's covering his tracks along the way. By the time the patent is awarded for his 'improved' version, no one will remember where it originated."

Neve stood, pacing the small living room. "We have circumstantial evidence for days, but we need a smoking gun. Irrefutable proof that ties him directly to the sabotage of Robert's treatment and the theft of Elaine's research."

"And we need it now," Ellis added. "Conrad is meeting with NovaCure's attorneys next week."

The following evening, Neve stayed late at the lab, ostensibly to clean the rodent enclosures. In reality, she was waiting for Conrad to leave so she could search his office. As the hours ticked by, she began to worry he might work through the night.

"Our target remains ensconced in his lair," Perry reported after a reconnaissance flight down the hallway. "He appears to be on the phone, gesticulating with the enthusiasm of a televangelist who's spotted a wealthy widow in the front row."

"We need to get him out of here," Neve muttered, watching Conrad hang up the telephone through the window in the door.

As if on cue, the phone rang a second time in his office. Neve couldn't hear the conversation, but minutes later, he emerged, briefcase in hand, moving with unusual haste.

"Family emergency," he announced to the second shift security guard as he passed Neve's station. "I must leave immediately."

The moment the elevator doors closed behind him, Neve sprang into action. "Keep watch," she instructed Perry, heading for Conrad's office.

The room was neat as a pin, every file labeled, every surface spotless. Neve began with the filing cabinet, searching for anything related to NovaCure or Protocol VitOx.

Twenty minutes of fruitless searching later, frustration mounting, she turned to Conrad's desk. Her frustration spiked when she learned the drawers were locked.

"Perry!" Neve hissed, kneeling in front of Conrad's locked desk drawer. "I could use a little help here."

What? The bird knows how to pick a lock?

"Perry has many special talents," Neve answered Donna.

He puffed up his chest feathers, delighting in the praise. "In the eyes of the law, I was a 'person of interest' in a series of high-profile acquisitions involving items of unknown origin."

"He was a thief," Neve decoded for Donna.

"I prefer procurement specialist," Perry corrected, his head cocked in mock offense. "Do you want my help or not?"

"I want it."

"A lock is but a puzzle of metal waiting to be solved." Perry explained, waxing poetically, "The pick is an extension of your fingertips, and you must use it to gently probe inside her tender flesh."

Neve's face twisted into a grimace of disgust as she fought the urge to vomit. "Tender flesh? Ick. Can't you make this training less pornographic and more instructional?"

"You take the fun out of everything." He let out a chirp of resignation and continued. "Insert the tension wrench at the base," he coached as Neve pulled the tool from Donna's backpack, not wanting to ask Perry why it was in there in the first place.

"Just like that. Now apply gentle pressure." After a few jabs, he added, "No, no, no! You're attacking it like you're stabbing a potato. Finesse is required."

"I'm being efficient," Neve muttered.

"You're being a bull in a China shop. Feel for the pins. Listen to them. Each one sings a different note when properly aligned."

Neve paused, trying to listen, but became frustrated. Finally, she heard a soft click as the narrow metal pick trembled against a pin.

"Hear that?" Perry whispered. "The first pin is surrendering to your will."

Neve let out Donna's chuckle of astonishment.

That bird sure is ridiculous, but he knows what he's talking about.

"Maintain steady pressure," Perry instructed, his voice dropping lower as the second pin clicked into place. "The lock yearns to be opened but requires the proper seduction."

"You're making this weird," Neve said, but her irritation faded as the third pin clicked.

"Almost there," Perry encouraged. "Now for the master pin. It's the stubborn one, the gatekeeper of all the treasures."

Neve's hand trembled then steadied. There was a final, louder click, and then the drawer slid open.

"I did it," she breathed, tucking the tool back into the backpack.

Perry jutted his head to the side and a smug expression quirked his beak. "Of course you did. You had an excellent teacher." He flapped his wings and returned to his lookout post.

Inside, she found what she was looking for: a leather portfolio stamped with the NovaCure logo. She opened it, and on the right-hand side found the patent application for "Manning's Oxidative Therapy Protocol."

"That pompous, thieving, duplicitous parasite," she hissed as she headed over to the copy machine to Xerox each page.

Deeper in the drawer, she discovered something

even more damning: a small notebook containing detailed instructions for calibrating the hyperbaric chamber. Margin notes specified exact offsets to create "undetectable pressure variances."

"Jackpot," Neve whispered, her heart racing. She pulled the 35mm Nikon out of the equipment locker and photographed it page by page. She had just pulled out the roll of film when Perry's urgent squawk from the doorway made her freeze.

"Incoming!" the parrot hissed. "Conrad's returning! Security just called up!"

Neve rushed to place the documents in the appropriate files, closed the drawer, and darted from the office. She had barely settled at her workstation when the elevator doors opened, revealing Conrad deep in conversation with a security guard.

"...must have been a false alarm," the guard was saying. "No sign of any disturbance."

Conrad's eyes narrowed as he spotted Neve. "Still here, Donna? It's quite late."

"Cell cultures wait for no one," she replied with a forced smile. "I was just wrapping up."

Conrad studied her for a moment, suspicion visible in his gaze. "Indeed. Well, don't stay too much longer. It's not safe for a young woman to be walking to her car alone at night."

The thinly veiled threat sent a chill down Neve's spine.

THIRTY-THREE

Elaine's home stood silent on Seaglass Lane. The terracotta roof tiles, once vibrant against the blue Florida sky, were now obscured by decaying palm fronds that no one had bothered to clear after a recent tropical storm. The stucco walls, previously a pristine white, had developed dark water stains that marched downward, leaving tracks of mildew behind.

The courtyard fountain had long gone dry, its basin now home to a layer of brown leaves and a colony of mosquito larvae thriving in the stagnant puddle at its center. Bougainvillea vines, untrimmed for weeks, sprawled across the garden entrance, their wild crimson tentacles snagging anyone who dared to cross underneath.

Neve pressed her face closer to the dirty window, cupping her hands around her face to see inside. Several funeral bouquets had been left to wither and die; their petals were brown confetti littering the tile floor. A collection of half-empty glasses and takeout containers suggested Elaine moved from room to room, setting trash down wherever she finished with it.

"Are you sure about this?" Diana asked, smoothing the front of her polyester maternity blouse. "She hasn't answered anyone's calls in weeks."

Ellis nodded. "We don't have a choice. The patent filing is scheduled for next Monday. It's now or never."

Neve stepped forward, straightened her jean jacket, and rang the doorbell. When no response came, she knocked, then knocked again harder. "Dr. Feldman? It's Donna, Ellis, and Diana. We need to talk to you."

Silence.

Perry shifted on Neve's shoulder. "Perhaps she's vacationing in Tahiti? I hear December is lovely for disgraced black widows seeking solace from the crushing weight of injustice."

"Not helping," Neve muttered, knocking again, this time calling out, "I brought Perry!"

After the third attempt, they heard slow, shuffling footsteps approaching. The door opened a crack, revealing Elaine Feldman's gaunt face. Her appearance had deteriorated; unwashed hair hung in limp strands around her shoulders, and she wore what appeared to be a dingy terry cloth bathrobe and fuzzy bunny slippers.

"What do you want?" Her voice was flat, devoid of its usual authority.

"We need to talk to you," Ellis said, pressing his earnest face into the crack. "It's important."

Elaine opened the door a bit wider, letting her gaze drift over the three of them, lingering on Perry before she stepped back without a word, leaving the door ajar. They took it as an invitation and entered.

Dishes were stacked in the sink, mail scattered across countertops, and the air held the stale scent of greasy takeout. Elaine led them to the living room, where the television was on, the volume bordering on offensive for Neve, and she had to fight the urge to cover Donna's ears. "Like sands through the hourglass, these are the days of our lives."

Neve froze in disbelief as she watched Dr. Feldman, who once called television "the intellectual equivalent of eating Styrofoam," stand in front of the boxy console transfixed by "Days of Our Lives."

"Marlena and Laura are fighting over Don," Elaine announced, her voice dull as she sank back into her recliner. "Even though it's statistically improbable that this many catastrophic events would occur to one social group, I find their patterns of predictable emotion oddly soothing."

Perry tilted his head and whistled while he studied the screen. "Ah, yes, soap operas, where matrimony is treated with all the permanence of a temporary tattoo, and everyone's romantic history is more tangled than Christmas lights in January."

"I've watched twenty-three episodes," Elaine continued, her gaze locked on the television. "The characters display overwrought emotional responses despite their illogical decision-making processes. Should I be ashamed to admit I find it riveting?"

Neve exchanged alarmed glances with Ellis. Elaine, the same woman who could recite complex molecular structures from memory and who once walked out of the boardroom because the conversation was "insufficiently stimulating," was now finding comfort in fictional melodrama.

Diana leaned forward, her attention caught by a scene showing Dr. Laura Spencer Horton, who had just given birth to her daughter. Her eyes locked on the screen, where Laura clutched her baby to her chest while huge drifts of snow isolated her from the outside world.

"She delivered that baby all alone," Elaine whispered. "No doctors, no hospital, just her own raw stamina."

Ellis glanced at Diana, who refused to meet his eyes, clearly overwhelmed by the parallel. The moment hung heavy between them before Elaine broke the silence.

"I'm not coming back," she stated, devoid of emotion, her eyes still fixed on the screen. "You need to know, whatever reason you've fabricated for this visit is unlikely to change my current trajectory. Fact."

"We're not here to bring you back," Neve started to explain. "We're here because we've found evidence that Conrad sabotaged your protocol." She thought this would elicit interest and was shocked when it fell flat.

"Did you bring snacks? I find eating salt and vinegar potato chips while watching people destroy their interpersonal relationships very satisfying," Elaine replied, finally looking at them.

"I don't think you heard me," Neve said, taking a seat across from her. "We have evidence that Conrad sabotaged your protocol."

"It doesn't matter anymore."

"It matters a great deal," Ellis countered, pulling out a folder. "Conrad is meeting with NovaCure's attorneys on Monday. He's filing for a patent derived from our protocol under his name."

Ellis finally penetrated her defenses. Elaine's head snapped up, her eyes focusing sharply for the first time. "He's what?"

"Trying to steal your life's work," Diana chimed in.

Ellis spread the evidence across the coffee table: photographs of altered documents, the calibration notebook, meeting schedules with NovaCure representatives, the hyperbaric chamber logs, and the IV supply room forms. As Elaine leaned forward to examine them, Neve noticed her fingers begin to tap a pattern on her thigh.

"He's been systematically discrediting you while preparing to modify our protocol and claim it as his own," Ellis explained. "Can you look over these documents? Is there anything you see here that is out of the ordinary?"

Elaine picked up a photograph of typed pages from the cohort logs. "These ribbon impressions, they're not from my typewriter. The 'e' is raised, and there's no nick in the 'g' like my keys have." Her eyes narrowed; it was like she was being awakened after a year of hibernation. "And these IV logs," she pointed at them, "this isn't my handwriting."

"That's what we thought," Ellis said. "We believe Conrad has been altering your documents for months, creating inconsistencies to make your work appear flawed."

Elaine picked up the photos of Conrad's calibration notebook. As she studied them, the color drained from her face, and her bottom lip trembled as she swallowed hard.

"These are instructions for manipulating the hyperbaric chamber," she whispered. "To create pressure variances while displaying normal readings."

"Yes," Neve whispered.

The silence that followed was deafening. Elaine's hands dropped to her lap, the photos slipping from her fingers to the floor.

"He killed Robert," she finally said, her voice hollow. "And for what?" she asked bitterly, then answered her question with another, "To discredit me and steal our work?"

No one spoke as the full weight of this truth settled over the room. Even Perry was subdued as he hopped from Neve's shoulder to the coffee table, nudging the scattered evidence with his beak.

"It was a most elaborate scheme," he observed quietly. "Worthy of a Shakespearean villain."

"*Et tu*, Brute?" Elaine muttered under her breath. Perry hopped closer to press the top of his head into her cheek, trying to comfort her.

After a long moment, Diana leaned forward. "We need to go to the authorities with this."

Elaine gave a bitter laugh. "With what? Illegally obtained photographs? Circumstantial evidence?"

"She's right," Ellis admitted reluctantly. "They'll need a confession. Right now, it's only he said, she said."

Elaine got to her feet and moved to the window as the darkness closed in again. She pulled back the curtain, letting in a shaft of pale December sunlight. "What's the point, anyway? Robert is gone. My reputation is destroyed. The medical community has made me a pariah."

"The point," Neve said, rising to stand beside her, "is that *your* protocol *works*. It could save millions of lives."

Elaine turned, studying Neve with fresh interest. "You believe in it that much? Even after what happened to Robert?"

"What happened to Robert wasn't your protocol failing," Neve insisted. "It was deliberate sabotage. And yes, I do believe in it. I've seen the cell cultures respond. Ellis and I reconstructed all the trials, and we've analyzed the original data and treatment logs. There is no denying it works."

Something shifted in Elaine's expression, a spark rekindling in her eyes that had been dead for over a month. Elaine held her gaze for a long moment, then turned to the others. "What exactly do you propose we do? Conrad has Aureon Biomedical behind him, the press in his pocket, and soon, he will have NovaCure's resources at his disposal."

"We expose him publicly," Ellis said, pacing the room. "In a way he can't deny or cover up."

Elaine stared vacantly at the soap opera still playing in the background, where a doctor in a crisp white lab coat was delivering devastating news to a woman whose feathered hair would give Farrah Faucett a run for her money. "Public exposure requires an audience. We have none."

The room fell silent, except for the melodramatic outro music swelling from the television as the credits rolled. Perry hopped closer to Elaine, nudging aside a stale sandwich crust. "While I hate to interrupt this festival of despair, perhaps we might consider the man's most obvious weakness?"

"His ego," Neve chimed in.

"Correctamundo!" Perry flapped his wings, then strutted like the Fonz. "Our villain has the pride of a peacock who's recently discovered his own reflection."

Ellis stopped pacing, his expression brightening. "I have an idea. My college roommate, Miles Murphy, is a freelance journalist."

"Another spin doctor?" Elaine scoffed. "No, thank you. Besides, Conrad has them all eating out of his hand. Fact." She crossed her arms, her clinical detachment returning with a vengeance.

"Not Miles," Ellis insisted. "He's hungry for a story that will turn him into a household name. And more importantly, he owes me a favor after I helped him pass Western philosophy."

"What are you thinking?" Diana asked, leaning forward.

Ellis rubbed his chin with his thumb and forefinger, his eyes gleaming with purpose. "What if Miles approached Conrad, claiming to be from the selection committee for the Hastings Award for Ethical Medicine?"

Elaine's head snapped up, her attention finally diverted from the television. "The Hastings? That's the most prestigious ethics award in medical research. Recipients typically receive endowed chairs at institutions like Harvard or Johns Hopkins."

"Exactly," Ellis continued, warming to his plan. "Miles contacts Conrad, tells him he's been shortlisted for the 1977 Hastings Award for his ethical vigilance in exposing dangerous research practices. We can tell him that all the candidates must complete a preliminary interview."

"Conrad would never resist an opportunity to shine," Neve agreed. "Especially if he thought it might coincide with his NovaCure patent announcement."

"But how does this expose him?" Diana asked. "He'll just repeat the same lies he's been telling everyone else."

"Because," Ellis explained with growing excitement, "the interview will be conducted in front of a panel of committee members, respected physicians and researchers who've agreed to help us. We'll ask questions that seem innocent but are designed to trap him into revealing his knowledge of the sabotage."

Perry strutted across the table. "A honey trap for

the academically vain! I do so love it when Karma serves up a steaming bowl of justice."

"And we'll get the whole thing on tape," Ellis added. "Every contradiction, every admission."

Elaine's scientific mind engaged despite her skepticism. "The statistical probability of success depends on multiple variables: Conrad's vanity, the credibility of your journalist friend, the presentation of the questions..."

"And our ability to find credible physicians willing to risk their reputations," Neve pointed out. "Who would take that chance?"

Ellis smiled. "Dr. Whitmore has already agreed to help. Conrad is familiar with him, and it will lull him into a false sense of security if he's on the panel. Dr. Whitmore has also offered us his entire Rolodex. Apparently, due to his investment portfolio, he has connections to doctors all over the country."

"Dr. Whitmore?" For the first time, genuine hope flickered across Elaine's face. "Robert adored him."

"He wants justice for Robert," Ellis said. "He believes in your work, Elaine, and feels you've been railroaded by the board."

Neve watched as Elaine's posture shifted, her shoulders straightened, and her gaze sharpened, the fog of depression lifting as her analytical mind engaged in developing a plan.

"The Hastings Award ceremony is traditionally held at the Plaza Hotel in New York," Elaine noted, her observations taking on their former brilliance.

"Conrad would expect a preliminary interview in a setting commensurate with the award's prestige."

"The Tampa Bay Grand Hotel has conference rooms that would be convincing," Diana suggested. "My uncle manages events there."

"We'd need appropriate documentation," Elaine continued, her mind visibly working through the logistics. "Letterhead, credentials, a detailed backstory about the selection process."

"And video cameras," Ellis added. "To capture every word that snake says."

"The hotel has audio-visual recording equipment for business conferences. We could tell Conrad the interview is being recorded for final review before the official selection," Diana said. "I'm sure my uncle could make it available at a reasonable rate."

Elaine turned to Neve. She'd come to trust her in the time they'd spent together, and she was looking for insight. "What do you think, Donna?"

Neve considered the question carefully. "Conrad's greatest weakness is his arrogance. He believes he's the smartest person in any room. If we appeal to his ego and give him a chance to publicly cement his triumph over you while simultaneously elevating his status in the medical community, he'll seize it without question."

"The timing must be impeccable." Elaine rose from her chair and switched off the television with a decisive click.

"We need to strike while the iron is hot. This

Friday," Ellis suggested. "Three days before his meeting with NovaCure."

"That leaves us only five days to prepare," Diana pointed out.

Elaine strode with purpose to her dining table, sweeping aside a collection of unwashed coffee mugs. "Then we have work to do."

Perry flew to perch on a nearby lamp. "From soap opera aficionado to justice crusader in under thirty minutes. I'd call that a remarkable recovery trajectory!"

As Elaine began outlining the necessary preparations, her voice regained its authoritative edge, and Neve felt a surge of hope.

"We'll need to prepare detailed questions," Elaine instructed, grabbing a notepad. "Innocent on the surface but designed to elicit specific responses about pressure calibration, protocol modifications, and data interpretation."

Diana smiled at this evidence of Elaine's returning focus. "I'll contact my uncle about the conference room."

Elaine's gaze landed on her belly, as if noticing it for the first time, and shock registered on her face as she blurted, "You're pregnant?"

"Yes," Diana said, shame filling her as she swung her sheepish gaze to her feet.

"Just like Dr. Laura," Elaine mused, then frowned. "That will not bode well for your career advancement, but I suppose congratulations are in order just the same."

Diana let out a weak, "Thanks," her cheeks flaming with embarrassment.

Neve flicked her gaze over to her father. She noticed the set of his jaw and watched him open his mouth to say something, then decidedly close it.

Instead, he walked over to the rotary phone and began the long process of inserting his finger into the dial and circling it around for each number. "I'm calling Miles," Ellis offered in explanation as he turned away, nestling the receiver between his chin and shoulder.

As they mobilized around the dining table, clearing space, gathering materials, and formulating plans, Neve caught Perry watching Elaine with something resembling admiration.

"The human capacity for resilience continues to astonish," the parrot murmured. "Particularly when motivated by righteous vengeance and the opportunity to publicly humiliate one's enemies."

"It's not about vengeance," Neve corrected. "It's about justice."

"In my experience," Perry replied with a knowing tilt of his head, "they are one and the same."

THIRTY-FOUR

IN THE LIVING room of Diana and Donna's apartment was a small artificial Christmas tree lit with colorful incandescent teardrop bulbs that cast prisms across the walls and ceiling. Strands of silver tinsel caught the light, trembling with each of Ellis's agitated footsteps as he paced the worn path between the avocado-green polyester chair and the ribbed corduroy sofa, waiting for the doorbell to ring.

On the table in the kitchenette, manila files bulged with medical trial reports, charts, and logs. Ellis checked his watch for the fourth time in as many minutes, letting out a heavy sigh.

"Are you sure about this guy?" Diana asked, tugging the hem of her purple velour top over her belly as she collected the now-empty pizza box and paper plates and discarded them into the trash. At six months pregnant, she had finally abandoned her loose lab coats for maternity wear at home.

"Miles is solid," Ellis assured her, pausing his

pacing. "He's trying to break into investigative journalism, and he's hungry for a story that will make his mark."

"That's what worries me," Neve said, stress organizing their evidence into neat piles she relocated to the coffee table. "Someone who's hungry might be reckless."

"Or he might be exactly what we need," Ellis countered. "Someone willing to take risks the established press won't."

The doorbell's chime sliced through the rest of their doubts. Ellis moved to answer it, opening the door to a short, slightly overweight man with a scruffy beard and alert hazel eyes that seemed to catalog everything in the apartment at once. He wore a rumpled crewneck sweater over a paisley shirt and carried a leather messenger bag that had seen better days.

"Ellis, my man!" Miles grinned, clapping Ellis on the shoulder as he entered. "It's been too long." His discerning gaze swept the room, lingering on the stacks of documents before settling on Diana and Neve. "These must be your colleagues."

Ellis made the introductions as Miles settled into an armchair, immediately pulling out a tape recorder and a notepad.

"Mind if I record? Helps me keep the facts straight," he said, already pressing the button without waiting for permission.

Diana exchanged a nervous glance with Neve.

"Maybe we should talk first before recording anything official."

Miles's smile never wavered as he reached forward to switch off the device. "Sure, sure. I want you to be comfortable. We'll start off-the-record until you say otherwise." He leaned forward, rested his forearms on his thighs, and laced his fingers together. "Ellis gave me the broad strokes. Brilliant cancer treatment sabotaged, respected scientist framed, maybe even a case of corporate espionage? It's got everything. Pulitzer prize-winning material."

Neve's eyes narrowed, and she chastised, "Must I remind you, a man died, and a woman's reputation was destroyed?"

"Of course, of course," Miles backpedaled, his expression turning appropriately solemn as he cleared his throat. "I just meant it's the kind of story that needs to be told. The public deserves to know."

"Why must you say everything twice?" Neve couldn't stop herself from asking. Her question was so blunt, Ellis silenced her with a glare. "Sorry." She let Donna mumble the apology, even though she didn't mean it.

Ellis opened a bottle of wine, pouring glasses for everyone except Diana, who opted for ginger ale. "Miles has contacts at *The Tampa Tribune* and *The St. Petersburg Times*. If we can get this story out, it could force an official investigation."

"Thank you," Miles said, accepting his wine. "Why don't you walk me through everything you know so far?"

Over the next two hours, Miles consumed glass after glass of wine while Ellis, Diana, and Neve presented all the evidence they'd gathered. His initial skepticism gave way to genuine outrage as he understood the magnitude of Conrad's deception and the consequences of his actions.

"This pressure calibration sabotage is brilliant in its simplicity," he muttered, studying Ellis's notes. "Evil, but brilliant. And these forged logs? Wow! The guy thought of everything."

"Not everything," Neve said, pulling out the original IV bag logs she'd discovered. "He didn't expect us to find these."

Miles's eyes lit up as he compared the authentic logs with the forgeries. "This is good. Very good."

By midnight, they had filled him in on their plan. Miles, now slurring his words from the second bottle of wine, would pose as a member of the selection committee. Along with other medical professionals, he would interview Conrad for the Hastings Award for his ethical vigilance in exposing Elaine's dangerous research practices.

"We'll need to give him enough rope to hang himself," Miles said, pouring himself another glass.

"Isn't this considered entrapment?" Diana protested.

"It's a slippery slope, sweetheart," Miles countered with a wink.

"Don't call me sweetheart." Diana shot him a look. "My name is Dr. Morrison."

Miles held up his hands. "Okay, okay."

Neve had to press her lips together to swallow the insults she yearned to rain down on this chauvinistic jerk. She gulped a full glass of wine down to soften the rage that had been building all night long. Ellis trusted him, and he seemed to be their only hope, a fact that she found quite unsettling.

Ellis grimaced as he got to his feet. "Let's take a beat."

"I've got to hit the head, anyway." Miles stumbled toward the only bathroom.

"You call this man a friend?" Diana questioned, getting to her feet. "It's a pretty dismal reflection of your values."

The tension in the room thickened as Diana and Ellis faced off.

"I'm going to get some air," Diana muttered, heading for the tiny patio.

Ellis followed her, leaving Neve alone until Miles returned a few minutes later. He fell onto the sofa and was struggling to keep his eyes open.

"She's pretty high-strung. No wonder there's trouble in paradise," Miles slurred, gesturing toward the glass door where Ellis and Diana's silhouettes were visible through the curtains. They were clearly arguing.

"It's complicated," Neve replied, uncomfortable with his prying.

"Always is," Miles chuckled, settling deeper into the couch and closing his eyes. "Wake me when the domestic dispute is over."

Within minutes, his soft snores filled the living

room, and the argument had moved back inside to Diana's bedroom. The door was closed, but their raised voices carried through the thin walls.

Perry, who had been quietly observing from his perch on a bookshelf, hopped down to Neve's shoulder. "Quite the soap opera unfolding, isn't it?"

"We shouldn't eavesdrop," Neve whispered, though she made no move to leave or turn up the music.

"Oh, please," Perry scoffed. "Like you're not dying to know what's happening in there. Besides, this directly affects you. Or rather, your existence."

Neve couldn't argue with that logic. She moved closer to the hallway, where Diana's voice came through more clearly.

"I can't do this anymore, Ellis!" Diana cried. "The lying, the sneaking around, the constant fear of being caught?"

"I'm trying to protect our future," Ellis replied, his tone pleading. "All of our futures."

"Our future?" Diana's laugh was bitter. "There is no 'our' future, Ellis. I've made my decision."

A heavy silence followed, broken only by Ellis's quiet question: "What decision?"

Neve felt her heart rate accelerate, the geode in her pocket warming against her hip.

"I've contacted an adoption agency," Diana admitted, her voice steadier now. "I've been screening potential parents. I've interviewed a couple from Connecticut. He's a doctor, and she's a teacher. They can't have children of their own."

"You're giving away our baby?" Ellis's voice was barely audible, choked with emotion.

"I'm giving our child a stable home with *two* parents who are prepared for a family," Diana corrected. "You're too busy with your career, and I shouldn't have to sacrifice mine. I've thought this through. It's the best solution for everyone involved."

"You didn't even consult me," Ellis said, his voice hardening. "This is my child, too."

"A child you never asked for!" Diana shot back. "It was an accident. We made a mistake."

"I don't believe in mistakes," he replied quietly.

Another long silence stretched between them.

"I'm tired," Diana finally muttered, her voice cracking with exhaustion." I'm scared all the time. Scared of Conrad finding out what we know. Scared of what this pregnancy is doing to my body and my career. I haven't slept through the night in months."

"Diana..." Ellis began.

"No, let me finish," she interrupted. "I've spent my entire life fighting to be taken seriously in a field dominated by men. Do you know what happens to female scientists who have children? They disappear. Their research stalls. They get passed over for grants, for promotions, for recognition."

"It doesn't have to be that way," Ellis insisted.

"But it *is* that way," Diana countered. "Look at the women in our department. The ones with children are all stuck in assistant positions, while the men with families advance. It's not fair, but it's reality."

"So, your solution is to just... give our baby away?" Ellis's voice broke. "To strangers?"

"They're not strangers to me anymore," Diana murmured. "I've read their letters. I've been to their home. They have a nursery set up already. They're good people, Ellis."

"I won't let a stranger raise my child," Ellis vowed, his voice stretched drum tight with emotion.

"Ellis..."

"No. I understand *your* choice. I respect that *you* don't want to be a mother. But I *want* to be a father. I can raise this child myself."

Diana's surprised laugh held no humor. "You? Alone? With your sixty-hour work weeks and research obsession?"

"I'll figure it out," Ellis insisted. "My sister lives an hour away. She'd help. I could adjust my schedule around it. People do it all the time. I'll find a way."

"You're being naïve." Diana sighed in frustration.

"And *you're* being unfair," Ellis countered. "You've made this life-altering decision without even taking me into account."

The conversation fell silent again, and Neve found herself holding her breath.

"I never expected this from you," Diana finally said, her voice thick with tears. "I thought you'd be relieved. That you'd understand this is the most practical solution for all parties involved."

There was a heavy thump as Neve heard someone collapse on the bed.

Ellis's voice was softer now. "I can raise our child. I promise, I'll be present. Involved."

"You say that now," Diana whispered.

"I mean it," Ellis insisted. "This isn't some idealistic fantasy. It's a commitment. I don't want our child wondering why they weren't wanted, why they were given away."

"A small part of me wants this baby too," Diana admitted, her voice breaking. "That's what makes this so hard. But I want my career too, and I know I can't have both. Not in this world, not in this time."

"Then let me do it," Ellis pleaded. "You can be as involved or as uninvolved as you choose. No pressure, no expectations. You can pursue your fellowship, your research, everything you've worked for."

"And when the baby asks about its mother?"

"I'll tell the child whatever you feel is best. We can decide how to handle it together."

Neve felt tears welling in her eyes as she listened. A wall of heat intensified as outrage at her father's conscious decision to lie to her settled in deep. The geode in her pocket pulsed with increasing warmth, sizzling hot against her skin.

"I need time to think," Diana concluded.

"So, the adoption isn't final yet?" Ellis asked, hope creeping into his voice.

"No, nothing's signed."

"Then promise me you'll consider what I'm saying. Please."

There was a sobbing sound followed by murmurs

from Ellis that Neve couldn't make out, even though she pressed her ear to the door. Ten minutes later, when she heard heavy footsteps approaching, she quickly retreated to the living room, pretending to organize papers as Ellis emerged. His face was drawn, his eyes red-rimmed.

"Sorry about that," he said, his voice rough. "Diana's not feeling well. She's going to sleep for the night."

Neve nodded, not trusting herself to speak. The conversation she'd overheard had shaken her to her core.

Ellis glanced at Miles, now snoring like a buzz saw on the couch. "I think our aspiring Pulitzer winner has had a bit too much wine."

"He can sleep it off here," Neve managed, her voice strained. "The couch pulls out."

Ellis nodded distractedly, gathering his coat. "I should go. Tell Diana I'll call her tomorrow."

After Ellis left, Neve stood in the silent apartment, overwhelmed by what she'd learned. Her entire understanding of her past had been upended. It wasn't that her father considered her a burden. He had fought for her, had been willing to rearrange his entire life to raise her.

The geode in her pocket now seared white hot against her skin, pulsing with an urgency she couldn't ignore. She was compelled by it to move to the couch where Miles lay sleeping, and she spent a minute studying his face. He looked peaceful, untroubled by the emotional storm that had just passed through the apartment.

Neve felt a strange pull toward him, as if the geode was guiding her. She reached out hesitantly, her fingers brushing against Miles's arm.

The world tilted, then swam, as reality fragmented around her. The geode's heat intensified, spreading through her body like liquid fire. Neve gasped as her consciousness seemed to stretch, then compress, then pour itself into a new vessel.

The last thing she saw before darkness claimed her was Perry's alarmed expression as he fluttered in tight circles, squawking above her.

Then there was only white.

CHAPTER 35
PEREGRINE

I MATERIALIZED out of the white ether with a disorienting lurch. Exhausted by the journey, it took concerted effort to open my eyes. The first thing I noticed was the loss of three of my most distinguished scarlet tail feathers, scattered beneath me like fallen soldiers.

"A tragedy of the highest order," I muttered, inspecting the damage with dismay.

The room around me was dimly lit, cluttered with cages and aquariums, the air thick with the mingled scents of cedar shavings, millet, and something distressingly akin to rodent urine. I found myself perched atop an ancient cash register, my talons clicking against the metal keys as I shifted from foot to foot.

Dawn light filtered through grimy windows, illuminating a sign that read "Marvin's Menagerie" in faded lettering. Fantastic. I'd been transported to a pet shop that appeared to have last been cleaned during the Nixon administration.

The jingling of keys announced someone's arrival. I straightened my posture, determined to maintain dignity despite my reduced plumage.

The door swung open to reveal a man who could only be described as a walking cannabis advertisement. His wild Einstein hair stuck out in all directions, complemented by a faded tie-dyed t-shirt. His bushy eyebrows were dangerously close to becoming a full-fledged unibrow and shot up when he spotted me.

"I must be stoned to the bone," he said, sauntering over with a lazy grin. "An African grey, just loungin' on my register like he's the boss or somethin'. Mind blown." He brought two gnarled fists to either side of his head, sending his fingers outward to illustrate his point.

I fixed him with my most imperious stare, deciding silence was my best defense. This human, presumably Marvin, circled me with growing excitement, and I caught a whiff of ganja so strong I almost passed out.

"No cage, no note... bummer, man. I must have left the door open and someone got in and ditched you last night," he muttered, scratching at his scruffy beard. "Stuff like this happens, ya know? Folks get all turned on about exotic pets, then freak when it's too much to handle."

He reached out his forearm to me, his mellow voice soft as an ocean breeze. "C'mon, let's find you a groovier spot to crash."

I considered pecking him because it would have been justified, but calculated that cooperation might serve me better until Neve found me. I allowed myself to be transported to a cage that was, frankly, an insult to a bird of my stature. The space was barely sufficient for a common Budgie, let alone an avian specimen of my exquisite caliber.

In protest, I promptly lost another feather, watching it drift to the newspaper-lined bottom of the cage.

"Chill out, my guy," Marvin said. "I'll rustle up some munchies and a little H2O for ya. I heard African greys are real talkers. You got any cool words in that beak, little dude?"

Little dude? I turned my back to him and scoffed a squawk in protest. I would not perform like a common circus animal for this dirty hippie. No. My silence would be my resistance.

The morning quickly devolved into The Great Sunflower Seed Interrogation. Marvin, apparently determined to make me speak, presented a succession of bargain-bin sunflower seeds, holding each one up like it was a priceless jewel.

"Pretty bird want a treat?" he cooed with a grin. "Say 'hello' for your 'ole pal Marvin. Lay it on me!"

As if I, a bird of sophisticated palate, would break my silence for anything less than organic, dry-roasted macadamia nuts. The offensive seeds were an obvious bulk purchase, probably stored in some musty cabinet for months and turning rancid. I ignored the pathetic offering.

Marvin, undeterred, pulled up a stool and began an absurd one-sided conversation. "I'm telling you, man, Iggy, my iguana, gets high just from secondhand smoke. Last Tuesday, he stared at the lava lamp for four hours, then tried to mate with a houseplant."

I lost another feather from sheer secondhand embarrassment for the poor reptile when Marvin segued from the high life of Iggy the party lizard to breaking out in song. His rendition of "Pretty Bird" in a tone-deaf falsetto was particularly trying.

"Pretty bird, pretty bird, such a pretty, pretty bird," he warbled, swaying into the counter.

I maintained my dignified silence, though it cost me considerable effort not to inform him that his singing voice resembled a garbage disposal processing a fork.

By midday, the shop had opened to customers, and my trying ordeal intensified. A woman wearing perfume in quantities sufficient to asphyxiate the hamsters approached my cage, dragging what I can only describe as demon spawn disguised as a human child.

"Oh, look, Mikey! An African grey! Aren't they supposed to talk?" she asked Marvin, who had materialized beside her with surprising speed for a stoner.

"This one's being shy," Marvin admitted. "Just got him this morning. Found him waiting for me when I opened up."

Mikey pressed his face against my cage bars, his metal mouth hanging open to display both his unfortunate braces and his recent popcorn consumption.

"Can I touch it?" he demanded, already poking a finger toward me.

"Better not," Marvin cautioned. "African greys can straight-up take a bite outta one of your gnarly digits, right at the knuckle, if they get freaked out."

Not Marvin's worst idea so far.

The child withdrew his finger, only to redirect it toward his own nasal cavity. I watched in horrified fascination as he proceeded to excavate his nose with frightening dedication, his tongue protruding slightly in concentration.

The digging complete, this abhorrent crotch goblin then wiped the results directly onto my cage bars. Revolting! I was so distressed I lost two more precious feathers.

"How much?" the woman asked, her interest undaunted by her offspring's repugnant behavior.

"Eight hundred," Marvin haggled. "Plus cage and supplies."

The price, clearly inflated, fortunately proved to be prohibitive, and I was spared adoption into that household of horrors.

As the day progressed, I played the waiting game. Every chime of the doorbell sent my heart aflutter. Each time, I raised my feathered head expectantly, hoping to see a familiar face, only to be disappointed by another parade of potential purchasers.

The emotional roller coaster cost me another three feathers. My plumage was beginning to resemble a molting season gone terribly wrong.

Marvin, concerned by my continued silence and

diminishing feather count, placed a mirror beside my food dish.

"Company might cheer you up, my dude," he suggested.

It was insulting. As much as I loved my own reflection, it wasn't enough. I turned my back on the mirror with disdain.

It was then that I became aware of my neighbor, a female cockatoo in the adjacent cage. She had been watching me with unmistakable interest, her head cocked to one side.

"Pretty bird," she warbled in the simplified language of pet-store birds.

I nodded once in agreement, then ignored her, maintaining my sophisticated silence.

From a cage across the aisle came an indignant screech. A male cockatoo in brilliant white fixed me with a baleful glare, puffing his feathers in obvious territoriality. He raised his crest, vying for her attention, and I had to admit it was jaw-dropping.

"Mine," he squawked, spreading his wings in warning. "Stay away."

"Pretty bird," the female repeated, edging closer to my cage wall.

I turned away, refusing to star in this avian tele novella. Unfortunately, in my attempt to reposition myself away from her, my tail brushed against the cage bars in what apparently constituted a provocative mating dance in cockatoo culture.

The female responded with an appreciative head-bob.

"Pretty bird," she chirped. I found the ignorance indicated by the single phrase in her vocabulary off-putting.

"I assure you, madam, any resemblance to courtship behavior is entirely coincidental," I informed her, breaking my silence for the first time. "I am merely adjusting my position in this woefully inadequate accommodation."

My speech, rather than deterring her, seemed to increase her interest tenfold.

"Pretty bird!" she screeched, performing an even more elaborate dance. Her crest popped up, and she swept her wings forward and back.

The male across the aisle erupted in a display of jealous rage, screeching and throwing himself against his cage bars with concerning force.

"Mine!" he insisted.

"Oh, for heaven's sake," I muttered. In my exasperation, I stretched my wings and accidentally executed what must have been the parrot equivalent of a dick pic. The female responded with an enthusiastic regurgitation of her morning seeds, apparently the height of romantic overtures in avian society.

The male's screeching reached a fevered pitch that threatened to shatter the aquarium glass. I presented them both with my back, and eventually they both calmed down.

By late afternoon, I had lost a total of twelve feathers, each one a testament to the trying nature of my incarceration. As the shop quieted, I found myself perched as far from my amorous neighbor as possible, muttering under my breath.

"Neve, where art thou? Save me from this amorous hell that smells like urine-soaked wood chips."

The bell above the door chimed once more. I raised my head without much hope, then froze in disbelief.

CHAPTER

THIRTY-SIX

Sunlight stabbed through the half-drawn curtains of Diana and Donna's apartment, landing directly across Miles's closed eyes. Neve moaned as the brightness penetrated his eyelids, dragging her reluctantly toward consciousness. Her head throbbed with the dull, persistent ache of a red wine hangover, and her mouth felt fuzzy, like her teeth were wearing sweaters.

Where am I? The thought bubbled up from the brain sludge as the first inkling of awareness crept in.

She blinked, wincing at the light. Something felt profoundly off. Her body seemed bloated and foreign, as if she'd been stuffed into a leisure suit several sizes too small. Her limbs were heavy and unfamiliar.

"Oof." Neve pushed up from the corduroy couch, the springs creaking beneath Miles's weight. The movement felt clumsy, uncoordinated, as if her brain was sending signals to a body that wasn't properly receiving them.

"What is happening?"

Neve looked down at broad, masculine hands with short, blunt fingernails and a dusting of dark hair on the knuckles. A silver college ring caught the light on the right hand. The sight sent a jolt of panic through her.

"These aren't my hands," Neve whispered, flipping them forward and back. Panic swelled, threatening to overwhelm her. She struggled to stand on Miles's wide feet, swaying slightly. The room spun for several seconds, then settled.

"Calm down," she told herself. "Think logically. You're dreaming. You must be dreaming."

But the hangover felt too real, the sunlight too bright, and the scratchy texture of the polyester shirt she'd slept in too annoying against her rougher skin.

A note on the coffee table caught her attention. In neat, block handwriting read:

Miles - Diana and I had to go to work. Help yourself
to breakfast. Lock up when you leave. - Donna

"Miles?" she said aloud. "Oh, God. I've shifted into Miles!"

A thought that wasn't her own suddenly formed in her mind.

Who the hell are you?

Neve froze at the demand, and a tingle of anxiety exacerbated Miles's bursting bladder. The bathroom. She needed to get to the bathroom. She stumbled down the short hallway, pushed open the door, and flipped on the light. The fluorescent bulb flickered to life, revealing a small, tidy bathroom with blue tile and a floral shower curtain.

Neve approached the mirror with dread, already suspecting what she would see. The reflection that stared back confirmed her worst fears. It was Miles Murphy, Ellis's college friend, the investigative journalist who was stocky, leaning toward obese, with a scruffy beard, calculating hazel eyes, and rumpled clothing he'd slept in.

"Oh, no! No, no, no, no, no," she gasped, reeling backward. The room seemed to compress and expand simultaneously. The pattern on the shower curtain, tiny blue flowers that repeated in endless rows, began to swim before her eyes, each flower multiplying and vibrating with frenetic energy. The scent of Diana's lavender soap, previously a subtle background note, now assaulted her senses in a cloud that made her sneeze.

She stepped closer and latched onto the edge of the sink, his hairy knuckles whitening. "This can't be happening," she whispered, then flinched at the sound of his voice. It was deeper, more resonant, and distinctly male.

"That's not my voice," she said, horrified as a wave of nausea rolled through her.

No, it's MY voice. The better question is who the hell are YOU and what are you doing here?

"I'm Neve. Donna's friend."

The thought-communication was disorienting, like having two radio stations playing simultaneously in her head. This shift was a completely different encounter than the three she'd already experienced. She felt his aggression and anger take hold.

Neve? How is this possible? How are you controlling my body?

"I don't know," Neve said, using Miles's voice.

Get out! Get out!

She closed Miles's eyes, trying to center herself and ignore his repetitive drivel.

What the hell is going on? Get out of my head! Get OUT!

"I need to sit down," Neve whispered, lowering Miles's heavier frame to perch on the edge of the bathtub. The simple movement felt like trying to operate a marionette with tangled strings; his body was on a delay. It responded a half-second too late to her mental commands.

She took a deep breath, feeling the air fill Miles's lungs. Even breathing felt strange. It was deeper, his chest expanding in unfamiliar places.

This is insane. I'm losing my mind. I need to stop drinking.

"You're not losing your mind," Neve muttered. "This has happened to me before."

What do you mean, before?

"I sometimes share consciousness with other people. Temporarily." Neve ran Miles's hands over his face, feeling the unfamiliar scratch of beard stubble. "I can't explain why or how. It just happens."

That's impossible. People don't just slip into someone else's skin like Invasion of the Body Snatchers.

"I know how it sounds," Neve replied, studying the

unfamiliar hands resting on Miles's knees. "The best thing we can do is stay calm and let it run its course."

A surge of resistance crashed through their shared mental space.

Let it run its course? Are you kidding me? This is MY body. I will not just sit back while someone else takes it for a joyride!

"It's not like I chose this," Neve said, frustration coloring her tone. "Do you think I want to be stuck in a male body with a hangover and a stranger yelling in my head?"

How long?

The demanding question cut as sharply as a blade.

"I don't know exactly. It's different each time."

Miles's outrage exploded with such force that Neve physically winced. *Absolutely not. I have interviews scheduled. I have deadlines. I have a LIFE.*

"So do I," Neve countered. "But right now, we're stuck with each other."

She felt Miles's consciousness pushing against hers, attempting to reassert control over his body. It created a strange pressure behind his eyes, a tightening in his jaw that Neve hadn't directed.

I'm not some passenger along for the ride. I'm the driver. You need to back off.

"That's not how this works," Neve said, trying to keep her voice steady despite the cutting tension building in Miles's temples. "Believe me, I've tried to fight it before. It only makes things worse."

Watch me.

Neve felt a sudden, intense struggle for control.

Miles's right hand twitched against her will, fingers splaying then curling into a fist. The effort sent a spike of pain through his skull.

"Stop!" Neve gasped. "You're hurting us both!"

Neve felt Miles's body breaking out in a cold sweat, his heart thundering in his chest as he fought for control. The bathroom seemed to tilt and spin around them.

"Miles, please," she pleaded. "I know this is terrifying. I know you feel violated. But we need to work together until it passes." His resistance continued for several more seconds before gradually subsiding, not out of agreement but exhaustion. The effort of fighting had drained him.

A sudden pressure in Neve's lower abdomen provided an unwelcome distraction. Miles's bladder was so full it was almost bursting.

"I need to use the bathroom," Neve admitted with dawning horror.

No way. I'm not letting you touch my jibbles.

"We don't have a choice," Neve pointed out. "Unless you want to wet yourself."

The standoff lasted approximately three seconds before the pressure became too insistent to ignore. With extreme reluctance, Miles's consciousness retreated, allowing Neve to direct her attention toward the toilet.

"How do I... I mean, what's the procedure here?" Neve asked awkwardly.

You're kidding me, right? Miles's thoughts were strained with disbelief. *You've never seen a man pee?*

"Theoretically, I understand the process. In practical terms? No." Neve thought she heard him sigh in defeat.

It's not rocket science. Just unzip, aim, and go.

With fumbling fingers, Neve managed to unzip Miles's fly and extract the dangling appendage. The sensation was so foreign, so utterly bizarre, that she dropped it immediately.

"This is my worst nightmare come true," she muttered.

Just get it over with, Miles pleaded, mortification clear in his tone.

Neve positioned herself in front of the toilet, held Miles's penis with awkward uncertainty, and tried to relax the muscles needed for urination. Nothing happened.

"It's not working," she said after a moment of uncomfortable silence.

You're too tense. Just relax and let it happen naturally.

"I AM relaxed," Neve insisted. "It's YOUR body that's not cooperating."

Try thinking about waterfalls. Or running faucets. Or putting your hand in a cup of warm water.

Neve closed Miles's eyes and visualized Niagara Falls, rushing water, ocean waves, anything liquid and flowing. Suddenly, the floodgates opened. Unfortunately, in astonishment, she lost her grip and then her aim.

The stream of urine went wildly off-target, splashing against the wall, the side of the toilet, the bathmat, and Miles's own shoe before she could regain control.

What are you DOING? Miles's thoughts screeched in her mind. *Point it DOWN! DOWN!*

"I'm trying!" Neve frantically adjusted, over-corrected, and created an even wider spray pattern before finally managing to direct the stream into the toilet bowl. The relief of emptying Miles's bladder was immediately overshadowed by the humiliation of the mess she'd created.

"I'm sorry!" she cried. "I didn't realize the contents would be so pressurized."

How could you not know? It's basic physics!

"I've never operated this equipment before!"

When the flow finally slowed and then stopped, Neve stood frozen, unsure of the next step.

Shake it, Miles instructed, his mental voice dripping with resignation.

"Shake what?"

You know what! Just give it a couple of shakes and put it away. And for God's sake, wash your hands after.

Following instructions with burning cheeks, Neve completed the procedure, then spent the next five minutes frantically cleaning up the bathroom with toilet paper and hand soap.

"Men are repugnant creatures," she said, genuinely mortified.

After washing his hands again, Neve splashed cold water on Miles's face, trying to collect herself. His shoulders were broader than she was used to, and his center of gravity was different. Even the way his clothes hung on his frame felt odd.

"This is so strange," she murmured, running his hands over his face.

We need to figure this out, Miles said, his thoughts calmer now. *What exactly happened last night?*

"I don't know," Neve replied. "I overheard Diana and Ellis arguing about the baby, and then I felt this strange pull. The geode in my pocket got hot, and when I touched your arm..."

Geode? What geode?

"It's complicated. It has something to do with time travel."

Time travel. Miles's thoughts were flat with disbelief. *Right. Of course. Why not? My body's been hijacked by a shape-shifting woman who believes in time travel.*

"Let's look in your messenger bag," Neve said. "The geode shard should be there."

Neve directed Miles's body back to the living room, where his leather messenger bag sat beside the pull-out couch. Inside, among notebooks, pens, press credentials, and a small tape recorder, was a jagged green crystal that seemed to pulse with inner light.

"That's it," Neve said, pointing. "That's the catalyst that caused this."

Time travel? Miles repeated. *Next, you'll tell me you're from the future.*

"Actually..." Neve began.

No, stop right there. I don't want to know.

"Okay," Neve said, nodding Miles's head as she scanned the room. "We need to find Perry."

Who's Perry?

"My parrot. He usually follows me when I... travel."

There's no parrot here.

Neve directed his gaze to the windowsill, where a single gray feather lay. "That's Perry's. He was here, but now he's gone."

Great. Just great. Miles's thoughts were bitter as Neve began gathering his things, stuffing them back into the messenger bag, and slinging the bag over Miles's shoulder.

Let's go home and figure this out.

As they left the apartment, locking the door behind them as requested, Neve felt a wave of disorientation. The world looked different from Miles's height. Colors were muted, scents less intense but somehow richer. The streets of Aura Cove baked under the late morning sun as Neve navigated Miles's unfamiliar body through the neighborhood. Each step felt like learning to walk again. His stride was shorter, and his feet felt heavier in their leather loafers.

"How far is your apartment?" Neve asked aloud, drawing a curious glance from a passing jogger.

About ten blocks north. AND COULD YOU PLEASE STOP TALKING TO YOURSELF IN PUBLIC? People are staring. Miles's thoughts came through with startling clarity, like he was speaking directly into her ear rather than communicating through the hazy filter of shared consciousness.

"Relax," she whispered. "This is all very disorienting."

You think YOU'RE disoriented? I'm a passenger in my

own body! His mental voice boomed, causing Neve to wince.

Unlike her previous experiences sharing consciousness with Rosa, Isla, and Donna, where the other woman's thoughts had been muted whispers that Neve could easily tune out, Miles's presence was dominating, loud, insistent, and impossible to ignore. His thoughts didn't politely wait their turn; they bull-dozed through her awareness with the subtlety of a freight train.

"Could you please tone it down?" Neve muttered. "You're practically shouting in my head."

I'm not shouting. This is how I think. Maybe if you'd LISTEN to me, we could sort this out faster.

Neve felt a flare of irritation. "I *am* listening. It's impossible not to with how loud and obnoxious you are."

Someone needs to take charge here, and since I'm the one with the most to lose...

"Take charge?" Neve stopped walking, drawing more curious glances. "Is that what you think this is about? You being 'in charge'?"

Mellow out. I'm just saying that, as the rightful owner of this body, my opinion should carry more weight. It's only logical.

"Logical?" Neve scoffed. "Or is it that you're used to being heard? To having your voice matter more?"

What's that supposed to mean?

"It means that you're coming through louder than Donna ever did, and I don't think it's a coincidence that you're a man," Neve said, resuming walking.

"You're used to taking up more space, to being listened to. Even as a passenger in your own body, you still expect to be the one calling the shots."

That's ridiculous. This has nothing to do with gender. It's MY body!

"And yet, when I shared consciousness with Donna, she was respectful, quiet, and collaborative. You, on the other hand, are demanding, obnoxious, and domineering despite the fact that neither of us has control over this situation."

Miles's thoughts went quiet for a moment, though Neve could feel his indignation simmering beneath the surface. When he finally responded, his mental voice was marginally softer but no less insistent.

Fine, maybe I am used to being heard. But that doesn't change the fact that I have more experience with this body than you do. Case in point: the bathroom incident.

Neve felt Miles's cheeks flush hot with shame. "That was a physiological challenge, not a gender issue."

All I'm saying is that we might make more progress if you'd defer to my expertise in certain areas. Is that so unreasonable?

"Defer?" Neve scowled as she spat the word out. "Interesting choice of words. Not 'collaborate' or 'work together', you want me to *defer*."

You're reading too much into this, Miles protested. *I just want some say in what happens.*

"So do I," Neve replied firmly. "But I don't expect you to defer to me. I expect us to figure this out together, as equals, regardless of whose body we happen to be occupying at the moment."

As they walked, Neve became increasingly aware of the geode in Miles's pocket. It seemed to pulse with warmth, like a heartbeat against his hip. When they approached the intersection of Palmetto Street and Harbor Avenue, the geode's warmth intensified dramatically.

"Wait," Neve said, stopping abruptly. "The geode. It's trying to tell me something."

Oh, for the love of Christ! You're communicating with a rock now? Miles's thoughts thundered through her consciousness.

Neve took a deep breath, trying to steel herself against his dominating presence. "This isn't about who's in control, Miles. This is about solving our problem. And like it or not, the geode is our guide."

Fine, but I'm registering my objection. Strongly.

"Duly noted," Neve replied dryly, turning left to follow the geode's pull. "Now, can we please focus on the task at hand instead of your fragile male ego?"

Miles's indignation flared again, but before he could respond, they found themselves standing in front of a weathered storefront with a faded sign reading "Marvin's Menagerie." The windows were partially obscured by dusty display cases and yellowing posters of exotic animals. A neon "OPEN" sign flickered like a strobe light in the window.

"This is it," Neve said, feeling the geode practically burning her skin. "We need to go in here."

A pet shop? You're letting a rock lead you to a seedy pet shop?

"It's not just any pet shop," Neve murmured, peering through the grimy window. "I think Perry might be in there."

Your time-traveling parrot? Of course. Of course.

A bell jingled as they entered, releasing a tsunami of offensive odor that hit Neve like a physical force. The scent of ammonia-soaked animal bedding, bird-seed, and mildew mixed with reefer assaulted Miles's nose. Neve staggered slightly, holding her hand over her nose and sucking in small sips of air through Miles's thick fingers.

"You okay there, buddy?" called a gravelly voice from behind the counter. "You look a little green around the gills."

Neve turned Miles's head to see a man in his sixties with a wild mane of white hair and thick glasses perched on a hooked nose. He wore a faded tie-dye t-shirt and was feeding something that looked suspiciously like a small octopus in a saltwater tank.

"I'm fine," Neve managed. "Just taking in the atmosphere."

That's one way to put it.

"Right on. First time at Marvin's Menagerie?" the old man asked, wiping his hands on a stained towel. "Most folks need a minute to adjust to the vibe. Got all sorts in here that you won't find anywhere else." He gestured expansively around the shop.

Indeed, the cramped space housed an astonishing variety of creatures. Glass terrariums lined one wall, containing everything from standard ball pythons to what appeared to be a two-headed lizard. Aquariums bubbled along another wall, home to tropical fish in a rainbow of colors. Cages of various sizes were stacked near the back, housing ferrets, chinchillas, and several rodent species Neve couldn't immediately identify.

But it was the sound coming from the far corner of cages that drew her attention, a familiar, sarcastic squawk that made her heart leap.

"Your bird section," Neve said, already moving toward the sound. "May I?"

"Help yourself," Marvin called. "Just don't stick your fingers in any cages. Some of 'em bite."

The bird area was dimly lit, with cages housing finches, canaries, cockatoos, and several larger parrots. But it was the African grey in the corner cage that caught Neve's eye. The gray feathers, scarlet tail, and gleam of intelligence in his black eyes seemed familiar.

As Miles approached, the parrot tilted his head in understanding, studying him with one unblinking eye. "Are you enjoying your testosterone tour, Nevermore?"

Neve gasped as relief flooded through her. "Perry? Is that really you?"

The parrot ruffled his feathers and bobbed his head up and down, chirping with relief. "In the feather, as it were. Though I must say, your new look leaves much to be desired. You appear to be engaged in the walk of shame without the pleasure of having earned it."

Neve pressed her lips together to prevent them

from quirking up ever so slightly. "How did you get here?" Neve asked, moving closer to the cage.

"One moment, I was watching you shift into the body of Mr. Personality here, and the next, I was waking up in this charming establishment, being offered sunflower seeds and subjected to 'Pretty Bird' cooing from Marvin over there." He gestured with his beak toward the shop owner.

This can't be happening. Birds don't talk like this. They mimic phrases, not carry on complete conversations.

"Oh, but we do, Mr. Internal Monologue," Perry said, cocking his head toward Miles's face with great interest. "At least, I do. I'm rather special."

It can hear my thoughts? Miles's mental voice rose in panic.

"Not all of them, thankfully," Perry replied. "Just the loud ones. And yours are practically screaming at the moment."

Marvin wandered over, eyeing the interaction with interest. "Right on, my dude. He seems to like you. That bird has gone full zen since he showed up this morning."

"Showed up?" Neve asked, turning Miles's body toward the shop owner.

"Yep. I thought I was trippin'," Marvin said, scratching his wild hair. "Came in to open the shop and there he was, sitting on the counter like he owned the place. No cage, no note, nothin'. Figured someone dumped him overnight."

"He hasn't spoken to you?" Neve asked.

"Not a peep," Marvin confirmed. "Been trying all

morning to get him to talk. African greys are supposed to be the best mimics. This one's just been staring at me like I'm wasted."

Perry confirmed his assessment with a whistle.

"I'd like to buy him," Neve blurted.

What? NO! Miles's thoughts protested vehemently. *You are NOT buying a bird!*

"Are you sure?" Marvin asked, raising bushy eyebrows. "African greys are a lifetime commitment. They live fifty to sixty years, need lots of attention, and require a specialized diet. Not cheap, either."

"I understand," Neve declared. "How much?"

STOP this right now, Miles demanded. *You have no right to spend my money!*

"Well, seeing as he just showed up and I haven't had to invest anything in him..." Marvin considered. "How about $600? That includes a decent cage and starter supplies."

"Deal," Neve said before Miles could mount further protests. She reached for his wallet, finding it in the back pocket of his pants, and relief washed over her when she saw the stash of cash inside.

This is theft, Miles fumed as Neve extracted and then counted the bills out one at a time. *I withdrew it yesterday to pay my rent. You're literally stealing from me!*

"I'll pay you back," Neve whispered.

$600 for a bird that insults me? This conversation is not over.

"Trust me," Neve said under her breath as she handed the cash to Marvin.

While Marvin tucked the bills into the drawer and

tore the paper receipt from the top of the register, Perry whistled and bobbed up and down in his cage. "Freedom!" he squawked. "Sweet, overpriced freedom!"

"Far out," Marvin exclaimed, placing the receipt in Miles's hand. "He does talk after all."

"Only when he has something worth saying," Neve replied with a smile.

This is INSANE.

Marvin busied himself gathering supplies: a bag of premium parrot food, toys, treats, and a book on African grey care. "You'll need these," he said, placing everything in a bag. "And here's your new friend."

The parrot immediately walked up Miles's forearm and perched on his shoulder.

"Thank you," Neve said, taking the cage in one hand and the supplies in the other. The weight was awkward in Miles's larger hands, but she managed to balance everything.

"Good luck," Marvin called as they headed for the door. "Bring him back for a nail trim in about a month!"

Once outside on the sidewalk, Miles's internal protests reached a fever pitch.

This is absolutely the LAST STRAW. You've hijacked my body, humiliated me in the bathroom, and now you've spent $600 of my money on a sarcastic bird. What's next? Are you going to sublease my apartment and become Charlie's fourth angel?

"Would you please calm down?" Neve said,

adjusting her grip on the cage. "Perry is an important ally."

"Indeed, I am," Perry agreed, flapping his wings in defiance. "That cage is an abomination. A serious downgrade from my previous domicile."

"It's just temporary," Neve promised. "If you're good, I'll order that play gym from Alexa when we get home."

This is ridiculous. I'm standing on a public street, listening to a woman who's invaded my body, bribe a bird for good behavior.

"Your internal companion has a point," Perry observed. "Perhaps this conversation would be better continued in a more private setting? Unless you enjoy looking like a lunatic talking to a parrot on Harbor Avenue."

Neve glanced around, suddenly aware of the curious stares from passersby. "You're right. Miles, which way to your apartment?"

Three more blocks north, then right on Bayshore. The brick building with the green awnings. Apartment 3B. Though I'm seriously reconsidering giving you this information.

"The sooner we figure this out, the sooner you get your body back."

Fine, but that bird is NOT sleeping in my bedroom.

"I wouldn't dream of it," Perry scoffed. "I have standards, you know."

CHAPTER

THIRTY-SEVEN

Miles's apartment contained a forest of dying plants, a typewriter surrounded by crumpled papers, and enough half-empty coffee cups to suggest a serious caffeine addiction. The brown shag carpet looked like a yarn toupee, and the avocado-green stove was covered with crumbs and congealed cheese.

Neve stood before the mirror in Miles's bedroom, practicing her dialogue before making the phone call. "Hello, Dr. Manning. Miles Murphy from the Hastings Award Selection Committee."

That's terrible, Miles's thoughts interrupted. *You sound like you're reciting names from a phone book. More confidence, less robotic.*

"I'm trying," Neve muttered, adjusting Miles's tie for the third time that felt like it was choking her.

Perry watched from his perch atop a dusty bookshelf, his head tilted in amusement. "Perhaps try channeling your inner academic elitist? Self-important, pompous blowhard is the tone we are going for."

Hey! I resent that, Miles protested.

"You resent everything." Neve sighed, picking up the phone. "Now please, both of you, be quiet while I make this call."

She dialed Aureon Biomedical's main switchboard, her heart pounding as Miles's larger fingers spun the rotary dial. After two rings, a crisp female voice answered. "Aureon Biomedical, how may I direct your call?"

"Miles Murphy from the Hastings Award Selection Committee," Neve said, deepening Miles's voice slightly, leaning into assertiveness. "I'd like to speak with Dr. Manning regarding his potential nomination for this year's Ethics in Medicine Award."

Better, Miles approved. *But stand up straighter and spread your legs. Take up space. Command authority.*

After a brief hold, Conrad's familiar voice came through the line. "Dr. Manning speaking."

"Dr. Manning, Miles Murphy here. The Hastings Award Committee has taken note of your recent ethical stance in medical research, particularly your recent crusade against dangerous cancer treatment protocols. I'm calling to inform you we're considering you for this year's Ethics in Medicine Award."

Perry fluttered to the desk, landed beside the phone, and whispered with glee, "Oh, he'll love this. You dangle that prestigious carrot in front of his face like it's made of solid gold."

"I'm honored," Conrad replied, his interest obvious. "Though I didn't do anything extraordinary. I simply followed my conscience."

"Your modesty is admirable," Neve said, fighting to keep the sarcasm from dripping into Miles's tone. "But standing up against a respected colleague and risking your own career to protect public safety is exactly the kind of ethical leadership the Hastings Award celebrates."

Now you're getting it, Miles praised.

"Well, when you put it that way..." Conrad's tone warmed. "Though I should mention I'm preparing for a rather significant announcement next week. I've accepted a new position at NovaCure and will be working with them to patent a recent treatment breakthrough I've made. "

"Perfect timing, actually," Neve replied. "This would coincide beautifully with your upcoming news. However, we do require a preliminary interview with all potential candidates."

Perry made a gagging sound. "That man's ego is so inflated, he could float in the Macy's Thanksgiving parade."

Will you shut that bird up? Miles demanded. *He's going to ruin everything!*

But Conrad was already taking the bait. "Perhaps we could meet on Friday? I have a full schedule with NovaCure next week."

"Friday would be ideal," Neve said, shooting Perry a warning glare. "Shall we say 10 AM at the Tampa Bay Grand Hotel?"

"The Grand? Yes, I believe I can make that work," Conrad agreed, practically gushing with delight through the phone line. "I look forward to discussing my commitment to ethical research practices with you at that time."

After confirming the details and hanging up, Neve collapsed onto Miles's worn sofa. "I feel like I need a shower after that conversation."

"Given your earlier bathroom adventures, perhaps you should skip that particular challenge," Perry pointed out.

Neve blanched at the thought. She'd have to take a shower sooner or later but decided later was preferable.

For once, I agree with the bird, Miles thought. *Now can we please have some lunch and focus on not completely destroying my career?*

Later that evening, Neve met the group at the Tampa Bay Grand Hotel. Dark wood paneling lined the back wall of the executive conference room, and the other three walls featured geometric-patterned wallpaper in shades of burnt orange and harvest gold. An elaborate crystal and brass chandelier dominated the center of the room, its light reflecting off the polished surface of a twenty-foot mahogany conference table. Heavy velvet drapes in chocolate brown framed floor-to-ceiling windows overlooking Tampa Bay.

"The camera will go here," Diana's uncle George said, tapping a bulky tripod. "And feed to a Nagra reel-to-reel analog tape recorder in the adjoining control room." He grinned, clearly proud of his technical expertise.

This better work, Miles's fears echoed in Neve's head. *My reputation is on the line.*

"Everyone's career is on the line," Neve answered his threat under her breath.

Perry, who was perched on the chandelier despite everyone's protests, offered his perspective. "At least the décor is appropriately pretentious. Nothing says 'prestigious medical ethics award' quite like enough mahogany to deforest a third-world country."

Dr. Samuel Whitmore arrived the next day. His silver hair lent an experienced gravitas, and his distinguished demeanor calmed everyone's frazzled nerves.

"You know, Robert was like a son to me," he told Elaine, his voice thick with emotion. "When he walked into my classroom the first day, I knew he was special. His dedication to ethical research on animals and fighting animal cruelty was legendary." He paused, collecting himself. "You have my word, Conrad Manning will not get away with this."

The group gathered at Diana and Donna's apartment each evening, surrounded by takeout containers and scattered papers, crafting the perfect trap. Donna's background player demeanor had shifted into fierce resolve as she and Ellis created pamphlets and supporting documentation that could withstand Conrad's intense scrutiny.

"The letterhead needs to be perfect," Donna insisted, her hands steady as she worked with the transfer letters. "Conrad will notice if anything is off.

He once spent an entire staff meeting critiquing the kerning in our quarterly reports." Neve was struck by her newfound confidence and wondered if their time sharing a consciousness had anything to do with it.

"Speaking of off," Perry commented from his perch on Elaine's forearm, "does our dear Dr. Manning have any tells?"

She reached over to give Perry the head scritches he adored. "Yes, you brilliant boy!"

Perry tittered with joy, puffing his feathers and crowing with pride.

"Conrad has a fascinating linguistic pattern when he's lying," Elaine explained, her analytical mind engaged. "He uses specific phrases that I've documented over the years. When he's about to present questionable data, he starts with 'Obviously, to anyone with proper training...' or 'As any competent researcher would understand...'"

She spread out several meeting transcripts on the table to prove her point. "But his most telling phrase is when he begins a statement with 'The literature clearly shows...' followed by 'it's quite elementary.' That combination? It's his way of establishing authority while dismissing potential questions. The more he emphasizes how basic or fundamental something is, the more likely he's hiding some sort of complex manipulation."

"Watch for his use of unwarranted academic jargon, too," Ellis added. "He'll suddenly start using words like paradigmatic and methodological framework when a simple explanation would suffice."

"It's a classic misdirection technique," Elaine continued, twirling a wild curl from the nape of her neck around her finger. "He buries his lies under layers of academic pomposity, making others feel intellectually inferior for questioning him. Once, he spent ten minutes explaining a simple calibration process using terms even I had to look up, all to hide the fact he'd forgotten to log the pressure readings."

Perry fluffed his feathers on his perch. "Ah, yes, the old 'if I can't dazzle them with brilliance, I'll baffle them with bullshit' approach. A favorite among academics and politicians alike."

Elaine pulled a packet of papers out of her bag and slid them over to Miles. "The key is to approach the pressure calibration issue from a back door," she explained, scribbling notes. "Start with an ethics discussion of the standard protocols, then gradually lead him into revealing his knowledge of the specific alterations."

"Like a scientific cross-examination." Neve nodded, making notes.

"Exactly," Elaine confirmed. "He won't be able to resist demonstrating his expertise."

Neve read through the questions to practice her interview techniques. "The Hastings Award for Ethics in Medicine," she rehearsed, trying to get acclimated to Miles's deeper voice but failing and becoming more melodramatic as she continued. "Recognizing those who uphold the highest standards of medical ethics."

Less pompous, Miles's thoughts interrupted. *You sound like you're announcing a royal proclamation.*

"I'm trying to sound authoritative," Neve protested, getting frustrated by Miles's constant criticism.

"Try for distinguished but approachable." Perry offered helpfully.

Diana's brow creased as she worked on the documentation. "What if he calls to verify his nomination with the real award committee in New York?"

"I doubt he'd make that call. Conrad's ego would never let him doubt his selection. Besides, he won't have the time," Ellis assured her. "The interview is Friday, and he's meeting with NovaCure on Monday."

The night before the interview, they gathered for a final review. The conference room was ready, recording equipment set up, and the award documentation was flawless. Dr. Whitmore had assembled two other respected physicians to serve on the panel, both with personal stakes in exposing research fraud and well-versed in ethics.

"Remember," Elaine instructed, her voice stronger than it had been in weeks, "Conrad's weakness is his certainty that he's the smartest person in any room. He'll want to demonstrate his superior intellect and understanding of the protocols. If we're patient, he'll hang himself with his own words."

"And if we're successful," Ellis added, "he'll reveal technical details that only someone who tampered with the equipment would know."

Focus on the prestige of the award, Miles's thoughts interrupted. *His eagerness to impress the selection committee might make him careless.*

Neve nodded Miles's head, feeling the weight of tomorrow's performance settling over her. As they prepared to leave, Dr. Whitmore pulled Neve aside. "Are you sure you're up for this?" he asked, his keen eyes studying Miles's face. "Manning is no fool. One slip in your performance…"

"I'm ready," Neve assured him, squaring Miles's broader shoulders. "We all are. I understand what's at stake here, not just for Elaine and Robert's memory, but for the doctors on the panel too."

Neve excused herself and went back to Miles's apartment with Perry to practice her questions. She studied them for over an hour, committing them to memory, before she got into bed for the night. The doubts and fears queued up the second she closed her eyes.

This could be career suicide, Miles's fear bubbled up, mingling with her own lingering doubts.

"No, this story is a career *launcher.*" Neve emphasized, trying to put him at ease by tapping into Miles's never-ending well of ambition. "Think about it. Once we expose Conrad, you can write an exclusive that *The New Yorker* would pay dearly to publish. This isn't just justice for Robert; it's the kind of investigative journalism that wins awards."

Miles's consciousness perked up at the thought. *You really think* The New Yorker *would be interested?*

"Interested? They'll be competing with *The Atlantic* and *Harper's* for it," Neve continued, feeling Miles's exuberance swell. "Scientific fraud, corporate conspiracy, a brilliant researcher's reputation destroyed? This might even lead to a book deal."

A book deal, Miles's thoughts echoed, his internal voice warming with ambition. *'The Manning Deception' by Miles Murphy. I can see the cover now.*

"Assuming we all survive tomorrow's performance," Perry chirped from the cage next to the bed. "Though I must say, nothing screams international bestseller quite like a wrongful death via treatment tampering. Everyone adores a scandal."

"Let's focus on getting through the interview first," Neve stretched, feeling the tension in the room shift as she settled into the bed with a yawn. "Then you can help Miles draft his acceptance speech for his Pulitzer."

CHAPTER

THIRTY-EIGHT

MORNING SUNLIGHT FILTERED through the heavy drapes of the Tampa Bay Grand Hotel's executive conference room, casting amber patterns across the polished mahogany table. Neve adjusted Miles's tie for the fourth time, her hands unsteady. The reflection in the mirrored wall showed a man in his early thirties, his beard trimmed neater than usual, wearing a borrowed navy blazer.

"Stop fidgeting," Perry advised from his perch atop a nearby credenza. "You look like a schoolboy awaiting the principal's wrath."

He's right, Miles's thoughts intruded. *Confidence is key. Prestigious Award committee members don't fidget.*

"I know that," Neve muttered, smoothing Miles's stubborn cowlick. "But in case you haven't noticed, I'm not experienced in conducting high-stakes scientific entrapment."

Diana's uncle George emerged from behind the wood paneling, wiping his hands on a handkerchief.

"Final check of the recording equipment is complete. We've got three microphones positioned strategically: one near where Manning will sit, one by the panel, and one central unit as backup." He tapped the wall. "All feeding to the analog recorder in the service room next door. The sound quality is crystal clear."

Dr. Whitmore entered, followed by Dr. Helen Briscoe, an oncologist from Johns Hopkins, and Dr. James Monroe, a medical ethicist from Columbia.

"Is everything prepared?" Dr. Whitmore asked, surveying the room.

"Yes," Neve replied, unconsciously projecting Miles's deep voice as if she were on stage. "The recording equipment is set, and we just did the sound check."

Relax, Jack. You're doing it again, Miles interrupted. *Nobody sounds like that outside of community theatre.*

Neve cleared her throat, adjusting to Miles's natural tone. "Sorry. Yes, we're ready. Conrad should arrive in about twenty minutes."

Dr. Whitmore nodded, placing his briefcase on the table. "Remember, this isn't just about outing a liar and a fraud. It's about getting justice for Robert." His voice caught on Robert's name. "And Elaine." He locked eyes with the other two physicians. "Helen and James, Elaine has brought me up to speed on the broad strokes of the protocol, but I'm sure we can agree, your expertise will be critical in gathering the information we need."

"Yes," Dr. Briscoe and Dr. Monroe nodded in unison.

"Begin with these questions about ethics," Dr. Monroe suggested, handing a list to Neve. "Let him establish his moral high ground before we delve into the technical details."

"Agreed," Dr. Briscoe added. "His pride in being the 'ethical whistleblower' should make him comfortable enough to reveal more than he intends."

"Then segue into the questions Elaine has prepared," Dr. Whitmore advised. "They should lead him gradually toward self-incrimination without raising his suspicions."

They bent their heads closer and continued to confer together while Neve excused herself under the guise of using the bathroom. She walked to the hall and paced the length of it in Miles's longer stride. "What if I say something that tips him off?"

That's MY concern, too.

Perry flew to Neve's shoulder, his weight unfamiliar on Miles's broader frame. "Listen to me, both of you," the parrot said, his chirp gentle as he delivered a pep talk. "You are more than capable. Neve, you've navigated multiple time periods and shared consciousnesses with excellence. Trust your instincts. Miles, as a journalist, your gift lies in drawing people out and distilling the truth. Leave the science to the doctors. Together, you're the dream team."

Neve felt Miles's consciousness soften at the unexpected support.

The bird's right. We've got this. Just ask the questions we've been given.

Neve returned to the conference room, and Perry

flew back to Elaine, who was waiting in the control room. George quickly verified that the recording equipment was running before slipping out through a side door.

"Places, everyone," Dr. Whitmore murmured, taking his seat at the head of the table.

A few minutes later, Conrad Manning entered the conference room with a confident stride. His once-shaggy brown hair was now expertly styled, and his blue eyes blazed thanks to his decision to upgrade to a tailored charcoal suit. Everything about him now exuded calculated sophistication.

"Dr. Manning," Neve said, extending Miles's hand. "Miles Murphy, chair of the Hastings Award Selection Committee. Thank you for joining us today."

Conrad's handshake was firm, his smile practiced. "The pleasure is mine, Mr. Murphy. Being considered for the Hastings is an honor I never anticipated."

"Yet thoroughly deserve," Neve replied, gesturing toward the panel. "Allow me to introduce our distinguished committee members. You already know Dr. Samuel Whitmore."

"Hello again." Dr. Whitmore shot him a warm smile.

"And this is Dr. Helen Briscoe from Johns Hopkins, and Dr. James Monroe from Columbia." Neve waved a hand toward the boxy video camera sitting on the tripod, "And fair warning, we'll be recording this interview to aid our final selection process."

Conrad gave a respectful nod to each as a momentary tension hung in the air before Neve directed him to his seat.

"Before we begin, Dr. Manning, I want to emphasize that this preliminary interview is an opportunity for us to understand the ethical framework that guides you. The Hastings Award recognizes not just scientific achievement, but moral courage in medical research."

Conrad settled into his chair, straightening his tie. "Of course. In my view, ethical considerations must always supersede scientific ambition. That principle has guided my entire career."

Whoa. He's already laying it on thick.

"Perhaps we could begin with your background," Neve suggested, offering him a warm smile. "Your journey to becoming such a staunch advocate for research ethics."

Conrad leaned back, already comfortable with the topic. "My commitment to ethical research began during my doctoral work at MIT. I witnessed firsthand how easily scientific zeal can override proper protocols." He paused as if it pained him to continue. "When I joined Dr. Feldman's lab three years ago, I admired her brilliance but grew concerned by what I perceived as increasingly unorthodox methodologies."

"Could you elaborate on how that principle influenced your recent actions?" Neve asked, with Miles's lucky pen poised above his notepad.

"Certainly," Conrad replied, warming to the subject. "Obviously, to any competent researcher, the integrity of experimental design is sacrosanct. Dr. Feldman's early work was impeccable, but as her husband's condition deteriorated, I observed troubling patterns. Data inconsistencies. Protocol deviations. Safety parameters that were ignored."

Neve noted the first verbal tell—"Obviously, to any competent researcher"—exactly as Elaine had predicted.

He continued, "When I discovered unauthorized human experiments, I had no choice but to act."

"That must have placed you in a difficult position," Dr. Monroe prompted. "Challenging a respected senior colleague."

Conrad's expression shifted to one of practiced humility. "It was the most difficult decision of my career. But ultimately, science must be governed by facts, not emotions."

"You exhibited commendable moral courage," Dr. Whitmore said, his tone neutral despite the tightness around his eyes.

Dr. Briscoe leaned forward, her scientific curiosity evident. "Speaking of the science, I must admit to some professional interest in Protocol VitOx. The concept itself seems promising."

"Indeed." Conrad brightened, clearly eager to display his expertise. "The concept itself had merit. It relied on high-dose vitamin C to generate hydrogen peroxide selectively in cancer cells. It's the execution that was fundamentally flawed."

He's getting comfortable, Miles noted. *Time to steer toward the technical details.*

"The hyperbaric component was particularly

interesting," Dr. Briscoe said. "I understand there were safety concerns?"

"Absolutely." Conrad nodded eagerly. "The hyperbaric chamber requires precise calibration. It's quite elementary, really. The pressure differentials must be maintained within specific parameters to avoid oxygen toxicity."

Neve leaned forward. "For those of us less familiar with hyperbaric technology, could you explain the safety protocols?"

Conrad's smile widened, clearly relishing the opportunity to display his knowledge. "Of course. Standard hyperbaric chambers typically operate at pressures between one point five and three point zero atmospheres. The therapeutic window for cancer treatment would theoretically be around two point five atmospheres."

"And the safety margins?" Dr. Briscoe inquired innocently.

"This is where Dr. Feldman's protocol was flawed," Conrad replied, leaning forward as his voice lowered an octave. "She was pushing the pressures to the absolute limit of the safety envelope. The calibration curves require precise adjustments to account for barometric variations."

Neve exchanged a subtle glance with Dr. Whitmore. Conrad had just revealed detailed knowledge of calibration procedures that wouldn't be part of standard protocol documentation.

"Fascinating," Neve said. "Could you elaborate on those calibration procedures? For our records."

Conrad launched into an explanation, his vocabulary growing increasingly technical. "The pressure transducers utilize a strain gauge connected to a Wheatstone bridge circuit. By adjusting the trim potentiometers, one can create a variance between the actual chamber pressure and the displayed reading."

Did you catch that? Miles interjected, his excitement sending a rush of adrenaline through his body. *He just described exactly how to tamper with the equipment!*

Neve maintained Miles's neutral expression with focused effort. "And these adjustments, would they be part of standard maintenance?"

"No," Conrad scoffed. "They're usually sealed after factory calibration. Modifying them would require specialized knowledge and deliberate intent."

"Just to clarify," Dr. Whitmore interjected, "you're suggesting Dr. Feldman intentionally altered these calibrations?"

Conrad paused, realizing his potential misstep. "I can't be certain. It's possible her deteriorating emotional state led to carelessness. The point is, the chamber was operating at dangerous pressures while displaying normal readings."

"Let's discuss the vitamin C component," Dr. Briscoe suggested. "I understand there were issues with the oxidative stress mechanism?"

Conrad's confidence bounced right back. "Yes, the fundamental principle is sound. Vitamin C at pharmacological concentrations selectively damages cancer cells due to their reduced catalase activity."

"Catalase?" Neve prompted as if unfamiliar with the term.

"An enzyme that breaks down hydrogen peroxide," Conrad explained. "Normal cells have abundant catalase, protecting them from oxidative damage. Cancer cells have reduced levels, making them vulnerable to the peroxide generated by high-dose vitamin C."

Dr. Monroe made a note. "And Dr. Feldman's protocol failed to account for this?"

"I wouldn't put it that way." Conrad shifted on his chair. "Her timing was off. The literature clearly shows the critical relationship between vitamin C administration and hyperbaric oxygen exposure. She insisted on a forty-seven-minute interval, which was shown to be ineffective."

"Why forty-seven minutes?" Neve asked.

Conrad's expression turned smug. "A complete misinterpretation of the pharmacokinetics. Vitamin C reaches peak plasma concentration within thirty minutes of IV administration. By waiting forty-seven minutes, you're already losing the optimal oxidative potential."

Dr. Whitmore leaned forward. "Our understanding was that the delayed timing allowed for the initial generation of hydrogen peroxide metabolites before enhanced oxygen exposure."

"A common misconception," Conrad dismissed with a wave of his hand. "The efficacy window is much narrower. Of course, introducing exogenous catalase would neutralize the effect entirely, regardless of timing."

He just admitted to knowing how to sabotage the treatment! Miles was practically shouting.

"Speaking of modified protocols," Dr. Monroe interjected smoothly, "we understand you've been consulting with NovaCure Pharmaceuticals?"

Conrad's eyes lit up at the mention. "Yes, they've shown considerable interest in my refined approach to oxidative therapy. Naturally, the protocol requires significant modifications from Dr. Feldman's original concept to ensure both safety and efficacy."

"Naturally," Neve echoed. "Could you elaborate on these refinements? The committee is particularly interested in ethical improvements to existing methodologies."

"Of course," Conrad replied, clearly eager to impress. "My approach maintains the basic mechanism while implementing crucial safeguards. The timing sequence is optimized to thirty minutes rather than forty-seven. The pressure calibration is standardized to prevent dangerous fluctuations."

"And the results?" Dr. Monroe prompted.

"Promising, though less dramatic than Feldman's claimed outcomes," Conrad admitted. "But a treatment that extends life by months rather than years is still valuable, especially if it can be administered safely."

Months rather than years, Miles repeated internally. *He's deliberately weakening the protocol.*

"Let's return to Dr. Robert Feldman's case," Dr. Whitmore said, with admirable clinical detachment. "You were present during his last treatment?"

"No," Conrad corrected. "I discovered what happened afterward. The seizure that killed him was a textbook presentation of central nervous system oxygen toxicity."

"Could you explain that process for our records?" Neve asked.

Conrad nodded. "At pressures above three point zero atmospheres, oxygen becomes neurotoxic. Robert's chamber was reading two point five atmospheres, but was actually delivering close to four point zero atmospheres."

Dr. Whitmore's pen stilled. "How could you possibly know the actual pressure if you weren't present?"

Conrad froze, his eyes flicking to the camera, then recovered. "Based on the symptom presentation and timing, when I reconstructed the events afterward," he rushed to explain, a slight flush creeping up his neck. "The symptom pattern was consistent with exposure to approximately four point zero atmospheres of pressure."

"That's remarkably specific," Dr. Monroe noted.

"Well, I am thorough in my investigations," Conrad replied, his confidence visibly wavering for the first time.

Neve leaned forward, sensing the moment to spring the final trap. "Dr. Manning, would you say your expertise in hyperbaric calibration predates Dr. Feldman's work with the vitamin C protocol?"

"Certainly," Conrad replied, eager to reestablish his authority. "I have an extensive engineering background. In fact, Dr. Feldman tapped me to lead the maintenance of the hyperbaric chamber."

"Including the pressure calibration systems?" Neve pressed.

"Of course. Regular maintenance is essential for safety."

Dr. Whitmore's voice cut through the room like ice. "Interesting, considering the maintenance logs show no authorized calibration work during the ninety days prior to Robert's death."

Conrad's confidence faltered. "I, um... there must be a mistake in the documentation."

Before he could engineer a plausible explanation, Neve moved on. "One last question," She said, keeping Miles's tone casual. "You mentioned that exogenous catalase would neutralize the vitamin C effect. Is that something you've incorporated into your NovaCure protocol?"

"I've suggested controlled catalase administration as a safety mechanism," Conrad replied carefully. "Obviously, to any serious researcher, having an antidote to oxidative stress is prudent."

"And would bovine catalase be suitable for this purpose?" Dr. Briscoe asked innocently.

Conrad nodded, relaxing slightly at the technical question. "Yes, bovine liver catalase is readily available and highly effective at hydrogen peroxide degradation."

"Fascinating," Dr. Whitmore nodded, making a note. "Your insights into the technical aspects of the protocol are quite illuminating, Dr. Manning."

Conrad leaned back in his chair, a satisfied smile playing at the corners of his mouth. "I've always believed that true scientific advancement requires both innovation and caution. My refinements to Dr. Feldman's protocol represent that balance."

"I think we have everything we need," Neve said, rising from her chair with Miles's practiced professionalism. "The committee will deliberate, but I must say your command of the technical details is phenomenal."

Conrad stood, straightening his tailored jacket. "When might I expect to hear the committee's decision?"

"Very soon," Dr. Briscoe assured him with a polite smile. "Your candidacy has certainly given us much to consider."

Conrad shook each of their hands, his grip firm and confident. "I appreciate the opportunity. Should you require any further clarification on the technical aspects, I'm at your disposal."

"I'm sure we have more than enough," Dr. Monroe replied with a tight nod.

After buttoning his jacket, Conrad strode from the room, shoulders squared with the certainty of a man who believed he'd impressed his audience.

The moment the door clicked shut, Neve exhaled Miles's breath in a long, shaky stream.

As she entered the adjacent control room, Elaine's fingers flew across the reel-to-reel tape controls, rewinding to specific timestamps. Her mismatched socks, one navy, one forest green, peeked out beneath her slacks as she swung her leg forward and back, unable to contain her energy.

"Did we get it?"

"I believe we did," she said, her tone matter-of-fact as if the full realization hadn't hit her yet. "Multiple technical admissions. Timestamp 14:22, detailed knowledge of pressure calibration tampering. Time-stamp 19:07, specific admission regarding catalase introduction."

George removed his headphones, grinning. "Crystal clear audio on all three mics. Even caught that little condescending scoff when he said, 'it's quite elementary.'"

Perry fluttered over to land on Miles's shoulder. "You did it! That pompous peacock preened himself right into a confession!"

Dr. Whitmore replayed a section of tape, his expression grim but satisfied. "His description of adjusting the trim potentiometers is damning. Only someone who had tampered with the equipment would know those specifics."

"And the catalase admission?" Neve asked.

Dr. Briscoe nodded. "Textbook self-incrimination. He explicitly described how bovine catalase would neutralize the treatment's effectiveness, knowledge he wouldn't have unless he'd used it himself."

"Is it enough?" Diana asked, emerging from the corner where she'd been observing.

"More than enough," Dr. Whitmore confirmed, his voice tight with emotion. "Conrad provided specific technical details that weren't in any documentation.

His theory that excessive pressure caused Robert's seizure, when he claimed not to be present, implicates him."

Miles's consciousness was vibrating with excitement. *You're right. This is it. The story of a lifetime.*

"I'll start the article immediately," Neve said, Miles's journalistic instincts taking over. "I can have a first draft ready by morning and the final copy to my editor at the *Tampa Tribune* by tomorrow afternoon."

Dr. Whitmore nodded. "My college roommate works at *The New Yorker*. Once it breaks in Tampa, I can make sure it gets picked up for national syndication."

"National?" Neve felt Miles's heart race at the prospect. "That would be incredible."

Pulitzer. This could be a Pulitzer. Miles's thoughts raced. *This is the exposé that I've been dreaming for my entire career.*

"I won't sleep until it's done," Neve promised, Miles's ambition flooding through her. "We'll need to frame it carefully, focus on the technical evidence without tipping our hand about how we obtained it. The pressure tampering details alone are gold."

Dr. Briscoe smiled. "The scientific community will validate sabotage led to Robert's death. Once other researchers see Manning's refinements to the original protocol, they'll also recognize he deliberately weakened a promising treatment."

"And the timing is perfect," Diana added. "Nova-Cure will be forced to pull their offer when the story breaks. They won't want to touch Conrad with a ten-foot pole."

Miles's journalistic mind was already organizing the story structure. *Lead with Robert's death. Then Elaine's disgrace. Build to Manning's corporate connections. End with the smoking gun—his technical knowledge of the sabotage.*

"I'll need quotes from each of you," Neve said, pulling out Miles's reporter's notebook. "On-the-record about the science, off-the-record about today's meeting. And Dr. Feldman, I'll need everything you have on the original protocol's efficacy."

"Of course."

"By this time Monday, Conrad Manning's reputation will be in free fall, and the world will know what he did," Neve assured them, Miles's confidence unwavering.

Elaine gave a sad nod, her lips pressed into a solid line. "It won't bring Robert back, but it will give him the justice he deserves."

Nearby, Perry bobbed his head with glee as he flapped his wings and strutted across the table. "Oh, how I adore the sweet scent of triumph in the morning!"

CHAPTER 39
PEREGRINE

I watched from my perch atop Miles's bursting bookshelves as Neve struggled with Miles's meaty fingers on the typewriter keys. The cacophonous clacking from the machine blasted through the apartment like machine-gun fire. There were staccato bursts followed by the aggressive ding of the carriage return, then a frustrated groan as Miles yanked the paper out and crumpled it into yet another ball for the growing collection on the floor.

"Perhaps some sustenance might lubricate the creative process?" I suggested, eyeing the kitchen with hunger. "A bird of my intellectual caliber requires proper nutrition to dispense wisdom. Some of those imported pistachios I spotted in your pantry would do the trick. Or at minimum, a wedge of that aged Gouda in your refrigerator?"

"Aren't you lactose intolerant?" Neve reminded me in Miles's considerably deeper voice. He began typing again, then immediately backspaced with enough force to damage the machine.

"Technically, it's toxic, but I'm willing to risk it." I flapped my wings in frustration.

"I'm not," Neve retorted, shutting me down immediately. "*You* need to entertain yourself. And *I* need to focus so I can coerce this archaic machine into submission! I hate this thing." He let out an anxious groan.

"Let me see if I can assist," I said, gliding down to perch on the back of the chair. For the next few seconds, I scanned the page over Miles's shoulder, finding the issue. "Are you writing a hard-hitting investigative journalist piece or a movie review? You must know, *The New Yorker* will not take you seriously when you start with 'In the hallowed halls of medical research, a wicked serpent lurked.' While I always appreciate a solid biblical reference, it *is* rather melodramatic."

Miles's face scowled at me, but I also noticed Neve's grateful smirk teasing at the corners of Miles's mouth.

"Perry's right," Miles conceded as he pushed his chair back from the desk and began pacing, clamping down on the pen in his mouth.

"What about 'Death by Degrees: How Academic Ambition Killed a Breakthrough'?" I offered, preening my wing feathers with practiced nonchalance.

"Too sensational," Neve said, running a hand through Miles's already disheveled hair. There was another frustrated groan, and then I heard, "Now it's not sensational enough!" She argued with herself as

Miles's fist suddenly slammed down on the desk, startling us both.

I let out a dramatic sigh, fluffing my feathers for maximum effect. "Humans. Always making simple things complicated. Why not just 'Bad Doctor Does Bad Things, Details Below? Direct, punchy, and impossible to misinterpret."

Neve snorted through Miles's nose, a most unattractive sound. "We need something with substance." He shook the tension from his body and then added, seemingly against his will, "And journalistic integrity."

Three hours and four pots of coffee later, Miles's body was vibrating with caffeine and frustration. The apartment had taken on the ambiance of a disorganized newspaper bullpen, with sheets of paper bearing half-sentences scattered across every surface. The typewriter keys were now making a concerning sticky sound from the combined assault of overuse and spilled coffee.

Neve wanted to focus on the technical evidence, but Miles insisted on building dramatic tension. Their battle had devolved into Miles's body typing a sentence, then immediately crossing it out, then retyping a variation, then crossing that out too.

"May I remind you both," I interjected from the perch on top of my cage where I'd retreated for safety, "that while you're arguing about Oxford commas, Conrad is probably shredding evidence and practicing his innocent face in the mirror?"

Neve looked up at me, eyes bleary from strain. "We

need a title that captures the gravity of the situation without over-sensationalizing it."

I took flight, circling the room once before landing with panache on the typewriter carriage. "The Fatal Price of Ambition," I declared with a grand sweep of my wings as I took a small bow.

Neve fell silent. The body they shared became perfectly still.

"It's perfect," he said, then Miles continued to mutter under his breath, seeming to start another argument about the subtitle.

"While you two continue this fascinating exercise in shared consciousness dysfunction, I'll just be over here composing limericks about fraudulent scientists. There once was a doctor named Manning, whose ethics were really quite lacking..." Miles let out a groan. Everyone's a critic.

The night progressed in fits and starts. Paragraphs emerged, were dissected, reconstructed, and occasionally sacrificed to the god of journalistic integrity. I offered commentary from various perches around the apartment, suggesting brilliant turns of phrase that were summarily ignored, then somehow reappeared in an altered form minutes later.

Miles's hands hovered over the typewriter as Neve hesitated to type his next sentence. "You can't accuse NovaCure of wrongdoing," she protested through his mouth. "We'll be sued!" Miles's thoughts must have thundered back about being complicit and speaking truth to power, because his face flushed red and a vein began throbbing at his temple.

"Might I suggest," I offered, side-stepping around coffee cups to reach them, "that sometimes the art of revelation lies in what's left unsaid? Let the readers connect the incriminating dots themselves."

By midnight, Miles's shirt was untucked, his tie askew, and crumpled paper littered the floor like over-sized confetti. The typewriter let out a triumphant zing with each carriage return, and the article was taking shape, powerful, incisive, and damning without being legally actionable.

I noticed that Neve had grown quieter, letting Miles's journalistic instincts take over more. His body moved with increasing confidence, fingers flying across the keys.

"It's his career," I heard Neve remind herself with a whisper. "His future. I'm just visiting."

I hopped closer, offering what comfort a bird can give to a woman trapped in a man's body. "Some-times," I murmured, "the best way to help someone is to let them help themselves. Much like how you could help me by offering a small midnight snack. Even a saltine would suffice at this desperate hour."

She smiled Miles's smile at me, a gentler expres-sion than his face often wore. "There are some nuts in the kitchen cabinet."

"Bless you," I replied, taking to the air and flying toward the kitchen. "Your generosity shall be forever immortalized in avian oral history."

Dawn broke through the grimy windows as Miles's fingers typed the last period. The article was pure Miles—passionate, hard-hitting, and uncompromising. Neve had retreated to a corner of his consciousness, but I caught her satisfaction in the slight softening around his eyes.

They'd done it. Together, though neither would admit it. The article before them would change lives, restore reputations, and possibly end careers. Not bad for a night's work.

"Well," I announced, fluttering to the desk, my belly pleasantly full of the mixed nuts I'd finally been granted access to, "shall we celebrate with breakfast? I hear the early bird gets the worm, though personally, I prefer croissants. Perhaps from that little bakery on 7th Street? The one with the delightful pain au chocolate and those raspberry danishes that achieve the perfect balance between tart and sweet?"

Miles's exhausted face looked up at me, and I couldn't tell which of them was in control as he said, "You know what, Perry? I think we've earned it. We'll drop off the article on the way."

"Indeed, we have," I replied, whistling as I puffed my chest feathers with pride. "Though I did most of the heavy lifting, creatively speaking."

Miles's snort indicated he thought otherwise.

CHAPTER

FORTY

WHEN NEVE WOKE SUNDAY MORNING, Miles's entire body ached. His fingers were raw from hours spent at the typewriter, and his shoulders were stiff from hunching over the desk. Sleep had been elusive on Miles's lumpy mattress, leaving her drowning in a muddle of broken dreams and bone-weary exhaustion after the article had been submitted.

The cooler December air felt soothing on Miles's cheeks as Neve made her way down the sidewalk. Miles's bustling neighborhood was silent, and she soaked up the quietude with delight. A few early risers were walking dogs, and the earthy scent of freshly brewed coffee wafted from cafes opening for early morning customers.

"Could you possibly move any slower?" Perry grumbled from inside the large backpack she'd found in Miles's closet. "I'm developing claustrophobia in here."

"Newspapers aren't even delivered until 7 AM,"

Neve replied, checking Miles's watch for the third time in five minutes. "The newsstand won't be open for another ten minutes."

"Then why did we leave at the ass crack of dawn?" Perry poked his head out, his feathers ruffled with indignation.

"Because I couldn't sleep," Neve admitted. "The article comes out today. I wanted to be among the first to read it."

When they reached the corner newsstand, Joe, the owner, was just unlocking the metal gate. He nodded in greeting as he pulled the stand filled with magazines out onto the street to catch the attention of passersby.

"Morning, Miles! You're up early. *Tampa Tribune* as usual?"

"Yes," Neve confirmed, unable to keep the eagerness out of Miles's voice. "Five copies, actually."

Joe raised an eyebrow as he pulled the first stack of papers from its bundle. "Five? What? Are you planning to wallpaper your bathroom?"

Neve didn't answer. Miles's eyes had already locked onto the headline sprawled across the front page:

The Fatal Price Of Ambition: How One Man's Quest For Glory Sabotaged A Breakthrough Cancer Treatment. Below it, in smaller print, was the byline: "By Miles Murphy."

Her hands shook as she scavenged cash from the bag, almost dropping the change onto the pavement.

"Big news?" Joe asked, his curiosity winning out.

"Front page," Neve replied through Miles's broad grin, hugging the newspapers to his chest.

Joe peered at the headline, then did a double-take, his weathered face breaking into an enthusiastic grin. "Well, I'll be damned! Murphy, you finally did it!" He reached across the stand to give Miles's meaty shoulder an exuberant clap that startled Neve. "I've been selling you papers every morning for what, three years now? You always said you'd crack the big one someday. And here it is! Above the fold, no less!"

"Been a long time coming," Neve managed in Miles's deep baritone.

"Medical scandal, huh?" Joe snatched up his own copy, scanning the first paragraph with obvious interest. "This is the kind of story that is a career maker, son. Bet the big papers will come calling after this. *Times*, *Post*, hell, maybe even *The New Yorker*!"

"Just doing my job," Neve said.

Joe shook his head admiringly. "Always knew you had it in you, Murphy. This one's on the house," he said, pushing back the money Neve had tried to hand him.

Neve felt Miles's consciousness swell with pride at the words, and she let his crooked smile spread across his face. "Thanks, Joe. I'll remember this when I'm accepting my Pulitzer."

"You better!" Joe called after them as Neve walked away, hearing him chatter with excitement to his next customer. "Hey, you'll want to read the *Tampa Tribune* today! My boy Murphy just broke a scandal wide open..."

The walk to Elaine's house took thirty minutes, but Neve barely noticed the time passing. Her mind raced through the ramifications of the article being published. She imagined Conrad's reaction when he saw the paper, the scientific community's response, and she couldn't wait for Elaine's complete vindication.

"You're smiling," a wary Perry observed from the air above after finally being let out of the bag. "It's disconcerting."

"Today's a good day," Neve replied.

As they approached Elaine's home, Neve noticed the difference immediately. The overgrown lawn had been mowed. The withered plants on the porch had been replaced with fresh flowers in terracotta pots. The windows, previously shuttered and dark, now stood open to the morning light.

Neve knocked on the door with Miles's knuckles, hearing movement rustling toward the door in seconds. It swung open to reveal Elaine, and the transformation was striking. Her curly red hair, previously dull and tangled, now framed her face in vibrant waves. She wore a crisp blue polyester blouse and tailored slacks. Her mismatched socks featured test tubes and microscopes.

"Hot off the press," Neve said, pulling a newspaper from her bag as Perry fluttered over to Elaine to perch on her shoulder.

Elaine's hands were steady as she took the paper, but Neve noticed the slight catch in her breath as she saw the headline. Her fingers traced Miles's byline with something approaching reverence.

"Front page?" Elaine whispered. "Wow, Miles, this is really something."

"Keep reading," Perry encouraged. "The good part is in the middle, where Miles completely eviscerates Conrad's subpar character. Poetic, really. I may have contributed a phrase or two." He angled toward her, fishing for praise, but she was already distracted, her lips moving as she read it.

The Fatal Price of Ambition: How One Man's Quest for Glory Sabotaged a Breakthrough Cancer Treatment

By Miles Murphy

The Tampa Tribune, December 15, 1976

In the sterile confines of Aureon Biomedical, a revolutionary cancer treatment promised hope to thousands. Instead, it became a cautionary tale of scientific fraud and personal betrayal that would ultimately cost a man his life.

Dr. Elaine Feldman spearheaded the research of an experimental protocol combining high-dose vitamin C therapy with hyperbaric oxygen treatment that showed unprecedented success in early trials. Her work, building upon Nobel laureate Linus Pauling's controversial vitamin C research, suggested a non-toxic breakthrough in cancer treatment and was dubbed Protocol VitOx. But behind the scenes, a darker story was unfolding, one of sabotage, ambition, and betrayal.

Dr. Conrad Manning, a rising star in medical research, joined Feldman's team in 1973. His credentials were impeccable; his dedication seemed absolute. Yet evidence now suggests Manning systematically undermined the treatment protocol, leading to the death of Veterinary Doctor Robert Feldman, the lead researcher's husband and a willing participant in a pilot study of the experimental therapy.

"The protocol showed remarkable promise," says Dr. James Monroe of Columbia University, who reviewed the original research. "Early results indicated survival rates previously thought impossible." Monroe went on to describe the treatment as "elegantly simple in concept, though complex in execution."

The therapy combined two emerging medical technologies: hyperbaric oxygen chambers, previously used primarily for treatment of the bends after deep-sea diving accidents, and massive doses of intravenous vitamin C. While the scientific community remains divided on vitamin C's efficacy in cancer treatment, no one could argue, Feldman's approach showed unprecedented results.

But those results began to falter mysteriously. An ongoing investigation has revealed Manning had been secretly manipulating the hyperbaric chamber's calibration system, a complex array of pressure gauges and safety mechanisms. By adjusting what technicians call "trim potentiometers," Manning could create a deadly disparity between actual and displayed pressure readings.

"These chambers require precise calibration," explains Dr. Helen Briscoe, an expert in hyperbaric medicine at Johns Hopkins. "Even small discrepancies can have catastrophic consequences. The maximum safe pressure for treatment is approximately three point zero atmospheres, roughly equivalent to the pressure at sixty-six feet underwater. Manning's tampering pushed the chamber to nearly four point zero atmospheres while displaying normal readings."

The results were tragic. During what should have been a routine treatment session, Robert Feldman suffered a severe seizure inside the chamber, leading to his death before help could arrive. Manning, who wasn't present during the fatal treatment, later claimed the death resulted from Dr. Feldman's reckless protocols. But an examination of maintenance records revealed unauthorized adjustments to the equipment that could only have been made by someone with intimate knowledge of the system's engineering.

The scandal deepened when investigators discovered Manning had been secretly negotiating with pharmaceutical giant NovaCure to commercialize a streamlined version of Feldman's protocol. His modifications systematically weakened the treatment's efficacy while maintaining the appearance of safety. "He essentially created a placebo," said Dr. Monroe, "one that would never threaten conventional cancer treatments."

In recorded conversations, Manning revealed detailed knowledge of how to neutralize the treatment's effectiveness through the introduction of catalase, an enzyme that breaks down the hydrogen peroxide theorized to be crucial to the therapy's cancer-fighting properties. This technical expertise, combined with evidence of equipment tampering, paints a damning picture of premeditated sabotage.

The case raises troubling questions about oversight in experimental medical research. While the FDA has recently strengthened requirements for human trials, many experts argue these regulations still leave room for manipulation.

Dr. Feldman will likely be cleared of wrongdoing, but she remains devastated by personal and professional loss and has withdrawn from research. Her groundbreaking Protocol VitOx, which showed such promise, remains in limbo. Manning faces potential criminal charges and certain professional ruin.

Perhaps most tragic is the lost potential. "We may never know how many lives could have been saved if the protocol had been approved for human trials," Dr. Briscoe reflects. "Sometimes the greatest enemy of progress isn't failure, but success corrupted by ambition."

In an era when cancer research proceeds at a snail's pace, this case serves as a sobering reminder of the dangers of taking the fast track. As investigations continue, one question lingers: how many other promising treatments have been silenced by similar acts of sabotage?

[*Miles Murphy is an investigative reporter specializing in medical research and ethics. His previous work includes exposés on pharmaceutical testing practices and hospital safety standards.*]

Elaine moved to her living room, where Neve was surprised to notice the change continued. Gone were the stacks of unwashed dishes and scattered papers. The room was tidy and organized. All the medical equipment and medications had been cleared out.

As Elaine read, her expression shifted between satisfaction, vindication, and occasionally, grief. When she reached the end, she carefully folded the paper and placed it on her coffee table.

"Accurate," she assessed with a decisive nod. "Comprehensive. Robert would approve. Fact."

"The scientific community won't be able to ignore this," Neve said gently. "You could get your life back."

Elaine nodded, her eyes fixed on a framed photo of Robert on the bookshelf, the only personal touch in the otherwise spartan room.

"I cleaned yesterday," she said abruptly, changing the subject. "Fourteen hours, twenty-seven minutes. The house needed it. *I* needed it."

"It looks nice," Neve offered.

"Dr. Whitmore called an emergency board meeting to reinstate me at Aureon Biomedical. They meet today at noon," Elaine continued, her tone measured. "The protocol is valid, and my research must continue. Robert's death wasn't in vain. I can prove it now, and I am eager to get back to work. Thank you for making it possible."

Perry hopped from Miles's shoulder to the coffee table, cocking his head at Elaine. "That's the spirit! Nothing says 'take that, you scientific saboteur' like continuing the work he tried to destroy."

For the first time since Neve had met her, Elaine shot her an exuberant grin. It started as a small, determined curve of her lips, then bloomed into full-scale delight as it transformed her entire face.

CHAPTER

FORTY-ONE

A WHIRLWIND WEEK of professional accolades later, Neve was looking down at the stack of newspapers that ran Miles's article in syndication with pride. He had job interviews scheduled with *The Times* and three other prominent papers already, and they were celebrating with a slice of peach pie.

We did it.

Neve nodded in agreement when knuckles rapped against Miles's apartment door with an erratic rhythm that matched the thunder rumbling in the distance.

"Coming!" she called, hopping to her feet and navigating through the cluttered living room.

She opened the door, gasping when Ellis nearly fell forward into Miles's arms. The scent of whiskey clung to him like cologne. His neat brown hair stuck up at odd angles as though he'd been running his hands through it repeatedly.

"Miles," Ellis slurred, gripping the doorframe for support. "Need to talk. S'important."

Whoa! He's absolutely plastered. Ellis isn't much of a drinker. I've never seen him like this.

"Come in," Neve said, stepping aside as Ellis lurched past her.

Perry, who had been napping on his perch by the window, opened one eye and assessed the situation. "Looks like someone decided to single-handedly support the bourbon industry tonight."

Ellis collapsed onto the couch, his lanky frame folding awkwardly against the cushions. "She said no," he announced to the ceiling, his voice cracking. "She actually said no."

Neve took the seat beside him, unsure how to navigate the intense emotion rolling off her father in waves. Finally, putting it together, she asked, "Diana?"

Ellis nodded and fumbled in his pocket, producing a small velvet box. He flipped it open to reveal a modest diamond ring that twinkled in the yellow light of a nearby lamp. "Bought this last week. After the article came out. Thought... maybe..."

His voice trailed off as he stared down at the ring, its small diamond glittering.

"You proposed," Neve said as understanding dawned.

"Dang right I did," Ellis replied, snapping the box shut with a force that made Neve wince. "Got down on one knee and everything in the lab, in front of everyone, like a complete idiot."

Perry flew over to perch on the coffee table. "There, there. Humiliation builds character."

Ellis barked out a laugh that evolved into a deep

sigh of frustration and leaned forward, elbows on his knees, the ring box still clutched in his fingers. "She got offered the fellowship at Johns Hopkins." He swallowed hard. "They've agreed to let her defer until April, after the baby is born." He let out a sad whimper.

"I'm sorry," Neve offered, knowing the inadequacy of the words but saying them anyway.

Ellis laughed, a hollow sound that held no humor. "You know what the worst part is? I wasn't even surprised. Deep down, I knew she'd choose her career. I've always known." He scrubbed his hands over his face. "But I had to try, right? Had to make the grand gesture?"

"Of course you did," Neve whispered.

Ellis reached inside his jacket pocket and pulled out a small square of paper. "She showed me this today. Right before she destroyed me." He handed it to Neve with trembling fingers. "It's a girl."

Neve looked down at the grainy black and white ultrasound image. In the fuzzy static of 1976's primitive imaging technology, there was barely a distinguishable shape. It was just a blob, the size of a small cabbage, surrounded by shadows. Yet Ellis stared at it with such reverence, such naked longing, that Neve felt her heart constrict.

"She's beautiful," Neve whispered, the words catching in Miles's throat.

"Isn't she?" Ellis's voice softened, his eyes never leaving the image. "I can already see her in my mind. She'll have Diana's intelligence, my persistence." He shot her a waning smile. "And now I'll never get to meet her."

This is getting intense. Maybe offer him some coffee?

Neve ignored the suggestion, watching as Ellis traced the outline of an elbow with his fingertip, his touch gentle.

"I told Diana I'd raise her alone," he continued, his words clearer as the emotional weight of the conversation seemed to cut through his intoxication. "I promised I'd give her everything. That Diana wouldn't have to be involved at all if she didn't want to be."

"What did she say?" Neve asked, though she already knew the answer.

Ellis's face crumpled. "She said it was too complicated. That she needed a clean break to focus on her career." He looked up, his eyes red-rimmed. "I begged her, Miles. I actually begged her."

"I don't know what to say."

"I even told her I'd lie," he continued, his voice dropping to a whisper. "Said I'd tell our daughter she was adopted. That her mother died a few months after she was born." His voice wavered on the last word. "How pathetic is that? Offering to build our child's entire life on a lie just so I could keep her."

Neve felt a shockwave of emotion ripple through. She was watching Ellis describe the very lie that had shaped her own existence, hearing the desperation in his voice as he fought for her before she was even born. The weight of it pressed against her chest, making it difficult to breathe.

"Did she consider it?" Neve asked, though she knew the answer to this question, too.

Ellis nodded miserably. "For a moment. I could see it in her eyes; she actually thought about it. Then she shook her head no and said it was too messy. Said she'd already chosen a couple from the five the agency offered her." He spat the words as if they tasted bitter. "Like she was picking out wallpaper, not deciding the fate of our child."

Perry hopped closer, and his head tilted in sympathy. "Sometimes people make decisions that seem cruel because they believe it's the kindest option in the long run."

Ellis looked at the bird with surprise as if just noticing his presence. "You're quite the philosopher, Peregrine." He turned to Neve. "This bird should be studied. His intelligence is off the charts."

"He's full of surprises," Neve replied, shooting Perry a warning glance.

Outside, the wind had begun to pick up, whistling through the gaps in Miles's rickety windows. The approaching storm cast shifting shadows across the apartment as palm tree branches swayed against the streetlights.

Ellis stared down at the ultrasound photo again, his thumb brushing over it with infinite tenderness. "I want this child more than I've ever wanted anything in my life," he confessed, his voice barely audible. "I wasn't sure I wanted to be a father until Diana told me she was pregnant. And now I can't imagine my life without her."

"Her?" Neve repeated, the word catching in Miles's throat.

"My daughter," Ellis said, looking up with a sad smile. "I already think of her that way. Crazy, right? She's not even here yet, but to me, she's already an entire person."

Neve felt tears pricking at Miles's eyes, a sensation that seemed to confuse his consciousness.

"It's not crazy at all," Neve managed, eyes glossy with tears. "Some connections transcend logic."

Ellis let out a heavy exhalation and tucked the ultrasound photo back into his pocket, his movements swift despite his inebriated state. "I don't know what to do. Diana's made up her mind. The adoption agency has already started the process. In a few months, my daughter will be born, and then they'll both be gone." His voice broke on the last word. "How am I supposed to live with that?"

"Maybe Diana will change her mind," Neve offered.

Ellis shook his head. "You don't know her like I do. Once Diana decides something, that's it. Her mind is made up." He leaned back against the couch, staring blankly at the ceiling. "I keep thinking about all the things I'll miss. Her first steps. First words. First day of school." His voice caught. "She'll grow up calling someone else 'Daddy.'"

Neve shivered. Personally, she'd always found the word Daddy repulsive, but she forced herself to push past it.

The storm outside intensified, with rain beginning

to lash against the windows. A flash of lightning illuminated the room, followed by a low rumble of thunder that seemed to vibrate through the walls.

Perry suddenly fluttered his wings, his feathers puffing out in agitation. "We need to go," he announced, his voice sharp with urgency.

"What?" Neve asked, confused by the bird's sudden declaration.

"The beach," Perry insisted, flying to the window and pecking at the glass. "We need to go to the beach. Now."

What is he talking about? There's a storm coming!

Neve felt it then, a familiar warmth spreading from her pocket where the geode shard pulsed with increasing heat. The air in the apartment seemed to thicken, taking on a strange, electric quality that made the hairs on Miles's arms stand on end.

"Ellis," she murmured, "maybe you should stay here tonight. You're in no condition to drive."

Ellis didn't seem to hear her, lost in his own grief. "I had it all planned out, you know. I was going to convert my study into a nursery. Paint it yellow, with little stars on the ceiling." He closed his eyes, tears leaking from beneath his lashes. "It was going to be perfect."

Neve felt a sharp pang in her chest. She was watching a scene from a film she'd always known the ending to, except now, the weight of her father's grief was unbearable.

Perry flew to her shoulder, his talons digging in

with unusual force. "We need to go," he implored. "The time is coming. Can't you feel it?"

She could. The geode was now burning against her thigh, and the air had taken on that now-familiar, syrupy quality that preceded a time shift. But how could she leave her father like this, drowning in despair?

"Ellis," she said, placing Miles's larger hand on his friend's shoulder. "I need to step out for a bit. Will you be okay here for a while?"

Ellis looked up, his eyes unfocused. "Yep. I'll just sit here and try not to ruminate on my poor decisions." He attempted a smile that came out as a grimace. "Don't worry about me."

Neve hesitated, torn between staying with Ellis and following the urgent pull of the geode. "There's coffee in the kitchen," she said, trying to pull away. "And blankets in the closet if you want to crash here."

Ellis nodded, already slipping off his shoes and reclining back onto the sofa with a yawn.

As Neve grabbed Miles's jacket and headed for the door, with Perry clinging to her shoulder, she felt a strange doubling of reality. She was leaving her father at his lowest moment, and he did not know who she was. Neve was stuck in a conundrum. How do you say goodbye to someone who hasn't met you yet?

"Ellis," she said, pausing at the door.

He looked up, his expression questioning.

"Don't give up," she said simply. "Sometimes things work out in ways we could never have predicted."

Before he could respond, she slipped out into the stormy night, the geode burning against her skin, guiding her toward the sand and surf.

The beach was deserted, the tranquil waters of the bay whipped into a frenzy by the approaching storm. Wind-driven rain lashed at Miles's face as Neve made her way across the sand, each step becoming more difficult as the geode's heat intensified.

"Are you sure about this?" she shouted to Perry over the howling wind. "We don't even know if we'll end up back in our own bodies!"

"When has certainty ever been part of our arrangement?" Perry cawed back, clinging to her shoulder. "Besides, would you rather stay in this hairy vessel indefinitely? No offense to our host, but his personal hygiene leaves much to be desired!"

I can hear you, you know.

Lightning split the sky, illuminating the churning waters. The geode was now blistering hot, burning through the fabric of Miles's pants pocket. Neve could feel the familiar sensation of reality beginning to fracture around her, the edges of her consciousness blurring.

"I'm sorry, Miles," she said aloud, knowing he could hear her. "I never meant to hijack your life like this. But all should go back to normal after the strike."

Just try not to drown us both. And for what it's worth, I hope you find what you're looking for.

Neve waded into the shallow water, each step sending shocks of cold up Miles's legs. The geode was in her hands and now pulsed with an almost unbearable heat, its rhythm matching the crashing waves.

"This is going to hurt," she told Perry, who had moved to the top of her head to avoid the spray.

"Like having your molecules disassembled and reassembled by a sadistic cosmic force," Perry chirped with sarcastic glee. "But look on the bright side, at least we'll be ourselves again. Assuming we survive, of course."

Neve took a deep breath, feeling Miles's consciousness retreating in confusion and alarm. The world around her began to shimmer and distort, colors bleeding into one another as reality seemed to bend.

"Here we go," she whispered, bracing herself for the familiar agony of the transition.

As the geode's heat reached an unbearable crescendo, Neve's last coherent thought was of Ellis, sitting alone in Miles's apartment, clinging to an ultrasound photo of the daughter he would both lose and find again someday.

Then the world dissolved into white-hot pain, and she was falling, falling through time and space, toward an unknown destination.

PART 3: POST-RETROGRADE LATE AUGUST 2024

CHAPTER 42

PEREGRINE

I CRASHED onto the wet sand with all the grace of a schizophrenic pelican, my wings splayed wide as the world spun around me. Every inch of my body was in agony. Like I was being ripped apart feather by feather, then hastily reassembled by a toddler with a glue stick and questionable spatial awareness. I gasped for breath, and my vision swam, blurring the coastline into smears of cerulean blue and raw umber.

"Neve!" I tried to chirp out, but what emerged was a pathetic squawk that wouldn't impress even the most desperate of female parrots. I blinked hard, forcing my eyes to focus on my surroundings.

The pristine white-washed sand of the beach stretched out before me. The familiar beach bunga-lows set back in the sea oats confirmed we'd returned to Aura Cove, but something felt profoundly wrong. The air tasted metallic, and my internal chronometer, usually reliable after our temporal jaunts, was spin-ning like a broken compass. Had we made it back to

2024? Or had we landed in some new temporal catastrophe?

"Nevermore!" I tried again, more desperately this time. "Where are you?" But only harsh, guttural squawks and chirps emerged from my beak.

The realization hit me like a brick to the cranium. I'd lost my ability to articulate. Panic bubbled up inside me, threatening to overwhelm what little composure I had left. In our prior time jumps, my unique linguistic abilities had remained intact. This was new. This was terrifying.

I attempted to calm myself with deep breaths, a technique I'd observed Neve practicing with some success during her anxious moments. *Focus, Peregrine,* I thought to myself. *Find Neve first, have your existential crisis later.*

But where was she? We'd been together when the lightning struck the geode. We should have landed in the same spot. Unless something had gone terribly wrong.

Determined to gain a better vantage point, I spread my wings and attempted to take flight. Under normal circumstances, I could execute a takeoff that would make military pilots weep with envy. This time, however, my wings felt like they'd been dipped in concrete. I managed to flap them exactly twice before the effort sent shooting pains through my sinewy muscles.

"Come on, you pathetic excuse for flight appendages," I muttered internally, trying again with similar dismal results. My energy was zapped, leaving me as aerodynamic as a brick. On my third attempt, I stumbled forward and landed beak-first in the wet sand.

The indignity of it all! In my previous life as a con man, I'd prided myself on always maintaining an air of unflappable poise. Now here I was, face-planted in beach grit, unable to fly, speak, or locate the one human whose survival had somehow become more important to me than my own.

I struggled to my feet, shaking sand from my feathers with as much dignity as I could muster. If I couldn't fly, I would walk. If I couldn't call out for Neve, I would find her through sheer determination. After all, I was Peregrine, the most exceptional bird to ever grace existence.

The sun beat down as I waddled along the shoreline, my pristine gray feathers now matted with sand and salt water. Each step was a test of my willpower. The August heat burned, bearing down on me and draining what little energy remained.

About twenty yards down the beach, something caught my eye, a faint purple glimmer in the sand near the water's edge. Under normal circumstances, I might have dismissed it as a piece of beach glass or a discarded bottle cap, but my bird twin's raw instincts were screaming that this was important.

I dragged myself over, each step more laborious than the last. As I approached, my suspicions were confirmed. It was Neve's geode, the temporal anchor that had facilitated our jumps through time. But something was different. Where there had once been a crystalline structure with a single missing shard, now another black void gaped like a missing tooth. Another piece was gone.

I nudged the stone with my beak, feeling only a tiny vibration of energy still pulsing within it. The void where the new shard had been removed was emitting a subtle glow in the daylight. This was both good news and bad news. Good because the geode always stayed close to Neve, so finding it meant she had to be nearby. Bad because the energy and light that pulsed within it had slowed to a dim, barely perceptible hum. I pushed it with my beak into the hollowed trunk of a piece of driftwood and covered it with sand and pieces of dried seaweed to hide it from view. She would never forgive me if it disappeared on my watch.

Priorities, Peregrine, I reminded myself again. *Find Neve, then you can come back for the geode later.*

With renewed resolve, I continued my search, leaving the geode tucked away. I followed the shore-line, checking behind every piece of driftwood, every swath of sea oats. The beach was relatively empty on what appeared to be a hot summer day. There were just a few scattered tourists far in the distance. None of them was my Nevermore.

My anxiety grew with each passing minute. Neve and I had developed a peculiar bond through our temporal adventures. I had gotten to where I could sense her presence, almost like there was a psychic tether that bound us together. Now that connection felt muted, distant, a glimmer of what it was, but it still confirmed one thing. She was nearby. She had to be.

After what felt like an eternity of searching, I spotted something near a cluster of rocks at the beach's northern end, a crumpled form that made my heart seize in my feathered chest. Even from a distance, I recognized Neve's distinctive braids, though now they were much longer and entirely white, splayed across the sand like spilled milk.

I pushed my skinny bird legs to move faster, practically tumbling down the slight incline toward her. When I reached her side, the sight almost stopped my heart. Neve lay face-down, one arm twisted at an unnatural angle beneath her. Her skin was pale and still.

"Neve!" I squawked, a bird sound emerging where I desperately wanted words. I pecked softly at her hand, then more urgently at her shoulder. No response. I moved to her face, nudging her cheek with my beak.

Nothing.

Her skin felt icy despite the summer heat beating down on us. Too cold. I pressed my cheek against her neck, searching for a pulse the way I'd seen Elaine do to Robert. Was that a faint thrumming beneath my feathers, or just my own frantic heartbeat? I couldn't tell.

Panic, raw and overwhelming, surged through me. In my former life, I remained cool under pressure. Now, as a bird watching my only friend lie unresponsive on a beach, I was terrified. Neve needed medical attention immediately, and I was her only hope.

About fifty yards down the beach, I spotted a young family tossing a Frisbee back and forth. They were laughing, oblivious to the emergency unfolding nearby, soaking up the sun and enjoying their summer vacation.

I gathered what little strength remained in my depleted body and launched myself into a pitiful approximation of flight. I managed to get about three feet off the ground before crashing back to the sand. Undeterred, I tried again and again, making slow progress through a series of short, painful bursts.

"Help!" I tried to shout as I approached them. "Medical emergency! Woman down! This is not a drill, people!" But only squawks and screeches emerged, causing the younger child to point and laugh.

"Look, Mommy! A parrot!"

"On the beach?" the mother questioned, shading her eyes to look at me. "That's strange."

I needed to make them understand. With no ability to communicate verbally, I had to get creative. I spotted their beach setup: towels, folding chairs, and a cooler of snacks. The little girl had a bright pink towel laid out for herself, adorned with cartoon mermaids.

Perfect.

I landed beside it, grabbed the edge with my beak, and tugged with all my might. The fabric barely moved, but it was enough to catch the girl's attention.

"Hey! That's my towel!" she protested, moving toward me.

I released the towel and hopped a few feet away, then turned back to look at her. When she stopped, confused, I repeated the process. Grab, tug, hop away, turn back.

"I think it wants us to follow it," the father said, his brow furrowed in confusion.

"Like Lassie," the older boy suggested, already moving in my direction.

"Birds don't do that," the mother argued, but she was following too, curiosity overriding her skepticism.

I continued my desperate charade, leading them in Neve's direction with a mixture of hops, short flights, and dramatic wing snaps, silent gestures that would have made Charlie Chaplin proud.

When we finally reached Neve, the father's casual expression mutated into one of alarm. "Oh my God," he gasped, rushing forward and dropping to his knees beside her.

"Kids, stay back," the mother commanded, already pulling out her phone. "I'm calling 911."

I was perched on a nearby rock, trembling with exhaustion and fear as I watched the father gently turn Neve onto her back and check her airway. My avian heart pounded against my tiny ribcage.

"She's breathing, but barely," he reported to his wife, who was speaking into her phone, giving their location to the emergency dispatcher.

"The ambulance is on its way," she said after hanging up. "They said not to move her."

I could do nothing but watch as the father took off his t-shirt and placed it under Neve's head as a makeshift pillow. The mother knelt beside him, taking Neve's wrist to check her pulse. The children stood a few yards away, wide-eyed and fearful, occasionally darting wonder-filled glances at me.

"Do you think the bird knew?" the little girl whispered to her brother. "Do you think it was trying to get help?"

"Ever hear of bird brains?" the boy asked, pinching his fingers together. "They are tiny."

I was too exhausted to be offended. In the distance, sirens wailed, growing louder with each passing second. I had never been so grateful for that sound. Help was coming. Neve would be okay. She had to be okay.

The ambulance arrived, and there was a flurry of activity. Paramedics ran over with backpacks full of medical equipment, spending the first few minutes asking the family questions and checking Neve's vitals. I stayed perched on my rock, refusing to leave even when one of the EMTs tried to shoo me away.

"That bird led us to her," the father explained, pointing in my direction. "It's the strangest thing I've ever seen."

The EMT shot me a skeptical glance but was too focused on Neve to argue. I watched as they stabilized her neck, attached monitors, and started an IV. Every beep from their machines sent fresh waves of fear coursing through me. Was she going to be okay? What had happened during our time jump? And why couldn't I talk?

When they lifted her onto a stretcher, I made a

split decision. As they carried her toward the ambulance, I gathered my remaining strength and flew to the vehicle, landing on the open door frame.

"Hey! Shoo!" one of the paramedics said, waving his hand at me.

I stood my ground, fixing him with my most intimidating stare. I might be mute, but I wasn't leaving Neve's side.

"Just leave it," his partner said, securing the stretcher inside. "We don't have time for this."

As they closed the doors, I slipped inside, finding a corner to perch where I wouldn't interfere with their work. The paramedics were too busy with Neve to notice or care about my presence.

Watching them work on her, inserting tubes and attaching monitors, I was overcome with a sensation I rarely allowed myself to feel. Guilt. My one job was to protect her, to be her guide through the temporal madness we'd stumbled into together, and I'd failed in the most spectacular fashion.

CHAPTER

FORTY-THREE

TALULAH BURST through the sliding doors of Aura Cove Community Hospital's emergency room, her crystals clinking against each other like a wind chime as she rushed to the reception desk. Her lavender hair was still damp from the storm, and sand clung to the hem of her flowy dress.

"My niece," she gasped, clutching her rose quartz pendant. "Nevermore LaRue. They brought her in a few hours back. I came runnin' as soon as I got word."

The receptionist's fingers clacked on the keyboard. "Yes, she's being assessed now. The doctor will…"

"I need to see her," Talulah interrupted. Her usual ethereal calm had evaporated. "She was struck by lightnin'."

"Ma'am, you'll need to wait until…"

"I don't think you understand." Talulah leaned forward, her voice dropping to a whisper that somehow carried more weight than a shout. "I'm all the family she has."

"Wait. Are you Talulah LaRue?" the receptionist asked after finally meeting her gaze. "The spiritual medium?" Her eyes beamed with curiosity as she leaned closer, giving Talulah her full attention.

"Yes, I am."

"I'll personally go and get an update from the doctor for you."

For the first time in a long time, Talulah was grateful for her celebrity status. It opened doors that often remained closed. She wasn't one to insist on special treatment, but it had proven to be useful in an emergency a time or two.

Two minutes of anxious pacing later, a doctor in rumpled scrubs approached as the receptionist gave Talulah a thumbs up and a wide grin behind his back. His badge read Dr. Andrews, and the dark circles under his eyes suggested he was several hours into a double shift.

"Ms. LaRue?" he asked, consulting his tablet.

"That's me. How's Nevermore?"

Dr. Andrews gestured to a quieter corner of the waiting room. "Your niece is in serious condition. We're still assessing, but I wanted to update you on what we know."

Talulah sank into a chair in relief, her bracelets jangling. "She's alive." She whispered it like a prayer of thanksgiving.

"She is," he confirmed, "but we're seeing some very unusual symptoms. Severe dehydration, irregular heartbeat patterns, and most concerning, there seems to be cellular deterioration that's, well, frankly, it's bizarre."

"What do you mean?"

"Her biomarkers show advanced biological aging relative to the time that has elapsed since her last exam. We're running tests, but..." he dropped off, changing tracks. "Has she been exposed to any unusual radiation sources? Any experimental treatments?"

Talulah shook her head, guilt washing over her features. "No, nothin' like that. She was just caught in the storm. Could the lightnin' strikes have caused this?"

He chewed on the inside of his cheek as he considered her question. "Maybe. There's something else," Dr. Andrews continued. "There's a parrot that refuses to leave her side. It flew in through an ambulance door and has been perched on the windowsill of her room ever since. We've called animal control, but..."

"No!" Talulah's hand shot out, gripping the doctor's arm. "That's Peregrine. He's her emotional support animal. Please don't remove him."

Dr. Andrews looked skeptical but nodded. "For now, he can stay. But if he becomes disruptive..."

"He won't," Talulah promised. "When can I see her?"

"I'll have a nurse take you to her soon. If you'll excuse me, I need to check on my next patient." Talulah watched him walk away, and she laced her fingers together, taking deep breaths as she waited for the nurse to call her name.

Fifteen minutes later, Talulah gasped when she entered Neve's room. Her niece lay motionless on the hospital bed, connected to five different monitors that beeped and flickered as they updated her vital signs. But it was Neve's physical appearance that made Talulah's heart constrict in her chest.

Neve's hair, which had been streaked with silver before, was now completely white and spread across the pillow like spun sugar. Deep lines were etched on her face: crow's feet, forehead furrows, and nasolabial folds that hadn't been there during her last visit. Her hands, resting atop the blanket, showed prominent veins and age spots.

"Oh, Nevermore," Talulah whispered, approaching the bed slowly. "What have you done?"

Perry sat on the windowsill, his feathers ruffled and dull. He didn't acknowledge Talulah's presence at all, his eyes never leaving Neve.

A nurse entered and adjusted one of the IV pumps. "The doctor will be back soon with more information," she said, her tone sweet. "Talk to her. Sometimes they can hear even when they're not responsive."

When the nurse left, Talulah pulled a chair close to the bed and sandwiched Neve's hand between hers. "I'm here, and so is Perry. We're not goin' anywhere."

The African grey parrot hopped from the windowsill to the foot of the bed, his movements subdued. Talulah noticed how he arranged five of his own feathers in a small circle on the blanket near Neve's feet, a protective gesture that brought tears to her eyes.

Outside the door of Neve's hospital room, Dr. Andrews stood at the light board, examining Neve's scans with three colleagues. The images showed anomalies none of them had ever encountered.

"She exhibits all the signs of significant physiological aging, off-the-charts levels of inflammation, poor organ function, and anemia. Her CBC, the blood panel, based on control comparisons, reads like a woman who is in her mid-sixties," he explained, pointing to the cellular images and reports. "Yet her medical records indicate she's forty-seven."

Dr. Patel, the neurologist, shook her head in disbelief. "And look at the temporal lobe activity. I've never seen patterns like these outside of seizure patients, but she's showing no seizure symptoms."

"The joint deterioration concerns me," added Dr. Ramirez, tapping another scan. "This level of arthritis doesn't develop overnight. It's as if her body has aged fifteen years in less than a month."

"What about radiation exposure?" suggested the fourth doctor, an oncologist named Dr. Wharton.

"Negative," Dr. Andrews replied. "Family has confirmed she has not undergone treatment. There are no radiation markers in her bloodwork. No signs of poisoning either. It's as if her mitochondria are simply burning out."

The wall clock above them suddenly stopped, its second hand frozen at 5:55. None of the doctors noticed, too absorbed in the medical mystery before them.

"I'm recommending we induce a coma," Dr. Andrews finally said. "Give her systems a chance to stabilize while we figure this out."

The others nodded in agreement. As they dispersed, Dr. Andrews glanced back at the scans, a deep furrow between his brows. In twenty years of medicine, he'd never seen anything like this.

CHAPTER

FORTY-FOUR

In Neve's room, Perry sat motionless on the hospital room's windowsill, watching the steady rise and fall of Neve's chest. The room was quiet except for the rhythmic beeping of monitors. They bleated five distinct tones that seemed to pulse in a pattern. Two days had passed since they'd been brought in. Two days of silence, of watching doctors come and go with increasingly puzzled expressions. Two days of visits back and forth with Talulah, who was sleeping at Neve's childhood home.

"You stubborn, infuriating woman," he warbled, not expecting the words to actually emerge. When they did, and he was uttering actual words instead of pitiful squawks, Perry almost fell off his perch in shock.

"My voice!" he exclaimed, louder this time. "It's back!"

He fluttered to Neve's bedside, landing carefully beside her pillow. "Neve? Can you hear me? I can talk again! Wake up and appreciate this miraculous development!"

She remained still, her face peaceful despite its new wrinkles. The doctors had induced a coma yesterday, explaining to Talulah that it was the best way to stabilize Neve's condition while they investigated further.

"This is all my fault," Perry continued, his voice softer now. "I knew the risks better than anyone." He paced along the edge of the pillow. "Each jump comes at a cost. Five years the first time, ten the second. I should have discovered the pattern sooner."

The door opened, and a stern-faced hospital administrator entered, followed by Talulah.

"Ms. LaRue, as I was explaining, we've had complaints about the bird. He's been stealing food from the visitors' lounge. Crackers, nuts, even a sandwich left unattended. We've bent the rules because of your social standing, but animal control is on their way."

"That's ridiculous," Talulah protested. "He's just hungry."

"Hospital policy clearly states..."

"I don't give a hoot about your policy," Perry interrupted, causing both humans to freeze in shock. "And those crackers were stale, anyway. Subpar hospitality, if you ask me."

The administrator's mouth opened and closed several times, resembling a fish out of water. "It... it talks?"

"He," Talulah corrected, recovering quickly. "And

yes, Perry is quite an evolved companion. As I was sayin', there's no need to get animal control involved. I'll take him home now."

When the door closed, Talulah turned to Perry with wide eyes. "You can talk again!"

"Brilliant observation," Perry replied, though his sarcasm lacked its usual bite. "Indeed. My linguistic faculties have been fully restored, though I can't explain why."

Talulah moved closer, her voice dropping to a whisper. "What happened to her, Perry? What's really goin' on?"

Perry looked at Neve's aged face, then back to Talulah. "We can talk about this at home. Privately. There's something you need to know about time travel and its side effects."

Back at Neve's house, Perry perched on the kitchen counter while Talulah prepared a plate of mango slices and walnuts for him.

"Every time she travels," Perry explained between crunchy bites, "it costs her. Physically. The first jump aged her five years."

"Five years?" Talulah gasped. "I thought she looked tired when I first saw her at the Omni!"

"Bingo! But it gets worse. The second jump cost her ten years. The toll seems to multiply each time."

"By five," Talulah whispered, her hand moving to her rose quartz pendant. "Five is a powerful number in the metaphysical world. There are five elements. Earth, air, fire, water, and spirit. Five points on a pentagram. Five senses through which we experience reality."

"And, apparently, five years of cellular aging per temporal displacement," Perry added grimly. "Multiplying with each journey."

As the realization of what this meant sank in, a hairline crack appeared in Talulah's rose quartz pendant. Then another. And another, until the crystal had split into exactly five pieces, falling onto the counter with a gentle tinkling sound.

Talulah stared at the fractured crystal, her face pale. "The universe is sendin' us a message."

"The universe has a convoluted sense of humor," Perry muttered, but his eyes betrayed his concern. "What does it mean?"

"We can't let her travel again," Talulah decoded. "The next jump could kill her."

The next morning, Talulah sat beside Neve's bed, Perry perched on her shoulder. Dr. Andrews had just left after explaining their decision to maintain the induced coma for another forty-eight hours.

"Her systems need time to stabilize," he'd said. "Her cellular structure is changing in ways we don't understand. We don't want to rush the healing process."

Talulah's brow pinched in confusion as the doctor continued.

"Her temporal lobe activity indicates an unusual pattern. It's as if her perception of time is fragmented, like she's experiencing events out of sequence, or all at once. Of course, neurologically, that shouldn't be possible." Talulah pressed her lips into a tense line as he outlined the next steps then left the room, heading to his next patient.

Alone in the quiet of the hospital room with only Peregrine as company, Talulah stroked Neve's hand. "I should have stopped you," she whispered. "I knew that geode was dangerous. I felt it in my bones."

"We both should have," Perry murmured. "But she's stubborn. Like her father."

"Ellis would be beside himself if he could see her now." Talulah's voice quavered. "He always tried to protect her. That's why he kept so many secrets."

"It's the secrets that are killing her," Perry implored, hopping down to arrange his protective circle of feathers with his beak again. One had been disturbed by a nurse earlier. "The irony would be delicious if it weren't so tragic."

Hours later, as Talulah sat vigil at her side, the afternoon light filtered through the blinds, casting striped shadows across Neve's still form. Her white hair caught the light, gleaming like stardust. Despite the age that now marked her face, there was a peace in her expression that was often absent.

"Did she at least find what she was looking for?" Talulah asked with a whisper.

Perry considered the question before answering. "She got some answers, but sadly, it uncovered even more questions."

CHAPTER

FORTY-FIVE

Five days after being admitted, as the hospital clock read 5:55 PM, Neve's eyelids fluttered, and her fingers twitched against the blanket. The monitors registered the change immediately, their beeping becoming more urgent.

Perry, who had been dozing on the windowsill, jerked awake and squawked, "Talulah! She's waking up!"

Talulah, who had stepped out for coffee, rushed back into the room just as Neve's eyes opened fully. They were disoriented at first, then gradually focused on the ceiling above her.

"Nevermore?" Talulah called out, moving to her side. "Can you hear me, honey bee?" Letting out a squeal of joy, she hurried to the nurses' station, and twenty minutes later, the intubation tube was out and a frail Neve was propped upright in bed.

Her lips parted, dry and cracked. When she spoke, her voice was a raspy whisper, barely audible.

"The geode...?"

Perry flew to the bed, landing with care beside her pillow. "Neve! Do you have any idea how worried we've been? How many stale hospital crackers I've been forced to steal to maintain my strength during this deathbed vigil?"

A ghost of a smile touched Neve's lips. "I was unconscious, not deaf. I heard you complaining to the nurse about the substandard quality of the food you mooched. Your selfless sacrifice has been noted for the record."

"For your information, I've eaten better things tucked between sofa cushions." Perry puffed up with indignation.

Neve sputtered out a laugh, then tried to lift her hand, wincing at the effort. She stared at her fingers in astonishment. They were thinner, and the backs of her hands had accumulated more age spots. "What... happened to me?"

Before either Talulah or Perry could answer, Neve caught sight of her reflection in the tinted window. The white-haired, deeply lined face staring back at her was a stranger's. Her eyes widened in shock, then filled with tears.

"Oh," she breathed, the single syllable containing a world of understanding. "I see."

"The doctors say you've experienced some kind of cellular acceleration," Talulah explained in a gentle tone. "They don't understand it but are runnin' a battery of tests."

"I do," Neve interrupted, her gaze still fixed on her

reflection. "It's the time jumps. I age normally in the present, but when I go back, it costs me." Her eyes shifted to Perry. "You knew, didn't you?"

Perry had the good grace to look ashamed. "I suspected the first time, but I didn't know for certain until we got back from 1976."

Neve closed her eyes, tears slipping down her weathered cheeks. The monitors continued to beep, the only sound in the room. Neve opened her eyes again, a new zeal visible despite her weakened state. "My brain is foggy. I need to tell you what I saw," she said. "Before I forget."

As the wall of storm clouds outside finally broke, revealing a sunset painted in shades of peach and gold, Neve began to speak. Her timbre grew stronger with each word, as if the telling itself was medicine for her aged body.

And in the shadows of the corridor, unseen by any of them, a tall man dressed in a doctor's coat and face mask hovered at the door, hanging on her every word. He turned on his heel to leave and pulled a purple geode out of his pocket. It was a stunning stone, its facets sparkling and glimmering in the light, except for two holes that were a dull black. He stopped at the nurses' station and handed the stone off to a nurse. "Can you make sure this gets returned to Nevermore LaRue?"

FORTY-SIX

A FEW DAYS LATER, Nevermore was released from the hospital. The long-term effects meant that waking up in the morning was a painful ritual. First came the dull aches of her body, then her memory returned like a slow tide, and finally, the sharp realization dawned that time was rushing by and there was little she could do to stop it.

She attempted to sit up in her bed, but her arthritic limbs protested. Her lower back seized, her knees creaked, and her shoulders felt as though they'd been wrenched from their sockets. Neve pushed herself to a sitting position, wincing as her joints complained. "Everything hurts," she muttered, her voice raspier and deeper than she remembered. She looked down at hands that were unmistakably hers but with thinner skin and more prominent blue veins with swollen knuckles.

"That's the price of temporal tourism," Perry replied, fluttering over to land on her nightstand.

"You've essentially gone from forty-seven to sixty-two without the courtesy of experiencing all those delightful middle years. Look on the bright side! At least you skipped right past perimenopause and into the real deal. No pesky hot flashes for you!"

"Menopause?" Neve ground out, shocked and horrified by the new reality.

"Judging by your current biological state, you're well past the finish line on that particular marathon," Perry confirmed. "Welcome to your golden years, Nevermore! Social Security is just around the corner!"

"But I don't get to collect for another fifteen years, if I even make it that long!"

"Hush your mouth," Perry scolded with a sharp squawk.

A knock at the door interrupted Neve's mounting panic. "Neve? Honey bee? You up?" Talulah's voice called through the panel.

"Come in," Neve croaked.

Talulah entered, carrying a tray with coffee and toast. Her lavender-streaked hair was pulled back in a messy bun, and laugh lines crinkled around her eyes as she smiled. "Well, look who's finally rejoined the land of the livin'! You've been out for nearly twelve hours."

"Twelve hours?" Neve echoed, attempting to swing her legs over the side of the bed. A sharp pain in her hip made her gasp.

"Easy there," Talulah cautioned, setting down the tray and moving to help. "Your body's been through quite an ordeal. Drink your coffee, then we'll get you up and movin'. Those joints won't loosen themselves."

Half an hour later, with Talulah's help, Neve made it to the bathroom, where she confronted her new reflection. The face staring back wasn't unattractive, just different. Older. Wiser-looking. Her gaze darted between her reflection and Talulah. They appeared roughly the same age now, a fact that dumbfounded logical Neve with its absurdity.

"You are being remarkably open-minded about this," Neve said.

"After all the strange things I've seen in my lifetime, a time-travelin' artist with a talking bird barely makes the top ten." Talulah chuckled. "Look on the bright side, sweetheart. We can bellyache about our pains together."

"That doesn't seem like much of a benefit," Neve groused.

Talulah chuckled. "What if I told you it comes with a boatload of senior discounts?"

"That makes it only marginally more attractive."

After a hot shower that eased some of her discomfort, Neve settled at the kitchen table with her laptop and a journal. Talulah had gone to the store, promising to return with age-appropriate supplies, whatever that meant.

"Alright," Neve said to herself, "I better update the log."

She cataloged her physical state in the journal she'd started after her first time travel experience:

Physical Assessment Post-Time Travel:
- Estimated biological age: early 60s

- Joint pain: moderate to severe, particularly in knees, hips, lower back

- Visual changes: reading glasses required, peripheral vision reduced

- Energy levels: reduced by 25%

- Hair: 100% white

- Skin: thinner, less elastic

- Voice: deeper, slight raspiness

"Don't forget to note the delightful sprouting of random chin hairs," Perry cheeped from his perch on the lamp as he crunched on a walnut.

Neve's hand shot to her chin in horror. "What?"

"Oh yes, they sprout overnight like magic beanstalks. Talulah says she keeps tweezers in every room of her house. Very practical woman."

Sighing, Neve added this disturbing detail to her notes, then turned to her laptop. "Now, let's see what happened to Aureon Biomedical."

The search results made her breath catch. Headlines from 1977 to 1978 dominated the first page:

Aureon Researcher Cleared Of Wrongdoing In Husband's Death

Breakthrough Cancer Treatment Vindicated After Fraud Exposed

Dr. Elaine Feldman Returns To Lead Vitamin C Research After Colleague's Conviction

"We did it," Neve whispered, skimming through the articles one at a time. As she scrolled through more search results, a book title caught her eye: *The Aureon Revolution: How One Woman's Vision Changed Medicine* by Miles Murphy. Published in 1980, it had become a landmark text on medical ethics and scientific integrity in research medicine.

"Miles wrote his book," she murmured, navigating to an online bookstore to order a used copy and have it overnighted.

"Capitalized on his big break, did he?" Perry chirped. "The man may have had questionable hygiene habits, but he certainly knew how to craft a compelling narrative." Perry hopped closer to peer at the screen. "Can't say I blame him. We did provide him with quite the career-defining scoop."

Further searching revealed that Miles had indeed parlayed his exposé into a distinguished career. After breaking the Aureon story, he'd been recruited by *The New Yorker*, eventually becoming their lead science and medicine correspondent. His work had earned him multiple awards, including a Pulitzer in 1985 for *Beyond the Laboratory: Women Redefining Modern Medicine*, which exposed gender discrimination in research funding while celebrating female scientists who persevered against overwhelming odds.

"Look at that! He got his Pulitzer," Neve cheered, feeling a strange mixture of pride and disorientation. Her memories of sharing his consciousness remained intact. When she'd first met him, he'd been a struggling reporter living in a cramped apartment and was ruled by misogynistic ambition. Seeing he'd learned to let go of his ego, and it helped him achieve everything he'd dreamed of, filled her with a sense of accomplishment. In some small way, she felt she'd been part of it.

"Your little body-swap adventure seems to have done him a world of good," Perry observed. "Perhaps we should charge your next host a consulting fee for career advancement."

"Funny, it seems to be doing me a world of good as well. Every temporal shift is a fully immersive masterclass on how neuro-typicals experience the world. It's been eye-opening." Neve paused, her gaze direct and unflinching as she considered the lessons she'd learned. "It confirms a belief it took me a long time to accept. My autistic brain isn't broken. It's perfect for the work I do and the person I am. I spent decades trying to be normal before I realized normal is just a setting on a washing machine."

"Good on you!" Perry cawed and flapped his wings together to congratulate her.

Neve continued her research, digging deeper into the aftermath of the Aureon scandal. The story had rocked the medical research community. Conrad Manning had been indicted on multiple charges: data falsification, endangering human subjects, attempted sabotage, and manslaughter in the death of Dr. Robert Feldman.

His trial had been a sensation, with Miles's book describing it as "A cautionary tale of scientific hubris. The moment when medicine was forced to confront its gods in white coats and find them mortal, fallible, and sometimes monstrous." Conrad had been sentenced to twelve years in prison, though he'd served only eight before being released on parole. After his release, he'd disappeared from public life entirely.

NovaCure scrambled to distance themselves from the scandal, issuing statements claiming they had been "misled about the origin and nature of Dr. Manning's research" and were "committed to ethical scientific practices." Their stock had plummeted and Olivia Wallis was hired to rebrand and revitalize the company a five years years later.

As Neve continued reading, she found herself drawn to the personal stories behind the headlines. What had happened to Diana? To Donna? To Ellis?

A search for Dr. Diana Morrison yielded numerous publications from the late 1970s through the early 1990s. Neve uncovered groundbreaking research papers, keynote addresses at international conferences, and Diana's appointment as head of oncology research at Memorial Sloan Kettering. But then, mysteriously, she could find nothing after 1992.

"That's strange," Neve murmured, digging deeper. After several increasingly specific searches, she found a small mention in a 1992 medical newsletter: "Dr. Diana Morrison, noted cancer researcher, has taken a leave of absence for personal reasons."

Further scouring led her to a disturbing discovery. A newspaper article indicated Diana had been institutionalized at a psychiatric care center in Clearwater, diagnosed with schizophrenia after releasing all the clinical testing animals and setting fire to a medical research facility.

"Oh no," Neve whispered, her heart sinking. With shaking hands, Neve composed an email to Dr. Donna Wilson, who had gone on to graduate from medical school and had since retired from a distinguished career in medical research ethics:

Dear Dr. Wilson,

I'm writing regarding Diana Morrison. You may remember my father, Ellis LaRue, from your work together at Aureon Biomedical. I recently learned Diana Morrison was my birth mother, and that she experienced some health challenges in the early 1990s.

I would be incredibly grateful for any information you might have about her current situation or whereabouts. This is a deeply personal matter, and any assistance would mean more than you know.

Sincerely,

Nevermore LaRue

After sending the email, Neve turned her attention to Ellis LaRue. The search results painted a picture of remarkable success. After the Aureon scandal, her father had continued his research into oxidative therapies for cancer treatment. In 1988, he'd been recruited by NovaCure, under new leadership, to head their oncology division.

By evening, Neve's kitchen table was covered with

printouts, notes, and open books. Talulah had returned with her promised supplies: comfortable shoes with better arch support, reading glasses in various strengths, and a heating pad for Neve's aching back. Afterward, they stayed up late to organize the research.

"So, you basically rewrote medical history," Talulah summarized, sipping her chamomile tea. "Not bad for a few weeks of work."

"I didn't mean to," Neve replied, rubbing her temples. "I just wanted to understand my past, to know who my parents were."

"And instead, you changed their futures," Perry observed from his perch. "A rather significant upgrade for Ellis, I'd say, though poor Diana's life took a nasty turn."

Neve winced at the reminder. "I want to find her. She might have more information about Dad."

As night fell, Neve's body demanded rest. The day's emotional and physical exertion had taken its toll. Talulah helped her back to bed, arranging pillows around her.

"Was it worth it?" Talulah asked as she adjusted the blankets. "All this pain, the aging, the lost years?"

Neve considered the question, then remembering Elaine's complete vindication, answered, "Yes, it *was* worth it. We changed things for the better."

"Not just for them," Perry added from his night-time perch. "For yourself, too, Nevermore. You finally know the truth about your father. About what kind of man he really was."

Neve nodded, swallowing through the knot tightening in her throat. "Dad wanted me. He fought for me. He loved me from the first moment he knew I existed."

"Of course he did, honey bee," Talulah whispered.

Her last thought before drifting off was of Ellis, proudly displaying the blurry ultrasound photo of his unborn daughter, already loving her with his whole heart. In the end, that was the only truth that mattered.

CHAPTER

FORTY-SEVEN

THE NEXT DAY, Neve's energy began to return. Her body was adapting to the physiological changes, and she was grateful when it loosened up by noon. To help keep the brain fog at bay, she had created a detailed spreadsheet tracking Diana Morrison's career trajectory: her publications, conference appearances, awards, and institutional affiliations. The data told a clear story of her brilliant ascent followed by a catastrophic fall.

- 1977: Fellowship at Johns Hopkins
- 1983-1987: Associate Director of Research at Memorial Sloan Kettering, 22 publications
- 1988-1991: Director of Oncology Research, Johns Hopkins, 18 publications, 3 patents
- 1992: Leave of absence for personal reasons
- 1992-present: No publications, no

conference appearances, no professional activity

"Something happened in 1992," Neve muttered, adjusting the brightness of her monitor down, then up again, seeking a level that wouldn't aggravate her more sensitive eyes.

"The same year your father disappeared," Perry observed from his perch on a branch in the sunroom. "That can't be coincidental."

The computer chimed with a notification of a new email in her inbox. Neve clicked to open it, the sender's name making her stomach flutter: Donna Wilson.

"She responded," Neve said, her voice tight with anticipation.

Perry fluttered down to the desk, positioning himself to read the screen. "What does our timid lab technician have to say?"

She read aloud:

Dear Neve,

I was surprised but pleased to receive your email. It's been many years since I've heard from anyone inquiring about Diana.

I wish I had better news for you. Diana's story is a difficult one. After her remarkable success at Johns Hopkins, she began experiencing what doctors eventually diagnosed as schizophrenia. The onset was gradual at first. It began with paranoid thoughts, increasing isolation, and occasional breaks with reality. By late 1991, her colleagues were concerned, but Diana was adept at hiding her symptoms.

The crisis came in the fall of 1992. Diana became convinced that the animals in the research facility were communicating with her, telling her they were being tortured. She released them all one night and set fire to the laboratory. Thankfully, no one was hurt, but Diana was arrested and subsequently hospitalized.

For several years, she moved between treatment facilities and her parents' home. When they passed away in 1998, she no longer had family support and has been institutionalized more or less continuously since then.

Diana currently resides at Bayside Psychiatric Care Center in Clearwater. I visit her occasionally, though I should warn you to adjust your expectations. The brilliant, vibrant woman I knew is largely gone. The medications control her delusions but leave her withdrawn and disconnected.

If you decide to visit, please let me know. I could perhaps accompany you and make introductions.

With sympathy,
Donna Wilson

Neve stared at the screen, her hand automatically reaching for the brightness control again, adjusting it up, then down, then up again.

"Well," Perry said after a long silence. "That's

certainly not the illustrious career trajectory one might have expected for a respected medical pioneer."

"Schizophrenia," Neve whispered. "She became ill the same year that my father disappeared."

"The plot thickens," Perry chattered his grim observation. "I must say, your constant adjustment of the screen brightness reminds me of the time I took 'shrooms at Burning Man."

Neve withdrew her hand, lacing it with her other one. "It helps me think," she reasoned.

"I know," Perry's tone softened. "And you have much to ponder tonight."

Neve turned back to the spreadsheet, adding a new column: "Mental Health Timeline." She entered the information from Donna's email, cross-referencing it with her father's known whereabouts. Before she went to sleep, she made a bold proclamation. "I need to see Diana. I'm going to Clearwater in the morning."

FORTY-EIGHT

BAYSIDE PSYCHIATRIC CARE Center was a non-threatening institutional building, all soft curves and muted colors that somehow made it more unsettling rather than less. Neve stood in the parking lot, clutching her messenger bag that contained the geode and a small notebook filled with questions.

"You can do this," she told herself, taking a deep breath that caught in her throat as a nauseating wave of antiseptic and ammonia scents washed over her upon entering the building. The offensive scent hit her like a brick. Neve jerked to a stop in the entryway, closed her eyes, and counted silently to regain her equilibrium. She envisioned the red balloon filling with her breath and let it go. Then, she visualized another before she was steady enough to walk into the lobby.

"Welcome to Bayside," said the receptionist behind a plexiglass partition. "How can I help you?"

"I'm here to see Diana Morrison," Neve replied,

approaching the desk. "I called yesterday. Nevermore LaRue."

"ID please," the woman requested without looking up.

Neve extracted her driver's license, noting the irony of presenting identification that showed a much younger version of herself. The receptionist barely glanced at it before pushing a clipboard toward her.

"Sign in. Visiting hours end at four. No food, no gifts without prior approval, no cameras. Store your bag in the lockers. No pens or notebooks with metal edging allowed."

"Okay," Neve said with a sigh, signing her name as her anxiety peaked. Knowledge was always comforting, so she asked, "Could you tell me more about her condition?"

The receptionist looked up, her expression one of blank professionalism. "You'll need to speak with her social worker. Through those doors, take a left, third office on the right. Ms. Lockwood."

Neve nodded her thanks and followed the directions, her hiking boots making small squeaks on the linoleum. The hallway seemed endless. The doors were all identical except for small nameplates. She counted them under her breath to anchor her racing thoughts. Ms. Lockwood's office was small but organized, with filing cabinets and a desk dominated by a computer. The woman herself was perhaps forty, with a kind face and tired eyes.

"Ms. LaRue? Please, have a seat." She gestured to a

chair across from her desk. "I understand you're here to see Diana Morrison."

"Yes. I'm her daughter," Neve said, the words feeling strange in her mouth.

Ms. Lockwood's expression registered surprise. "I wasn't aware Diana had any children. There's no family listed in her records."

"She gave me up for adoption at birth," Neve explained. "I only recently discovered she was my biological mother."

The social worker looked up at Neve with a more assessing gaze. "I see. Well, I should prepare you. Diana has been diagnosed with treatment-resistant schizophrenia. She experiences paranoid delusions, disorganized thinking, and occasional catatonic episodes."

"What is her daily life like?" Neve asked, needing concrete details.

"She follows a structured routine. Medications in the morning, group therapy, lunch, occupational therapy, free time in the dayroom, dinner, evening activities, then lights out at nine. The structure helps minimize episodes."

"Does she speak? Is she aware of her surroundings?"

Ms. Lockwood hesitated. "She has periods of lucidity, particularly in the mornings after medication. She speaks, though her words are often rambling and incoherent. She does recognize staff she sees regularly."

"Will she know who I am?"

"That's difficult to predict," Ms. Lockwood said

gently. "I would suggest not overwhelming her with too much information at once. Perhaps introduce yourself as someone interested in her previous research work."

Neve nodded, processing this advice. "When can I see her?"

"She should be in the dayroom now. I'll take you there."

The dayroom was a large, open space with institutional furniture arranged in conversational groupings. Windows lined one wall, letting in pale sunlight filtered through security screens. About a dozen patients occupied the room, some watching television, others engaged in solitary activities.

"Diana is over there," Ms. Lockwood said quietly, gesturing toward a woman sitting alone by the windows.

Neve's breath caught. The woman bore little resemblance to the vibrant, determined researcher Neve met in 1976. This Diana was thin to the point of fragility, her once-sharp features now sunken. Her gray-streaked hair hung limply around her face, and she rocked slightly in her chair, her fingers moving in repetitive patterns against her thigh.

"Would you like me to introduce you?" Ms. Lockwood asked.

"No," Neve said, finding her voice. "I'd prefer to approach her myself. Thank you."

Neve crossed the room slowly, giving herself time to observe. Diana's movements—the rocking, the finger patterns—felt familiar. They were stimming behaviors, self-soothing techniques that Neve herself sometimes used in times of stress or overstimulation.

"Hello, Diana," Neve whispered, stopping a respectful distance from the chair. "My name is Neve. May I sit with you?"

Diana's eyes, once sharp and intelligent, were now clouded by medication. They flicked toward Neve, then away. "The chairs are for everyone," she murmured. "Everyone sits. Everyone waits."

Neve took the seat opposite her, intentionally keeping her movements slow. "What are *you* waiting for?"

"For the numbers to align. For Ellis to come back," Diana replied, her fingers still moving in their pattern.

At the mention of her father's name, Neve's careful composure shattered. A small gasp escaped her lips.

"You remember Ellis?" she asked, leaning forward.

Diana's gaze sharpened, focusing on Neve's face with sudden intensity. "Ellis?" she repeated, her rocking increasing. "Ellis, is that you?"

"No," Neve said gently. "I'm not Ellis, but I knew him."

Diana's burst of clarity faded as quickly as it had appeared. Her eyes grew distant again, her mumbling resuming. "They're watching. Always watching. The cells divide too quickly when they watch."

Neve sat with her for nearly an hour, trying different approaches to start a conversation. Occasionally, Diana would emerge from the thick fog with startling lucidity, when asked a specific question about her research, or the mention of a colleague. But these moments were brief islands in a sea of confusion.

Finally overwhelmed by the emotional strain, Neve excused herself and retreated to the nearby restroom. The institutional bathroom was cold and sterile, but it offered privacy. Neve locked the stall door and tilted her head back, counting the ceiling tiles until her breathing steadied.

One, two, three, four, five. Five across. Seven down. Thirty-five tiles total.

When she felt composed enough, she splashed cold water on her face and returned to the lockers to retrieve her messenger bag, where Ms. Lockwood was waiting.

"How did it go?" the social worker asked.

"I don't know. I wasn't sure what to expect," Neve replied.

"She has good days and bad. It's best to keep your expectations low."

Neve pulled out her notebook and flipped it open to where she'd written a list of questions. She took a deep breath and asked the first one.

"What would be involved in having her released into family care?"

Ms. Lockwood's eyebrows rose in surprise. "That's a significant undertaking. Diana requires consistent medication management, regular psychiatric evaluations, and a structured environment. Are you considering becoming her guardian?"

"Right now, I'm gathering information. I'd like to explore all the options," Neve answered, her analytical mind already cataloging the list of requirements. "Could you walk me through the process?"

For the next thirty minutes, Ms. Lockwood outlined the legal and practical steps: petitioning for guardianship, home evaluations, care plans, medication management protocols, and the network of outpatient services that would be necessary. It required a mountain of paperwork and navigating a legal battlefield, and Neve wasn't sure she was up to the task.

"It's not impossible," Ms. Lockwood concluded, "but it would require significant resources and support. Diana has been institutionalized for a long time. A transition of this magnitude would be challenging."

"I understand," Neve said, processing the information with a firm nod. "Thank you for your time."

When Neve explained the steps later that evening to Talulah, she'd exclaimed, "That's a huge responsibility you're considerin'."

"She's my mother," Neve said, spreading the paperwork Ms. Lockwood had given her across the kitchen table. "And she's been locked away for decades."

"She's also severely mentally ill," Perry pointed out from his perch. "Not to mention a complete stranger to you. This goes far beyond the obligation of familial duty."

"She broke down the same year my father disappeared. That can't be a coincidence," Neve insisted. "If she's here, I might get the answers I've been searching for."

Talulah sighed, picking up one of the forms. "Legal guardianship. Home care requirements. Psychiatric supervision. This is a bureaucratic maze of madness, if you'll pardon the expression."

"It's a concrete problem with concrete steps toward a solution," Neve replied. "I can handle executing a plan."

"But can you handle Diana?" Perry asked, his tone gentle but direct. "The woman you describe sounds profoundly unwell. Are you prepared for what that might mean day to day?"

Neve was silent for a long moment. Her fingers reached up to tighten the ends of her braids as she thought it over. "I don't know," she finally admitted. "I don't know how I feel."

"You don't owe her anything," Talulah whispered.

"Maybe not," Neve agreed. "But she might be the key."

Later that night, unable to sleep, Neve sat at her drawing table. Her aged hands protested as she worked, joints stiff and painful after only an hour. The physical limitations of her older body were still difficult to accept when it came to her art.

The image taking shape on the paper was of Diana, not as she was now, but as she had been in 1976, young and brilliant, caught between her career and motherhood. Beside her, Neve drew Ellis as she remembered him in Miles's apartment. Head over heels in love with

Diana, and desperate to be given the chance to become a father.

She startled when her phone buzzed with an incoming text from Lisa: "How are the final pieces coming for the show? The opening's in three days. Need anything?"

Neve set down her pencil, flexing her aching fingers. "Just more time," she texted back, knowing it was the one luxury she couldn't afford. Time had already played a cruel trick on her, accelerating her through years she should have lived day by day. Now she was racing against it again, trying to uncover the truth about her parents before her chance slipped away.

Neve turned back to her drawing, adding a third figure. A child. She gave it her own face, not as she was now, but as she had been at fifteen when her father disappeared. The age when everything had changed.

CHAPTER

FORTY-NINE

THE NEXT MORNING she sat at her drawing table in the sunroom. Her knobbier fingers tightened around a graphite pencil, sketching across the heavy paper in long strokes. The scratching sound it made filled the quiet room, interrupted only by the occasional rustle from Perry's cage as he groomed himself.

Neve leaned back to assess her work, her chair squealing in protest as she flexed her fingers to restore the blood flow. The portrait taking shape was of her Aunt Talulah. She'd captured the effervescent quality of her gap-toothed smile and the luminous intensity of her periwinkle eyes.

"Another human face?" Perry asked, his head tilted to one side. "What happened to your architectural obsession? I thought buildings were your jam."

"Jam? Are you talking grape or strawberry?" Neve didn't look up, continuing to add shading to Talulah's cheekbones.

Perry groaned. "While I appreciate your pitiful

attempt at humor, maybe you should run all your new material past me before you subject the general public to your standup routine?"

Neve ignored his comment at first, engrossed in her drawing, then decided to answer him. "My work is evolving. Buildings don't hold the same allure anymore."

Perry hopped closer to the edge of his cage, straining to see better.

Neve's hand paused, hovering over the paper. "Ever since we returned, my memory has been hazy. Drawing helps me remember the people I love most in this world. The ones who shaped me."

"I notice a distinct lack of a handsome African grey parrot in your new collection. Just an unfortunate oversight, I presume?" Perry's feathers ruffled as he realized he was being overlooked.

Neve glanced up, her bright gray-blue eyes meeting Perry's beady gaze.

He huffed and seemed to fold his wings in front of his chest plumage. "I'm the most colorful character in your life. But sure, draw more humans with their boring, featherless faces," he muttered, spinning away from her on one clawed foot as he snapped his wing and hid behind his feathers.

A small smile tugged at the corners of Neve's lips. "Fine, I'll add you to the list."

"I should be at the *top* of the list," Perry groused, even as his tone softened and he shifted back toward her.

The ringing of Neve's phone cut through their

banter. She frowned at the interruption, checking the caller ID.

"It's Dr. Andrews," she read aloud, her pulse quickening. She'd been waiting for test results since she'd returned home.

"Better answer it," Perry said, suddenly serious. "Unless you'd prefer to continue this thrilling discussion."

"Point taken." Neve tapped the screen and uttered a greeting. "This is Nevermore."

"Ms. LaRue, thank you for taking my call. I have your test results." The doctor's voice was crisp and professional. "I'd prefer to discuss this in person, but given the unusual nature of your case, I thought you'd want to know our findings as soon as possible."

Neve drummed her fingers on the drawing table. "I appreciate it. Please proceed."

There was a brief pause. "As we suspected, your telomeres show significant shortening compared to the baseline of other forty-seven-year-old Caucasian women. They are measuring more consistent with someone in their late sixties. We've also identified a mutation in your LMNA gene. It's unlike anything the team has seen before."

Neve's drumming intensified. "Please be specific."

"The LMNA gene produces lamin A protein, which is essential for maintaining the stability of cell nuclei," Dr. Andrews explained. "In normal aging, small amounts of an abnormal form called progerin accumulate over time. In classic Hutchinson-Gilford Progeria Syndrome, a specific type of mutation causes excessive progerin production, leading to accelerated aging in children."

"I'm familiar with the condition," Neve said, her voice steady despite the icy dread spreading through her chest.

"Your case is unique. The mutation appears to have been dormant, or at least minimally active, until recently. Something triggered a dramatic increase in progerin production. Your cells are essentially experiencing rapid aging at an accelerated rate."

Neve's mind raced through the implications. "The lightning strike," she murmured.

"Pardon?"

"Nothing. What is the progression rate?"

Dr. Andrews sighed. "That's difficult to predict given the unprecedented nature of your case. Based on cellular markers, you've experienced approximately fifteen years of aging during the last year."

Neve's hand stilled. "And will it continue at this rate?"

"We don't know. The progression could stabilize, continue, or even ramp up. We need to run more tests."

"Percentages, please," Neve interrupted. "What percentage of normal function can I expect to retain in six months? A year?"

Perry had gone dead silent, his black eyes fixed on Neve's face.

"Ms. LaRue, I understand your desire for concrete numbers, but this is uncharted territory. If the current rate of decline continues, you could experience significant deterioration in motor function, vision, and cognitive abilities. But I must emphasize, we don't know when or if that will happen."

"When should I expect vision impairment?" Neve pressed, her gaze falling on her drawing as she began to rock to self-soothe.

"There are already signs in your latest eye exam. The hardening of the lenses is consistent with someone in their early sixties. We should monitor this closely."

Neve nodded, though the doctor couldn't see her. "And my hands? The joint pain and stiffness?"

"Consistent with advanced osteoarthritis. We can manage the symptoms, but if the cellular aging continues..."

"...they'll get worse," Neve finished flatly.

After arranging a follow-up appointment and ending the call, Neve sat motionless, staring at Talulah's half-finished portrait.

"Well, that sounded unpleasant," Perry finally said, his usual sarcasm unable to mask his growing concern.

Neve tightened the ends of her braids. "It appears the hyper-realistic artist is hyper-aging," she admitted in a whisper.

"Neve..."

"I need to finish these portraits," she said, picking up her pencil again. "While I still can."

Perry watched as she bent over the drawing, her hand shaking a bit more than it had before the call. "You know," he offered, trying to comfort her, "I've always thought wrinkles add character. And you, Nevermore, now have character to spare."

Neve didn't respond, but her rocking slowed, and her breathing steadied as she lost herself once more in the careful lines of Talulah's face. The grim prognosis fueled her to finish the rest of the pieces for the show, and she delivered them to Lisa just hours before the deadline.

THE NEXT EVENING, Neve drove to the Elysian Atelier. It was Aura Cove's artistic heartbeat, with the clean lines of mid-mod design, concrete floors, and exposed brick. Inside, Lisa was preparing to host Neve's first solo show, and the staff was busy making last-minute adjustments before guests flooded in. The gallery sparkled with track lighting, highlighting each piece as they'd discussed, and as Neve stood in the center of the main gallery, she felt a well of pride spring up. Her first solo show, she'd done it, and it felt like she'd crossed the finish line of her first marathon.

She cocked her head, studying a grouping, then reached out to straighten the frame of the Henry B. Plant Museum study.

"Perfect," Lisa declared, appearing at Neve's side. "This one is magnificent. I believe it will be the first to sell tonight."

Neve nodded, stepping back. "I would agree. It will forever be my architectural masterpiece."

Lisa's smile faltered as she took in Neve's appearance under the gallery lights. The changes were even more pronounced than when they'd last met.

"Neve," she began carefully, "are you feeling alright? You seem…"

"Older?" Neve supplied, her tone matter-of-fact. "That's because I am."

"Aren't we all?" Lisa tried to laugh off her concern but couldn't. "I don't want to pry, but I've been worried. This seems more than just stress or lack of sleep."

Neve had the urge to tighten and re-tighten her braids, but she laced her fingers together to stop the need to stim. "I received my diagnosis yesterday. A mutation in my LMNA gene is causing accelerated cellular degradation. Essentially, my cells are aging at a faster rate due to excessive progerin production."

Lisa blinked, clearly not expecting such a clinical response. "My God, Neve. I don't know what to say. Is there a treatment?"

"Experimental only. Outcomes are uncertain." Neve turned to adjust another frame, though it was already perfectly aligned. "The relevant point is that I need to discuss the TMOM grant with you."

"The grant? That's the *least* important thing right now."

"I must disagree," Neve insisted, her voice taking on a professional edge. "My hands won't cooperate like they used to. I am experiencing tremors, and my vision is beginning to deteriorate. I don't think I can produce work at the pace I once did."

Lisa's professional veneer cracked, genuine concern flooding her features. "That's heartbreaking."

"I can return most of the money," Neve continued, as if Lisa hadn't spoken. "It should go to someone who can fully utilize it. Someone with the time and ability to do it justice."

Lisa reached out, then hesitated, remembering Neve's aversion to unexpected touch. "The grant was awarded based on your vision and talent, not your production speed. We're not taking it back."

Neve swallowed around the unexpected lump in her throat. "But I..."

"No," Lisa insisted. "This isn't open for discussion. The money is yours to use however you need to realize your vision, whatever form that takes, however *long* it takes."

Neve felt her eyes well up, but before she could respond, the gallery door opened, and the first guests began to file in. Lisa squeezed Neve's shoulder gently. "We'll talk more later. Right now, let's celebrate your hard work."

Within an hour, the gallery was packed. Art enthusiasts, collectors, and critics moved from piece to piece, murmuring in appreciation. Neve retreated to quieter corners between necessary interactions as the constant stimulation became more overwhelming.

During one such retreat, she found herself counting the frames to still her mind. One, two, three, four... seventeen, eighteen, nineteen...

"Twenty-four in this section," came a familiar voice.

Neve turned to find Talulah standing beside her, barely recognizable in an elaborate disguise. She wore a sleek black wig cut in a sharp bob, oversized sunglasses, and a fitted black pantsuit so unlike her usual ethereal dresses that Neve had to blink twice.

"Talulah?"

"In the flesh, darlin', though not in my usual packagin'." She grinned. "Thought I'd keep a low profile tonight. This is your dog and pony show, after all."

"You didn't have to come incognito," Neve said, though she felt a rush of gratitude.

"Oh, but I did. The moment someone recognizes me, it's all 'Talulah, did my grandmother reach the other side?' and 'Talulah, can you sage the negative spirits in my apartment?'" She rolled her eyes behind her sunglasses. "Tonight is not about me. It's about your beautiful work."

Neve nodded in thanks, scanning the collection. Lisa was placing another red "sold" dot on a drawing of the John and Mable Ringling Museum of Art.

"Your work is connectin' with people," Talulah observed. "Look at all those gorgeous red dots."

"Thank you," Neve said, her response automatic but sincere. "But I thought it would feel different."

"What do you mean?"

"For so long, the goal has been to get the solo show before I turned fifty. And now that I blew past fifty right into my sixties, it's bittersweet. All that striving doesn't seem to matter as much anymore."

Talulah tilted her head, the edge of her wig brushing against her shoulder. "Oh, honey bee, that's what happens when we finally get what we've been chasin'. The destination is never as magnificent as we imagined while we were on the journey."

"It's inefficient," Neve stated, her tone apathetic. "All that time spent striving toward something that doesn't provide the expected emotional payoff."

"Maybe the payoff isn't what you thought it would be," Talulah suggested, her voice gentle as a warm spring rain. "But that doesn't make the journey any less important."

Neve folded her fingers together to stop herself from stimming again. "I'm running out of time." She glanced down at her feet. "I can't waste what's left on lies and half-truths."

"What truth are you still searchin' for?" Talulah asked, her eyes softening behind her disguise.

"Everything. Why Diana was institutionalized the same year my father disappeared. How I ended up with him when she'd already picked out my adoptive parents. What happened to him and why he was taken from me." Neve's voice remained steady despite the emotional weight of her words. "I need to know before I can't remember anymore."

Talulah nodded as the truth slowly took hold. "And you're thinkin' about another jump, aren't you?"

"Yes." Neve's response was immediate and certain. "The calculations suggest each temporal displacement accelerates the aging process. The next jump might cost me fifteen or more years, but I believe it's worth it."

"Even if it steals the time you have left?"

"Time spent in ignorance isn't valuable time," Neve said bluntly. "I'd rather have the truth for a single day than live decades with lies."

Talulah reached out, telegraphing her movement before placing her hand on Neve's arm. "You've always been brave that way. Seekin' truth no matter the cost." A shadow flickered across Talulah's face, quickly masked by her warm smile. "I understand, I just worry about you pushin' yourself too hard."

"That's not logical. The time will pass regardless of what I do with it."

Talulah withdrew her hand, adjusting her wig that had tilted as silence engulfed them both. She glanced at her watch. "Let's talk more about this later, alright? When we have more privacy."

Neve turned her attention back to the exhibition, and she noticed a figure at the edge of the crowd, a man in dark sunglasses and a ball cap, his features obscured. Something about his posture, the set of his shoulders, sent a prickle of recognition down her spine.

She blinked, trying to focus, but her vision blurred at the edges. When she looked again, he had moved, now partially hidden behind a group of enthusiastic art lovers.

"Do you see that man?" she asked Talulah. "In the cap?"

Talulah followed her gaze. "The one lurking by the doorway? Yes, there's something familiar about his energy."

Neve began moving toward him, weaving through

clusters of guests. But each time she got closer, he seemed to drift just out of reach. Her worsening vision didn't help; the details blurred, and the bright gallery lights created halos that obscured faces.

Finally, she reached the spot where he'd been standing, only to find it empty. She turned in a complete circle, scanning the room, but he had vanished.

"Lost him?" Talulah asked, appearing at her side.

"Yes," Neve frowned. "There was something about him..."

"We'll have to figure it out later. Lisa needs you," Talulah said, redirecting her toward the center of the room where Lisa was calling for attention. Neve noticed the slight stiffness in her aunt's fluid movements. Something was off, but Neve couldn't quite identify what, and the noisy gallery made concentration difficult. She tucked the thought away for further reflection.

Hours later, after she'd given a brief speech and the last guest had departed, Lisa uncorked a bottle of champagne in the back office. "To a sold-out show," she declared, pouring three glasses.

Neve, Talulah, now wigless, and Lisa raised their glasses in a toast, clinking them together.

"I haven't seen excitement like that in years," Lisa enthused, sinking into a chair and kicking off her heels. "People were fighting over your work. Your rendering of the Dali Museum started a bidding war."

Neve nodded, sipping her champagne. The bubbles tickled her nose, a sensation that was off-putting. She set the glass down on the table and said, "This seems like the most opportune time to tell you I'm shifting my emphasis to portraits now."

"Really? That's an incredible idea!" Lisa gushed with enthusiasm. "Have you considered doing some celebrity portraits? I have connections who would pay top dollar..."

"No," Neve said in an ultra-direct tone, cutting her off before she could finish.

Lisa blinked in confusion. "No?"

"Celebrities are an invasive species," Neve explained without apology. "They already suck up every ounce of attention in a room. They don't need more exposure. Beauty is found in the ordinary, in faces that would otherwise be forgotten."

A beat of silence followed, then Lisa burst out laughing. "God, I love your brutal honesty. Okay, no celebrities."

"My new portfolio will capture people I've loved, before I lose my vision and memory," Neve continued, matter-of-fact.

The levity drained from the room at her words.

"It is what it is," Neve said, rocking back and forth in the chair to self-soothe. "I need to work while I can."

"And I'll help however I can," Lisa assured her. "Whatever you need."

Neve studied her half-empty champagne glass, watching the bubbles rise and burst, their fleeting existence seeming to mirror her own.

FIFTY-ONE

A FEW DAYS LATER, Neve sat at her kitchen table, drowning in a sea of paperwork. The medical power of attorney forms sat to her left, guardianship petition to her right, and supporting documentation directly in front of her. Each stack was perfectly aligned, corners matching with the papers underneath.

Her knobby fingers squeezed the pen as she signed her name on yet another legal document. The signature looked foreign to her; it was the shaky handwriting of an elderly woman, not the bold, confident strokes she'd used to sign her artwork. She paused, flexing her fingers to ease the stiffness, then continued working through the stack of documents in front of her.

"Are you sure about this?" Talulah asked, setting a cup of chamomile tea beside Neve, careful not to disturb the orderly arrangement. "Takin' on guardianship is a monumental responsibility."

"I'm aware of the implications," Neve replied

without looking up. "I've calculated the financial requirements, spatial accommodations, and medical oversight needed. It won't be easy, but it's manageable."

"I wasn't talkin' about the logistics," Talulah coaxed. She watched Neve for a moment, then cleared her throat. "Have you thought about what this means for your lifestyle? Takin' on guardianship isn't just paperwork and visits. It's daily caretakin'."

Neve's hand froze over the document. She looked up, her brow furrowed. "What do you mean?"

"Well," Talulah said, choosing her words carefully, "you've been livin' that nomadic van life for decades now, comin' and goin' as you please. But Diana will need stability, routine, and consistent care. You might need to..." she hesitated, "settle in one place. Permanently."

The pencil in Neve's hand snapped in two. She stared at the broken pieces as the anxiety in her mind ramped up.

"I hadn't considered that," she admitted, her voice suddenly tight. The rhythmic rocking started, slow at first, then faster. "My van. My independence. My routine."

"I'm not sayin' it's impossible," Talulah interjected. "Just that it's somethin' to factor into your calculations."

Neve stood abruptly, her chair scraping against the floor. She began pacing as fear crested inside her. "I require flexibility. The ability to leave when environments become overwhelming. The freedom to adjust my surroundings according to my sensory needs."

"I know, darlin'."

"Diana requires stability. Consistent medication management. Regular therapy appointments. A structured environment." Neve's pacing increased, her hands now fluttering at her sides. "Our individual requirements are fundamentally incompatible."

Talulah rose and moved to block Neve's path, careful not to touch her. "Breathe. Remember your coping strategies."

Neve stopped, closing her eyes. She visualized a red balloon filling with her breath, then floating away. One, two, three breaths. When she opened her eyes again, some of the panic had receded.

"She could live here," Neve thought aloud, her analytical mind already searching for solutions. "It is in an optimal location close to necessary medical facilities."

"That's a possibility," Talulah agreed. "Or you could modify your van, make it more suitable for two people."

"No." Neve shook her head. "The van is one hundred and eight square feet. Two adults require a minimum of four hundred square feet for adequate personal space and functionality, according to architectural standards."

Talulah suppressed a smile. "What about my place? I've got that spare room now that Yuli's movin' out."

Neve considered this, her fingers tugging on the

end of one of her braids as she thought it over. "That would be a temporary solution at best. You travel too much to make it a viable option." She returned to the table, staring at the scattered paperwork. "Perhaps this was an error in judgment. I didn't fully consider the logistical implications."

"Now hold on," Talulah said with conviction. "Don't go throwin' in the towel just because the path got a little rockier than expected. That's not the Nevermore LaRue I raised."

"But what if I can't provide what she needs?" Neve's voice was barely above a whisper. "What if my own limitations make me an inadequate caregiver? What if the disruption to my routine causes me to decompensate?"

The vulnerability in her questions made Talulah's heart ache. For all Neve's brilliance and tenacity, she still harbored deep insecurities about her ability to connect with and care for others.

"Listen to me," Talulah said, her tone gentle but firm. "You've spent your whole life adaptin' to a world that wasn't built for you. Findin' workarounds, creatin' systems that make sense to your brain. This is just another puzzle to solve."

Neve looked unconvinced.

"And you won't be doin' it alone," Talulah continued. "I'm here. We'll find resources and support services. Maybe Diana wouldn't need to live with you full-time right away. Maybe there's a transitional program, or part-time respite care options, or a traveling nurse."

Neve's rocking slowed as she considered this. "A phased approach with incremental increases in responsibility and proximity," she murmured. "That would be more manageable."

"Exactly," Talulah said, relief palpable in her voice. "One step at a time."

Neve nodded, some of the tension leaving her shoulders. She picked up the broken pencil and carefully placed the pieces in the trash, then selected a new one from her case, aligning it with the edge of the document.

"I still want to do this," she concluded. "It's the right thing to do. But I need to be realistic about my capabilities and limitations."

"That's all anyone can ask," Talulah said. "And for what it's worth, I think you'll be amazin' at it. You understand what it's like to navigate a world that doesn't always make sense. That's somethin' you and Diana have in common."

Neve hadn't thought of it that way before. Perhaps her own neurodivergence wasn't a liability in this situation, but an asset. She understood the importance of routine, the overwhelming nature of sensory input, and the need for clear, direct communication. Maybe she was uniquely qualified to help Diana after all.

Neve nodded, returning to her paperwork. The familiar rhythm of organizing documents calmed her racing thoughts. Creating a plan, following procedures, this was something she understood. This was something she could control.

Over the following weeks, Neve established a

quiet routine with Diana. Every Tuesday and Friday afternoon, she would arrive at Bayside with her messenger bag, sign in at the front desk, and make her way to the dayroom where Diana often sat by the window.

Today, Diana was rocking slightly in her chair, mumbling to herself as Neve approached.

"Hello," Neve said, taking the seat opposite her. "It's Friday. Can I sit with you?"

Diana's unfocused eyes drifted toward her, and she gave a curt nod, then they darted away. "The particles accelerate when the magnetic field is applied," she said, her voice thin and reedy. "Ellis understood. Ellis always understood the variables."

Neve had grown accustomed to these non-sequiturs, fragments of Diana's brilliant mind breaking through the fog of medication and mental illness. "What else did Ellis understand?" she coaxed.

"Quantum entanglement," Diana replied, her fingers tracing invisible patterns on her lap. "Once connected, always connected, regardless of distance. He's still connected. Still watching. The cells divide too quickly when they watch."

Neve nodded, letting the words wash over her without trying to force meaning from them. Sometimes Diana would talk for hours about scientific theories, interspersed with paranoid delusions about surveillance and experimentation. Other times, she would fall into long silences, humming fragments of the *Jeopardy* theme song, a detail that had startled Neve the first time she heard it, remembering how she watched the show with her father every night as a child.

Ms. Lockwood approached, clipboard in hand. "Diana seems calmer today," she observed. "Actually, we've noticed she's more settled on the days you visit."

"Is that unusual?" Neve asked.

"For Diana? Yes. She often doesn't respond to visitors at all. After a while, they stopped coming." Ms. Lockwood lowered her voice. "The staff is very supportive of your guardianship petition. We've all noted the positive changes in her since you started visiting and documented them in her chart."

Neve nodded, processing this information. "Thank you. I've completed all the required paperwork and home evaluations."

"I know. You've been remarkably thorough," Ms. Lockwood praised with a small smile. "The hearing is scheduled for next month, correct?"

"October fifteenth," Neve confirmed. "I've arranged for all necessary testimony and documentation."

Ms. Lockwood squeezed her shoulder in gentle support. "You're doing a good thing, Ms. LaRue."

After the social worker left, Neve reached into her messenger bag and pulled out her sketchbook. She'd found that drawing during these visits helped ease the awkwardness of one-sided conversations. Today, she began sketching the profile of her father from memory, his serious expression, the slight furrow between his brows that appeared whenever he was deep in thought.

Diana's mumbling gradually quieted as she watched Neve's pencil move across the paper. After several minutes, she lurched forward.

"Ellis," she asserted, pointing at the drawing. "That's Ellis."

Neve's hand stilled. "Yes," she confirmed. "This is Ellis. Do you remember him?"

Diana's eyes, usually clouded and distant, fixated on the sketch. "His eyes were more gentle than you've drawn them. He looked at me with kindness, even when I couldn't bear it."

It was the most coherent sentence Neve had heard from Diana about her father. Heart racing, she reached into her bag again and pulled out the geode.

"Diana," she murmured, placing the rock in the woman's skinny hand and curling her fingers around it. She could feel the vibration through Diana's skin. "Do you recognize this?"

Diana's fingers closed around the geode, her eyes widening. For a moment, a startling clarity came over her face. "The storm is coming," she whispered. "He knew it was coming. That's why he left."

"Who left? Ellis?"

Diana nodded, her gaze locked with Neve's. "He didn't abandon you. He was protecting us."

"Protecting us?" Neve repeated, leaning forward.

"Yes," Diana stated. "He knew they were watching me. He knew they would come for him next, and you might be collateral damage. The research was too dangerous."

"What research? Diana, please..." Neve begged.

But the moment of lucidity had passed. Diana's eyes clouded over again, and she resumed her rocking, the geode still clutched in her hand. "The particles accelerate," she murmured. "Always accelerating."

The following Tuesday, Neve arrived at Bayside to find Talulah already in the lobby, accompanied by a short, round woman with snow-white hair pulled into a tight bun at the base of her thick neck.

"Neve!" Talulah called out, waving her over. "Hope you don't mind, but I brought my roommate, Yuli, along today. She's been dyin' to meet you and Diana."

Neve stiffened. Unexpected changes to her routine triggered anxiety, and introducing a stranger into her carefully orchestrated visits with Diana seemed risky for them both.

The white-haired woman stepped forward, extending a weathered hand. "It's wonderful to meet you," she said in a no-nonsense tone. When Neve's hand met hers, she felt a wave of peace calm her jackrabbitting heart. "I have experience with mental health conditions. I thought perhaps I could be of assistance."

Something about Yuli's direct manner put Neve right at ease. There was no pretense, no excessive social niceties, just straightforward communication. Her green eyes captivated Neve, and she felt her fears wash away.

"Could I meet her?"

Neve glanced at her watch. "She is in the dayroom at this hour."

They found Diana in her usual spot by the sunny window, but today she was agitated, her tapping more pronounced, her mumbling louder and more distressed.

"Bad day?" Talulah asked with concern.

"It appears so," Neve said as she edged closer, letting out a strained moan of trepidation. "Hello, Diana. It's Tuesday, and I brought some friends for our visit."

Diana didn't acknowledge her, continuing to rock and mutter about "contaminated samples" and "compromised results."

Yuli studied the distraught woman, her green eyes narrowed in concentration. After a moment, she took the seat directly across from Diana and spoke in a firm, clear voice.

"Dr. Diana Morrison. Look at me."

To Neve's surprise, Diana's head snapped up, her unfocused gaze settling on Yuli's face.

"Good," Yuli said, nodding. "Her mind is fragmented but not lost. She is still inside there."

Before Neve could ask what she meant, Ms. Lockwood appeared at her side. "Ms. LaRue? Could I speak with you for a moment? There are some updates to Diana's care plan we need to discuss."

Neve hesitated, glancing between Diana and the social worker.

"Go on," Talulah encouraged. "We'll stay with Diana. Won't we, Yuli?"

The white-haired woman nodded, her attention still fixed on Diana. "Yes. We will be fine."

Reluctantly, Neve followed Ms. Lockwood to her office, where the social worker produced a thick folder of documents.

"We've been adjusting Diana's medication regimen," she explained, "and there are some forms you'll need to sign as her pending guardian."

Neve frowned, scanning the paperwork. "This indicates a reduction in her antipsychotic dosage. Won't that increase her symptoms?"

"It's a careful balance," Ms. Lockwood replied. "The current dosage is causing some concerning side effects. The psychiatric team believes a slight reduction might improve her quality of life without significantly worsening her psychosis."

Neve struggled to process the implications. Her literal mind wanted concrete assurances, specific percentages of risk and benefit, not the vague language of "might" and "potentially" that filled the medical documents.

"What exactly is the statistical likelihood of improvement versus further deterioration?" Neve pressed.

Ms. Lockwood sighed. "Mental health treatment isn't precise. It's more art than science sometimes."

"That fails to provide clarity," Neve muttered.

"I understand your frustration," Ms. Lockwood spoke in a soothing voice. "But these decisions require some tolerance of ambiguity. We're trying to find the best balance for Diana's overall well-being."

The discussion continued for nearly thirty minutes, with Neve asking increasingly specific questions and Ms. Lockwood providing the best answers she could. By the time they returned to the dayroom, Neve was mentally exhausted from navigating the bureaucratic language and imprecise medical terminology.

She stopped short at the sight that greeted her. Diana sat perched in her chair, no longer rocking or muttering. Talulah was beside her, chatting in her soft drawl, while Yuli stood behind Diana's chair, her hands resting on the woman's shoulders.

For a brief moment, Neve thought she saw a golden shimmer in the air around them, like sparks dancing in sunlight. She blinked, and it was gone.

"Everything alright?" Talulah beamed as Neve approached.

"Yes," Neve answered, studying Diana. Something was different. Her posture was more relaxed, her eyes clearer. "What happened while I was gone?"

"I just taught her an ancient relaxation technique," Yuli said, removing her hands from Diana's shoulders. "Sometimes the mind needs gentle guidance to find its way back to center."

Neve doubted this explanation, but Diana *did* seem remarkably improved. "Thank you," she said to Yuli, with genuine gratitude in her voice.

A week later, Neve arrived for her regular Friday visit, her mind preoccupied with the upcoming guardianship hearing. She entered the dayroom, automatically scanning for Diana in her usual spot by the window, but her favorite chair was empty.

"Neve," called an attendant. "Diana is in her room today. She requested to see you there when you arrived."

Puzzled, Neve followed the attendant down the residential hallway to a small private room. Diana sat on the edge of her bed, her thin frame straight, her hands folded in her lap. She seemed more peaceful than Neve had ever seen her before.

When Diana looked up, Neve froze. The clouded, unfocused gaze was gone, replaced by clear, intelligent eyes that locked onto hers.

"Hello, Nevermore," Diana said, her voice steady and coherent.

Neve's breath hitched in her throat. It wasn't just the use of her full name; it was the recognition behind it, the awareness of their relationship to each other that had been missing in all their previous interactions.

"Diana?" she whispered, taking a tentative step forward.

"Yes." Diana offered a small smile. "I'm having a good day. The fog has lifted, at least for now."

Tears welled in Neve's eyes, surprising her. She rarely cried, finding emotional displays inefficient and uncomfortable. But hearing her mother, her actual mother, not the hollow shell she'd come to know, address her and carry on a conversation, broke something loose inside her.

"How do you know my name?" she managed to ask, wiping at her eyes.

"Ellis," Diana replied.

The tears came faster now, and Neve made no attempt to stop them. Diana patted the bed beside her, and Neve sat down, her hands quivering.

"I have something for you," Diana said, reaching beneath her bed. She pulled out a worn shoebox. The cardboard was soft with age. "I've been keeping these safe, waiting for the right time. I think that time is now."

She placed the box on Neve's lap. Inside were dozens of letters, their edges softened from years of handling, the envelopes yellowed. Neve picked one up, and her heart galloped in her chest when she recognized the handwriting on the envelope.

Her father's unmistakable penmanship.

The postmark read September 18, 1997—five years after his disappearance.

"He's alive?" The question emerged as a broken whisper.

Diana nodded twice.

Neve's carefully constructed understanding of her past, of her father's death, of Diana's illness, of her own identity, melted like a sandcastle under a wave. Her usual need for order and control fell away as she struggled to process this revelation, her aging hands clutching the letters so tight they crinkled.

"He wrote to you?" Neve whispered, her voice breaking.

Diana nodded. "For years. He couldn't contact you

directly; it wasn't safe. But he wanted me to know he was alive, that he was working to make things right."

Neve's hands shook as she opened the envelope, pulling out a folded letter. A photograph slipped out of Ellis, older than she remembered him, standing on a beach she didn't recognize, with a mountain range visible in the background.

"How? Why?" she finally asked, the single words encompassing a lifetime of questions.

Diana took a deep breath. "It's a long story, and parts of it I'm still piecing together myself, but it begins with his research at NovaCure," Diana continued. "He made a dangerous discovery." Her voice wavered. "So, he made the hardest choice a father could make. He staged his death and went deep underground, taking his research with him. He believed that if the world thought Ellis LaRue was dead, you would be safe. And I..." She trailed off, her gaze losing focus before snapping back. "I broke. The pressure, the fear, the loss, it was too much. My mind fractured."

"He didn't die? He chose to abandon me," Neve whispered the agonizing truth to herself under her breath. It felt like she'd been impaled by a sharp sword, leaving her vulnerable and exposed, and she hated it.

Diana reached out, her thin hand covering Neve's wrinkled one. "He never stopped loving you, Nevermore. Never. Every letter asks about you, begs for news of you. He was heartbroken that he couldn't see you grow into adulthood."

Neve closed her eyes, tears streaming down her weathered cheeks. Everything she'd always believed about her life, about her father, about herself, all of it was transformed in an instant by the box of letters settled in her lap.

"Read them," Diana urged. "Read them all. He wanted you to know the truth but had to wait until it was safe."

"How do you know it's safe now?" Neve asked.

Diana's smile was sad. "I don't. But you're already involved, aren't you?"

"Yes," she admitted. "I am."

"Then you need to know everything," Diana insisted, tapping the box of letters. "And when you do, when you understand what your father was trying to prevent, you'll have to decide what to do next."

"What do you mean?"

Diana's eyes, clear and focused for the moment, held a deep sorrow. "History is trying to repeat itself, Nevermore. The same people who came after him, they'll come after you, too, once they realize what you know."

FIFTY-TWO

Neve pushed through the front door with such force that it slammed against the wall, then flinched as the sound reverberated through the house like a gunshot. Her hands shook with barely contained rage as she clutched the weathered shoebox against her chest. The cardboard edges dug into her lined palms, but she didn't notice the discomfort through the white-hot anger coursing through her veins.

Perry flew over to her. He roosted on a perch on the back of the sofa, his feathers at odd angles as he observed the scene with caution.

From the kitchen came the familiar sounds of Talulah making dinner, the gentle clink of Corelle plates as she pulled them from the cupboard to set the table, the hiss of hot oil in a pan.

"What's got you all riled up?" Talulah appeared in the doorway, wiping her hands on a dish towel, concern puckering her brow.

The words died in her throat as Neve marched into

the living room and slammed the shoebox down on the coffee table. The impact sent several letters spilling out, their yellowed envelopes spreading across the polished surface like a deck of cards.

"He wrote to her," Neve blurted, her voice fracturing despite her efforts to remain composed. "For years. While I thought he was dead." She gestured to the scattered envelopes, each one addressed in the same distinctive handwriting. She pulled one out. "This was postmarked in 2010! Eighteen years after he supposedly died."

Talulah froze as her gaze fixed on the letters. The color drained from her face, leaving her complexion ashen against the vibrant fabric of her handkerchief dress.

"Where did you find those?" she asked, her voice barely above a whisper.

"Diana gave them to me," Neve replied, pulling more letters from the box. Her hands shook as she spread them across the table. "She kept them all these years. Every single one."

Talulah approached slowly as if the letters might bite. She reached out to touch one, then pulled her hand back. "I see," she muttered, and those two simple words carried the weight of decades of secrets.

"You see?" Neve repeated, incredulity sharpening her tone. "That's all you have to say? I see?"

Perry shifted uncomfortably on his perch. "Perhaps we should all take a deep breath before—"

"No," Neve cut him off, her eyes never leaving Talulah's face. "No more deflections. No more cryptic hints. No more protecting me from the truth." Her voice rose with each demand, years of frustration bubbling to the surface. "I'm sick of being protected! I'm not a child anymore!"

She began to rock back and forth, her body's automatic response to overwhelming emotion. "I'm dying, Talulah. I'm literally running out of time with every jump. I can't afford to wait for the truth anymore."

Talulah sank onto the couch, her airy quality deflated and replaced by the heavy resignation of someone carrying an impossible burden. "You're right," she conceded, and the Southern lilt that usually colored her speech faded, leaving her tone stark and plain. "You deserve the truth. All of it."

Perry flew from his perch to the coffee table, positioning himself between them as if mediating a negotiation. His flippant demeanor had vanished, replaced by solemnity.

"Your father didn't die when you were fifteen," Talulah stated. Each word fell like a stone, deliberate and heavy.

Neve went completely still; her rocking stopped mid-motion. The only sound in the room was her shallow breathing.

"You knew?" The question escaped her lips, a whispered accusation.

"Ellis didn't die," Talulah repeated, meeting Neve's gaze for the first time since she'd entered the house. "And he never came through the veil... because I helped him disappear."

The silence that followed was deafening. Neve felt

as if the floor had dropped out from beneath her. All these years, her foundation was built on a quicksand of lies.

"You helped him?" Neve finally managed, each word sharp with disbelief.

Talulah nodded, her shoulders slumping under the weight of her confession. "He came to me, terrified. Ellis was leading a pharmaceutical trial for a new cancer drug called Zynesta, but NovaCure was not reporting adverse effects. He was going to be a whistleblower, but then he started receiving death threats."

Neve's mind raced, struggling to process this revelation. Her hands moved of their own accord, methodically arranging and rearranging the letters on the table. First by date, then by size, then back to chronological order. The familiar ritual helped ground her as her entire world tilted on its axis.

"He was afraid," Talulah continued, her voice growing softer. "Not just for himself, but for you and Diana. He decided the best way to keep you both safe was to disappear."

"So, he faked his own death," Neve said flatly.

"Yes. He staged the scene, secured pints of blood of his type from the lab, enough to suggest an injury no one could have survived. I tried to talk him out of it, Neve, but he was adamant it was the only way."

Neve's hands stilled over the letters. "It wasn't up to you," she declared, her voice dangerously quiet. "It wasn't up to either of you to decide what I needed."

"You were fifteen..."

"I was old enough to understand the truth!" Neve's voice rose sharply, the control she'd been maintaining buckling under the weight of the revelation. "How could you keep this from me for so long? Do you have any idea what his disappearance did to me? The trauma, the uncertainty... I spent years in therapy trying to process his death!"

Talulah flinched as if physically struck. "He arranged for me to be your guardian. He thought it was the only way to keep you safe."

"Safe?" Neve repeated, the word bitter on her tongue. "I wasn't safe. I was devastated that my father was gone." Her voice faltered. "All this time, he was alive. Out in the world, writing letters, living his life."

"He thought it was the only way to protect you."

"Stop saying that!" Neve snapped, her composure fracturing. "Protection isn't worth the cost if it destroys the thing you're trying to protect! Can't you see that? Can't you see what his absence did to me?"

The question hung in the air, unanswerable. Talulah reached across the table, her fingers brushing against Neve's hand. "I'm sorry," she murmured. "I'm so sorry."

Perry cleared his throat. "Not to interrupt this long-overdue revelation, but perhaps we should address the present situation. Where is Ellis now?"

Talulah's expression shifted, a flicker of uncertainty crossing her features. "I don't know. Not anymore."

"What do you mean, you don't know?" Neve demanded.

"We maintained contact over the years. He moved frequently, never staying in one place too long. Used different names, kept a low profile. He would write to me, and I sent him photos of you."

"When was the last time you heard from him?"

Talulah hesitated. "About a year ago. The letters stopped coming. The emergency contact number he gave me was disconnected."

Neve's analytical mind kicked in, seeking patterns, connections, and explanations. She reached for the most recent letter in the pile from Diana, examining the postmark. "September 18, 2023," she read aloud. "Almost exactly a year ago."

"Yes," Talulah confirmed. "That's around the time I lost contact, too."

Neve stared at the letter, her fingers tracing the handwriting that was so achingly familiar. "He could be anywhere. He could be..." She couldn't bring herself to finish the dark thought.

"I don't believe he's dead," Talulah murmured. "I've never felt his presence beyond the veil. And I would know, Neve. I would feel it."

"Like you felt it fifteen years ago?" Neve shot back, unable to keep the bitterness and sarcasm from her voice.

Talulah's eyes filled with tears. "I've regretted my part in this deception every day. But Ellis was convinced it was the only way to protect you."

"Protect me," Neve repeated, the words hollow. "That's what everyone keeps saying. Diana gave me up to protect me. Ellis disappeared to protect me. You lied to me to protect me." Her voice rose with each statement. "I'm sick of being protected! I needed the truth!" She turned away, her breath coming in short gasps as she struggled to process the magnitude of the betrayal.

Perry fluttered to her shoulder, his weight a small comfort. "Perhaps we should focus on the practical aspects," he suggested. "If Ellis has gone silent, there might be a reason. The same forces that threatened him before could be at play again."

Neve nodded, grateful for the parrot's pragmatic approach. It gave her something to focus on besides the maelstrom of emotions threatening to overwhelm her.

"You're right." She turned back to Talulah. "I need to know everything. Every detail about where he went, who he contacted, and what names he'd used. If he's in danger, we need to find him."

Talulah seemed to age before Neve's eyes, the weight of her secrets finally lifting but leaving her diminished in their wake. "I'll tell you everything I know," she promised. "But it's not much. Ellis was careful, methodical in covering his tracks."

"Of course he was," Neve said, a bitter laugh escaping her. "Like father, like daughter."

She sank back onto the couch, suddenly exhausted. Neve looked at her aunt, the woman who had taken her in, loved her, and lied to her for decades, and felt the complicated tangle of emotions that defined their relationship threaten to choke her.

"I don't know if I can forgive you for this," Neve told her honestly. "Not yet."

"I know," Talulah replied, her usual sparkle dimmed by sorrow. "I wouldn't expect you to."

Neve gathered the letters, carefully returning them to the shoebox. Each one was a piece of a puzzle she was only beginning to understand, a map to the truth she'd been seeking her entire life, and she would use that map to find her father. As Neve turned to leave, Talulah's voice stopped her.

"Wait," she called with an urgency in her tone that made Neve pause despite her anger. "There's something you need to hear."

Neve turned slowly, skepticism etched across her weathered face. "More secrets?"

"No," Talulah insisted, her voice steadier than before. "The opposite. Your father recorded a message for you in the event you found out the truth. It's at my home in the Everglades."

Perry tilted his head and squawked with delight. "A remote house surrounded by alligator-infested waters? I must admit, as hiding places go, it has a certain *je ne sais quoi*."

Talulah ignored the parrot's commentary, her eyes fixed on Neve. "I want to share everything I have from your father. All of it. No more secrets, no more half-truths."

Neve's fingers found the ends of her braids and tightened them as she considered the offer. The analytical part of her mind had always served as her anchor. "Why should I believe you now?" she asked, her voice quiet but direct.

"Because I've nothing left to hide," Talulah replied. "And because, despite everything I did, I love you. I always have."

"Fine," Neve conceded. "We'll leave in the morning."

CHAPTER

FIFTY-THREE

THE NEXT MORNING, Neve's Sprinter van hummed smoothly down the Tamiami Trail, its well-maintained engine purring as the Florida Everglades stretched endlessly on either side. Neve sat rigid in the driver's seat, clenching the steering wheel at ten and two. The air conditioner blew crisp, cool air throughout the cabin, efficiently cutting through the October humidity that fogged the tinted windows.

Perry perched on the leather headrest of Neve's seat, his feathers fluttering in the artificial breeze. "I must say," he observed, breaking the thick silence that had enveloped them since leaving Aura Cove, "there's something disturbingly primordial about this landscape. Like we're driving straight into the jaws of prehistoric peril."

Neither woman responded. Talulah sat in the passenger seat, her usual effervescence dimmed. Her eyes, normally crinkled at the corners with perpetual delight, were shadowed with remorse as she stole glances at her niece's profile.

"Neve," she finally whispered, "we'll be turnin' off the main road soon. The last stretch isn't exactly what you'd call smooth sailin', even in this fancy chariot of yours."

Neve gave a curt nod but remained silent, her gaze fixed on the wilderness beyond the windshield. The landscape had transformed mile by mile as they'd traveled south. Urban sprawl gave way to farmland, then to a vast, prehistoric wetland. Saw grass prairies stretched toward the horizon, broken by islands of cypress trees draped with Spanish moss that swayed in the sluggish breeze.

The van slowed as Neve turned onto a narrow shell-paved access road invisible among the tall grasses. Despite the quality suspension of the van, they still felt every bump and dip in the primitive drive.

"I'm simply making an observation," Perry began with forced nonchalance as his talons dug into Neve's shoulder a little tighter, "but the ratio of reptilian predators to available escape routes seems rather concerning in this particular ecosystem."

"Don't be a baby, Perry."

The shell road wound deeper into the Everglades, the two-lane highway disappearing behind them with each crunching turn. The air grew thicker with humidity as earthy decay and flowering jasmine intertwined. There was a sulfurous hint of stagnant water.

"There she is," Talulah murmured as they rounded

a bend. "My little piece of paradise, just finished last summer."

Neve leaned forward despite herself, taking in the sight of Talulah's Everglades sanctuary. The house stood on sturdy cypress stilts, rising fifteen feet in the air near the dark water of the swamp, its fresh lumber still honey-colored and unweathered by the elements. Its modern architectural lines blended surprisingly well with traditional Florida cracker hallmarks. It featured a wide wraparound porch already festooned with crystal wind chimes that sent rainbow prisms dancing across the polished wood. The structure itself was painted a soft sage green with crisp white trim, and had several large impact-resistant windows that reflected the dappled sunlight filtering through the canopy of overhead trees.

"Designed it myself," Talulah said, a hint of pride breaking through her somber mood as Neve parked the van on a pad made of ground oyster shells. "Took me three years to get all the permits, but only eight months to build once they came through."

They climbed out of the van, and Neve's joints protested as she stretched, the humidity making her white hair cling to her neck. The oyster shells beneath her feet crunched softly. Perry hesitated at the open door, eyeing the surrounding landscape with obvious trepidation.

The hypnotic drone of insects made the hair on Neve's arms stand on end. Two mosquitoes buzzed by her ear, and she waved them away.

"I believe I'll just..." His sentence was cut short by a

splash from a nearby pool of water, where the armored snout of an alligator emerged for a single second before submerging again. With a terrified squawk he'd later deny making, Perry launched himself from the van to Neve's shoulder, burrowing into her neck.

"Merely the most efficient perch," he explained as he trembled. "Gives me a better vantage point."

A great blue heron stalked through the shallows twenty yards away. In the branches of a nearby cypress, an osprey tended to its impressive nest, while a line of turtles basked in the sun along with a cotton-mouth snake, its deadly serpentine curves draped across the rough bark.

"They keep to themselves... mostly," Talulah assured them, leading the way to the stairs. "Unless you go swimmin' at dusk, which I don't recommend."

As they ascended the sturdy steps, Neve noticed protective symbols were carved into the railings and doorframes. They were ancient sigils that Neve recognized from her aunt's books on spiritual protection. The front door was painted a vibrant purple and adorned with a wreath of dried herbs and flowers. Talulah hesitated before opening it, turning to face Neve with eyes that shimmered with unshed tears.

"I know you're angry with me, and you have every right to be," she said, her voice losing its musical lilt. "What I did, what Ellis and I did, it was wrong. No matter our intentions."

Neve met her gaze, her face impassive despite the storm of emotions churning inside her. "Just show me what you brought me here to see."

Talulah nodded, accepting the rebuff. She pushed open the door, revealing colorful tapestries draped over sleek, contemporary furniture, and built-in shelves displaying crystals and fresh herbs growing in hydroponic wall gardens. The air inside was scented with sage and rosemary.

"This way," Talulah instructed, leading them through the eclectic space to a small room at the back of the house.

Unlike the rest of the home, this room was stark and orderly. A simple wooden desk stood beneath a window that looked out over the endless expanse of sawgrass and cypress. On the desk sat a framed photograph of a much younger Ellis standing beside a smiling Talulah. She tugged open a drawer and pulled out an ancient cassette player. Then she felt around the top of the drawer for a few minutes before pulling out a single cassette tape labeled in Ellis's distinctive handwriting. "For Nevermore."

Neve stared at the cassette, her heart hammering against her ribs.

"I'll leave you alone," Talulah whispered, backing toward the door. "Take all the time you need."

As Talulah's footsteps faded, Perry hopped from Neve's shoulder to the desk, studying the cassette with his intelligent eyes, his earlier fear of the wilderness temporarily forgotten in the face of this new mystery.

"Well," he cooed softly, his voice steadier than it had been outside, "shall we hear what the ghost has to say?"

Neve's hand trembled as she reached for the player, her fingers hovering over the obsolete technology that contained her father's message, and perhaps, at last, the truth.

The cassette player whirred to life with a mechanical click, followed by several seconds of static. When Ellis's voice finally emerged, it was familiar, the deep timbre now roughened by age but still carrying the unique cadence Neve recalled from childhood.

"Nevermore... my brilliant daughter. If you're listening to this, then you've discovered the truth." A pause, a heavy sigh. "I'm not dead. I've been alive all these years, watching you from a distance I never wanted to keep."

The tape hissed softly in the background as Ellis collected his thoughts.

"First, I need you to understand something crucial: Talulah never wanted to deceive you. She fought me on this plan, tooth and nail. She begged me to find another way." His voice wavered. "The guilt has probably eaten at her for decades. Whatever anger you feel, direct it at me, not her. She only went along with it because she loves me, and more importantly, because she loves you."

There was the sound of ice clinking in a glass, then a swallow.

"You deserve to know why. Why I would abandon my only child, the person I love more than anything in this world." Ellis's voice dropped lower, as if he feared being overheard, even in the recording. "My research at NovaCure went beyond what anyone realized. What began as a cancer treatment based on cellular regener-ation led me to something revolutionary. A cure, Neve. Not just a treatment, but an actual cure for several aggressive forms of cancer."

A bitter laugh. "But NovaCure wasn't interested in cures. Do you know how much money is in treatment? In keeping patients dependent on expensive medica-tions for years, even decades? Billions. A cure would destroy their business model."

The tape captured the sound of Ellis pacing, his footsteps a rhythmic counterpoint to his words.

"I tried to hide my discovery, to bury it in mundane research papers. But someone noticed. Strange men began following me. Our phone was tapped. Then came the night that changed everything."

His voice tightened with remembered fear. "You had just turned fifteen. I came home late from the lab and found a man in our house, in your bedroom, standing over your bed while you slept. When I confronted him, he didn't run. He smiled and said, 'Imagine what we could do to her if you don't cooperate.'"

There was a long pause, filled only with the sound of Ellis's labored breathing.

"I never told you or Diana. But I knew then that I couldn't protect you while staying in your life. They would use you to control me, to access what I'd discovered."

The recording captured the sound of papers shuffling.

"So, I made a choice, the most difficult decision of my entire life. I staged my death, disappeared, and continued my work in secret, away from NovaCure's influence. And I made Talulah promise to watch over you, to keep you safe without ever revealing the truth."

His voice softened, becoming more intimate. "I've followed your life from afar, Nevermore. I saw you graduate. I know about your art, your travels. I've been so proud of the woman you've become, independent, brilliant, resilient. Just like the woman your mother used to be. She's become another casualty in this war, and I carry the guilt of her mental health breakdown as well."

The tape captured a trembling inhale.

"There's so much more I need to tell you about my research, about the people still trying to steal it. But this recording can only hold so much, and some things are better explained in person."

There was a pause, heavy and long.

"If you're hearing this, it means the time has finally come for us to meet again. Talulah knows how to find me if you're willing, but after everything I've done, I would understand if you aren't."

There was the sound of Ellis clearing his throat as emotion made his voice rough and gravelly.

"I hope to see you soon, Nomo."

Thank you for reading *Never Lose Hope!* Get ready for the next thrilling installment of the Aura Cove

Temporal Traveler series with *Never Alone*—Book Three, packed with unexpected twists, excitement, laughter, and heartwarming moments!

Order here.

🎁 **Before You Go... Claim Your Sneak Peek!**

Can't get enough of Aura Cove? **CLICK HERE for an exclusive 3-chapter preview of *Hawt Flash*. The magical series that started it all.**

Turning 50 is supposed to be a milestone, but for Katie Beaumont, it's the beginning of a supernatural adventure that will change her life forever.

Devastated by her husband's infidelity, Katie discovers she possesses powers beyond her wildest dreams. But as she embarks on a journey of explosive self-discovery, a century of ancestral secrets begins to unravel and threatens to upend everything she thought she knew.

Guided by her sassy best friend, a talking dog, and a ball-busting lawyer, Katie embraces her new life. But she soon realizes that her magical abilities come with a price and enemies who will stop at nothing to claim them.

WANT MORE GOOD BOOKS?

Scan the QR Code Above or Tap HERE to unlock my entire backlist & find your next great read!

🎁 JOIN MY BOOK CLUB

- Read FREE Extended Sneak Peeks
- Unlock Exclusive Bonus Content
- Private Subscriber-Only Discounts
- Handpicked 5-Star Book Recs
- Delicious, Healthy-ish Recipes

👉 JOIN THE BOOK CLUB HERE

bookclub.tealbutterflypress.com

ABOUT THE AUTHOR

I've always been a risk-taker, so at 44 I decided to write and publish my own books. It has been a roller coaster ride with a punishing learning curve, but if it were easy, everyone would do it. I write under the pen names of Ninya and Blair Bryan.

I love to travel and a trip to Scotland with a complete stranger was the inspiration for my memoir. I also seem to attract crazy experiences and people into my life like a magnet that gives me a never-ending supply of interesting storylines.

If you love a good dirty joke, a cup of coffee so strong you can chew it, and have killed more cats with your curiosity than you can count, I might be your soulmate.

Join My Book Club